HE BRUSHES HIS FINGER OVER MY CHIN. "WHEN YOU WERE HUMAN, I always said you were my greatest creation. Now you truly are."

His expression always contains a hint of pain. I remind him of his wife. My mother. I wish I could remember her. I wish I could remember myself.

Most of all, I wish to claw the heart from the wizard who did this to my family.

He is monstrous.

Praise for **MONSTROUS**

"Like a literary mad scientist, MarcyKate Connolly takes bits from classic fairy tales and legends and uses them to assemble a creation that is wholly original and wonderfully strange. Subversive, bewitching, and whip smart, *Monstrous* is a marvel of storytelling alchemy."
—Anne Ursu, author of *Breadcrumbs*

"This is a dazzling and unique once-upon-a-time about a girl who is part dragon, part bird, part cat, all hero."
—Natalie Lloyd, author of *A Snicker of Magic*

"A smart, ambitious adventure, led by a heroine whose differences only enhance her humanity."   —Emma Trevayne, author of *Flights and Chimes and Mysterious Times*

"From its first line, *Monstrous* had me in its grip. This remarkable, absorbing debut will enchant readers."
—Rebecca Behrens, author of *When Audrey Met Alice*

"Readers seeking a lengthy, thoughtful novel, particularly those who appreciate careful world-building, will find this worth their time."
—*BCCB*

"A likely read-aloud that has its share of guts, blood, and grim reality within this fantasy land, *Monstrous* will keep young readers thinking about trust, good and evil, friendship and loyalty, and devotion to community."   —ALA *Booklist*

"Magic, fantastic creatures, mythology, and a bit of Mary Shelley's *Frankenstein* combine here for an exciting . . . tale."
—*School Library Journal*

"Connolly invokes fairy-tale elements with ease, and…the formidable theme of sacrifice resonates far beyond the final page."
—*Publishers Weekly*

MONSTROUS

MarcyKate Connolly

HARPER

An Imprint of HarperCollinsPublishers

Library of Congress Cataloging-in-Publication Data
Connolly, MarcyKate.
  Monstrous / MarcyKate Connolly. — First edition.
    pages cm
  Summary: Kymera, who has a raven's wings, a snake's tail, and
a cat's eyes and claws, loves the father who brought her back
to life after a wizard killed her, but she begins to question his
motives, especially after she connects with a boy in the town
from which she is rescuing sick girls.
  ISBN 978-0-06-227272-0
  [1. Fairy tales. 2. Monsters—Fiction. 3. Magic—Fiction.
4. Wizards—Fiction. 5. Dragons—Fiction. 6. Identity—
Fiction.] I. Title.
PZ8.C765Mon 2015   2014013835
[Fic]—dc23   CIP
                                                           AC

Typography by Torborg Davern
15 16 17 18 19   OPM   10 9 8 7 6 5 4 3 2 1
❖
First paperback edition, 2016

To my parents,

for never doubting that if I pursued my dreams,

I would catch them.

DAY ONE

I WILL NEVER FORGET MY FIRST BREATH. GASPING. HEAVING. DELICIOUS.

When I opened my eyes, the colors of the world swarmed me, filling up all space with hues and objects for which I had no name.

Three seconds later, I passed out from sensory overload, or at least that is what Father says. He fixed me up and when I woke the second time, the world became a more comprehensible place. The object hovering over me was a face, the circles within it were eyes, and the warm, wet drips leaking from them were tears.

The crease across the bottom that widened under my gaze was a smile.

"You're alive," Father said.

Even now, hours later, he mutters it still.

DAY TWO

I LEAN BACK AGAINST THE WILLOW AND HOLD OUT MY ARMS, STUDYING them under the waning sunlight. The thin red lines marking the sections of my body have faded to nearly nothing; all that remains are the many shades of my flesh and the tiny metal bolts fastening tail to spine, joint to wing, and neck to shoulder, along with a dull ache.

Father, his silver hair flapping in the summer breeze, lays out logs and strange steel pipes in the field. They will be used for my training. He has not told me what I am preparing for, only that he will when I am ready. He waves when he notices me watching.

I am sure I will be ready soon. Father is astonished at my progress. Yesterday, I mastered walking within one hour and running in two, and now I can even jump to the lowest branch of the willow with ease.

Father says his biggest coup is my speech. He managed to preserve that part of my brain, so I talk just as I did when I was human.

Before.

My only regret is he was not able to carry over my memories. I know nothing of who I was. Nothing of my mother. Even my memories of Father are out of reach.

But I do not need them to know how precious I am to him. Every time he looks at me, his face fills with surprise as though I am some kind of miracle.

I suppose I am.

The maze of tones on my arms, legs, and torso fascinates me to no end, because my face is only one plain shade of porcelain. Father says I must look as human as possible from a distance, but no one will see my arms or legs under my cloak. When I bore of studying my arms, I tuck my long, dark locks behind my ears and curl my green tail up to get a better look. It has a three-pronged point at the end. A barb, Father called it. He said I need to be careful not to swish too hard or I might sting myself or him.

I run a finger over the iridescent scales surrounding the hard brown spikes. I rather like the scales. They are lovely in the last beams of the day. I wonder what the barb does, and I tap it ever so gently—

DAY FOUR

I SIT BY THE FIRE IN OUR LITTLE RED COTTAGE, PESTERING FATHER WITH questions while I toy with the end of my tail. He dances around the answers, just as my fingers dance around the stinging tip. I am much more cautious now. The venom puts people to sleep. The last time, I pricked my finger and did not wake up for half a day.

A lesson well learned.

"Why do you not have a tail, Father?" I ask.

He gives me the same response he gives to all questions along these lines. "I am not special like you, Kymera. Most people are not. You have a purpose. Your parts will aid you."

"How?" I frown at the barb, then shake my tail as if to make it frown back. Instead, the scales glitter in the firelight.

"I will tell you when you are ready."

Frustration warms my face, but when he reaches over and places his hand against my cheek, I lean into the affectionate gesture. I am becoming fond of this place, with its worn wooden walls, high hedges, and rose garden. Even the tower beside the cottage feels like an old friend.

Mostly I cannot help but stare at Father—the man who made me—and memorize every line and plane of his face. That, too, is nearly as worn as the walls, but radiates a kindness, a warmth that even the fire cannot match.

A yapping brown dog with sparrow wings skids to a landing by Father's plush armchair. Pippa. He calls her a sperrier.

I call her delicious.

But I am supposed to pass as human, and humans do not eat sperriers or terriers or any other animal they care for as pets.

Pippa keeps her distance from me, venturing into the same room only when Father is around. I swish my tail in irritation. I am hungry.

Crash.

A book falls off the shelf behind me and Father sighs. It is a volume he gave me on my first day of life. Its cover is frayed around the edges, but the words are lovely, full of magic and life and mystery. He calls them fairy tales. They are supposed to be a part of my education. I rise—more carefully—to retrieve the volume. I have not yet gained control over all my parts and it worries him. I return it to the shelf, wiping my dusty hands on my dress.

I do not want Father to worry. This is the fifth time he attempted to reanimate me and the only time he succeeded.

I have not yet asked what happened to my other bodies. For now it is enough for me to know I am alive and strong, though perhaps more clumsy than I would like.

He created me for a purpose—a noble one, he claims—with the tail of a snake, the wings of a giant raven, and the claws and eyes of a cat. Much to his dismay, I have not yet mastered flying, either. But I am rather good at knocking things off shelves.

Father suffered for me and I hope I can live up to his expectations.

"Kymera, come sit. You are making Pippa nervous with your pacing." He pats the chair across from him. Pippa squirms in his arms, as though she is considering taking flight again.

I bare my teeth at her and hiss as I sit in what I hope is a ladylike fashion. Pippa leaps up to the rafters. I giggle.

"You should not do that. This is the one place you will find other hybrids. Pippa is a kindred spirit."

She whines as though she understands his every word. I roll my eyes.

"I am better than a puppy with wings. You made me so." I grow bolder at his smile. "Why did you create me?"

His eyes soften. "Kym, you are my daughter."

"Yes, but what drove you to try over and over? If you cannot tell me my purpose, at least tell me that." I blink, switching from yellow cat's eyes to my blue human irises.

He is more accommodating to my requests when I wear those.

He sighs. It is working.

"Most of your human parts come from my daughter. A year ago, a wizard abducted you. Your mother attempted to stop him, and the wizard murdered her in the ensuing struggle. He vanished and only later when he was done with you did I find your body. After that, it became my life's work to bring you back." He settles deeper into his chair, and the flames in the fireplace recede to embers. Fury builds inside me. The cat's irises slide back into place, and the claws in my hands ache to unsheathe.

"What sort of person would murder the child of a good man?" This question pains Father, but I do not regret asking.

"Wizards are naturally power hungry, but this one was also driven mad by grief. He lost his own daughter to illness not long before and is so jealous that he steals any other girl who crosses his path and kills her. I suspect he aims to work some sort of dark magic to bring his lost child back."

"But how?"

"Humans may not have magic in them, but young blood is a powerful ingredient in black-magic spells. From what I hear, his magic has only gotten darker since he lost his child, and he needs a steady supply of sacrifices for his spells."

"I was one of those sacrifices."

Father bows his head.

"Then you saved me." The emotions swelling in my

chest confuse me. Pride and love for my father, grief for my mother, and a raw, burning hatred of the man who destroyed everything I must have once loved.

"It was tricky work and I could not bring you back exactly as you were. Your memories I could not salvage." He sighs. "With each attempt, I lost more and more of your original body. I did manage to preserve the speech center of your brain, and words will come back to you as you need them. And most importantly, I made you stronger each time. I just needed to find the right combination of parts." He brushes his finger over my chin. "When you were human, I always said you were my greatest creation. Now you truly are."

His expression always contains a hint of pain. I remind him of his wife. My mother. I wish I could remember her. I wish I could remember myself.

Most of all, I wish to claw the heart from the wizard who did this to my family.

He is monstrous.

DAY SEVEN

"AGAIN, KYMERA."

I growl as I lunge back into the training grounds Father set up for me. I leap over the obstacles, rows of bars increasing in height, then unfurl my wings and swoop down into the maze of hedges surrounding our home. Father says they are for protection against the wizard. We do not want him and his magic to reach us. To travelers on the outside, the hedge and our home are barely visible, concealed by a thick span of pine trees.

But not to me. Now that I am flying well, I have learned the secret routes in and out. I can fly above and see as far as the city of Bryre on the horizon in the east and the green rolling mountains to the west. A river winds through the forest, a sparkling blue to rival the sky. Dots of deeper blue pepper the far horizon to the north between the large swaths of forest that threaten to swallow everything. Something about the landscape and the city makes my heart swell every time I view them from above.

They are precious to me—or at least they were to the girl I was before. The ghost of that memory haunts me.

I hit the ground at a run and close my eyes. My other senses guide me through the maze. I know it by heart now. The crisp smell of pine from the forest fills my nostrils, but I follow the savory aroma of Father's stew cooking over the fire. My belly rumbles with hunger and I move faster.

If we are not finished training soon, I swear I will eat Pippa in two bites and suffer the consequences.

I slide to a halt at Father's feet and he beams at me.

"Perfect," he says, stroking my hair. "That was the fastest yet. You will do well, my child."

My stomach growls again. "May we eat now, Father?"

His eyes glitter. "Soon. You have one more task."

I swallow my groan. If I do this well Father will be proud. Perhaps tonight he will tell me my purpose at last. I force a smile.

"Now, you must get some practice hunting. You will need stealth and cunning to complete your mission. This will be an excellent place to start."

"Hunting," I repeat. My instincts flare at this word, teasing some buried primal urge.

"Go into the forest and bring me a rabbit. We will put it in our stew."

My mouth waters at the mention of our supper.

Cat's eyes in place, I put my nose to the air as I fly over the hedges and land in the forest proper. Pine and loam, game and fear—these are the smells that greet me.

Father brought home rabbit for my very first dinner, and I remember the scent. I also recall the meat was tender and tasty. All the more reason to do this swiftly.

Flying in the forest is not easy. The trees are close, and the branches grasp at everything in their path. I jog over the leaf-covered ground instead, hoping I can find the rabbit and return to Father before it gets dark. Hunger claws at my belly.

I smell all manner of creatures in the undergrowth and trees, but they flee before I can get close. I realize too late that it is my fast, heedless pace that scares them off.

I will never catch a rabbit if I keep on this way.

I slow, then flutter between the trees. I cannot fly quickly, but it keeps my feet off the ground. The animals will not hear me coming. Is this what Father means by stealth?

Suddenly the warm, fearful scent of a rabbit consumes my senses. My eyes lock on the small creature hopping through the crackling leaves.

Mine.

My predator instincts guide me on what to do next. I float closer and closer. The rabbit crouches in a hollow at the base of a tree, flattening its body to the ground in an effort to blend in. I hear its heart thump against the damp earth.

I pounce, my teeth tearing into the soft flesh of its neck. A tiny part of my brain cringes, but it is all I can do not to devour the animal raw right here in the forest. I must bring the rabbit back to Father.

Hot blood dribbles over my chin, staining the collar of my pale green dress. I try to wipe it away with my sleeve but it coats that, too. What will Father say now that I've ruined my dress?

I swallow the bite I took and spit out the fur. The small eyes are no longer lit with the fires of life. A strange surge of hunger and revulsion courses through me. I killed it because I wanted to eat it, but I am no longer sure this is right. I scramble to my feet, panicked. Did Father intend for me to kill it? Or was I wrong? My only thought was hunger, not to kill.

I stare at the limp, bloody creature in my hands. There is no help for it now. I must return.

I walk back through the forest, slower than before. I fear what Father will think when he sees I killed it. But how else would we eat it? He must have meant for me to do so.

I shiver. How will killing an animal prepare me for the mission he has planned?

I am lost in my circling thoughts when I reach the part of the forest where our hedge begins. I brace myself and launch into the air. Father is speaking to a strange man in front of our cottage. How did he get past the hedge? Father never mentioned any human friends.

The stranger's wide-brimmed hat is pulled down over his eyes. I alight on the ground and run toward them.

"Father!" I say, holding up my rabbit and praying I did

the right thing. "I have got it."

The strange man yells. Father's expression turns from shock to horror to fury in three seconds flat. "Get in the house! Now!"

My smile disappears and I flee inside, flinging myself to the floor by the fire. Tears stream down my cheeks, washing away some of the rabbit's blood.

I chose wrong. I should not have killed the rabbit. I crawl to the window to watch him speak to the other man.

The stranger waves his arms, his tanned face contorted in shapes that make no sense to me. Father shouts back.

Oh, I have done something very bad! Confusion burns through my limbs as I crouch by the window, transfixed by the scene in the yard. The urge to flee tugs at me fiercely, but I have nowhere to hide.

The stranger turns to leave, but Father grabs his arm. The man is much larger than Father, but he calms at his touch. Father speaks to him so low I cannot hear, and when he releases the man's arm, the stranger has changed.

He is now quite happy to stand in our front yard and talk to Father. He even laughs, then takes his leave.

I skitter back to my chair by the fire, all thoughts of dinner forgotten until now. The rabbit rests on the bricks by the fireplace, waiting to be skinned. I hope that is not a part of my training, too.

When Father enters the house, I am relieved to see his expression is no longer the furious one from moments ago. He is back to his usual soft, kind look. I smile tentatively as he approaches.

"You must be more careful, my dear. We cannot have anyone seeing you, not without your cloak."

"Why?"

"The humans are different from you. What you are will frighten them. When they are frightened they lash out like a cornered dog. I would not have you get hurt."

"Was that man afraid of me?"

Father chuckles. "Yes, very much. Most humans will not react well to a girl with wings and blood dripping down her chin." He pats my head and picks up the rabbit. "Excellent work. Though next time, try to bring back the whole rabbit, not a half-eaten one."

I blush.

"Go wash up and I will finish fixing our dinner."

I head for the bathing area, but glance back. "Will you tell me my purpose tonight, Father?"

He shakes his head. "No. But you are almost ready. Tomorrow."

I cannot smother the pout that forms on my lips. I did disappoint Father. I am sure of it. If not, he would tell me what I want to know tonight.

DAY EIGHT

I STAND IN THE GARDEN SURROUNDED BY THE ROSEBUSHES FATHER planted. I water and whisper to them every day. Some are yellow and pink, others white, but my favorite are the deep crimson blossoms. I practice my words at them the most and I suspect they grow bigger because of it. Everyone needs someone to talk to. I have Father, but the roses only have me.

The door of the cottage squeaks open and I grin at Father. Watching the roses always makes me happy. It does not hurt that today is my final day of training.

Tonight, at last, I will understand my purpose. I am floating at the prospect.

He hands me my cloak. "From now on, my child, you must take care to always wear this when you leave the safety of our cottage." He swings it over my shoulders and fastens it at my neck. It catches on one of the bolts, but Father fixes it.

"So the humans will not see the parts that would scare them?"

"Yes."

"Was it my wings or the blood that frightened your friend?"

Father laughs. "Both, I imagine."

"I am sorry. I did not know he would be here."

Father pats my shoulder. "Neither did I. He will not drop in uninvited again. You do not need to worry."

"Oh, good." I skip toward the hedge. "What are we doing for my training today?" Each day has brought different tasks. At first, an obstacle course to test my coordination. Then my speed and efficiency. Then hunting. I have not yet decided whether I like hunting. Though I am quite sure I like rabbit.

"Today, we will see how you do with blending in and being stealthy."

"But I did stealthy yesterday," I say as we enter the path in the hedge.

"That was with rabbits. Today, we will see how you do with humans." He takes me by the shoulders. "Humans fear what they do not understand. They will not understand you. They will be frightened if they see your tail or wings, and you must take care to conceal them."

He adjusts my cloak and I stand up straighter.

"Keep your wings furled close to your back, like a

second skin. Keep your tail beneath your skirts and do not let it slip out for any reason."

I curl my tail around my thigh. "Like this?"

He holds me at arm's length to inspect me. "Exactly. You always were a fast learner, my dear." He turns back to the path, but I pause.

"What if someone does see my wings or tail? What should I do?"

He is at my side in two steps, gripping my shoulders hard. "You will do what your instincts demand—then you will flee. Fly straight here before they can follow you. Do you understand?"

Father's eyes have a look I have never seen in them before. Intense. Determined. Yet something there reminds me of the rabbit I cornered yesterday. I cannot help wondering why.

"I understand."

His grip relaxes and we continue down the path. "Good girl. I knew you would."

"What will my instincts do in such a situation?" I am afraid to ask. I am unsettled by what my instincts did to that rabbit.

"You need not worry. They will take over."

"That *is* what worries me."

"You are not a mere human. You have animal parts and they know what to do. Your barbed tail will neutralize any threat and your wings will help you escape." He tousles my black hair. "You are the perfect creation. I should know; I made you."

Father's explanation sounds simple. Instinct should not be hard to master.

When we reach the forest Father checks me one more time. He leads me in a new direction, one we haven't taken before on our walks.

"Where are we going?" I ask.

"To the road. We must see how well you can stay hidden in plain sight from travelers."

"Will I be doing a lot of hiding in the days to come?" I say, hoping for a hint of my purpose.

"More than I wish, but yes."

"Will I ever be able to walk freely among humans?" I speak the words without thinking and my heart hitches as I utter them. The human girl I once was must wish this. But surely I do not. I only need Father and my roses to be happy.

"I do not know, Kymera, but this is not the time to worry about it. We have more pressing concerns." He points to a man and a wagon pulled by a small horse. "Your next training session has begun."

Heat rises up my back and down to the barbed tip of my tail. I will meet this challenge, whatever it is, and make Father proud.

"What must I do?"

He smiles. "Get by him without attracting attention."

The distance between us and the man grows shorter with every step. I focus on keeping my tail secure and my wings as flat as possible. I hold my breath until I begin to feel dizzy. He tilts his head at us, then returns his attention to the road and his horse.

I did it! I want to leap in the air with joy, but I resist for fear of alarming the man we passed. I bubble over on the inside.

"Well done, girl," Father says. "Now, keep that up along this entire road."

"How many more will we pass?" I squint at him in the sunlight. This is the most open space I've been in yet. It is as though the sun has direct access to my skin, even through the suffocating cloak.

"As many as it takes to reach Bryre's gates and back."

We pass several more men and horses and wagons on the dusty open road, as well as a handful of women and children. They come in an assortment of shapes and sizes and colors, but not one of them in as many colors and shapes as me. Not one with a tail. No wings in sight but those of the birds circling overhead. No cat's eyes to see in the dark, no armored scales or claws.

I am very different from these people.

In more ways than just appearance. Something about them, the way they move, perhaps, is different. Their shoulders are more bent and bony. Their skin is dirtier. Their eyes less gleaming than Father's and mine.

I halt in the middle of the road as I recognize the expressions for what they are. They are depressed. Burdened.

"Why are these people unhappy?" I ask Father.

"It is the wizard's doing. He spoils their crops and steals their children. The people are miserable. They need a savior." He takes my chin between his thumb and forefinger. "They need you. In your first life, your friends and neighbors in the city were precious to you. You were well known for your kind nature. Do not forget that. Even if they fear you, curse you, or attack you."

"I will not forget it. Ever." It is true. The spark of a long-distant memory kindles at Father's words. I cannot remember names or faces, but that emotion, that drive to do what is best for Bryre, remains inside me. I want to help these people. I want them to smile at the sun's rays and have all the roses they need to be happy. This is the first hint at my purpose.

If it is to help them, I will do it with joy.

We approach a turn in the road and Father slows his pace.

"It is time to see how you fare on your own," he says, leading me toward a small grove of trees near the bend. "I will rest for a few moments in the shade, hidden by the trees. You, my dear, will wait several paces before the turn. When you hear someone approaching, walk around the corner in time to pass them."

I frown, not quite understanding Father's reasons. "But they will not see me until they are right on me. The trees block that small stretch of road."

"Exactly. They will be surprised. You must keep your wits about you and not let them know what you are."

I am still confused, but I do as he says and walk to the point farthest from the bend where the trees conceal me from approaching travelers. I close my eyes and listen, letting my animal senses take over.

A hawk flies above, air rushing over its wings. The sun beats down on my face, making me wish I could remove my cloak. But Father has been clear about that. Behind me, the rumble of the last horse and cart retreats. The breeze rounds the corner and flows over me. I smell cinnamon and musk. One is a man, the other I suspect to be a woman. Uneven footsteps approach. I creep forward and moments later a young woman hurries around the corner, eyes cast down and hands clenching her cloak closed, without giving me a second glance.

I frown. Her movements remind me of the rabbit's. Quick and panicked. Something inside rears its head. This woman is scared. I must know what frightened her. I continue around the bend, ignoring Father's instructions. I will go back once I determine the cause.

I see only a young man. He does not look frightening. I pause, making sure no one else is in sight.

When I turn back, the young man grins. Something about it chills me. Perhaps it is that strange glint in his eyes. Or the manner in which he walks toward me. His gait appears nonchalant, but it is faster than I think and he stands in front of me before I have taken two breaths. Before I decide what to do.

I should have run back to Father. Where is he? Why did he leave me to face this unsettling man alone? How will this help save the unhappy people?

"Hello, miss," the man says. His breath smells bitter and strange. "It is far too hot for a girl so pretty to be wrapped up in that cloak." His unpleasant smile widens and my heart races. I do not want to be near this man. "Why don't you take it off?"

I shake my head. "I must go." I head to the trees, but he grabs my wrist, twisting me back around.

It takes me a full five seconds to realize my tail has whipped around and stung the man in the center of his chest. By then his body has hit the ground and the smile has slipped off his face. My hands shake so hard, I have trouble retracting my claws. When did those come out?

Footsteps echo behind me. I hiss, spinning into a crouch.

It is Father. I straighten and my pulse reverts to its normal pace. "I did not mean to sting him. It just happened." I gape at my hands. "I am not even sure how."

He pulls me into an embrace and I breathe in his honeyed smell. A heaviness descends on my chest. "Did I fail my test?" Father pushes me back and cups my face in his hands.

"You were perfect."

I stare at the motionless man on the ground, stunned. "I was?"

"Yes, my child. That man was a threat and you nullified it." He glances down. "Quite efficiently, I might add."

"How did I know to do that?"

"That, my dear, is instinct."

Instinct is an odd thing. I am sure I will be on intimate terms with it soon, but I am uncertain how I feel about my body reacting without my consent. The man no longer looks at me in that unpleasant manner, but I feel sorry for him. He had no idea what I could do. He would not have approached me if he had known.

I suppose that is what stealth is. Both reaching something

undetected and hiding in plain sight like I did today.

My head begins to hurt.

"Come, help me move him to the side of the road."

I tilt my head. "Why?"

Father grimaces. "So if another traveler comes down this road before he wakes, they will only think he is a stupid drunk. No one needs to know what you are capable of yet."

I grab his legs while Father takes his arms, and we drag the limp body into the shade of the trees. The ground under my feet rumbles and when I have set the man down, I wander back to the road.

Two black horses tear down the path, their heavy hooves churning the dirt into dust clouds. Behind them a man in a cart struggles to maintain his hold on the reins. The hitch snaps and the horses' speed increases. I gape, shock rooting me to the spot, as they barrel toward me.

"Kym!" Father shouts, dragging me off the road. My heart flails in my chest as the huge animals race by us. My cloak billows in their wake. Father clutches me to him until I stop shaking.

"Next time," he whispers, "if something that large bears down on you, run. Promise me."

"Yes, I will," I say, troubled. "Should instinct have guided me to do that? Why did it fail me?" Indeed, all I felt was frozen, unmovable.

"Sometimes, when we are caught by surprise, it can mute our natural instincts. That is why you must take care, my dear, to always be aware of your surroundings. Never let your guard down for a moment."

"I promise." I mean it. This strange world outside our cottage requires the utmost attention to navigate, and I am determined to do it well.

Muffled cries reach my ears and I pull away from Father. The cart has overturned, but the driver is nowhere in sight. Before I can say a word, Father hurries to the cart, muttering under his breath. My legs still tremble, but I stumble after him. That poor man must be trapped beneath the cart. He needs our help.

Father reaches it before I do and struggles to lift it. I grab the edge of the wooden frame and together we push it back onto its wheels. It does not seem too heavy to me, but Father heaves with the exertion.

The man underneath gasps with relief as the sun pours over him again.

"Thank you, thank you," he says as Father helps him to his feet.

"Your horses have run toward the mountains. I imagine you will need a few more men to round them up."

"Yes, of course." The man appears rather dazed. He thanks Father again, then limps back toward the city gates, cradling one arm close.

Pride swells in my chest. Father saved that man, just like I will have to save the rest of the unhappy people in Bryre.

We retreat back down the road toward our forest, arm in arm.

"Do you think he will get his horses back?"

Father laughs. "Eventually, yes."

"I did well today?" I ask.

"Oh yes. You exceeded all my expectations."

My steps suddenly feel lighter. Father is happy with me. Can there be any better feeling?

"You will tell me my purpose tonight?"

He squeezes my arm and pats my hand. "Yes, my dear. Tonight you will learn what I created you to do."

I smile at him so wide I can feel the sun on my teeth.

I am finally ready.

That evening, after the stew is eaten and the dishes are scrubbed, Father sits me down by the fire. Pippa lies at his feet, scrutinizing my every move. I suspect the sperrier sleeps with one eye open for fear I will devour her.

She is no longer in danger from me, though I do enjoy teasing her. She would be too stringy for my taste.

Every night thus far, Father and I have read fairy tales together by the fire. But tonight I do not retrieve the worn volume from the shelf. Tonight I have other concerns. My mission, my purpose.

I sit next to the hearth at Father's feet and curl my legs beneath me. It is difficult to prevent my tail from swishing. Father gazes at me with adoration. He is as eager for me to begin my work as I am.

"Now, Kymera, do you recall what I told you before about the wizard?"

"He killed me and Mother. He kills other people's daughters."

Father nods. "He has cursed Bryre with a creeping, evil disease brought on by magic and transmitted like an infection. It strikes only young girls, leaving the adults and boys to be unwitting carriers. The wizard only had to curse one innocent traveler on his way into the city to send the disease spiraling along its path. The people of Bryre have no choice but to quarantine those infected."

"What about me?" I ask. "Could I become infected?"

"No," Father says, smiling. "I was sly with you. You are not just a young girl. You are bird, snake, and cat, too. The curse will not touch you."

I grin. Father thinks of everything. He will keep us one step ahead of this wizard.

He sighs and leans back in his chair. "Trouble is, the usual nurses fear to enter the quarantine hospital. Only those with no children of their own dare to care for the poor girls as they wither day by day, and only guards without families will protect them from the wizard. Stealing the girls from the hospital and holding them in his prison is child's play."

My skin tingles. "Did the wizard hold me in that prison, too?"

Father's face softens. "My dear, I do not know. I only found you after he was through with you."

"Do you know where this prison lies?"

"I do. The prison is hidden in plain sight in the middle of the city, just like you were on the road this afternoon. I have drawn you a map." He pulls a folded piece of paper from the book on the table beside him and hands it to me. "This will lead you to the girls. You will free them. You will be the one to stop the wizard."

DAY NINE

THIS IS MY FIRST TRIP INTO THE CITY. I TUCK MY CLOAK BETWEEN MY
wings and fly down the forest path, buoyed up by my purpose. The sun set hours ago and the moon winks down as
though it knows and approves of my task.

This will be a good night. I will not fail Father. I will
save the other girls from the prison and Father will give
them the antidote to the wizard's disease. He cannot save
them without me. He needs me.

This is why he gave me fairy tales to read. I must learn
about wizards and magic to understand the canny nature of
our enemy.

According to my books, wizards are a wily, unpleasant
lot—trapping maidens in towers, bewitching entire villages,
spoiling the land so nothing can grow. It does not surprise

me in the least that one has found a new way of terrorizing the people of Bryre.

I will do everything in my power to stop the one who killed me and my mother. Who is killing Bryre's girls now.

Father told me how the wizard plagued them for months, then disappeared not long after my death. The evil man only hid so he could devise new plans to torment the city and resurfaced less than a year later. It is up to Father and me to keep them safe.

The tall trees thin to new growth with sparser foliage and I settle back onto the path. Father's parting words echo in my ears.

Do not let anyone see you.

I will not fail him in that, either. I gather my cloak around me, pulling up the hood to hide my face and tuck-ing my tail close to my back. My cat's eyes see clearly even without the moonlight. No traveler can sneak up on me.

The trees are now behind me and rough cobblestones pass beneath my feet. I break into a run, reveling in the night breeze over my face. When the walls of the city come into view, I slow and slip into the trees surrounding them. I know there will be guards, but Father showed me how to put them to sleep. Between my tail and the vials of sleeping powder tucked into my belt, they are no match for me. I purr, content in the knowledge that I am a well-planned creation.

I close my eyes and use my heightened senses to tune in to my surroundings as Father taught me. The guards at the eastern gate snore. Crickets chirp in the trees and field around the city. A hundred sleepers breathe out as one, like a whisper spoken just for my ears. Somewhere inside the walls a child cries, and I fight the urge to fly to it and snatch it away from its undeserving parents. No child should have to suffer. Another guard paces along the length of the wall above me. Though Father gave me the means to defend myself, I have no wish to hurt the guards if I can avoid it. We all want to keep Bryre's children safe.

Still, I hold my breath until he is out of earshot.

Alone again, I leap to the top of the wall, skitter across, and drop down to the other side.

Landing in the soft grass makes me want to remove my slippers and curl my toes into the earth, but I suppress my instincts. I cannot lose sight of my mission.

I remain crouched in the grass as I take in the city with my blue eyes back in place. It is endless. Buildings made from red bricks and dark wood go on for miles in neat little lines intersected by other roads and houses. Trees and flowers, their muted colors shimmering in the moonlight, adorn all of them. I thought our cottage and yard were big, but this is enormous in comparison. How many people live in this one place?

I could stay here drinking it in for hours, but I remove Father's map from my pocket instead. The best route to reach the prison house and not attract attention is marked.

Without hesitation I melt into the shadows.

As I wander through Bryre, I notice some things out of place. Not all the houses are as neat and bright as I first thought. Many gardens have fallen into a sad state, choked with weeds and debris. The windows of some houses are boarded up, like they've closed their eyes and gone to sleep. They feel hollow, and I walk through these sections as quickly as possible.

I round the last corner on the map, and a glittering fountain comes into view, so different from the streets I just passed. Cherubs spout water into the sky, laughing as it falls back to their faces. They are so lifelike that I reach out to lay a hand on one, just to be sure it is marble. It is cool and wet beneath my palm. Despite Father's repeated reminders to stay hidden beneath my cloak, I dip my tail in the water and splash the cherubs. A laugh escapes my throat and I slap my hands over my mouth.

It is quiet enough here in the middle of the night that a mere laugh could have the entire city after me.

Footsteps echo down an alley on the other side of the fountain. Fear slides up my scales and my claws snap forward unbidden. If I am caught, Father will be found out. And the wizard will exact yet another round of revenge. I cannot allow that to happen. I pull the hood down to conceal my face, tuck my tail under, and take cover in the shadows of the nearest building.

I do not breathe at all.

Moments later, a figure about the same height as myself dashes into the square, rounds the fountain, then ducks into the alley beyond. The boy—and I am certain it must be a boy—did not even sense my presence.

But I saw him. And smelled him—a faint trace of

cinnamon lingers in the air, and his chestnut-brown hair streaked with moonlight still dances in front of my eyes.

What could a boy be doing out this late at night? Father said a curfew forced all children to be inside by sundown. Dark magic is the most powerful in shadows and moonlight, and the risk of catching the disease curse is greater at night. It is well past that time, and something in my brain tells me the boy is my age. He definitely should not be out.

But I am not here to rescue a boy. I am here for the girls the wizard locked up. The map guides me past the fountain and down the street the boy came from. Like him, I run. The buildings on these streets are larger than the cottages I passed before. More of them rise for two or three stories and have sturdy brick facades. These do not look like homes.

The building marked on the map as a prison comes into view. A square brick structure with two floors and ivy crawling up the sides. It looks like the other buildings around it. Hiding the girls in plain sight. Clever and diabolical. I wonder if there are charms to keep intruders out, but nothing holds me at bay when I approach.

Now all I have to do is get past any guards the wizard may have stationed here. I expect they will be wily, but Father prepared me for this as well. I make my way to the back of the building, checking carefully for any prying eyes or the telltale sounds of nearby guards. When I am sure I am alone, I fly up to the roof and quickly furl my wings, crouching close to the shingles. Below my feet, many hearts flutter in silent slumber. All those girls.

Emboldened, I pry up several shingles as quietly as

31

possible, and poke my head through the rafters. Two shadows move in the darkness. Guards. No sign of the girls. Perhaps they are in the next chamber. I can sense they are close.

I unlatch one of the vials from my belt and toss it into the room as Father instructed. Plumes of white dust blossom when the glass shatters, filling the space in seconds. The shadows cease moving as the white dust dissipates. It looks as though their dark forms absorb it, but I am sure it is a trick of my eyes.

In a few moments, they sleep soundly on the floor.

I land softly on the stone floor of the room. The guards' faces are slack and loose. They do not look like bad people. I wonder why they work for the wizard. A spell, most likely. Father says magic can do any number of unexpected, tricky things.

The room is more of a hall extending in each direction, with torches in holders along the walls. The door I seek is on the inner wall. The locks are no match for my claws and I am inside in two minutes flat.

Nothing Father told me prepared me for this.

Row after row of cots fill the room, and sickly girls in a wide range of ages sleep on them. The youngest cannot be more than seven and the eldest eighteen. The tang of blood hangs in the air like mist and it threatens to overpower my animal senses. These girls are not merely sick; the curse has taken its toll on their bodies with boils, bloody rashes, and fevered dreams. I stumble between the rows in shock. I cannot count how many girls are here, but the enormity of my task hits me full force.

I can take only one each night.

Stealth and time are on our side, Father said.

How—How can I choose just one? One poor soul to rescue from this nightmare?

A noxious sensation fills my innards and I rush to the nearest chamber pot to heave my supper.

I was once here. This is where I died.

Father claims he does not know, but in my gut I have no doubt. Did he choose not to give me my memories after all, knowing he would send me back to this horror? If so, it was a true kindness.

I rise from the floor, the sickly feeling replaced with a ferocious desire to rip apart the wizard who stole, poisoned, and tortured these girls. I will save them. Even if it takes the rest of my life to do it.

I gaze into the sleeping faces, wondering which one should go first. It is cruel to make me choose. Why did Father not give me guidance on this? Why did he not tell me who needs to be saved most?

I am surprised to realize my face is wet. I touch my cheek.

Tears is the word my mind brings forth. People cry when they are sad.

Yes, I am sad. This awful place makes me sad.

A child in the corner catches my eye. Streaks of damp line her dirty cheeks. She has been crying too.

I will take her first.

I creep closer. She is a small thing and should be easy

to carry. Under the dirt, disease, and darkness, her cheeks bloom with a hint of pink. The same color as the roses in my garden. Her hair is a tangle of golden curls, framing her face in a manner not unlike the cherubs at the fountain. She sucks on her thumb as she sleeps, a continuous, unconscious motion.

Yes, this child deserves to be saved the most. Tonight is her night. Our night.

My arms slide under her slight body and I scoop her up. Her head lolls. Then her eyes pop open. Her fingers fall away from her mouth.

"Hush," I whisper, realizing too late that I left my cat eyes in place over the human irises. A soft whine grows in the girl's chest as she struggles in my arms.

She must not wake the others.

My tail whips forward and stings the girl's chest. Shock registers for a moment—then she goes limp in my arms. I know it is a necessary evil, but I wish I did not need to put her to sleep. I wish to talk to her, tell her how much better her life will be now. That she is safe and when she wakes she can play in my rose garden.

Her sweet face again reminds me of the marble cherubs.

When I get home, I will ask Father if I can have a fountain for my garden. I think these girls would love it while they stay with us.

I tiptoe to the door of the prison room, dodging back into the corridor with the sleeping guards just as the sounds of shuffling feet echo down the hall. I fly through the hole in the roof, replace the shingles, and retrace my steps through the winding streets. The girl is tucked into my cloak. She can breathe, but she will not be easy to spot.

Neither am I. The shadows welcome me like an old friend. By the time I reach the walls, my arms begin to tire. Father is waiting; I must go faster. I pause in the cool grass below the parapet, listening for any approach.

I hear nothing but the snoring guards at the gate.

With one jump, I reach the top of the wall. I turn my cloak around, tying it in a makeshift sling to hold the child.

I stretch my wings and take off into the night.

DAY TEN

FATHER WAS PLEASED WITH THE GIRL I CHOSE. HE PATTED HER HEAD AND
mine when I brought her home and laid her out in the guest
room in the tower over his laboratory.

"You have done well, my child," he said, then bade me
leave so he could do his work to cure her. I wanted to stay
and watch, but Father insisted I needed my rest.

Now, the next day, I still glow with his praise. I did
well. I saved that girl. I wonder if she will like my roses.

I consider the blossoms as I water the bushes. I will
pluck two and give them to her. It will make her simple
room lovely. Roses make everything a little better.

I roll the word *rose* around in my mouth, repeating it out
loud several times as I cross the yard. Something about the
sound of it is pleasing. Soothing, almost.

I climb the stairs of the tower attached to our cottage, where the girls will sleep at the top. The same tower where Father worked so hard to create me. The stone steps do not creak, but sometimes the wooden exterior sways a bit in a strong wind. The winding stair is dotted with small round windows through which streaks of sun light my steps.

The room at the top is sealed by a heavy wooden door, and I use the key hanging from a peg on the wall to open it. When I enter the whitewashed room, the girl is already awake and sits up, her legs dangling over the side of the bed. Her slight form is lit up by the sun streaming through the window behind her. She sniffles and wipes a tear from her cheek. I remembered to keep my cloak pulled close; I am sure she cannot be crying at the sight of me.

"What is the matter?" I ask. She cries harder and makes no answer. Her dainty yellow curls cling to her damp cheeks, and her thin arms wrap around her middle. Her skin is only one unbroken color, and not a single stitch or bolt holds her together. My hand runs over one of the bolts securing my neck to my shoulders before I realize what I do.

Of course, she does not have a tail or wings either, and I am growing rather fond of mine. They are quite useful.

I step closer and I am pleased to see that all traces of the cursed disease have vanished. No more boils and rash, and her fever has all but disappeared. Father is very good at what he does.

Her tears seem endless. I cock my head at her, then hand her the roses. The blossoms are a peach color with a darker red hue creeping up the sides of the petals. Father calls them blush roses.

She does not take them.

I lay them on the bed beside her, perplexed. She sniffles again and picks one up, twirling it between her tiny fingers. She knows how to avoid the thorns. She must like them. I smile hesitantly.

"Mama . . ." she whispers as more tears slip from her eyes.

"Mama?" I echo.

"I want my mama."

Something primal rears inside me, full of grief and other emotions I do not understand.

Mama. Mother. She misses her mother.

Did I miss mine when I was in that awful prison? I wish I could remember, but at the same time I am grateful I do not. I do not wish to experience the pain this child is in.

I drop to my knees before her. "You are safe," I say, but even I understand it means nothing to her. She eyes me, then the rose again.

"Mama loves roses," she whispers.

"Do you like roses?" I ask. Her face twists and the tears come full force again. She shakes her head back and forth and hurls the rose across the room. Petals burst all over the floor.

I do not understand this child or her strange emotions. Why would she throw such a lovely thing away?

"Kym!" Father says from behind me. "What are you doing?"

I spin. Father appears concerned. Perhaps he thought I was crying. "I brought our guest flowers." I frown at the broken blossom on the floor. "But I do not think she likes them."

"Kym, you cannot get attached to the girls. Now, put her to sleep and come with me."

I bow my head. "Of course, Father."

The girl flung herself upon her pillow in such a manner that she will not see me. I sting her without a second thought and follow Father from the room.

I halt in the doorway, an odd feeling coiling inside my chest.

Mama. That word, something about it—

Shimmering blue silk skirts. I can feel the fabric between my fingers, and see how it moves like water around the feet of a woman. *Mama*.

The primal feeling from moments before returns in a flood, threatening to choke me. I cling to the doorframe, and my claws snap into place, driving into the wood.

It fades as quickly as it came. No more silk, no more woman—nothing but the fading sense of a familiar presence.

I run down the stairs. The sight of Father at the bottom calms me.

He stoops to run his hands over the floor. I tilt my head and watch. I have not seen him do this before. But then again, I do not spend much time in the tower. I prefer the garden or a chair by the fire in the cottage.

Father mutters as he pulls on a hidden latch in the floor,

which slides away to reveal stairs. He notices me staring. "Come on. You have something on your mind. You may ask me while I work."

This pleases me. Father is a creator—a scientist, he says—but I have never watched him make things before. I scamper down the stairs after him. My hands shake and I wonder if it is from what just happened in the doorway.

"What are you making today, Father?"

He winks. "You eat so many eggs that we need a few more chickens."

I giggle. I have been eating a lot of eggs. They are my favorite, next to rabbit.

When we reach his laboratory, I gasp. It is a mirror image of the room upstairs, before it was whitewashed and prepared for the girls. But this room is different in so many ways. The floor and windowless walls are all cold, gray stone. Along the wall are long, rectangular stone boxes. Shelves filled with all sizes of odd glass jars line the walls. Some contain dried herbs, others hold eyes and tongues and fleshy things I do not recognize, all suspended in murky liquid.

Despite its underground location, the hidden tower room has a high ceiling. A dozen skeletal specimens of creatures from my fairy tales hang above my head. I reach up, wondering, and touch my finger to the tip of a fish tail attached to the hips of a human-like skeleton.

Father *tsks* at me. "Kym, please, no touching. They are quite fragile."

I do not answer as I circle the room, examining each

in turn. One is huge and equine on the lower half with a human head and torso. Another has a catlike skull, but the body of a much larger beast and eagle claws. Most are combinations I cannot name. I am determined to scour my books for every one of them.

"What is this?" I ask, pointing to one that has a human skull atop an animal's frame with an insect-like tail. The stinger at the end reminds me of my own.

"That is a manticore."

"What is it doing here?"

His expression turns grave. "They are all here for safe-keeping. And for me to study. They helped me determine the best way to connect your parts, Kymera."

A chill slithers over me. "You killed them?"

"Oh, no, my dear. I tried to save them. The wizard draws magic from these animals. Some people grind their bones for the magic residue that clings to them, but I could not bear to let that happen to such creatures."

"You protect them?" I say, relieved.

"Exactly." Father slides a lid off one of the strange gray boxes and reaches inside.

"What are those?" I ask.

"Cold boxes. They preserve things. Like this." He pulls a stiff, half-rotted chicken carcass from the box and places it on the stone table in the center of the circular room. A pair of fuzzy, hoofed legs follows.

Curious, I sidle up to the box and press my palm to the side. I yank my hand away. It is indeed cold. Very cold.

Freezing, says the corner of my mind.

"How does it do that, Father?"

"Some would call it a charm."

"But I thought that was magic." My fairy tales include mention of all sorts of spells and incantations. Wizards cast dark enchantments in the dead of night by waving their arms over a cauldron and channeling the evil magic into terrible deeds.

He smiles. "Indeed, a charm is magic. But I did not say I call it that, just that some people would. There are other nonmagical ways of doing amazing things." His smile falters. "I am afraid my science is about as misunderstood by the people of Bryre as your true form would be. They fear everything they do not understand. That is why they forbade the practice of magic within the city walls years ago, and much of science, too."

"What is the difference between science and magic?" I do not wish to confuse the two and mistake an innocent man for the wizard.

"More than you think, but less than is visible to the naked eye. Magic is an essence that can be wielded; science requires a knowledge of the physical elements. Both can be used to manipulate the world you see around you. A spell cannot be cast with science, but you can still make unusual things happen."

"Like me?"

He glances up from the stiff chicken. "Precisely."

My face lights up with understanding. It is beginning to make sense.

I position myself on the other side of the table to watch

Father work. He murmurs and moves his hands quickly. It is mesmerizing, but not enough that I forget the question troubling me since I spoke to the girl upstairs.

"What did my mother look like?"

Father stops what he is doing and pales deeply. "Oh, Kym. Why must you ask that?"

My face warms. "I think I might remember her. A little."

"What do you mean?" Father frowns.

"That girl. She mentioned her mother. And then I saw something in my mind. A glimpse of a woman in blue skirts. It was so real, I could almost feel the fabric between my fingers." I am not sure how to voice that roaring feeling inside when I had the vision, but I hope my stumbling words give Father enough to go on.

Father leaves the chicken and pulls me into an embrace. "My dear child, your mother was the loveliest creature. Your eyes are just like hers, and you have her sweetness, too. If you saw something it is only a snippet of memory your brain has retained. Do not be troubled by it, and do not search for more like it. Any memories you have left will be scattered and confusing. It will only grieve you to glimpse what you cannot have back."

The truth of Father's words chills me. Whatever my mother was to me once is lost forever.

He returns to his work, and I watch in silence for several minutes, my mind wandering back to my travels the night before.

"Are you certain the curfew is still in effect?"

"Without question," he says, then pauses. "Why do you ask?"

"Might the king have changed his mind?"

"That is unlikely, given the wizard's continued torment of the people." He places his hands on the edge of the table. "Why, Kymera?"

I am suddenly uncomfortable. He gazes at me with a strange intensity and I know I must tell him about the boy I saw run by the fountain. Part of me resists. Part of me wants to keep that secret, that boy, to myself.

But Father has been so good and generous to me, I cannot keep anything from him. He must know all about the mission. I do not want to make any errors that might allow the wizard to proceed with his horrible scheme.

"Kymera?" He stares harder than before.

"There was a boy. I think. He ran by me. At the square with a cherub fountain."

Father's hands tighten around the edge of the table, causing threads of blue veins to pop out on the skin. "Did he see you?" he whispers tightly.

A twinge of fear shivers down my spine. I shake my head. "I hid in the shadows. He had no idea I was there. It struck me as odd because of the curfew."

His hands loosen their grip, but his eyes get a faraway look in them, like he is no longer in the room with me. "Yes, that is odd. I am glad you told me." His eyes meet mine. "If you see anything else out of place, you must tell me. Above all, you must not let this boy or any other human see you. Do you understand, Kymera?"

"Yes, Father. I will stay hidden. I promise."

"Good girl. Now hold this." He gives me the cold, fuzzy legs, guiding my hand to press them to the chicken body. Both are mangled, but as Father mutters and sprinkles them with herbs from his shelves—pepper to warm, aloe to heal—they thaw and change form before my eyes. The flesh is soft and warm now.

My father is truly an amazing man.

He fastens the legs to the chicken with tiny bolts and resumes his muttering.

"How long can we keep her?" My thoughts return to the girl sleeping in the top of the tower. "Will they all come and live with us?"

Father looks aghast. "Of course not. Where would we put them all? We do not have room for that many girls." At my crestfallen expression, he pats my shoulder. "Do not worry. She and all the others you fetch will go to a wonderful place. Much better than anything here."

"What about their mothers? Can they go, too? The girl said she misses her mother." The remnants of the memory pinch inside my chest, but I swallow the feeling down.

Father's face goes slack for a split second. "Not yet. Perhaps when the wizard is gone they can join them."

I smile. "I think she would like that." I run my finger over the outline of the chicken's hoof while Father continues to fuss over the creature. "Tell me about the place we will send her."

He chuckles. "I wondered how long it would take you to ask that." He shakes his head. "Belladoma is the most beautiful city in the world. It lies beyond the western mountains. The ruler is a kind, powerful man. He has a soft spot for young girls in trouble. They will be in the best of hands. The wizard would never think to seek them there. Belladoma's alliance is with me, not the city. He is far too single-minded and focused on Bryre."

I frown. I feel . . . responsible. For the happiness of the girl upstairs and the others in that prison. "But will they have roses?"

"They will have roses and posies and sunflowers and petunias and hyacinths and every flower you can imagine. They will stay in the palace with the king as his special guests."

I have not seen the palace in our city yet, but I plan to find it on one of my excursions. I imagine it must be very fine. How much more lovely must this one be in such a rich, happy kingdom!

"Does Belladoma have creatures like them?" I motion to the skeletons on the ceiling. "And dragons or perhaps griffins?" Father's fairy tales tell of such creatures, but I have seen none in Bryre. Not even here in the laboratory. They are supposed to be both wise and fearsome.

Father grows serious. "I am afraid not. The last griffin died more than a century ago, and dragons have been hunted to the brink of extinction for their magic powers. More so than my friends here. They leave their bones behind, but dragons do not. They are pure magic, right down to their marrow."

"Who hunts them?" I wish to throttle anyone who would do such a thing.

46

"Who do you think?"

I hiss. "The wizard."

Father considers the contents of a cold box. "Not just him, but he certainly has had his share of dragons' blood."

My claws snap into place. "Why?"

He closes the cold box and examines his shelves instead. "It is how wizards got their powers in the first place. Dragons and humans once lived together in harmony. The dragons each shared an affinity with different elements—rock dragons with the earth, water dragons with the rivers, and so on. Eventually those who lived with the dragons began to absorb some of their magic. Those dragon riders became the first wizards."

"That does not make sense at all. If they were friends with the dragons, why would the wizards hunt them?"

Father turns to face me. "Well, my dear, that is the tricky thing about power. People tend to want more of it. These wizards were still human, after all. They discovered that when the dragons died, all their powers transferred to those closest to them. And if they killed the dragons themselves, it sped up the process. Dragons can live for hundreds of years. Why wait around for one to die, when you could kill it right away? The more magic the wizards absorbed, the easier killing dragons became. They have all but disappeared now." He taps a finger to his chin. "Though I did once hear a rumor that a dragon lived somewhere in the vicinity of Bryre. It would not surprise me at all if that was the reason our wizard came here in the first place."

"What an awful thing," is all I can say through my

scowl. Poor dragons. Trusting those men to be their friends, even sharing their magic, however accidentally, only to be murdered by the very same.

Father pulls a few bottles off the shelves and begins shaking drops on the chicken's patched-up body. The flesh sucks them in like the sponges I use to wash the dishes.

"Are there fountains in Belladoma? The laughing cherubs on the one I saw last night were so funny." I need to change the subject before I get angry. Despite what the wizards may have done, I must save the people of Bryre, tonight and every night.

"There are fountains and pools and gardens. Everything is green and bright as the mountains you must cross to get there."

My chest swells with pride. We will take these girls to that paradise. We will save them all. "I wish I could see it. It sounds perfect."

Father stops his work to squeeze my shoulder. "Someday, my dear, you will."

My eyes widen. "Really? I can?"

"Of course. After the wizard is gone, we will spend the rest of our days there."

"When can we take the girl? I want to see it!"

Father's face darkens. "You misunderstand, child. We cannot take her there ourselves. It is too long a journey and we are needed here. My friend Darrell will take her."

Disappointment sets in. Father's friend . . . "Is that the man who was scared of me?"

Father snorts. "It is. But as long as you don't appear as

fearsome as the first time, we will not need to worry about that happening again."

"I will not, I promise." I clasp my hands behind my back. "If we cannot go with them, can I at least have a fountain? For my garden?" I switch to my blue irises and smile hopefully.

"Bring back a few more girls and I will see what I can do."

"Thank you, Father!" I flap my wings happily, sending a plume of herbs skyward from an open bottle on the nearby shelf.

"Yes, yes, now go take this chicken"—he places the stirring beast on the stone floor—"and introduce her to her new friends."

I marvel at the creature pecking at the floor of the tower. Father is good at fixing broken things. I believe he could fix anything. Even our broken city.

While Father returns to the cottage, I let the chicken out in the yard and it clucks and paws the ground with the others. They move fast with their hooves, sometimes galloping in spurts when they get too excited. Just as they begin to do now. I sniff the air. Something has changed; a faintly recognizable odor pierces the hedge.

Someone is coming. I run inside to alert Father and grab my cloak. I do not wish to frighten anyone. I must be presentable. I fasten the clasp around my neck, but the bolts still show. I frown, not wishing to remain hooded on such a warm day.

"Father!" I cry. "Someone is coming through the hedge."

He appears in the hallway. "Thank you, my dear." He pauses when he sees me holding my cloak up over my neck, the only way I can think of to hide the bolts and not wear a hood.

"Wait here, I have something that will help." He vanishes into his bedroom. I barely have time to wonder what he could be fetching for me when he reappears holding out a strip of black satin with a red carving of a rose affixed to it.

"It is beautiful," I breathe.

"I gave it to your mother, long ago," he says as he fastens the choker around my neck. It covers the bolts perfectly. I run my finger over the carving. I will cherish this; it is all I have left of my mother.

Father takes my arm, leading me into the yard to greet our guest. A man drives a small cart that has a box with bars on the back into our yard. I startle as I recognize him.

It is the same man I terrified the other day. I grip Father's arm tighter. Given his reaction, I am more than a little wary, despite what Father says.

He slides off the cart, waving to Father and tipping his wide-brimmed hat to me. "Allo, there, Barnabas. Is this your little secret weapon?" The man winks and something tightens deep in the pit of my stomach. He may be Father's friend, but something about him does not sit well with me. Perhaps it is just leftover uneasiness from the first meeting.

Father pats my arm. "She is indeed. My greatest creation yet."

The man approaches and peers at my face, his eyes widening. "Barnabas, you have outdone yourself. She looks completely different, except for those eyes."

"Yes, she is different enough that the city dwellers will not recognize her if they catch a glimpse."

I squeeze Father's arm. Why should this man be surprised by how I look?

"It is a pleasure to meet you," he says, his hazel eyes meeting mine. His face is dusty and lined, though he is younger than Father. He does not appear to remember me from our first meeting. I am less wild now than at our initial encounter. Perhaps he did not get as good a look at me as I feared.

The man bows and pries my hand off Father's arm to kiss it. I do my best not to pull away, but my claws unsheathe on instinct at the unfamiliar touch.

"What is this?" he yells as he jumps back.

Oh no, I have been bad again! I retract my claws and smile widely, hoping he will calm down as fast as the last time. Father places a hand on his shoulder with a firm grip. "It is all right, Darrell. There is nothing to fear. It was just a trick of the light."

The man's expression slackens. Then he chuckles and wipes his brow. "Well, that right scared me. Sorry, young lady, I must not be getting enough sleep." He adjusts his hat. "Where is our cargo?"

"Kymera, go and fetch the girl, will you? Be sure she is asleep. Darrell will be taking her on a long journey." Father gives me a meaningful look and I know what he wants me

51

to do. I wish the girl did not have to sleep all the time, but Father has his reasons. It is for the best.

I retreat to the tower, glancing over my shoulder to see the heads of Father and the man bent together in deep conversation. The man frowns in my direction more than once. I wonder if he really believes my claws were just a trick of the light.

I climb the tower stairs, smiling at the knowledge of Father's laboratory hiding in the basement. The girl still sleeps and I lift her easily. I take the second rose left on the bed and tuck it behind her ear. She will have many flowers and joys where she is going, but I hope she will keep it and remember me and Father and all that we have given her.

When I return, Father and Darrell lean against the metal bars of the strange cart. Father beams at me as I near. Darrell smiles, but not in the same kind way as Father. Try as I might, I am not warming up to this man.

Darrell opens a section of the bars and gestures for me to place the girl inside. A few pillows and some straw line the bottom. Not as nice as the room I prepared in the tower, but fewer frills are needed for traveling. I rest her body on the pillows, smoothing her hair and clothes.

"Perfect," Darrell says as he closes the door of bars and secures a sheet of canvas over them. "She'll be right safe in there." He turns to Father. "A pleasure doing business with you all, but I must be off. Those mountains won't travel themselves." With a tip of his hat, he jumps up to the seat atop the cart and whips his horse.

"Come, Kymera, it is time to start dinner." Father squeezes my shoulder and heads into the cottage.

I watch the cart disappear into the thick hedge, then close my eyes and wait until the smell of the girl and the strange man dissipates.

DAY THIRTEEN

TONIGHT, THE MOON IS AN AIR DRAGON, CHASING ME HOME AS I RUN through the trees. In my books, dragons like to eat maidens. My latest rescue is secured around me by my cloak, sleeping soundly. She has pretty red locks that float like wisps in the night air. I am the hero who stole her out of the claws of the dragon. Yet I feel for them both. The dragon must be starving, but the girl surely does not wish to get eaten. I, a creature stronger than the humans, will lead the dragon-moon astray and into the path of other prey. Perhaps a nice fox would do.

I dodge another moonbeam. Then I halt in my tracks near the opening to the hedge surrounding our home.

What was that noise?

I hold my breath and wait—

Squawking.

It sounds like our chickens. But why would they be awake at this time of night? They never rise before the sun. I flutter a few inches off the ground so I can pass through the hedge without making a sound. I am not sure why—they are only chickens, after all—but something inside my brain insists caution is the best idea.

I pause at the edge of our yard, jaw dropping open.

The girl I took last night trips and stumbles around the yard. The goat-footed chickens zoom after her, pecking at her feet and making the terrible noise I heard from the woods. Her brown hair whips around her shoulders and face as she dodges their beaks.

How did she get out? I must stop her—if she leaves the safety of our home, the wizard could get her. I cannot let that happen.

I untie my cloak and set my sleeping burden down softly on the grass.

"Stop!" I yell as I take to the air and swoop toward the girl. When she sees me, her eyes go wide and she screams. The chickens swarm and overwhelm her. She falls to the ground, but the chickens do not stop pecking. I try to shoo them, but they are so frenzied, they even peck me. A bead of blood blooms on my hand. I stare at it for a moment, then realize specks of blood cover the screaming, crying girl before me. I throw my head back and howl, claws drawn and cat's eyes out.

The chickens flee.

The girl raises her head from between her arms.

Something in her sharp blue eyes makes my breath choke off. Her gaze is not like that of the other girls. It is . . . stronger. *Fierce* is the word that pops into my head.

She scrambles to her feet and runs toward the hedge. "Stop!" I cry. "Stop! You cannot leave. It is for your safety. The wizard might capture you!"

I am not certain, but I think the noise she makes in response is a laugh. I fly into her path, stopping her before she reaches the hedge.

She skitters back, looking wildly about for another route to escape. "Don't touch me," she cries. "He can't have me."

"I am sorry, but that is exactly why you must stay." My tail swings out and stings her in the arm. Father was right; they never understand what we do for them. She slumps to the ground, but I sting her other arm for good measure. She must have woken up early in order to get loose like that, so I suspect a stronger dose is necessary until we can get her to Belladoma and true safety.

I scoop her up and take her back to the tower. Scratches and peck marks cover her body. I will have to ask Father for a healing salve. The poor thing had no idea what she was doing.

But what I do not understand is why the goat-chickens attacked her. What did she do to provoke them?

I set her down in one of the four beds in the tower room, tucking a blanket around her limp body. When I reach the yard again, Father hovers over my latest retrieval.

"Ah, there you are, girl. What happened out here?"

Father gestures to the torn-up front yard and the wandering chickens.

I frown. "I am not sure. When I arrived home, I found last night's girl running around the yard with the chickens chasing her and making a horrible noise. I had to sting her—twice!"

Father rubs his chin. "Hmm. We shall have to be more careful. Perhaps you should dose them more often, just to be safe. Bring this one inside, and then we will have to round up the chickens."

"Of course, Father." I pick up the red-haired girl, then pause. "Why would she try to leave?"

He puts a hand on my back between my wings and guides me toward the tower. "She wanted to return to Bryre, no doubt."

My brow furrows. "But why would she want to go back to where the wizard held her captive?" Indeed this seems quite at odds with her words.

"She has family there, my dear. And love of one's family can make people do the most incredible things."

I smile. "Like bringing your daughter back to life?"

"Exactly. But in this girl's case, we must do what we can to protect her from herself. She must not return to Bryre until we have stopped the wizard. We cannot expect the girls to always understand, but we must help them anyway."

Pride swells in my chest and buoys me up the stairs. Yes, we have a noble purpose. The humans may not understand now, but one day they will see how much we do for them.

I lay the girl in her bed and tuck her in just like I did for the one who got loose. That girl's pecked-up arms remind me of another lingering question.

"Father, why would the chickens attack her?"

He shrugs. "I cannot say for certain. But I would guess she tried to climb over the hedge by the chicken coop. Sometimes the best route can be the least obvious one, but not in her case I am afraid. She must have given them quite a start. They probably thought she was a fox."

I brush a wayward lock of mussed-up brown hair from the runaway girl's face. "Poor thing. At least the chickens alerted us. I might not have come home so quickly had I not heard them screeching from the woods."

"Yes, that is lucky. I am afraid I am too sound a sleeper for my own good sometimes. And my old body cannot rise from bed so fast anymore."

I take his arm and we retreat down the staircase. "Do not worry, Father. I will keep an ear out for them in case they sound the alarm again."

He pats my hand. "I know you will. I can always depend upon you, my dear."

DAY SEVENTEEN

I HAVE NO TROUBLE GETTING INTO THE CITY NOW. I CAN CLOSE MY EYES
and see it laid out before me. The twists and turns of the
map have become raised and ridged planes instead. On my
mental map, a red dot hovers.

The palace. I have not yet set eyes on it, but I know
where it lies. Tonight, I will find it. And I will fetch another
girl.

This afternoon, I read a tale that brought Bryre's palace to mind. A lonely princess locked in a tower for her
own protection, trapped by her parents' fears of a giant.
It seems even giants need brides, and this one—a mean,
nasty brute—wanted a royal one. They built her a tower
so high that the giant could not reach her, but they always
feared he would come back. She was perfectly safe—and

miserable—until one day she found a way out, and snuck into the main palace during a masquerade ball. There was a handsome prince and dancing and roses, and of course they fell in love. They eloped, but on their wedding night, her groom transformed—into that giant.

Strange how her seeming freedom turned out to be everything she had been raised to fear and hate.

I set out on my usual path through Bryre's streets and alleys, but then veer west. Inspired by the tale, the hidden part of my memory conjures up all sorts of grand things at the word *palace*. Gold, marble, peacocks, coins, jewels. Images swirl in my brain, just out of reach. I need to see them for myself.

I must be extra careful not to disturb the king or his court. I doubt they would take kindly to me poking around. But I will be cautious. If I am caught, I will simply put them all to sleep.

Besides, I only want to see it for a few minutes. I suspect they have a beautiful garden, even bigger than the one Father made for me. If I love my simple roses, how much more will I delight in royal ones?

I keep to the dark corners of the unfamiliar alleys. While I could take out any guards, I prefer to avoid them altogether. Soon, I smell something new. The city has a scent all its own, but it is earthy and musky. This is . . . spicy. Sweet. Fragrant.

I must be getting near.

My breath quickens. I move faster.

Moments later I see the gates, curled wrought iron rising

to meet the tops of the trees. Two guards patrol the perimeter, and I suspect more wait in the guardhouse nearby. I halt, keeping to the shadows. Then another scent intrudes: bread baking, dusted with cinnamon.

The boy I saw the other day smelled just like that. I drop into a crouch, becoming one with the shadow of the building I hide behind. I close my eyes and let my ears take over. Footsteps. Fast ones. The boy is running right this way. My heart stutters. Why would he come here?

He moves swiftly past my hiding place and stops at the end of the alley, remaining out of the guards' sight line. He glances around furtively and presses two bricks into the wall. To my shock, a hidden door opens and he slips inside.

The wall begins to close behind him, but I lunge forward and pry it open wide enough to step through. My curiosity increases by the second. I must know where he is going. The walls are smooth on either side, with an empty torch holder at the front. I slide my cat's eyes into place and tiptoe down the dark stone hallway. It slants down for a time, then suddenly slopes back up. My skin tingles with a strange sense of recognition.

A sudden faintness stops me in my tracks and I press my hand against the wall to steady myself. In my head, I hear the sounds of laughter and feet pounding the dirt of the tunnel. The shadows of two figures bounce along the walls as they run. The scene lasts for only a moment, but it leaves an unsettling feeling in its wake.

For reasons I cannot explain, I am certain this takes us right underneath the gates of the palace. My heart thrums in my chest. Who is this strange boy, out after curfew with access to secret passages? And where did I see a passage like this before?

The sound of stone scraping against stone echoes down the corridor. The boy has exited the tunnel. I sprint to the end and slowly push the barrier open. Claws at the ready, I edge out into the night and flatten my back against the wall of what I believe is the far side of the guardhouse.

The courtyard is immense, filled with the wonderful aromas I caught on the wind earlier. Roses and other flowers paint rainbows across the yard. Rows of tulips are closed up tightly for the evening, but the night-blooming primroses and moonflowers blossom in a full array of delicate yellow, pink, and white. I want to touch and smell them all and forever fix them in my memory, but now that I am not alone I force myself to be cautious. Perhaps I can come back here another night and take more time with them.

A path edged by fragrant purple four-o'clocks leads to a long, fancy building at the far end. Both building and path are lined by sculpted hedges in all sorts of fantastical shapes and sizes. A girl with a fish tail, a man's torso on a horse's body, a winged horse—I stare, transfixed. They are like the skeletons hanging in Father's laboratory, but fleshed out in foliage. They are like me. They are hybrids.

They are beautiful.

Perhaps, one day, there will be a sculpture of me here for saving the girls from the wizard.

A creak echoes down the path, and my focus sharpens.

The boy opens a door in the side of the palace, likely one used by servants. I sneak closer, bounding from hedge creature to hedge creature to stay hidden.

As I near the side door, I hesitate to listen for the guards. I can sense them outside the gates, unaware that a boy and a girl have snuck past them. Still, my growing uneasiness about the palace does not abate. That strange vision with its disconcerting familiarity has only made it worse. Something is wrong here.

I follow the boy through the servants' door. Shadows hang in the air, covering the fine tapestries on the walls and alcoves. If I did not know better, I would think I had the wrong palace. This one is deserted. I tune in to the boy's footfalls and slink down the marble corridor, enveloped by the welcoming darkness. He takes turn after turn as though he knows where he is going. I am perplexed.

Who is this boy? And what can he be doing? He cannot be here to enjoy the garden as I am, but I hear no telltale noises of thievery. He has not touched a thing. He walks with confidence through the halls. I cannot smell other people, nor hear the normal sounds of life or even slumber that I expected.

When the sound of his steps cease, I approach with even more caution. I must get close enough to see what he is about. Otherwise, I will be up for days burning with curiosity. I come to an ornate doorway, and peek inside. Two carved marble thrones sit on a dais at the front of the room. The marble hall is dark, save the beams of moonlight shafting in through the high windows. I imagine long tables overflowing with food and wine, and people in beautiful costumes dancing and laughing before a regal king and queen, just like they did in the story I read this afternoon.

Tonight there is only the boy. And me, spying on him.

He approaches the dais, but kneels at the bottom step. Decorative roses are carved into the marble edge, and he presses the second to last one on the left. It sinks into the rim. A marble panel slides out of the step base, startling me. The boy pauses for a moment and I pray he did not hear me jump. I hold my breath and count to ten, waiting for his alarm to pass.

He takes something out of his cloak—a slip of paper—and places it in the hidden compartment. When he pushes it back in, a click echoes in the hall, much louder in the emptiness than it should be.

This boy knows secrets about the palace.

I vanish into my corner, covering my face with my hood. He must not see me at all. But I cannot help peeking a little.

The boy takes off down another passage. I marvel again at the complete absence of people. The gardens are well cared for; someone must live here. Father never said a word about the city no longer having a king. My misgivings curl around me like a cloak.

Maybe the paper the boy left will shed some light on this mystery. As his footfalls grow fainter, I leave my shadows and creep across the huge ballroom to the dais and the thrones.

A slow smile inches across my face. I have never

encountered a place quite like this. At least, not that I remember. I wonder if my past self ever visited the palace. That might explain the odd feeling I had in the tunnel. Did I love it as much as I do now? The shadows and marble and moonlight make for an extraordinary combination. And the garden!

But I must focus. If I am wrong and this place is not as empty as I believe, I could be caught at any moment. I hurry to repeat the motions the boy made to open the panel in the bottom step. When it slides out, I snatch the paper.

More girls sick. K suspects wizard. Will remain where he is. More guards.

My heart flutters. This boy is delivering a message—about my own mission. I sit on the steps, reading it again and again until I can recite the words by heart. Father will want to know about this. If the boy took such pains to hide it, it must be important.

The question is, who is he delivering the message to in an empty palace?

I run a clawed finger over the marble veins in the steps when I am overcome with a wave of dizziness and light. A child's laughter echoes in my ears, and sun spills onto the floor instead of moonlight. A golden-haired little girl, so clear, swings in front of my eyes as though we dance together. She bows, and the vision vanishes.

I return the paper to its hiding place and push the panel back with trembling hands. What is that child doing in my head? Who is she? And why does this odd protective urge linger in my chest?

The moon is higher in the sky—it is getting late. I must rescue a girl and return to Father before dawn breaks. I sneak back through the halls, fearing guards will descend any second.

But without the mysterious boy's footsteps to guide me, I take a wrong turn and end up in a long, wide hallway. Huge, crooked portraits line the walls for as far as I can see in the darkness. Pieces of the marble floor are cracked and stick up at odd angles like some creature tried to burst through. Chills ripple over me, as I realize the walls have holes too, and from them dark twisting roots creep to the floor, leaving whole sections in rubble.

What happened here?

Whatever it was, and whatever this is, it must have something to do with why the palace seems all but abandoned.

The urge to run is overwhelming. I backtrack through the halls as quickly as possible. Finally, I reach the garden and its wondrous flowers and hedges. I attempt to gain entrance to the tunnels the same way the boy left them, but all my efforts come to naught. The wall of the guardhouse is frustratingly unmoving. I patiently track the guards' patrol, then leap over the palace walls when they are out of sight. I take off at a run to the prison and I am almost at the cherub fountain when a voice calls out.

"Hey! You there!" I stumble at the sight of the boy at a crossroads. Luckily, my tail is curled around my thigh and does not slip out. Fear fills every muscle in my body, freezing me where I stand for one long torturous moment.

His brown eyes warm and widen in surprise, and I thank my good sense that my blue eyes are in place. Messy chestnut locks ring his face, lending him a wild look.

Instinct takes over and I bound down the road, away from the boy. He cannot see me. He cannot talk to me. Father will be furious.

"Wait!" he calls. His feet pound after mine, but I am much faster and round the fountain first, dodging down an unfamiliar alley. This boy, however intriguing, must not know where I am headed. He could be working with the wizard for all I know.

When his footfalls no longer trail after me, I lean against a building and catch my breath. Adrenaline leaves my legs rubbery and weak. I must be more careful. What if he saw me coming out of the palace?

I will rest for a few more minutes, just to be sure he is gone. Then, and only then, will I resume my task.

DAY EIGHTEEN

WHEN I WAKE ON THE FLOOR OF THE TOWER ROOM, FATHER WAITS IN THE armchair in the corner, studying me carefully. The limp bundle of girl remains on the bed where I placed her last night. I waited a long time before fetching her and was so exhausted that I must have fallen asleep as soon as I set her down.

"Something troubles you, my dear," Father says.

My face burns and I take a seat on the edge of a bed. My dreams were plagued with images of the strange boy, and the haunting vision of the little blond girl. I cannot lie. Father can see into the recesses of my mind and sense everything I know.

"That boy," I say, fearing his anger. "He saw me on the way to the prison. He called for me to stop."

Father grabs my arms. "What? How could you let some-one see you? Did you speak to him?"

I flinch. "I ran. I hid. He did not catch me."

The tension in Father's shoulders relaxes. "Good. You are certain he did not follow you to the prison?"

"I am certain," I assure Father.

"You must be careful, Kymera. If anyone else were to find the secret prison, they would be in danger, too. Only you can go in and out safely."

Shame slinks through my belly. For some reason, I do not like the thought of the boy getting caught by the wiz-ard. I brush the strange feelings away as Father paces the circular room. He taps his forefinger to his chin as he often does when he thinks hard about something.

"What I do not understand is why the boy was out after curfew. The king's proclamation allows for no exceptions."

My face reddens. "I might know something, but I can-not make sense of it."

Father stops and stares. "Well, go on, child."

I clasp and unclasp my hands. They are sweaty, which strikes me as odd.

"I am not sure the king is in power anymore."

"What?" The look on Father's face makes me want to giggle. Confusion, mixed with fear and a tinge of happiness. So much conflict in the span of a mere two seconds.

"The palace is empty."

"Tell me, how do you know this?" he whispers.

"I am sorry, Father, but I had to see it for myself. All the fairy tales revolve around a palace, and after all you've told me of our city, I could not help it. But when I arrived, no one was there. Except that boy." I frown, realizing how much this could upset Father. I wish I had held my tongue.

"No one? What do you mean, no one?"

"The only guards were at the gates, there was no heavy breathing of sleep—one of the halls even seemed to be falling apart. That boy knew secret ways in and out." My hands quiver as the uneasiness from the night before descends again, and I clasp them together.

"What did the boy do in the palace?"

"It was all very strange. I followed him to the throne room and watched him open a panel in the dais stairs. He hid a note there and ran off." I grin. "But I am sly and I read his note. I put it right back. No one will know."

"What did it say?" Father's voice is throaty and he seems to be having trouble swallowing.

"The meaning baffles me. It said: 'More girls sick. K suspects wizard. Will remain where he is. More guards.'"

Father's hands shake, but then he laughs out loud, startling me. "He is running away. The king is running away and using a mere boy to deliver secret messages for him. No wonder the city council still makes a show of entering the palace every day. They are only there to retrieve messages, not truly holding court." He sighs and runs a hand through his silvery hair. "Kym, our king is a grand fool. If you can intercept his messages, he has no hope of keeping them from the wizard. He may as well deliver them right to his doorstep. And sending a boy! After curfew! As though no one would notice."

70

I am pleased Father is amused by my discovery. "The king must fear this wizard."

"Indeed he does." Father's face takes on a grave expression. "The wizard sacrificed his daughter, too. The crown princess."

I suck in my breath. "Oh, the poor girl." I picture a girl in fine clothes, withering in the prison under the wizard's thumb. It breaks my heart. In a way, it reminds me of that fairy tale about the princess in the tower. "I wish I had been alive in time to save her."

Father cups my cheek. "You would have done a fine job of it, too, I am sure. But we can only save those who remain. Mourning the lost will not help those who can still be found."

I am lucky to have such a wise, kind father. It fuels my boldness.

"Father, was there another girl? A small, blond one who I may have played with?" I cannot hide the tremor in my voice.

"Another girl? No, my dear. You are my only child. We lived in Bryre but briefly, and after that it was only you and I and your mother here in our cottage."

Mother. That word again. Every time I hear it, the hollowness inside me expands. I do not know about magic, but words are powerful things indeed.

"Why do you ask?" Father says.

"It was another sliver of memory," I say. "I could have sworn it was a little girl."

"Perhaps it was a memory of you looking in the mirror,

71

or a friend you made when we were in Bryre."

"Yes, that must be it," I agree. "When can I hunt down the wizard? I want to destroy him." The remnants of my shattered memories may be all I have to remind me who I was before, but I know who I am now.

The vehicle of the wizard's destruction. Every day I embrace this more wholeheartedly.

"In good time, child. I am still trying to find him. It seems he and the king are well hidden both from each other and from me."

"I know you will find him." If anyone can do it, it is Father. I just hope it is soon.

I flutter through the moonlit woods with a heavy heart. Even though he is no longer upset, Father's words still ring in my ears.

How could you let someone see you?

How could I, indeed? I had not meant to, but I have not seen many humans aside from Father and this boy. I must have stared too long at him in the palace and somehow caught his attention. He would not have noticed and followed me otherwise. My curiosity will be our undoing.

Our work is too important for me to risk. I must push the boy out of my head. It is, according to Father, the only way. I do not see any other.

So why is my pulse pounding and my breath shorter than usual?

Pausing at the edge of the city walls, I check for guards, then bound up to the walkway at the top. I take a deep breath, inhaling the glorious scent of roses beneath as the night blooms waft upward.

Though I saw it for only a moment, that face is etched upon my heart, with lines and planes different from Father's. Younger. And . . . handsome. Yes, that is the word. *Handsome.* And his expression, a mix of shock and something I cannot identify. Perhaps no one looked at my former self in such a manner so I have no word for it in my lexicon.

But I must push him out of my thoughts. I do not know this boy, and Father is certain he will be trouble. He will cause us to fail. Or worse, he might be working with the wizard. Why else would someone be out after curfew lurking around the palace? Yes, the boy cannot be up to anything good.

My mind flits back to the prison filled with girls in pain. I jump down and run so fast through the alleys that I may as well be flying.

I slow as I reach the square with the fountain, now wary of entering an exposed place. I slink through the shadows, losing a feather or two to the rough stone walls. The welcome cool seeps through my wings and cloak to my taut muscles and flaming skin. A familiar scent meanders through the square—that of baking bread.

A flush creeps up my patchwork neck and I switch to my cat's eyes. Before I can complete a scan of the square, the boy steps around a column and approaches the fountain. The smell of bread grows stronger.

I freeze, switching back to my human eyes. I will myself

to blend into the black shadows surrounding me.

When he reaches the fountain, he stops and rests some-thing on the rim. The playful cherubs block my view of it. My throat closes. I am trapped. If I move an inch he will see me.

The boy tosses something into the fountain, then runs a finger through the waters. He raises his eyes and—to my shock—meets mine without flinching and winks. Before I can recover my senses, he bows, then runs off down his usual alley.

All instincts are on alert. Is this a trap? What did he leave at the fountain's rim? How did he know I was here? I curse myself for my stupidity. Despite my efforts, I have not been cautious enough. I am not good enough to fulfill the mission Father created me to complete.

I am a failure.

I close my eyes, listening to the night sounds and sniff-ing the breeze to ensure the boy has truly left. The echoes of his steps and his familiar scent fade as he travels away from me.

I breathe out slowly. He saw me. How strange are his manners!

What did he leave on the fountain? Curiosity rears its head, too powerful for me to resist. I must know.

I leave the safety of my shadows and circle the fountain, the cherubs happily spraying me as I pass.

There, on the edge of the fountain, is a perfect red rose. Its scent must have mixed in with the other roses in the area, masking it from me until now.

The boy who smells like bread and cinnamon left me a rose.

I pick it up, wary of thorns and barbs. I press the crimson petals to my nose. It tickles, but smells divine. The warmth on my neck rises to the crown of my head.

I like this flower. I like this boy. Someone working for the wizard would not leave a gift like this. Would they? I must ask Father, I know, but part of me resists. What if he thinks the flower is under a spell? What if he makes me get rid of it? I want to keep it, smell it, and stare at it as long as it lasts.

It is the loveliest thing I have ever seen. That boy left it for me. It is mine. I should not have to give it up.

Perhaps I will tell Father in the morning. Tonight, it is just for me.

A smile creeps over my face and I dip my hand in the water, swirling the images of shining coins at the bottom. I wonder what those are for. Father will know.

I tuck the rose into my thick, braided hair and hurry to the prison.

Tonight, a new pair of guards is posted outside, and I am forced to circle around. I watch their patrol carefully and time my own movements to evade their notice.

On the roof, it does not take me long to pry the shingles up. More shadows than before are posted in the girls' room. I count at least five tonight. I toss down the vial of powder and watch the smoky plumes curl around all the bodies in the room, girls and guards alike. Soon they all slumber, and I can go about my business.

75

I have devised a system for deciding which girl to take each night. I go bed by bed down the line. It is fair and requires less thought.

These girls, they are beginning to unsettle me. While I am grateful not to be a weak child anymore, sometimes I wish I could remember what it was like to be completely human. To have a simpler life, free from the call of duty, and the strange impulsive tugs of animal instinct.

One where I could meet a boy offering roses by a fountain without fear of the repercussions.

As I gather the girl in the designated bed, I realize another child has already taken the place of the one I took the night before and each night before that. Every bed in the prison is filled again. I gape for a moment too long and hear the creak of the front door opening below. The guards posted outside return for the change in shifts, just like they do every two hours.

Instinct takes over. I bolt through the rafters.

The second I hit the trees beyond the walls, I wing home, letting the night air wash away my fear that all my efforts to save the girls of Bryre and defeat the wizard will come to naught.

DAY TWENTY-ONE

I LIE ON MY BED, ALLOWING THE MORNING SUN TO WARM MY NAKED, mottled arms. I stretch toward it, grinning as I recall the secret stashed beneath my pillow. I reach under it to retrieve the latest rose. The boy has left one for me at the fountain for the past several nights. The petals of this one are flattened, but the scent lingers. I press it to my nose and remember the boy.

Brown hair, brown eyes. Everything about him suggests warmth. I am warmed just thinking about him.

He is an odd one, though. Each night I follow him to the palace, staying hidden in the shadows, while he sneaks in and hides a note in the throne room. I memorize them all, and by the time I reach the fountain, a rose awaits me.

I have been exceptionally careful, and the boy has not

spotted me again. But he knows I am out there, since he keeps leaving me the roses.

The notes are almost as strange as the boy. Father is delighted by them, though I cannot decipher their meaning yet.

Disease spreading. Move D to first position.
Two guards deserted, need more recruits.

"Kymera!" Father calls for me and I shove the flower back into its hiding place. I do not want to tell him about the roses yet. He would not be happy that a boy is leaving me gifts.

"Coming!" I call back, and throw on my clothes. Father depends on me to feed the chickens in the yard each morning and I am a little late. Their hooves scratch the earth with impatience.

I fly to the kitchen and grab the bucket of feed. It always fills overnight, but I never see Father do it. I must ask someday where we keep the feed in case I ever wake first.

When I toss the feed into the midst of the chickens, they commence a riotous squawking and look ridiculous with all the fuss they make. Feathers dot the yard, amid the grass and dew and sunlight. I cannot help laughing. I love these chickens. And the eggs they give us. I must collect a few right after I water my roses.

Pippa amuses herself by digging in the soil at the far end of the garden while I water the red-, pink-, and blush-colored blossoms. She has learned not to chase the chickens while they feed, though it took a lot of pecks and blood to get there.

She whimpers at something lodged in the dirt and bats it with her paw. Then she scrabbles at it even more determinedly. I pause in my task to see what she has found. Her furious digging kicks up dirt every which way, so I can barely see into the hole she is making. I shove Pippa aside.

"Bad Pippa! Bad!" I growl at her, certain she has ruined my lovely roses. The sperrier slinks back but continues to whine. "Go away! Shoo!"

A good chunk of the roots at this end of the garden have been torn up. I huff as I press the soil back on top of them, ready to eat Pippa out of spite.

I stop.

Something else lies in the dirt. Chills shiver over me as I reach my hand between the twisting roots and hit something hard and unyielding. I tug, but it does not give way. I yank harder, then fall backward into the pile of dirt Pippa left behind, holding the strange thing in my hand.

Except it is not so strange. In fact, I know exactly what it is.

A bone.

It is long and white and resembles the arm of the mermaid hanging in the tower laboratory. Curious, I put it next to my forearm—it is almost the same size. What is this thing doing beneath my roses?

I scramble in the dirt on my hands and knees. I dig around the roots until I feel more bones under my fingertips. I brush off the dirt, revealing a rib cage and another bit of arm.

I keep digging until my dress is caked with damp soil, then stand back to survey my work.

It is a skeleton and it does indeed remind me of Father's creatures. The top appears human, but the bottom looks like a larger version of the pygmy goat legs Father uses to make the chickens, hooves and all. Only one thing is missing.

Its head.

Despite the warm sun, goose bumps pop out on my skin. My gut feels as though it is filled with the earthworms dancing through the soil, whispering that this is not right. A headless skeleton does not belong under my rose garden.

Something is wrong.

I hurry back toward the house, only to be stopped by the empty egg basket at the door. Father will need the eggs for breakfast. He is waiting for me. I fly to the coop and grab a few as fast as I can.

Father rests by the stove, the pot already boiling. I toss the eggs in, snarl at Pippa to scare her out of the chair next to him, and take a seat. He kisses my cheek, eyes widening at my appearance.

"Good morning, my dear. What on earth have you been up to?"

I wipe my dirty hands on my dress. "It was not me, Father. It was Pippa."

He reaches down to scratch her head. "What did she do now?"

I pick at the dirt under my fingernails and frown. "She

was digging in my garden. At first I thought she was just going to spoil my roses, but she found something." That shivery feeling returns but I shrug it off. "It was a skeleton, like one of those creatures in your laboratory."

Father's face softens. "My dear, I am sorry. I did not ever expect you to find that. Yes, a faun was buried near where your garden lies. He was . . ." He glances away momentarily. ". . . a close friend. He was the first hybrid I knew to die in the wizard's never-ending search for more power. I buried him there, some time ago, and planted the roses over his grave. Both as a tribute and to keep his bones from being used by others."

"But . . . where is his head?"

"The wizard took it as a prize. But I take heart that I managed to salvage the rest of him." He sighs heavily and leans back in his chair.

My poor father. How much he has suffered! I throw my arms around his neck, wishing I could squeeze all the sadness out of him. He hugs back, then sets me in my chair again, dusting the dirt from his shirt.

"I see you had another successful evening," he says, unhappiness lingering in his gaze.

"Is she awake yet?" If Father wishes to change the subject, I will not press him. I cannot bear to see him upset.

He shakes his head. "No, she slumbers still. We will check on her at midday."

The girl I rescued last night had a pretty ring of dark curls around her face. It is very similar to my own hair, and I am determined to arrange mine in the same manner. It framed her sleepy expression so prettily. Perhaps that boy would like it, as long as the rest of me stays hidden beneath my cloak.

Father opens a book as we wait for the eggs to cook. I watch them bobble in the boiling water, but sneak a few glances at him. The book is worn leather and has an embossed dragon on the cover. Of all the creatures I have learned about, those fascinate me the most.

"Is that a book about dragons, Father? Will I get to read it, too?" I ask hopefully.

He glances up from his reading. "This is not a storybook for you, I am afraid. You would find it a bit dry. It is for research only."

I frown. "What are you researching?"

"Dragons, and their movements over the years. Like I said, there are no stories here."

Disappointed, I change the topic to another that has been troubling me for days.

"Father?" I say.

He looks sideways at me. "Yes?"

"Am I like her?"

He frowns. "Like who?"

"Your daughter. The one who was human."

He closes the book and removes his glasses. "Oh, my dear, you are just like her because you are her. You think like her, speak like her, even move like her."

"Do I look at all like her? Darrell seemed so surprised by me the other day that I wondered."

He smiles. "Of course, some parts of you do. Much of your face and skull had to be replaced, but your eyes are hers. Your hair is a different color, but I daresay I like it much better."

I twist a long black lock around my finger, watching the way the light reflects off bits and pieces of it. "What color was it before?"

"Gold like the sun. Now you are dark like the night. Fitting, is it not?"

My breath hitches in my throat. "Will I ever be able to walk into Bryre in daylight without a cloak like I did before?"

"Now why would you want to do a thing like that?"

I twist my hands together in my skirts. "I wish to know more about the people there. You told me I loved them before. I want to see the city with the sun shining down on the fountains and the flowers and—"

He cuts me off with a wave of his hand. "No. You are a hybrid. You shall never walk among the humans. You are better off not wishing for it."

My face burns with shame. Despite what Father may think, I do wish for it. I appreciate what I have gained in my new life, but I cannot help wanting to know what I lost. I may be a hybrid now, but they are nearly extinct as well. "Why do you think ill of them? Are you not human too?"

"Of course I am. But you are not. I have told you before, they fear what they do not understand, and a girl with wings, a tail, and a cat's claws and eyes would terrify them." He cups my chin as tears form in the corners of my eyes. "They would undoubtedly lash out at you, and that is something I could not bear."

I stare down at my twisting hands. He cannot be right about all of them. It cannot be true about that boy. He leaves me roses. He wants to know me. "Surely, they are not all bad. I am part human, too."

"No, my dear, they are not all bad. But the ones who strike out of fear are in the majority. Even if you found one or two who did not fear you, they would be overwhelmed by the others."

"What do you mean?"

Father sighs. "Let me be clear. If the humans find out what you are, they will kill you. They will hunt me down and kill me for creating you. Anyone caught sympathizing with you would be murdered as well."

My entire body grows cold. "Are they so vicious?"

"Yes. They are ruthless. Stay as far from them as you can." He cracks his book again but then closes it halfway to examine me. "You have not seen that boy again, have you?" His eyes narrow and I cannot meet them.

"No," I lie. "I have not."

Satisfied, he returns to his book and we wait for breakfast to finish cooking.

If there was any doubt I have to hide the roses from Father, it is gone. His words tear apart my insides. I cannot believe what he said is true of the boy. If the humans caught me, I could defend myself. That is why Father gave me the claws to fight, the tail to stun, and the wings to flee.

I want to please Father, but it is no longer the only thing I desire.

I want to see that boy again.

DAY TWENTY-FOUR

IN MY BOOKS, THERE IS ALWAYS A PRINCE, AND HE ALWAYS HAPPENS upon the damsel in the most unexpected places. As I flutter between the sunbeams shafting through the forest, I cannot help but wonder if I will meet my prince here, like this. Does that boy ever wander through this forest? Could a creature like me even have a prince to call her own?

Perhaps somewhere out there is another hybrid like me. Or maybe Father could make me a prince.

By the time I reach the river that meanders around the edge of our woods, the sun is at the very top of the sky, smiling down at me. I usually love days like this; everything in the forest is bathed in warmth and I can drink it in. But today my unsettled thoughts hang over me like a shadow.

Of course, this is the first time I have wandered off

without a task from Father. He is away at a market, he said, foraging for the materials he needs for his experiments. He will be back by dusk, but the afternoon is mine. And I want nothing more than to read my books by the river. I settle onto an outcropping of rock that glitters in the sunlight, and crack my book.

A yapping sound disturbs me. My keen ears perk. The sound gets louder and I scowl.

Pippa.

That blasted sperrier followed me.

She bursts through the foliage, then skids to a stop, eyeing the rock I perch on warily. She growls.

I stick out my tongue. "There is not enough room for you up here, anyway." She paces for a few minutes, the rumbling in her tiny throat unceasing, then finally curls up near a bunch of ferns about ten yards away.

I settle into my seat, a depression on the boulder that just fits me, and let the stories paint pictures in my mind.

In this one, the miller's daughter loves the king's youngest son. Trolls and gremlins roam the land and wizards make deals, extracting promises no one can keep. Though the prince is handsome and brave, and the girl is fair, it does not end well.

One look at the multicolored skin of my arms, and the weight of my tail curled around my leg, remind me of how different I am from the girls in these tales and the girls I save each night. Father says I am perfect, but would a prince agree if he knew what I am made of? Would he value me for the usefulness of my parts, or for the contents of my heart?

Or would he only value me as a prize to slay like the monsters in the story?

My fairy tales have shed no light on this subject.

Father gave me them to educate me about the behavior of humans and their many odd customs. And the trickiness of wizards. In my books they never fight fair. I must be prepared when I meet my evil wizard.

The sun has traveled a great distance in the sky. I should go soon to be sure Father does not beat me home. He might not view my newfound freedom as fondly as I do.

But I am not quite ready to leave this place yet. I stretch out on the rock and stare up at the blue sky through a web of leaves from an overhanging tree. Everything is sunny and bright. I could bask in it forever.

Even the rock beneath me is warm.

And moving.

Before I can get my bearings, I'm tossed off and roll to a stop at the base of a thick oak. I rise to my feet slowly, trying to understand what is in front of me amid Pippa's furious yapping.

The rock has a face. And feet.

And teeth.

The rock unfurls in my direction, drawing itself up into an enormous beast.

A dragon.

My claws unsheathe while my heart shudders against my rib cage. Heat blazes over every inch of my skin.

It is a creature out of my fairy-tale books. I thought they were long gone from Bryre and the surrounding cities. But what I mistook for granite shining in the sun is actually gleaming scales. Sunlight flares off them in every direction, lending the beast a glowing aura. Two knobs of rock open and blink at me with pale yellow eyes. Wings, five times the size of mine at least, expand from his body and flap, sending waves in the opposite direction of the river flow.

His head swoops down, the eyes studying me. They blink once, twice. I do my best not to breathe. The dragon could swallow me whole and not think twice about it. And still be ravenous.

Pippa yips one last time, before she turns tail and flees into the forest. The dragon does not pay her a whit of attention.

The giant nose sniffs the air. It presses close to my ribs and inhales. Blood rushes to my head, instinct screaming through every pore. But instinct is useless here. He would catch me before I took flight and fighting is out of the question.

The dragon breathes out, humid air rushing over me.

You smell odd.

I gape at the beast. How did that voice get in my head? Did he just speak to me?

I sniff the air; the dragon's scent reminds me of the deep forest after a heavy rain. Dark and dank. But with a hint of metal.

"Y–you smell odd, too," I whisper back.

The head rises up, above the stonelike shoulders and trees, and opens to let out a sound like boulders falling.

Is he . . . is he laughing?

The head returns and the pale eyes hold me in their gaze once again.

What are you?

My windpipe narrows to a pinhole, but somehow I manage to squeak out, "I am Kymera."

Ah, a chimera. I see. Part human, part bird?

"And snake." My tail slides out, trembling.

The head rears back, then slowly inches forward again.

Sister.

The strangest feeling comes over me. Relief, as though a long search is over. But I do not believe the feeling is my own. It comes from the dragon.

I've been looking for you. Your strange scent called me out.

"Why?" I cannot fathom what a dragon would want with me in particular. But I cannot shake the feeling I got from it. Mixed in with the relief is something else. Something I feel, too. "You are lonely."

The giant head nods, scales glittering. He is awfully pretty, even if he does have me trapped against this tree.

Not many like me are left. The mouth makes an awful hissing sound. *Wizards.*

Hatred fills me. This time the feeling is already there, just magnified by the creature's own. A growl escapes my mouth.

You hate them too? The head tilts.

"More than anything."

We must protect each other, sister.

Warmth fills my chest at the mention of that word again.

"From the wizard?" I ask.

He hisses again. *Yes. They take our blood, they take our magic.*

Chills trickle up my legs. Father mentioned dragons' blood being used in potions. What a horrid thing to do to a creature.

"I am going to kill the wizard. It is my mission."

You are most unusual. If I did not know better, I would swear the dragon raised an eyebrow.

"Thank you." I pause, realizing I do not know what to call him. "What is your name?"

You may call me Batu.

"Batu," I repeat, testing the word out loud. "It suits you."

His snout opens wide in what I hope is a grin. *You and I, we are very alike, sister.*

Yes, we are alike. Alone and feared. And we both hate the wizard with equal ferocity.

There is only one way to protect each other. The dragon settles back on his haunches, but his height still rivals the treetops.

"Tell me. I will do it." I am drawn to this majestic creature who has named me kin, who has also suffered at the hands of wizards. Surely Father would approve—he has done what he can to protect many hybrids. Protecting a dragon is just as worthy a cause.

A blood oath. Together we will be stronger. Batu punctures the paw of his front foot with a claw. Shimmering blue blood beads between the scales. I do the same, but yelp at the pain in my hand. My blood is red, and does not shimmer as the dragon's does. I am somewhat disappointed by this.

Batu holds up his huge paw.

Place your hand on my paw, and when our blood mingles, it is done.

I do not understand how this will protect us, but I am not well versed in the ways of dragons. I confess, mostly I am just relieved it does not want to eat me.

Still, this creature stirs up something primal, a need hovering just below the surface of my mind.

I place my hand in his paw. The trickle of blue blood is cold and thick, yet once it meets mine, something changes. A thousand pins prick my hand, rippling down my arms, tail, and body.

We must keep each other secret to keep each other safe.

I yank my hand away, frowning at the lingering pain. "You mean not tell anyone?"

The massive head nods.

"No one at all?" I am not sure I can keep such a secret as this from Father.

No one!

The force of his thought shoves me against the tree. "At least allow me to tell my father," I plead.

No one, the dragon think-speaks again, though softer this time.

"But we're working against the wizard. You hate him, too. If we all work together, surely we could defeat him. You are huge!"

The nearest eye blinks slowly. *Size and power are not*

always related. Though yes, once, I might have defeated the wizard.

"Why not now?"

He killed too many of my brothers and sisters. They were the strong ones.

"But how do you know if you have never tried? You will not be alone. Like you said, we will be stronger together."

I can make no promises when it comes to wizards. He pauses, the giant stone face hovering above my head, and inhales deeply. The pale eyes flare and turn to slits. *I must go.*

"Wait! How will I find you again?" I ask, hoping I have not pestered him too much about telling Father. Now that I have stumbled upon this strange creature, I must see him again.

Next time you are in the woods, come to the river, and I will find you. Good-bye, sister.

The dragon folds in on himself, returning to the rock formation I mistook him for earlier. His skin does look exactly like rough granite.

That is, until he shimmers in the sun and vanishes from sight.

The huge beast, nowhere to be seen. I test the air where he was moments before—nothing at all. Just empty space.

That emptiness fills my chest now too. I liked that dragon. He was different and powerful—like me. He called me sister. Until now, I have not had much in common with, well, anyone. Except Father.

Now I share a blood bond with a creature more extraordinary than anything I could dream up from the pictures in my books.

But where did he go? How did he disappear? And, most importantly, when can I see him again?

I trudge through the forest as dusk swiftly approaches. I must return home before Father, but part of me is afraid. It is bad enough that I have not told him about the boy and his roses. Keeping a real, live dragon a secret? Unthinkable! Especially when he could be an ally in our fight against the wizard.

Yet the thought of telling Father when the dragon was so serious—and stern—sends a sick feeling swimming through my gut. The next time I see Batu, I will do my best to persuade him to let me tell Father. Together, the three of us could certainly rid Bryre of the wizard.

Maybe it would not be so bad for me to tell Father first. He would know what to do, and he might be able to explain what this blood bond is about. But telling him I met a dragon also means admitting I left the safety of the cottage in daylight without his permission. Perhaps I can find another way to bring it up.

I will protect the dragon with everything I can, though my silence I cannot guarantee.

The sick feeling moves up my chest, settling around my throat as the word *sister* bounces inside my brain. I never had a sibling before. I don't think I realized how much I wanted one until now. That word, *sister*, conjures thoughts of shared secrets and comfort. I wonder if the dragon thinks of sisters that way too.

My ears perk up. Footsteps tromp along the path behind

me, crunching the leaves in a regular pattern. I leap up to the branches of the nearest tree. I smell Father before I see him. My heart lurches into my throat. I do not want him to discover I have been out without his permission. I launch into the air and wing toward home. The hedge is not far and I am running into the house within minutes.

Now if only I can catch my breath before he enters the cottage, he will never know. Pippa yaps at me as I settle into her favorite armchair. I pull out the book I was reading at the river and skim the chapters, hoping for one with dragons.

I want to know everything about them.

The cottage door creaks open as Father steps inside. He sniffs, then tilts his head in my direction. "Have you started supper yet?"

Drat. I forgot all about that. The pot for our vegetable stew hangs empty over the hearth. I close my book guiltily; I will have to return to it later. "Forgive me, I got caught up in the book you gave me." I hold it up and smile, blue eyes firmly in place.

"No matter, child, we will eat a little later tonight than usual. I did have something at the market, anyway. Be a good girl and peel the carrots, will you?" As I return the book to its place on the shelf, Father stops and stares at me with amazement. "My dear, where have you been?"

A hot blush creeps up from my neck bolts. "What do you mean? I have been here, of course." The lie tastes sour on my tongue.

"Your skirts and feet are caked with mud!" Pippa sniffs

me for good measure, then slinks away as soon as she sees my gaze.

"I . . . must have gotten them dirty while I was watering my roses." My mind and heart race each other, though my stumbling tongue does all the work. "I may have been day-dreaming. I did not even notice!" I laugh at my supposed foolishness, certain the color of my skin will give me away.

Father shakes his head. "Well, my dear, you are tracking mud all over the floor. I will handle the stew, while you clean up. A muddy dinner would not be very tasty, now would it?" He kisses my forehead, and I can hardly believe he does not feel the heat of my skin.

He believes me. I lied and he does not even question. This is almost worse than keeping secrets.

I hurry to the washroom and clean as best as I can. When I return to the kitchen in a deep blue dress and black leather slippers—dirt free—Father has the stew bubbling over the fire. The aroma fills me with warmth and guilt. I should have been home earlier and made dinner for Father. He walked half the day at least. His old bones must be very tired.

"Father, please sit," I say, shooing Pippa off his armchair. She growls and hides under the chair. "I will stir the stew."

He smiles warmly. It makes me feel even worse. "Why thank you, Kym. I think I shall." He scratches Pippa's ears, then settles into his chair. I scoot mine closer to the fire and stir our dinner every few minutes.

"Did you find what you needed at the market?" I ask, racking my brain for a way to bring up the dragon without letting on that I left our yard.

"Some of it, yes." His fingers tap the arm of the chair. "Others are harder to find. More scarce."

"Like what?" He plans to go out more often now that I have become self-sufficient, and I am quite curious about his trips.

"Well, I did get the gecko's tail and the hawthorn, ash, and rowan seeds I needed. They are key ingredients in the process of building hybrids. And you never know when we may need more chickens."

Indeed, the chickens can barely keep up with enough eggs to feed Father and me as it is.

"Can I go with you next time?"

He laughs. "No, I am afraid not, and you know perfectly well why."

I scowl. "They do not like hybrids either?"

"They do not. There is a reason the half-breeds—centaurs, fauns, and mermaids—always kept to themselves. Those that remain now hide."

"As do dragons," I add.

"Yes, if any still live."

I open my mouth to say the words, but the odd feeling from earlier returns full force, squeezing my vocal cords in place. My skin tingles with invisible pinpricks. I can do nothing but flap my jaw and cough.

Terror trickles up the scales of my tail to my spine. I spoke fine seconds ago, but now when I try to speak about the dragon, I cannot utter a word.

That feeling, rearing up like a living thing in response. Could it be magic? Could the dragon have spelled me with that blood bond?

Batu may have called me sister, but he does not trust me. My heart sinks; I was going to tell Father. I suppose the dragon had reason. I will have to ask him to undo this.

I stir the soup a little too hard and broth sloshes onto the fire. "What was it you could not get?" Relief floods my bones. My voice returns now that I have relinquished the thought of telling Father about the dragon.

He sighs and clasps his hands over his belly. He glances sleepily at the stew I am stirring. "Tears."

"What?" *Tears*. I have seen those. The girls who stay with us cry all the time. I wish I could comfort them, explain what we do. But Father does not want me to talk to them. Only rescue them and keep them asleep as long as possible.

"They have powerful properties when shed by powerful creatures. I used the last of my stock creating you."

A shiver wriggles down my spine. "You used tears to create me?"

"Yes, there is a spark of life in them. Every time we cry, we die a little. A tiny piece of our life exits with that drop. I needed quite a lot to bring you back."

"But the people in this country are sad all the time. Tears cannot be that hard to come by."

His eyes droop further but he still manages to chuckle. "Human tears are a dime a dozen. These are special."

"How so? Whose tears are they?"

He yawns wide and Pippa does the same beneath his chair. For a moment, I do not think he heard my question.

"Dragons'."

My hand freezes over the pot. No wonder they are scarce.

This unsettles me deeply. To get tears from dragons, they would have to be made to cry. I do not like the idea of purposefully making dragons unhappy.

And I do not know what to think of Father using them to bring me back.

Suddenly, I am glad I could not tell Father about my rock dragon after all.

DAY TWENTY-NINE

I LEAP UP TO THE CITY WALLS, SKIN TINGLING WITH ANTICIPATION. EVERY
night, the boy has left a rose by the fountain. The blossoms
have taken up residence between the pages of a book in my
room, and thoughts of the boy and his warm eyes follow me
wherever I go. I hunt for our dinner and I feel him watching. I soar over the hedge and he is there in the sky, too. In
the garden I wish to share with him, there is no escape from
his shadow.

All day I wait until I can return to the city and glimpse
him again. And hope for another rose.

I suspect he pilfers them from the palace garden when
he goes there to leave a message in the throne room. I only
tail him from afar, then sneak in once he is out of sight, for
fear he might catch me. If he did, I doubt he would continue

to leave me roses. I do not want to risk that.

I wish Father had not forbidden me to talk to the humans. Sometimes I feel like that princess in the tower from my book—locked away from the world. But this boy has sparked my curiosity; I am half desperate to know him. He has some connection to the king, that much is clear from the messages I intercept. Is he a prince or a servant? Or something else I have no word for yet?

His message from last night made Father shake his head.

Wizard evades guards again. Move D to second position.

What is D, and what is the second position? Father said he didn't know the answer when I asked what it meant, but he did get a faraway look in his eyes.

The winding streets and shuttered buildings pass as I glide to the square with the fountain—our fountain. Every once in a while, snippets of conversation reach me through an open window. It is not until I hear a familiar name that I halt my swift progress.

"That Barnabas. I always thought the king was a simpleton to put any faith in him. Swore up and down he could rid us of that menace and now we're right back where we started," a woman says. I hover outside the window, watching two woman wash dishes. Barnabas. Darrell called Father by that name. Could they be talking about him?

The other woman snorts. "I heard he made outrageous demands of the king. Marta said he burst out of the palace gates, raving like a loon about firstborns and broken wagers.

He's right crazy, but even he knew enough to get out while the getting was good. If he was still around, I'd bet he'd be blamed for all our girls getting sick."

"He'd do well to stay gone. The likes of him aren't welcome in these parts anymore." The woman waggles a huge ladle at her friend. I shrink back against the wall of the house. Could their Barnabas and mine be the same? Did Father have a falling out with the king? He never told me he knew the king. Of course, I never asked. Now, I will make a point of it.

I slip into the alley, but slower than before. I do not like hearing others speak that way of Father. He is good and kind, but they make him sound like a madman who ran out on a city that needed him. Perhaps they meant another Barnabas.

A churning in the pit of my stomach tells me they did not. What was Father's life like before I died? Before he brought me back to life? Did Father warn the king not to make the deal with the wizard? Did he try to stop the wizard with his science and fail when things went south? It sounds like something he would do, and he didn't have me to help him then. I do not know much aside from the fact that he is a doting father, a brilliant scientist, and a man with a noble mission.

Knowing that much is enough. Father can explain it. These women are just gossiping. And gossips are often wrong.

Of course, if Father is keeping secrets, he is not the only one. I have yet to tell him about my rock dragon. Guilt has calcified into a hard point in my stomach, but I cannot break my silence. I am physically incapable of speaking when I have a mind to tell him about Batu.

Now, every time Father enters a room and I am reading one of my fairy-tale books, I jump. Though truth be told, I have not learned much. My books tend to cast dragons in a villainous light, but I am certain my rock dragon is not the sort who would destroy a village or eat hapless maidens.

No, Batu is different.

He called me sister. Each time I whisper that word aloud, something buzzes inside my heart and thrums all the way to my fingertips. We are connected now, the dragon and I, and not only by the blood bond.

We both hide in the shadows of the world, lingering on the fringes and longing for the sun. The dragon knows what it is like to be feared and hated, just like the city folk would hate me if they found me out.

Perhaps dragons are just misunderstood.

I continue to the fountain with a little less spring in my step. Father and the dragon will both have to wait. If the boy maintains the same schedule as the last week, he will be here soon. My mottled skin turns pink in some places and red in others. I tug my cloak closer. He does not need to see the strange tones that comprise my body. In fact, the boy does not need to see me at all.

I hear the spattering of the fountain's waters and pause. Caution is the watchword, tonight and every night. I creep over to the fountain, circling the edge, just to see if the boy arrived before me and left another flower.

"You," a soft voice says from the shadows. I whirl, keeping my back to the fountain. My tail is tense and wound so tight around my thigh that my toes begin to go numb. I have to concentrate to prevent my claws from spiking out.

The boy steps out of the alley not ten feet from me, closing the gap further. My breath stutters as though a lump prevents it from passing. Is this a normal reaction for a girl surprised by a boy? Everything in me screams it is.

No words will form on my lips. He steps closer, holding out a hand, palm up. His other hand remains behind his back, but I already know he holds a rose. The scent matches those I keep hidden in my room.

"Please don't run away this time," he says. His voice has a pleasant tone, with a slight rough edge. A shiver runs up my spine with every word. I rather like it.

Father would not. He would be furious that I stand here, staring at the strange boy out after curfew and radiating warmth in the middle of the night.

I take a step back, keeping close to the fountain.

"Please, I just want to talk to you." He inches forward.

I bite my tongue and insist my feet stay in place. Part of me aches to talk to him, but instinct screams to flee. To get as far as I can from the very awake, very aware, human boy. This is different from my interaction with the girls. Getting nearer to me is not something that ever crosses their minds as a good idea.

He takes another step. In a few paces he will be right in front of me, close enough to touch. Close enough to hand me the rose himself.

"What is your name?" he asks. I purse my lips and shake my head. Father would not want me to tell him that. It might be dangerous. I cannot risk him discovering Father's plan. Or what I am.

"I'm Ren." He points to his chest. I remain silent. My throat is so dry, I could not talk even if I wanted to.

"I've never seen you in the city until recently." He pauses, his brow furrowing. Another step. "But something's familiar about you."

And then another. The scent of baking bread rolls over me stronger than before. I want to close my eyes and breathe it in, but that is out of the question. I have not yet determined whether he is friend or foe.

One more step and we will be inches apart. My hands quiver beneath my cloak. My claws ache for release. My knees bend without my willing it, ready to launch into the air at the slightest provocation.

He moves the hand behind his back and holds out the rose as he takes the final step.

I cannot help it; I skitter back, gripping the edge of the fountain. Water splashes my fingers, but can do nothing to cool my burning skin.

He holds up both hands, one still clasping the rose. It is red. It is perfect. "Don't run, please. Can you speak?"

I hold my breath and stare at the petals of the rose. A drop of water from the fountain hits one and rolls off, leaving a deep red trail in its wake.

I realize I am about to let him come closer. What will happen? What does he intend to do? Panic surges inside my chest as he closes the space between us.

Instinct takes over. My tail whips out from beneath my cloak and stabs Ren in the leg. His smile fades as his eyes lose their focus. He stumbles and sways, and I catch him before his head hits the rim of the fountain.

I am hyperaware of three things: Ren is in my arms, he is unconscious, and it is my fault. I press my hand on his chest—his heart beats against my palm. He will wake like the girls always do, but seeing this boy limp and up close affects me differently. I rescue them, but I rendered him vulnerable. Robbers might find him. Or worse, the wizard.

This was wrong of me. I need to maintain greater control. Ren is nothing to fear. I pry the rose from his hand and tuck it in my braid. Then I hoist the boy up in my arms and head for the palace. He will be safe in the garden until he wakes tomorrow.

I stop in the alley just beyond the guardhouse, and push in the two bricks that open the secret passage. I hurry through the tunnel, and in minutes step out in the moonlit garden. Ren does not stir. His stillness worries me, but his chest rises and falls as he breathes. Satisfied, I set him on a carved marble bench beside a bush of sweet roses. Before I can think better of it, my hand traces the line of his jaw. I want to commit every facet of his face to memory.

On the other nights I only sensed him or saw a quick glimpse; this is different. His skin is browned by the sun and, before he fell asleep, I saw that his eyes are rich like the soil in my garden. His hair is the same color, but streaks of sunlight run through it.

I must not see him again. This was dangerous. Too dangerous. I cannot confide in Father about it.

Settling back on my haunches, I take in the beauty of this garden one more time. As I gaze at the roses, the world fades, leaving the same rosebushes, but bathed in the sunlight of high noon. A man describes them to me, his hair dark and his bearing regal. He has such kind blue eyes that I instantly trust him. Indeed, a sense of overwhelming gratitude fills me in this vision.

"I know how much you love roses," the man says. The sun sparkles off dewdrops that cling to the petals, lending the roses a magical feel. The memory is so vivid that I reach out, but it is gone startlingly quickly.

It is only me, and Ren, and the silent flowers in the moonlight.

It takes me a few moments to get my bearings. Have I been to this garden before? The scene in my mind appeared nearly identical, right down the curling wrought-iron gates. I can believe I loved it, and I would not be surprised if I had befriended a gardener in a past life.

Still, the feeling the man was something more is unshakable. And it troubles me. These visions or memories or whatever they are come upon me so unexpectedly, yet not one of them has included Father. Have I just forgotten my memories of him entirely? That makes me feel even worse. Surely he has noticed when I explain the glimpses my brain gives me that he is not in them.

Perhaps I should not pain him any longer by recounting them. Yet I am now terribly curious to know how I could have possibly been in the palace garden.

I run from the palace, heading straight for the prison. Over the last few days the wizard has stationed a pair of guards outside as well as those he has inside the walls. They patrol around the prison every half hour. The wizard knows someone takes his girls.

He must never find out who.

I circle the shadows until I am in the guards' blind spot, then fly up to the roof. Between my cloak and the darkness, they have yet to see me. I move a few shingles aside and drop down into the rafters. I have not made the mistake of entering by the wrong room again since that first night, but the guards have caught on. From my perch on a high beam, I can see four guards below, settled in corners of the room.

Do they not realize they are no match for me? Or does being in the wizard's thrall make them determined to thwart me? Perhaps only the few remaining wish to try.

I pull a vial from my belt and toss it in the midst of them. One guard hovers over a girl, and looks up as I drop down to the floor. He tries to yell, but it only comes out as a strangled whisper. The others slump in their chairs as the mist overtakes their senses.

The nearest girl succumbs to the sleep, coughing as she rolls over. She is a small slip of a thing with an angry rash creeping up her neck, but I like the look of her nonetheless. Tonight, I will save her.

DAY THIRTY

I SWING BY MY GARDEN TO PLUCK A COUPLE OF ROSES SPECKLED WITH gleaming dewdrops. Then I head straight into the tower. I hope the girls like them as much as I do, though they have barely done more than sleep and cower from me. At the very least, the roses will brighten the space. I thrust open the door to the tower room and arrange the flowers in the small vase I have set up on a side table. Light from the windows streams in through the curtains, illuminating the two sleeping figures with blankets tucked up around their ears and an empty bed.

I stop short. Only two girls sleep here. The one from last night is missing. I fly back down the stairs, blood pounding in my ears.

The wizard has found us.

But why would he take only one?

"Father! Father!" I scream. I must be sure he is safe. I must inform him of the missing girl immediately.

He wanders out of the cottage, his face creased with surprise and concern. "What is it, Kym? What is wrong?"

I land before him and throw my arms around his neck. "Father, the girl I rescued last night. She is gone!"

He pats my back, just between my wings. "Ah, I was hoping to catch you before you went to the tower." He pries me off his neck and holds me at arm's length. My tears blur his form into silver streaks. "I am afraid the girl did not make it."

"What do you mean?"

He leads me into the cottage and sits me by the fire. "Kymera, the wizard is very powerful. This girl was already so far gone, had already suffered so much at his hands. She did not survive the night."

My entire body goes numb with the chill that creeps over me. "She is dead?" I whisper.

He nods, scratching Pippa's head.

"How?" I remember worrying over Ren, how pale and lifeless he was. "Did my sting kill her? Was it me?"

In the moment he hesitates before answering, I hear the truth he does not say. It *was* me. It was my fault. I killed her. Horror grips me in its cold, stinging embrace. I may be sitting by the fire, but even that blaze cannot warm me.

"No, of course not. It was the wizard. The wasting disease he cursed her with had wreaked havoc on her body. She would not have lasted much longer anyway."

But I sped up the process. He will never admit that. Father does not wish me to be troubled by unhappy thoughts. But it is true.

My insides feel as though they've been hollowed out. That girl is gone because of me. She'll never see my roses or taste the freedom of Belladoma.

"Where is she now? May I say good-bye to her?"

Father startles. "Oh, Kym. I am sorry. Darrell already took her away. She will be buried in Belladoma, far from the wizard's reach. He will not be able to use her ever again."

"She is already gone? Why would he take just one girl?"

Father grimaces as though he ate a rotten egg for breakfast. "Most humans do not like to travel with the dead. It makes them uncomfortable."

I stare at my hands, then glare at my tail. Both refuse to stop shaking.

"Should I only take the ones who are less sick, Father? So they do not die?" Another tear rolls down my face. I do not think I can stand it if it happens again.

"That might be for the best. Just to be safe." He pats my head and hands me a bowl of porridge. "Eat. You need your strength for tonight."

I pick at the porridge. I am not hungry in the least. All I can think of is that poor, small girl and her pale, yellow face. And Ren. I left him alone. I pray he is all right.

I have to wonder—if my sting affected that girl so adversely, could it hurt him, too? Or any of the other girls?

Injuring them is the last thing I want to do. Nor would Father. I watch him putter around the hearth. He soon settles down with a book. Yes, Father would have taken precautions. My sting cannot truly injure; it only causes a deep sleep to fall over them. This unfortunate girl was an exception.

Still, worry for Ren pricks at my heart.

By the time I force down the gruel, I have made up my mind. I must make sure Ren is safe. I will seek him out tonight. I will talk to him. I will know him, like I never got to know that girl.

After lunch, Father left me by the fire reading my books to go to a market in a village beyond the forest and river. It is far enough away that he will not be back until I have left for Bryre and my nightly rescue.

Which means the afternoon is entirely mine.

I start out pruning my roses, trying to focus on the blossoms. But the lovely colors and sweet scent do not soothe me as they usually do. My mind feels scattered, unable to focus. The back of my neck tingles, and suddenly my vision is no longer my own.

Rose petals, my favorite blush ones, fall to a white marble floor. A shrill sound pierces the air and lingers like smoke. A woman slumps amid the petals but I cannot see her face. Just her golden hair and fine blue silk dress.

It is the woman whose image my mind conjured the first time I considered the word *mother.*

I want to reach out, to turn her and see her face, but the memory fades too quickly. It leaves only a loneliness that curls itself up next to my heart and makes itself at home.

Familiar surroundings are the last things I want now, but I hardly know where to flee.

I find myself wandering through the hedge and making my way toward the river. My thoughts rush like those waters.

I do not wish to be alone. I seek the solace of another creature who understands me and what I am.

A creature who called me *sister.* The word has been roaming through my brain ever since, almost as much as *mother.*

Did that girl who died last night have a mother who will miss her? Or a sister who shared her secrets? I would cherish all the girls like sisters, if only Father would let me. If only that little one had not died. If only I had some way to fix it. To bring her back.

An idea wafts through my head and solidifies more with every step. If the dragon finds me today, I know what I could ask. If I can find the courage.

I settle on the bank of the river, resting back in the soft green moss and dangling my legs in the water. I squint at the sun as the clouds make shapes in the bright blue sky. It feels so wrong that everything can be sunny and bright when I am hollow inside. That poor girl can no longer enjoy this. Nor will she ever see her family again, or run through the streets of Bryre. My chest tightens. Just like I will never see my mother—the woman in that memory—again. The broken pieces of my mind play a cruel trick as they sort themselves out, showing me glimpses of a past I can never recover.

Tears spill over my cheeks and onto the moss. I close my

eyes to stop the torrent, but my eyelids are useless to hold it back. I will flood the riverbanks if I do not stop soon.

A warm blast of dank air brushes across my face, chilling the drops on my cheeks.

Why do you cry, sister?

I scramble to my feet and come face to face with my rock dragon. Batu is just as humongous and magnificent as the first time, but now he seems less fearsome. His wings are furled close to his body, like a shimmering cloak. His scaly head, larger than my entire body, is bent close to the ground to keep me at eye level. I am so relieved to see him that I nearly burst into tears all over again.

"A girl died. I fear the fault is mine."

The giant snout nudges my chin. *It is not your doing. Only the wizard goes around killing girls.*

"I know, but I was trying to save her and I may have been overzealous."

Sometimes, all you can do is try. Sometimes it is not enough. Neither is your fault.

I sink down on the bank again. From this vantage, the dragon blocks the sun from my line of vision and it surrounds him with a halo of glittering light. It is so lovely I wish to reach out and touch it.

But since I also wish to keep my hands, I refrain.

"My father brought me back with a spark of life. But he cannot bring the girl back because he used it all up on me."

A sharp gust of dank air is my only response. I try to read the expression in the pale yellow eyes, but without success.

Your father did this? Do you know what he used?

I nod miserably. I do not like that a dragon had to cry for me to be reborn. "He told me dragons' tears are the most powerful and can bring people back to life."

Batu's head rears back. *Where did he get this knowledge?*

"From the markets, I think. That is where he finds these things. He uses his knowledge for good, for science. We only want to thwart the wizard—"

Your father plays with dangerous forces, sister.

I suck in my breath. "He knows what he is doing, and it is all for the good of Bryre. If I could tell him about you, we could all work together."

Batu shakes his enormous head. *No, sister. We have a bond, a blood oath. You must not break it.*

"I cannot break it even if I wanted to. Just thinking of doing so makes my tongue freeze."

I am sorry. This is the only way for us to be safe. The wizard has eyes and ears everywhere.

"Father would be so kind to you, just like he is kind to the girls we free from Bryre." The image of the poor child from last night vaults to the forefront of my mind, and my hands quiver. I was not half so kind as Father when I stung her. More than anything I wish I could take it back, undo what was done.

What exactly are you doing with the girls from Bryre? Has the city become so corrupt that they require rescuing?

"The wizard sent a curse into the city that sickens the girls. They have to be quarantined to contain the spread of the disease, but the wizard steals them from the hospital and imprisons them. Each night I sneak into the city to free the girls and bring them to Father. He has a cure for the disease, and we keep them safe and hidden." I clench my fists. "Soon, we'll find that wizard, and we'll make sure he'll never harm another girl again."

Your father cures them, does he? Intriguing. Not many men would go to such lengths for strangers.

Pride blooms in my chest. "My father is not most men."

Batu flaps his wings as he settles back onto his haunches, yellow eyes considering me.

Sister, if I could give you my tears to bring the girl back, I would. But I fear I cannot. They have all been spent weeping over my fallen brothers and sisters.

This beast is truly a mind reader. I have been dying to ask, but could not find the nerve. It did not seem right. "You cannot cry for a human child?"

You can only cry so much until your life is wept away.

My tears spring forth again, shattering the glittering image before me. My faint hope of catching up to Darrell and the girl withers. I brush the tears away.

"What happened to your brothers and sisters?" I ask. I cannot help but wonder about this dragon and how he came to be as lonely as I am.

The wizard happened. He huffs, air ruffling the waves of the river. *Once, rock dragons filled the mountain range.* Batu flicks his tail in the direction of the peaks. *Fire dragons nested in volcanoes, water dragons in rivers, and nearly invisible air dragons in the clouds. The rock dragons and water dragons lived in harmony with men, though the air dragons kept to themselves and fire dragons had too hot a temper. But then men discovered they* could take our magic by killing us. *The power corrupted them, making them greedy for more. Our numbers dwindled and the men who had become wizards began to fight among themselves, killing each other to gain more power. By that time, my clan had only a dozen members left. We roamed across all these lands and ones far away, keeping on the move. But the wizards picked us off, until there was only a single wizard. Always hunting, always chasing.*

Anger flares up my neck. I *hate* that wizard.

Batu exhales again, curling his wings around his body. *I do not know what became of the other wizards. They either fled from that one's power, or he consumed them in his greed. One wizard was more than enough. I was the youngest in my clan, a mere draglet when we were first on the run. Sometimes we remained in one place for years, other times only days. Each time, the others protected me, so I could escape. Until the last time. My sister fought the wizard, and when I tried to help her, she brought the mountain down around them to keep me out and give me time to flee.*

Batu hangs his huge scaly head. *They were braver than I. Now I am alone, punishment for my cowardice.*

I place a tentative hand on his snout. The rough, granite skin is oddly warm. "I do not believe you are a coward. You only did what was necessary to survive. And I am very glad you did."

He huffs twice, then leans into my hand. I smile slowly, warmth filling my insides. I may not have a complete human family anymore, but I believe I have found a friend.

When I sneak into Bryre, I run straight to the hidden entrance to the palace. I am more convinced every day that something strange is going on in the city—and it cannot only be because of the wizard. An empty palace, crumbling in places, with a well-maintained garden? Bizarre. Someone is here during the day and keeps the grounds. But why? And for whom? Does the council parade into the palace each day to keep up appearances for the people of the city, as Father suggests? The mystery of Bryre's palace is far stranger than anything in my fairy tales.

And the notes Ren leaves—what can they mean? Father understands some of them, but others stump even him. I want to know more.

I prowl the garden, hunting for some sign or scent of Ren. The only trace is the smell of bread clinging to the bench where I left him. I sneak inside the palace walls, but tonight not even a note awaits me.

He is gone. He must have woken up perplexed and gone on his way. Perhaps he will still stop by the fountain.

I hope I have not scared him off.

When I reach the fountain, I sit on the rim, dangling my legs in the water. One is darker skinned than the other, but I will cover it before Ren appears. If he says anything, I can always claim it is a trick of the light, or a wayward shadow. He does not need to see what I am truly made of, that I am not like the other girls who live in Bryre.

Sometimes I wish I was more like them, but then I wouldn't be able to help Father in his mission. I may look different, but I have abilities they could hardly dream of. If only what makes me special did not also set me apart. I have more in common with a dragon than I do with Bryre's girls.

"You came back."

The warm voice from behind startles me out of the fountain with an undignified splash. I hit the ground hard, but manage to keep my wits—and tail and wings—close about me. I did not even smell his approach. I was too consumed by my circling thoughts to pay attention to what was happening in the present.

I will not make that mistake again. It could have been a dear one.

Ren holds out his hand before I can even take one full breath. I raise my eyes, and put my palm in his.

His warm, strong fingers pull me up. I do not require his assistance to stand, but I accept it more out of curiosity than anything. Is this how a boy normally treats a girl who falls off a fountain? I have a niggling feeling most girls do not fall off fountains, but I push that aside.

Ren is here. Ren is alive. Ren is warm and fascinating and he holds another rose out to me with a sheepish grin.

"I, uh, I'm not sure what happened last night. My memory is a little cloudy. I thought I saw you and gave you this, but I couldn't remember when I woke up." He runs a hand through his hair. It is a not a gesture I have seen before, but my brain provides an answer to the mystery of its meaning. Ren is nervous. For some reason, I feel like I am soaring over the treetops even though my feet touch the ground.

I reach out with my free hand and take the rose, bringing it to my nose to breathe in the aroma. "Thank you," I say. A creeping redness rises on my neck. He still holds my hand and I have made no move to release it. I rather enjoy both the creeping glow and the pressure of his hand in mine.

"I'm Ren," he says, and I do not let on that my memories of the previous evening are far less clouded than his.

"My name is Kymera," I say. This is the first time I have introduced myself to a human. It is an odd sort of thrill, as though we have entered into some kind of secret partnership.

"Kymera," he repeats. "I like it. It suits you." I love the way my name rolls off his tongue. I want to hear him speak it in his warm voice a hundred times over. Not knowing how to respond, I just smile. He takes this as a positive sign.

"Something about you is so familiar, but I can't quite place it," he says. "Are you new in Bryre?"

"I do not live in Bryre. I live outside the city."

"I thought as much. Everyone who lives in Bryre knows not to be out after the curfew."

"You are out after the curfew."

He laughs. "True. And I can't tell you why, either. So I suppose I shouldn't pressure you. Wouldn't be fair, would it?" He winks and I laugh with him.

"It would not." Yes, I like Ren very much. His warmth, his laugh, and his voice make me feel like I am floating.

He squeezes my hand. "Since you're new to our city, would you like to see something?"

"What is it?"

"Well, it won't be much of a surprise if I tell you, would it?"

I giggle. I cannot help it. "I suppose not."

He gestures with his head toward an alleyway. "Trust me?"

I do. In spite of all Father's misgivings, I trust this boy without hesitation. Now that I have spoken to him, I am positive he cannot be in league with the wizard.

I squeeze his hand back. "Yes."

"Keep up," he says as he takes off at a run, pulling me with him. I keep pace effortlessly. In fact, I am faster than he is. But I do not want to outrun him. I just wish to remain here, running side by side and hand in hand with Ren through Bryre. The breeze is just the right temperature to keep us cool and the moon above provides enough light to keep us from stumbling.

As we pass buildings I do not recognize, I wonder where Ren is taking me. Should I be concerned? The buildings grow farther apart and seem more run down. Bricks tumble into weed-filled flower beds, and broken windows wink as we run by. Not a soul breathes in this section of town. Even the guards keep their distance, as far as I can tell. When he stops, I cannot help gaping. A huge gnarl of vines and thorns rises in front of us. It appears to be swallowing a building whole. And the ground. The green vines and black thorns, dotted with an occasional blossom, spread over everything in view. To my right lies a steeple; the tip still struggles to remain above the climbing vines. Plants in the shapes of small, blocky houses line the edge of what was once the road. And the street is now a nest of creeping thorns twisting together amid overturned cobblestones.

"What is it?" I ask, unable to keep the astonishment from my voice.

"It's the back of the palace and the neighborhood that

once housed most of its servants."

I shudder. I never went that far back in the palace. I only ever saw that one hall where the roots of this plant must have been punching through the walls and floor. I did not stop to explore more for fear of neglecting my real duty.

"It is horrifying."

Ren nods. "But here's the strange thing. It's not just any thorny plant. It's part briar patch, part creeping vine. No one has ever seen anything like it." Ren is animated as he talks, waving his free arm about. He retains a firm grip on my hand with the other.

"Why does no one cut it back?"

"Cutting it does nothing. You trim it, and it's back doubly strong the next day. We tried burning it once, but it grew right back in three days. Three days!"

"Incredible," I say.

"It sure is." He leans over. "Can you keep a secret?"

My face burns with his closeness. "I can."

"It's gotten bad enough that it's taken over the living quarters of the palace. Completely torn them apart. Even swallowed up a servant while he slept. And it creeps further into the palace every day. You can't tell from the front gates. Most people don't have a clue how rampant this is. They only know they had to evacuate this section of the city due to pests of some kind."

This explains why the palace is empty at night. These briars are far more pervasive than I realized. They forced the king to leave and seek safety elsewhere.

"That is the secret? That this exists?"

121

"There's more to this"—he waves his hand at the thorny monstrosity—"than just overfed flora. There's dark magic at work. Someone wants to get to the king."

I gasp. Ren's words leave no doubt. This must be the wizard's work. No wonder they have not been able to get rid of it.

"Who?" I ask.

"No one knows." He shrugs, but the sparkle in his eyes reveals that he holds something back. I bet he thinks it's the wizard too. Or he really does work for the wizard and enjoys showing off his master's accomplishments. But that does not seem likely.

"How do you know all this? It is quite a story you tell." I do my best to laugh off the question, but still hope for an answer.

He waggles a finger at me. "That I can't tell you. Not yet."

Ren drags me back down the alleys, away from the strange, viney briars. He slows when we approach the cherub fountain again. Our fountain.

He smiles apologetically. "I must take my leave. Will I see you tomorrow?"

"Yes." I can hardly speak. I do not want him to go.

"Wonderful," he says. He runs down the alley, glancing over his shoulder to wave as he goes.

I stand like a statue at the fountain's rim, waiting until the warm smell of just-baked bread fades from the night air.

DAY THIRTY-THREE

BENEATH THE WILLOW IN THE YARD, I WATCH THE SUN RETREAT OVER the hedge, lighting all the trees on fire. Father has been out at the markets most of the afternoon. He is always looking for more ingredients for his experiments, and he has the best luck finding them in the outlying villages and traveling markets. Despite the guilty weight of secrets, I wandered toward the river again the moment he was out of sight in the hopes I might see my dragon. I've yet to find Batu first, but he is as good as his word and he never fails to find me.

But our encounter was fleeting today, as they often are, and I was unable to convince him that Father is on our side. The only one Batu rivals in suspicions is Father himself.

Now back home in the fading light, I scour my fairy tales and other books of Father's for details about rock dragons. While Batu answers most of my questions, an unbiased opinion might shed greater light on the mystery he poses. What I've uncovered thus far is pitiful. They prefer rocky places. They're loners. And they're presumed extinct.

When I tire of reading I collect my books and head for the tower. Soon it will be time for me to return to Bryre. I will see Ren again. *Warm* is the word that makes me think of him. It fills me up inside until I'm so full I swear I could overflow. Between Batu and Ren and Father, I almost feel like I have a whole family.

But Father would not approve. Meeting Ren every night is very bad. Leaving the safety of our cottage to seek a creature whose existence I have hidden from Father is even worse.

The worst part is I know, without question, I will do both things again. Father cannot force me to remain alone forever.

That first night with Ren, I forgot all about the child I'd killed. By the time I reached the prison, my melancholy returned in full force. I took the girl with the pinkest possible cheeks. But each night since, I've found Ren waiting with a rose at the fountain after he has delivered his messages, charming me more with every meeting.

Ren's most recent note said *Rumors of a beast in the streets. Return D to first position.* Father's brow clouded over when he heard this and I detected a hint of disappointment in his expression. I fear what they mean by a beast. That they mean me. Could the man I stung on the road during my training remember me? Could he have seen more than I thought?

Most of all, I fear what Ren would think if he could see my many and varied parts. Would he hate me as Father suggests? My wings and tail, and the shades of my skin, are an invisible wall standing between us.

When I reach the lower level of the tower, faint sounds of crying curl down the spiral staircase. I wish I could comfort the two girls upstairs, but my presence always upsets them more than anything. Father asked me to stay away, except to give them their nightly dose of venom.

Even though their cries pinch my heart, I obey him. I must obey him about something. Between Batu and Ren, I am toeing a very fine line.

I set down the books and take the watering can into my garden to care for my roses. The reds and yellows flame in the dying light. I caress a few of the petals and coo at them. I know they appreciate the attention; they get bigger and lovelier every day.

When I catch my thumb on a thorn, the monster briar patch Ren showed me comes to mind. Strange that a plant would take over so fast. I wonder if Father has any idea about the briar or why the wizard sent it.

The sound of feet crunching over branches and leaves alerts me to Father's approach through the hedge. I run, throwing my arms around him as he enters the yard.

"Oh! My dear girl!" He hugs me back. "What have I done to deserve such a welcome?"

"I missed you." It is true. I find I do not like being alone if I can avoid it.

Balancing my duty to Father and our mission with my need to be near Ren becomes trickier every day.

I lead him into the house. He hangs his traveling cloak on the wall hook and rests on the chair by the fire. Pippa yaps over and over until he lets her land on his lap and rubs between her ears.

I remain standing, a question on the tip of my tongue.

"Did you want something, Kymera?"

I take that as an invitation to sit next to him. "I came across something odd when I was in Bryre the other day. I thought you might be able to explain it."

He waits for me to continue. Pippa glares at me from under Father's arm.

"I stumbled over the most bizarre plant. It reminds me of my roses, but it is . . . more . . . fearsome? The thorns are black and plentiful and there are vines winding around all of it. The blossoms made me think of my roses, though. It appeared to be eating the palace and the entire neighborhood that lies behind it! Have you ever heard of such a thing?"

A flicker of concern crosses Father's face, then a frown. "It sounds like a rather aggressive briar patch. Perhaps the city folk have been leaving their waste for it to consume. That would explain the overgrowth." A smile tugs at his lips. "Though I am sure you must be exaggerating a little about the palace."

"No, not at all! It has eaten an entire street! It must be the wizard's doing."

Father frowns deeper. "The night is well known for playing tricks on people's eyes, even those with eyes as sharp as yours. Besides, what would the wizard do with a plant? And why would he waste time with it when he already keeps himself busy torturing Bryre's girls? It does not make a whit of sense."

"But I have seen it with my own eyes. It is real, I swear it."

"My dear, I do not doubt that is what you think you saw. But I am certain you are mistaken."

How can he not believe me when I am his eyes and ears in Bryre? "But Father, I—"

"No, enough. You are only to worry about the girls. Leave Bryre's flora and fauna alone, however strange. You must not stray from your mission." He pats my shoulder and smiles, a bit sadly I think, as he rises from his chair.

I smile back, but I thrum inside. I am not exaggerating. A few more months and it will swallow the palace whole.

But soon Father places his cool palm on my cheek, and my worries fade into mist.

Of course, Father is right. Rescuing the girls comes above all else. Father is always right.

A gnawing ache fills my innards as I wait by the fountain. Father would be furious if he knew what I was doing. But when Ren's baking-bread smell wafts over me, I forget everything else.

I wheel around, grinning from ear to ear. Ren grins back and grabs my hand. The feeling of his skin on mine makes me shiver pleasantly. A wash of red spreads from my fingers to my temples. Something about him is oddly familiar and yet so foreign at the same time.

"Come," he says. "I have something special to show you tonight."

He pulls me through alley after alley and it does not take me long to realize where we are going.

The palace.

When we arrive in view of the gates, I am breathless and gape up at the intricate scrollwork. I never took the time to examine the gates before. I was too concerned with following Ren and seeing the gardens beyond. Even deserted, the palace is beautiful. Ren signals me to remain quiet as he leads me to his secret entrance. I feign as much surprise as I can when the wall opens to reveal the passage, and I purposely stumble as though I don't know the way by heart.

The roses and hedges are just as impressive as they are each night. Exquisite. Breathtaking. Gorgeous. A hundred words fill my brain at the sight of them. Ren weaves between the giant hedge monsters, careful to stay out of the line of sight of the guards in the guardhouse. He stops in the corner of the garden, where a blanket has been set up on the grass encircled by rosebushes and tall hedges. There is a basket with bread and cheese and sausage for us.

"Do you like it?" he asks, sneaking me a shy, hopeful glance. I realize with a jolt that his skin is as red as mine. It makes me blush harder.

I inhale the scent of the roses and the cool night air. It's perfect.

"I love it," I say.

He sits on the blanket and pats the spot next to him. "Come sit," he says. "Are you hungry?"

I was nervous about meeting Ren again and only ate a little of the stew Father made for dinner. The cheese and sausages smell divine. I sit, tucking my legs under my skirt along with my tail, careful not to let my cloak come loose. That would be disastrous.

He hands me a hunk of cheese and takes one for himself.

"Where did you live before Bryre?" Ren asks.

I fumble with the cheese. I was not prepared for this.

"The forest?" I cannot admit I really am from Bryre. That would reveal too much and spur an avalanche of unanswerable questions.

Ren laughs. "But where in the forest?"

"I am not sure. Just not here. We only came to live in this forest recently."

"You switched one forest for another?" He raises an eyebrow.

"Something like that," I say, forcing a smile. Ren is close enough that his breath whispers over my face when he speaks, making every nerve in my body flare. I fight the urge to reclaim his hand. It is too easy to be here with him. I must think of Father and my mission.

Yet here I stay, planted next to Ren on the blanket.

"Have you always lived in Bryre?" I ask, desperate to direct the conversation away from myself.

"Yes, I live on the edge of the city with my parents. My father is the king's steward and I'm his page boy." He leans closer. "That's how I know all the ins and outs of the palace."

"Where is everyone? Won't the king and queen be angry we are trespassing?"

Ren shakes his head. "Can you keep another secret, Kym? A big one?"

"Of course," I say.

"Bryre is plagued by a wizard."

"A wizard?" I know enough to understand I should be surprised at this revelation, even if the expectation was not written all over Ren's face.

He chews his lip. "I hope that doesn't make you think twice about staying here. He really doesn't bother us too much."

I dig my nails into my palms to stop myself from gasping out loud. The extent to which the wizard bothers Bryre is no small thing. But it warms me to think Ren does not want to scare me off.

I wish I could tell him I am working to outwit the fiend right now. But I stay silent. I will not betray Father, no matter how much I like this boy.

"He must not be a very powerful wizard."

Ren snorts. "Remember that monster plant I showed you?"

I nod.

"That's the wizard's work. We're not sure how he got it into Bryre, but he sowed those seeds when we weren't looking, I'm sure of it." He leans in conspiratorially. "No one lives at the palace anymore, not after that plant devoured a servant. The council insisted the king go into hiding. They're afraid the wizard will get to him here. The briar patch is just the beginning." Ren's hands clench into fists. I don't like to see him unhappy. I place a tentative hand on his arm. His skin is warm and soft through the fabric of his shirt. He glances up at me and smiles. It is suddenly stifling in my cloak.

"What is it like being the king's page boy? Is it exciting?" I'm not sure what a page boy does.

He picks a bit of crust off his bread and tosses it in his mouth. "It's a fine job. The king's a good man. I'm lucky that way. Not all kings are kind," he says. "And with the palace empty and the king hidden, well, let's just say things are more exciting now than they were a couple years ago."

"How so?"

"For one thing, there was no curfew when I started serving the king." He stretches his legs and leans back on his elbows. "Now that there is, I have special dispensation to ignore it." He grins.

"Why is there a curfew?" I already know the answer, but if I were who I claim to be—a girl just moved to Bryre—I would not. And I can't help but be curious to hear Ren's version of the story. I wonder if the girl who was once me is in it.

Ren's face clouds over and I wish I had bitten my tongue instead.

"The wizard steals and murders young girls, but first he makes them sick with an infection curse. I don't understand why. It just seems so . . . senseless." He lies back on

131

the blanket and closes his eyes. "Curses are stronger at night and the infection more likely to be passed then. They can't stop the disease from spreading entirely, but the curfew has slowed it. Just not enough." The urge to tell him I rescue those girls is nearly overwhelming, but one tricky thing prevents me. I'd have to tell him how.

And that would mean revealing what I am. That I am among those murdered girls. I cannot gauge how he would react to that, let alone to the fact that I am part animal. My strange parts brought me closer to Batu, but I suspect they would not do the same with Ren.

"I am sorry. Were . . . were any of the girls people you knew?"

He nods, but says nothing more.

It only takes a moment for me to decide, but it feels like an eternity. Ren's chest rises and falls as he breathes. A lock of his brown hair tumbled across his forehead when he lay down, shielding one of his eyes. I should not want to be close to Ren. I should not want to know him.

But I do.

I lie next to him and rest my hand on top of his. His skin is cold, but he does not seem to notice.

Hundreds of stars glitter down on us from the night sky. I wonder what the view is like from up there. How wonderful it must be to see everything. If I could do that, maybe I could see the wizard and stop him before he hurts any more girls. Put an end to this city's pain. To Ren's pain.

"When I was little," Ren says, "my grandfather died. My mama told me his soul had become a star and he'd always watch over us. I like to think those girls got to be stars, too."

"I like that very much." If Father had not brought me back to life, would I be a star now? I squeeze Ren's hand and he turns his head to look at me. My breath falters and I fix my gaze on the sky again.

"I lost my mother to a murderer. It was senseless too."

Now he squeezes my hand back.

I blink rapidly as my eyes grow warm and wet. The truth of my words hits me full force. I only have my father left. And the dragon who calls me sister. I wonder if Batu's brothers and sisters are stars now. He grieves like Ren does, I can feel it when the dragon speaks to me in that strange way of his. Will he ever join them? Will I?

I cling to Ren's hand, unable to answer my own questions and afraid to ask him. One look makes it clear he is troubled enough.

He could not help me anyway. He knows less of me than I do. But after this night and sharing the sky with Ren, I have gained something else.

New memories.

I may not have my mother or the memories of the girl I once was, but I'll always have the stars.

DAY THIRTY-SIX

FATHER REMAINED AT HOME TODAY, DUE TO EARLY-MORNING SHOWERS, but I itch to escape from the hedge that pens me in. Perched on the top of the tower, I can see fog cloaking the trees. Sunlight pierces through it, setting the entire woods aglow.

I want nothing more than to read my book in a patch of sunlight with the fluffy fog clouds swirling at my feet.

But Father will not like me wandering about aimlessly as I intend. I fly to the ground as a plan takes shape in my head. Pippa nips at my feet just before my toes touch the soil, then follows me into the tower.

She does not, however, follow me into Father's laboratory. She never goes down there. It is the only thing Father has managed to train her to do. She sits at the top of the stairs and whines at me. I waggle my fingers at her as I descend into the laboratory.

Father is in the corner, fiddling with something in one of the cold boxes. When he hears my footsteps he slams it shut and whirls around, but not before I catch a glimpse of the contents. It almost looked like a child's hand, but that can't be right.

"Kym," he says, "what brings you down here, my dear?" He leaves the cold box behind, clutching a goat leg in one hand for the chicken that lies on the table in the center of the room. I frown. I must have seen wrong.

He wipes his hands on a nearby rag and looks at me expectantly.

"Father, I wish to have fish for dinner."

He chuckles and returns to the chicken with one leg yet to be affixed. "Do you now?"

"Yes, and I wish to catch it myself. May I go to the river?"

He raises a silver eyebrow. "Kym, the river is no short distance away. And it is daylight. What if a traveler saw you?"

"I would do just as you taught me: sting him and flee."

"Still, I do not like having you out during the day. You never know who may be about."

"Please?" I blink, setting my blue eyes into place, then batting my eyelashes with my hands clasped neatly in front of me. He sighs.

"No, Kymera. It is too dangerous. But I will offer you a compromise because I confess I would not mind fish for supper either." He takes a bottle off the shelf and continues his work. "I am almost out of some ingredients. I need to go to a market this afternoon, and I will bring home a nice fish or two for us."

I cannot hide my disappointment. "Do you not trust me to go out on my own, Father?"

"You, I trust. It is everyone else I worry about." He sets the bottle down and comes over to hug me instead. "When the wizard is defeated, you will be able to travel much more freely, I promise. Though you will still have to be cautious around the humans."

"I hope we defeat him soon," I say, my words muffled in Father's shoulder. He pats my wings.

"Me too, my dear, me too."

With a heavy heart, I fly out of the tower basement, scaring Pippa away from the edge of the stairs. "Go away," I say. She whines and flies alongside me all the way to the garden, despite my orders. I sigh and scratch her behind the ears. To my surprise, she lets me.

"I bet you want to go to the river, too, don't you?" I ask her, but she makes no reply.

As I prune my roses, my mind spins with strange ideas. What did I see in the laboratory? What could Father possibly be keeping in there? Gradually, a new plan sprouts. It is a wicked idea, but so tempting that I do not think I can pass it up. I will have my afternoon out yet, but I must satisfy my curiosity first.

By the time the roses are pruned and watered, Father leaves his tower, cloak in hand. "I shall not be gone too long," he says, waving. "There is a market just an hour's walk from here today. I shall be back in time to cook the fish for dinner."

I smile and wave in response, waiting patiently until his honey-sweet scent has faded and I am certain he is deep in the woods proper.

I fly to the tower, and when I try to open it, I find it locked. At first my stomach sinks; but of course Father locked it. We do not want any of the girls to wake up and escape. That would be disastrous. I pick the lock with my claws and let myself into the hall.

The door to the hidden room is also locked and I assume it is for the same reasons. Though it does strike me as odd Father would need to lock them both. The entrance to the hidden room is hardly visible if you do not know where to look.

But this I unlock as well and head down the cool stone stairs.

It looks much as Father left it—the shelves are in their usual disorder, and the hybrid skeletons hang just as they should. The chicken he worked on no longer rests on the table; it must be in a cold box, waiting for the last ingredient he fetches now. I run my fingers along the foot bones of the lowest-hanging skeleton. A minotaur, I think, with a bull's head and great horns at the top of its skull. A couple of its toes are missing.

For reasons I cannot quite explain this makes me shiver. I do not recall that there were toes missing before, but surely I overlooked it.

I peek in one of the cold boxes and find the chicken

half complete, as I suspected. Next I zero in on the cold box Father had open when I surprised him earlier. I only want to know what I mistook for a hand.

But this cold box does not open for me, nor my claws, nor the great strength Father blessed me with. The chill I felt moments before returns full force, making my hands quiver. Try as I might, I cannot get them to stop.

Father does not want me to look in this cold box. It is the only explanation. But why? What would he hide from me?

Suddenly, the skeletons above do not look as friendly as I thought. Their gaping mouths are mocking, and their hollow eyes bore into me. Nothing welcomes me here today.

I stumble back up the stairs and slam the door of the tower, locking it behind me, then hurry to collect my cloak and my book. Nothing will chase away these fearful thoughts better than a run through the forest.

Before long, I fly through the trees with puffs of white fog trailing after me. The sun beats down, eating away at the fog little by little. Playing with it cheers me and when I tire, I take out my book and read as I meander toward the river.

"Once upon a time," I say, skirting a low bush, "there was a man with two daughters . . ."

What would it be like to have a human sister? Someone to laugh with and share all my secrets. A hollow twinge pricks my chest. The sisters in this story are close in age, but opposite in temperament, yet they are so dear to each other, they give up all to keep each other safe in a dangerous world.

But the story distracts me only temporarily. The lingering questions of what Father could be hiding in the laboratory plague my thoughts and follow me all the way to the river. The flowing water shimmers and foams as it rushes past the remnants of the morning's fog. I shoot into the sky, reveling in the currents, and survey the open areas for any hint of a human who might glimpse me. The only ones I spy are far to the east on the road near the city. I alight on the bank again, shedding my cloak and setting my book upon it. I will read another story while I wait for Batu, and then fly home.

Father will never know.

I sit as close to the edge as I dare, dipping in my tail and watching the fish with their gleaming scales soar through the churning river. I wonder what it feels like to swim. To be fully enveloped in the water. I imagine it's cold.

The water tugs at my tail while I wait. A fish brushes against it, tickling, and I jerk back instinctively.

The bank shifts under the sudden movement and I plunge into the water headfirst.

Freezing. Despite the warmth of the sunlight on the waves, the water is so cold I can barely move. Fish scatter from my thrashing limbs and tail as my lungs ache for real air. I cannot resist the urge to gasp.

Water rushes in, choking, smothering me. Horrible, horrible water. I claw at it, desperate to get out and find real air. The current drags me farther along. Which way is up? I cannot even tell.

Something yanks me from the flow. Everything rushes

around me in the opposite direction, and then—air. The warmth of it folds over me, rushes into my lungs, and flushes the unwelcome water out in huge gasping coughs. The something gently rests me on the moss a safe distance from the river bank.

When the water is finally gone from my lungs, I risk a glance at my savior.

Batu's pale yellow eyes gaze at me with what I take to be concern.

I leap to my shaking feet and throw my arms around his snout. "Thank you," I whisper.

Without this dragon all of Father's work to bring me back to life would have been for naught. I was so foolish. I have to be careful, not just for my sake, but for Father's.

I take it you have not yet learned how to swim, sister.

I hug him more tightly in answer. The sound of falling boulders—laughter—follows.

Perhaps next time try when it has not been raining and the water is not so high.

I release his head and sink to my knees. My hands still shake and my claws refuse to retract.

"I do not think I will try swimming again. I never intended to. I fell in." I curl my hands in, trying to force the claws back inside my fingers. "I must be more careful. There is too much at stake."

The dragon's massive head tilts questioningly.

"My father. He has sacrificed so much for me. He would miss me. And we have not yet thwarted that awful wizard."

The dragon hisses dank air in my direction. *Do not speak of him. He toys with dark forces and has many under his sway. You never know who may be listening.*

Dark forces. That sounds oddly like something Batu said about Father once. I shiver, though whether it is from the cool breeze and my soaking dress or Batu's words, I cannot tell.

"How can you tell them apart from the rest of us?"

You cannot. That is the problem. Not until they betray you. The wizard is a master of secrets.

The locked tower door and cold box flash to the forefront of my mind, along with the split-second vision of a small hand. Or was it? I no longer know. Father may have secrets, but they're in service of defeating the wizard, of that I am sure.

"Did someone betray you?"

Batu's expression darkens. *Many humans have betrayed dragonkind, and their fellow humans when under the thrall of a wizard. Magic can make a man do things he would not do otherwise. Long ago, I trusted humans. Lived with them, even. When our riders first began to change into wizards, they enchanted whole villages to hunt us down as we fled. Humans and hybrids we had coexisted with for years were suddenly our enemies.*

"That is horrible. And the hybrids, too? You'd think they would stay away from wizards."

This was before they were hunted by the wizards themselves. A centaur village lived near the mountain where my clan first hid, and rivers like this one teemed with merfolk. At first they helped us, warned us if any wizards were in the region. They were friends. Until the wizard enchanted them. They led him right into our cavern and he murdered half my clan before we could escape. Later we heard how he repaid those he kept in thrall—he killed them, too, to take what meager magic he could from their bones.

I shudder. "They have no choice?"

None. Most do not even know they are enchanted, have no memory of what they do, until it is much too late.

"That is why you do not want me to tell anyone about you?"

Batu nods. *You say you go into the city often, sister?*

"Yes," I say.

Be ever on your guard. There is something evil at work in Bryre, and it reeks of the wizard.

"That is exactly why I must go. I can fight against him, in a way the humans cannot. It is my duty to help them."

You are brave for one so small. Batu huffs, but I believe it is with approval. *If you must go into the city, then come to the river as often as possible. The thrall enchantment has an odor I will never forget, and I can warn you if you stink of it.*

Fear creeps over me. "I do not smell of it now, do I?"

He shakes his huge head.

I am relieved, but still a bit confused. "Are there other ways to be certain? My father, for example, he hates the wizard even more than both of us combined! He lost everything because of him. And while he does go to the traveling markets, he never goes into the city. Surely he cannot be in the wizard's thrall."

You can never be truly certain, even with your father. Remaining hidden is the only way to stay completely safe.

"That, and I need to stay out of the water."

The dragon chuckles in his stones-grinding way, and it makes me smile.

"Thank you again for dragging me out." I kiss the side of his snout. It may be a trick of the light, but I swear that, just for a moment, his gray granite scales take on a faint reddish hue.

DAY THIRTY-EIGHT

TONIGHT, REN LEADS ME ON A SHORTCUT THROUGH A PART OF THE CITY
where I haven't ventured yet—the other side of the abandoned neighborhood that lies between the palace and the
outer wall of the city. This part has not yet been swallowed
by the briar, but it surely will be soon. The walls are more
run down than the rest of the city. Vines burst through in
patches as though they're reaching out to the trees beyond.
Bits of thorn peek over the top of the wall and wind down
to the mossy forest floor on the other side. Crumbling
pieces of stone and mortar lie scattered all over the ground.
The moonlight cloaks the whole scene in silver and shadow,
giving it a ghostly cast.

If I did not know better, I would think the vines had a

mind to rip the city apart, brick by brick. It makes me cold just thinking about it.

When we pass the palace gates, I begin to babble on about the garden in an effort to put the briar and all other unpleasant thoughts from my mind. After my failed attempts to find out what Father has been doing in the laboratory these past few afternoons, I have felt more talkative than usual. I suspect I simply wish to think about anything else. Father would only admit he was making more chickens.

"Why do you think they keep up the garden?" I ask. Ren's hand is warm in mine and I wonder if he feels my pulse fluttering in my fingertips.

"Appearances, mostly." He has been all smiles, but now his face creases for a moment. "The people of Bryre don't know their king is in hiding, just that the palace is closed to all but council members."

"What reason do they give for closing it?"

"Mourning. For the girls the wizard murdered."

I am sorry I asked. I should have guessed as much. I squeeze his hand, willing his smile back to his face. "Of course."

"May I ask you something?" Ren says. His face twists in a strange manner.

"You may."

"Why do you come into the city each night? I know I said before that I shouldn't pry, but I'll tell you what I do, if you'll tell me. I worry for you. The wizard steals young girls, and usually at night." He grasps both my hands and

145

stops my breath with a single look. "I've grown fond of you, Kym, and I'd hate for anything to happen to you."

My head spins. Ren is fond of me. How wonderful is that? But I cannot betray Father, not for anyone. Even Ren.

"I told you before that I work for the king as his page boy," he continues. "That is true. But I am also responsible for delivering messages between the king and the city council. They're the reason he's hiding. They're afraid the wizard will find him too easy a target if he remains in the palace. And with the rate that briar patch is growing, I daresay they may be right." He pauses and looks at me hopefully.

"My father is very . . . overprotective," I say. "He will not let me go into Bryre during the day. But when he's asleep, I sneak out. I love the city, its alleys and roads and fountains. It is the only time I get to see even a hint of other people. I just wish I could visit more during the daylight."

"Please be careful. I confess, I rather like seeing you here at night. But it's very dangerous."

I grin. "Not very dangerous. I have you to protect me, do I not?"

"Always." Ren picks up the pace again. "But even I can't protect you from the wizard's disease curse."

"This curse—how does it work? Do you know?"

"Sort of. It only attacks Bryre's girls. But anyone can carry it unwittingly."

I smile. "Then you need not worry about me. I am not one of Bryre's girls."

Surprise lights Ren's eyes. "You aren't, are you? Though

146

if you come here often enough the spell might take you for one."

"I doubt the curse is that smart," I say, and Ren visibly relaxes.

He stops before an unusual building. It begins as a square, but the top takes off into spires and huge colored windows with wrought-iron filigree covering it all.

I step forward to the gates. "What is this place?"

Ren laughs at my expression. "It's called a church. Do you want to go inside?"

"Very much."

He opens the heavy door for me. Then he takes my hand and guides me inside. "What do you think?"

Rows of benches fill most of the space, leading up to a marble dais. Huge tapestries depicting dragons, merfolk, and centaurs line the walls between the windows. Hundreds of candles almost burned down to the ends of their wicks give the space a soft, glowing atmosphere.

"Lovely," I breathe. Ren squeezes my hand and tugs me toward the windows.

The moonlight teases his hair with faint colors, only a shadow of what the sun would do with the colored glass, but the effect is still breathtaking. I hold up my hands to see the effect on myself. It reminds me of the differing hues of my skin hidden beneath my cloak. I pull my hands back. Even that is too close a hint of my true nature.

"When you said how much you liked the topiary figures, I thought you might like the windows here, too," Ren says.

The windows are not mere colored glass as I'd first thought. They're scenes of creatures, just like my books, but gigantic and lit up like jewels. I gently press my hand against one of a dragon. Its silver scales remind me of Batu.

"Why are these here?" I ask. "And the hedge creatures at the palace? Who were they?"

Ren smiles, but with an odd expression on his face. "They're just decorations, Kym."

"What?" I know for a fact that is wrong.

"They existed once, or something like them. But they're gone now."

"But you said there's a wizard around here? And magic? Aren't these creatures magic?"

"The only magic left in this world is dark and rotten." Ren scowls, then lifts his gaze back to the dragon on the pane in front of us. "Maybe it wasn't always that way, but it is now."

My breath catches in my throat as I recall Ren's face the other night in the garden. "You lost someone to the wizard's magic. Who was it?"

His head snaps up and his grip on my hand tightens.

"I'm sorry. You do not have to tell me," I say, regretting my impulsive words.

His hesitation hangs in the air between us, thick as fog.

After a moment long enough to make me think I've ruined our entire evening, Ren speaks again. "I was wondering," he says, "do you like music?"

Music. I have heard of it, of course, in my books. They play music at balls, but I do not quite understand what that means. "I'm not sure. What is music?"

"You're serious?" Ren's expression turns into disbelief. "You don't have music where you're from?"

"Not that I'm aware of, no. Will you show me?"

His grin reappears and relief rolls over me. "Come on."

Ren leads me down a hallway lined with shadowed tapestries at the very back of the church, until he finally turns in to a room. Moonlight spills in through high windows, revealing strangely shaped objects hanging on the walls and standing in the corners. Ren lights the candles resting on a nearby table. "What are these?" I ask, running my hands over one with many strings pulled taut across a hole cut in the middle. I yank my hand back as the strings vibrate and the sound resonates in the air.

"Instruments. That one is a lute. Nothing to be afraid of." He winks and runs his fingers over it too, but in a different manner. The sound is more pleasant this time.

"How did you do that?" I stare at the lute and Ren in amazement.

"It takes practice to play an instrument. I only know a little of this one."

He pulls another instrument off a hook on the wall. It looks like a bunch of reeds of different sizes tied together. He hands it to me.

"What do I do with this?" I turn it over, confused.

He tilts it toward my lips. "Blow across the reeds."

I do, but the sound wilts. I laugh and hand it back to him. "I am no good at music."

"I'll make a musician of you yet." He sits next to me on

the bench, the warmth of his leg seeping through my cloak and skirts. If only I could take off my cloak, be closer to Ren. But he'd see my wings and my bolts.

He'd know I am different. I don't want to find out if Father is right, if he'd hate me. My heart is all too human; he never needs to know my body is not.

"This is a pan flute. I'm good at this one." Ren puts it to his own lips.

The sound curls around me—*melody*, according to the words in my head. It lilts and weaves and sounds so sad, I nearly cry.

So *this* is music.

The tune rises and falls, as Ren moves along to the rhythm in his head. He and the music are one; it changes his whole appearance. The entire room hums, nudging my heart with the hint of a memory.

All this from the boy who smells of baking bread and a bunch of reeds tied together by string.

Perhaps music is a sort of magic.

The sound slows until it comes to a single haunting note. It echoes off the walls, resonating in my head and my soul. My hands quiver. If music is a form of magic, it is a powerful one indeed. I'm certain it is a good one, too. The wizard could never create anything as beautiful as this.

Ren sets the flute down on his knees. The silence makes me ache for more.

"That was lovely," I whisper.

He smiles, but with a hint of sadness. "I learned how to play with . . . with the person I lost."

I place a comforting hand on his arm, fingers trembling. "I am sorry, you do not have to—"

"No," Ren says, the sadness leeching further into the lines of his face. "I have enough secrets as it is. The person I lost was a good friend. The best of friends, really. She was one of the first victims."

"You miss her." It is not a question. I take his hand. "What was she like?"

"She always had a kind word and smile for everyone she met. I can't even remember a time when we weren't friends. It's been months, but it's still strange without her." His eyes meet mine, searching. "You lost your mother. Do you have that empty spot, too?"

I do. The hollowness has been growing for some time. Yes, something is missing inside me. Empty. A space that was once filled and now is not.

"Yes," I whisper.

We sit there for some time, our hands intertwined, not speaking. Our pulses beat with the same rhythm.

For a few moments, just before the candles finally burn out, I think perhaps that empty spot can be filled.

DAY THIRTY-NINE

THE SUN WAKES ME MUCH LATER THAN USUAL TODAY, CREEPING OVER my face and clearing the shadows away like cobwebs. I throw off the covers with a start. It is nearly noon. Father didn't even wake me to feed the chickens.

Could he know why I arrived home so late this morning? That I lingered too long with Ren and his music? I still rescued another girl. That is all that really matters.

I slip into my pale blue dress and tiptoe out of my room. I peek around the corner to take in the kitchen and sitting room. Father nods off in his chair, a book open on his lap, with Pippa snoring beside him.

No hint at all that he is angrily waiting for me to wake up.

I snatch an apple off the counter and sneak past Father to

the front door. My roses must miss me. I should be sure they have enough water. The door squeaks as I open it.

"Kymera? Is that you?"

I flit to his side, smiling as innocently as I can.

"Well, I see you finally decided to join us. In another hour I was going to send Pippa in there after you."

"Thank you for letting me sleep in, I did not intend to do so."

He reaches out to take my hand. "Are you all right, my dear? Are you having trouble sleeping?"

"Yes," I say, latching onto the excuse. "I fear I am."

"Come and sit. What troubles you?"

Though I started out with a lie, many things have troubled me of late. "I have rescued so many girls from the wizard's secret prison, but more girls are there each night. How does he get them into the prison without anyone finding him out?"

"Ah, that is a good question. The wizard has many people under his sway. They do his bidding and deceive the people they love, often without even realizing it. Those are the ones who take the girls from the hospital when he has sickened them enough, and who you must outwit and avoid each night. Then they leave them in the prison for him to toy with at his leisure. You never know who you can trust. This is why it is so important you only go to the city during the night, when no one will see you. Even if the guards expect you, the darkness gives you the edge you need."

A cold knot forms at the base of my spine. "He uses them and they don't even know it? How?"

"Magic, my dear, can do many things. Controlling people's behavior is only one of them and not the most impressive, either."

I swallow the sand coating my throat. This confirms what Batu told me a few days ago. The wizard keeps the guards in his thrall. I wish I could tell Father about him, but the blood bond restrains my tongue. I do not like keeping secrets.

"That is awful," I say, balling my fists into my skirts.

"It is. And it is why we must stop him. Why you must stay a secret and continue rescuing those girls. Only then can we stop him from sacrificing them for his dark magic."

If only that did not mean avoiding Ren, too! For one long, horrible moment, I consider not stopping by the fountain to see him ever again.

The hollowness inside swells, threatening to swallow me whole.

I cannot fathom it for long—it is too awful. Like it or not, right or wrong, I must see Ren. Every fiber of my body hums at the expectation, and silences at the thought of life without him in it.

"Father . . ." I am not sure how best to put my next question into words. "Is there something wrong with me? Something missing?" I need a way to explain the empty feeling in my chest that persists no matter how many roses or Fathers or Rens or Batus I put into it.

"Wrong with you?" Father places a hand on my cheek. "No, Kym, you are perfect."

"But I do not feel perfect. Something is missing."

Father's face twists. "Ah, yes. Your memories, I suppose." He sighs. "That is my biggest regret. That is a part of you I cannot bring back."

"I am not sure that is it." I frown. Indeed, I suspect my memories are coming back, piece by piece, despite Father's assurances that it is impossible. Either that or I am going mad. Those are the only explanations for the visions that occasionally take over my head.

"But what else could it be?" Father says.

"I don't know," I admit. "I guess you must be right."

I twist the lace edging on my sash. He is not right. Of that I am certain. The knowledge makes my hands feel weak.

Father is *wrong*.

It is not the memories that left a hole in me, but the things in the memories. Those lost pieces of me that once made me human. The memories of Father that I cannot access. The tantalizing shadows of my mother, but never her face. An entire life that I may as well have never lived for all I can remember of it.

"Can you tell me more of my former life? Of my mother?" I wish to ask so much more—how did I befriend a gardener in the palace? Who was that little blond girl? But I will start small, for now.

My best pleading look falters as Father turns away, covering his face with his hand. It breaks my heart—for both of us. What he cannot bear to say is exactly what I need to know most.

This emptiness is something Father cannot fix.

The moon hangs low and bright over the city as though I could fly up and touch it. I feel like I'm flying all the time now when I'm in Bryre.

Because of Ren.

Father would disapprove, but I can't help it. My chest stretches full whenever I see Ren, filling up the hollow in my heart however temporarily. Sometimes, I fear I might explode. I wonder if the once-me ever felt this way.

I draw circles around the moon's reflection in the fountain. Ren is late and I grow more concerned by the second. If I am not back by dawn, Father will be angry. Worse, he'll know something other than my task keeps me lingering in Bryre.

Suddenly, the world in front of me vanishes and I am in a bustling marketplace, filled with all sorts of people and colors and smells. Carts and horses mash together, but I wander through them as though I know where I am going. Someone's hand is in mine, warm and soft and confident. I cannot see the person's face, but there is a faint scent of bread baked with a dusting of cinnamon.

My heart stutters in my chest. Though I cannot see his face, I have no doubt the person walking with me in this sliver of memory is Ren.

Voices echo down a nearby alley, wrenching me back to the present, the sense of happy contentment fading all too quickly.

The once-me, she knew Ren. She knew him and cared for him—

Unless Father is right, and it is just my imagination making sense of fragments. But it felt so real—they all have—that I cannot discount any of them entirely.

The voices grow louder. I scramble behind the fountain and crouch low. My cloak covers all but my eyes and I peek over the brim. I recognize Ren's voice, but who is he talking to this late at night?

He comes into view whispering close to a girl's ear. Her cloak lies about her shoulders and she giggles at something he says. A burning sensation spreads over my chest.

I do not like this girl, with her pretty yellow curls, rosy cheeks, and pale blue eyes. She could've stepped out of one of my fairy tales.

I do not like her walking and talking with Ren in such a familiar manner. Not when he was supposed to meet me.

She has no tiny screws at the base of her neck to hide. Her skin is one creamy shade, not the rainbow of pinks and browns that make up mine.

She is unabashedly human, and I am . . . not.

Jealousy.

Yes, that is the word my brain supplies and I think it fits.

They walk closer, passing right by the fountain and my hiding spot. Has Ren forgotten me already? Has this pale creature bewitched him? Why else would he bring her to our fountain? The burning turns into pinpricks, as though the seams that hold me together are coming undone.

It is all I can do not to throw myself on the two of them and rip their eyes out. My fingers ache with the pressure of

157

the claws inside begging to be released. Why would Ren do this to me?

I remain hidden as they head down the alley opposite the one leading to the prison. A moan wells up inside my chest and I'm unable to strangle it. It slips out and echoes off the fountain's waters.

Ren chose the pretty girl over me.

Is he taking her to the palace gardens? Or the church with its myriad colors? Will he share his music with her like he did with me?

I thought there was something special between us. Something that would not be easily forgotten.

What did I expect? Father warned me it would be this way. That the humans would not understand or appreciate me. No human would want a hybrid like me.

I thought Ren liked me, that he was fond of me. Tears flood my cheeks, and the moon quivers in the sky. I thought Ren was my friend. But he is not. He has already forgotten me.

I know what Father would say. He'd tell me that now, I must forget all about him.

I rise from my hiding place and run to the prison. I'll take the first girl I see and fly home. I will not wait for Ren at the fountain again.

Shame replaces the tears as I run. I have been distracted lately. I've been neglecting the purpose for which I was created. I have betrayed Father. I have betrayed the mother I can't remember. I have betrayed myself.

For a fickle, foolish human.

I break into the prison, but tonight I'm so angry that I let my fury move me. I do not use Father's sleeping powder; I climb in through a window, taking the guards by surprise at their post. All seven fall to the floor, unconscious before the ones guarding the girls' room have the door open. I howl at the moon that lights the place, and one of the remaining guards runs away and into the street. Those who are left have swords drawn in shaking hands and attempt to circle me. I dive through them, tail thrashing from side to side, and they tumble like stones to the floor. The girls in the next room whisper and that gives me pause. I do not want to do the same to the girls.

I pull Father's vial of powder from my belt and toss it into the room. The girls gasp when it shatters, but soon all noise dies down.

I duck inside the room and sting the nearest girl just to be sure she has no chance to wake on the flight home. Tucking her under my arm, I pull my cloak close and flee the prison.

For a fleeting moment I consider hunting down the man who ran off. I would know him by the smell of his fear, like the rabbits I hunt for dinner. But there are so many people and so many fluttering pulses in each house I pass, that it would take me all night to do it.

No, it is more important that I get this girl to safety. I vanish into the shadows, swallowed up by Bryre's alleyways.

Behind me, I hear the sound of my name on the wind.

"Kym! Kym!"

I ignore it. I will not abandon my mission again.

DAY FORTY-TWO

I'M EXTRA ATTENTIVE TO FATHER TODAY. I HAVE BEEN SULKING IN MY garden for the last few days. My roses are the only thing that brings me joy lately. Father senses something altered within me, but does not press. He has no idea it has anything to do with the boy he forbade me to see. He'd be disappointed if he did.

I cannot let that happen. Father needs me. And I need him.

I do not need Ren.

This vision I had of Ren and me together has only made it worse. The once-me may have known him. I wonder if he chose that girl over me in my former life, too? Or was I the close friend he still mourns? Given the wizard's history, I suspect he has lost many friends, not just the girl I once was.

It is very hard not to think of Ren.

It pains me to think his name, as though it holds a sort of magic. When I work in my rose garden, the scent reminds me of him. I've taken his pressed flowers from between the covers of my book several times just this morning. He filled me up and now I feel hollow again. The emptiness is worse. It is a strange thing how one person can gut another so thoroughly.

I do not like it at all.

I repeat Father's tale of the wizard over and over. The wizard would murder every girl in Bryre to sate his thirst for dark magic. He would suck the magic marrow out of Batu. He would incinerate Father. He would destroy Bryre, brick by brick. He would kill me—for the second time.

I will fill up the gap in my chest with my purpose. Father depends on me. I must save the children and find the wizard to destroy him. Only then can Father and I be truly safe.

I tug at a weed and toss it in the growing pile. I wonder how Batu fares lately. I've been neglecting him, too. Father has not gone to a market all week, so I have not been able to venture near the river to see Batu for days. Instead I've moped around my garden, dreaming of my nightly meetings with the boy I should never have spoken to in the first place.

Pippa whines from her hiding spot in the shadow of the hedge. The earth under my knees rumbles and I sniff the air. Darrell has come for the girls. I could smell him a mile away. I wrinkle my nose, but rise to greet him as his cart rolls into view. He is Father's friend; I must be nice.

And keep my extra parts hidden. Father has been quite adamant about that. I pull my cloak around me, tucking my tail up and flattening my wings against my back.

Darrell tips his hat as he pulls the horse and boxlike cart up to the house.

"Good afternoon, Miss Kym," he says. "Is your father around?"

"Of course, I'll get him and your cargo." I turn in to the house faster than I should, but I'm still uncomfortable around most humans.

Everyone but Ren.

Father is by the fire, reading a book. "Darrell has arrived," I say.

He closes the book. "Wonderful. Get the girls, will you? Give them an extra dose. We would not want them to wake up early and be scared."

"Of course. Darrell wants to talk to you, I believe."

Father gives a long sigh. "Ah yes. He usually does." He heaves himself off the chair and it hits me how fragile he is. He's strong, to be sure, but his work takes a toll on him. All his late-night experiments in the tower basement claim something of him. But he always seems the most tired on the days Darrell comes to visit.

A pang of guilt slams into my chest. How could I have ever doubted Father for a second? Whatever he is hiding in the laboratory is part of his larger plan, I am sure. As always, he will tell me when I am ready for it. If he hasn't told me yet, the fault must lie with me.

And I have not been as reliable as I'd like of late. Whether

I want to admit it or not, Father has undoubtedly noticed. I will do better, keep my focus keenly on the mission, and then Father will see fit to share more of his secrets.

I head for the tower room. One girl sits up on the bed, taking in her surroundings. It's a charming room, with bright white walls and lace curtains. Every morning I bring our guests fresh roses from my garden, though they are not awake enough to know it is me who does it. As Father requested, I have not been talking to them.

After Ren's betrayal, I cannot help thinking Father is right to warn me from getting attached.

I pat the child on the arm. She tilts her head to look at me, sucking on her thumb. She is one of the youngest girls I have rescued.

"Did you eat your lunch like a good girl?" I ask, though I can see the bread and cheese I brought in earlier remains untouched. She twirls her hair with her free hand and shakes her head.

"Are you hungry?" I push the plate toward her. She eyes it warily before reaching out to snatch the bread and stuff a bite in her mouth. I wait until she's chewed it, then unfurl my tail. Her eyes widen and she skitters back on the bed toward the window, as though she wants to escape.

She will. She just doesn't understand that yet.

"You need to go to sleep for your journey. Don't worry." I smile at her and she whimpers. I don't understand humans. I want to help, but somehow they never realize it's help I'm giving. One day, she and all the other girls will understand.

My tail whips around, green scales flashing, and the girl

slumps forward on the bed.

The others will wake soon, so I repeat the action with them, then scoop up the first and carry her outside. Father and Darrell are in the middle of a heated discussion, but I hear only the end of it.

"You will get your reward in due time," Father says.

"That time better come soon." Darrell's face is twisted in a way I have not seen before. I do not understand his expression, but I understand his words. What did Father promise him in return for his help?

Father's face brightens when he sees me. I place the girl on the makeshift cot attached to barred walls in the back of the cart. Darrell's eyes burn into my back as I retrieve the next two girls from the house. I place them each inside the cart, strap them in for the journey, and wrap blankets around them. Even though they fear me, I feel a sisterly affection for them. They were miserable in that prison. I want them to be safe and happy.

Darrell climbs to his perch and whips his horse. I watch the girls go until they disappear into the hedge.

Father starts up the steps and I catch his arm. "Three more. How many have we saved now?" I ask.

He beams. "Well over two dozen. You are doing a wonderful job, my dear." He kisses my forehead and warmth fills me. Father is proud. I will do anything to keep it that way. He will never know about the secrets I keep from him. About Ren and Batu.

"What is Darrell's reward, Father?" I ask.

He looks startled for a moment, but recovers. "Ah, you

heard that, did you?" He sighs. "Darrell is not like us. He is a mercenary sort of man. As long as we pay him well, he will keep our location and mission secret."

I help him into his chair by the fire while I digest that. "He doesn't care about the girls?" This puzzles me. How could anyone not care about them with their sweet, child-like faces?

"He simply cares more about himself. Do not trouble yourself about him. Once our mission is complete, Darrell will be out of our lives. But for now, he is a valuable ally." Father opens his book to where he was reading before.

"Is his reward gold or silver?"

"That is my concern, child, not yours. Now don't you have a city to sneak into tonight?"

I grin for his benefit. "I do indeed."

"Then you had better have some dinner. You will need your strength."

Father always has my best interests at heart. So I obey.

By the time the sun sets, I am desperate for some kind of solace. For someone who understands my loneliness.

I do not head directly to Bryre. My feet take me to the river, the call of my dragon brother too strong to ignore. I hover above the path, moonlight and the faint sound of rushing water guiding my way. Shadows swirl around me, but their strange shapes do not frighten me.

I have nothing to fear from the monsters in the woods. I am a monster. Humans cannot offer me anything lasting, not anymore. I am too much animal and instinct. Too many broken pieces sewn together.

My books have never mentioned whether dragons come out at night, but every fiber of my will calls for Batu. Even though it's outside of our routine, I hope he will find me by the river tonight.

When I reach the river, I close my eyes and give myself over to my senses. An owl hoots from a tree across the bank. The water next to me ripples merrily along, paying no heed to my inner turmoil. The scent of night-blooming flowers floats through the air from somewhere deep in the forest. And there—a dank, dark, slightly metallic smell hangs in the air.

I open my eyes and find Batu coalescing before me.

Sister, he says.

Tears fill my eyes as a leathery wing curls around me. I feel more at home now than I ever have in the cottage. Father loves me, has sacrificed so much for me, but even he cannot fully understand what it is like to be what I am. To have human desires and fears, but to be so different from them in ways that are utterly insurmountable.

Batu, however, does. He too lived among the humans, cared for them, and was betrayed by them.

He puffs dank breath over me. *What is wrong?*

I rest my head against his wing. The moonlight glints off it in a way different from the sun. Instead of silvery bright, he is now a charcoal-and-diamond hue.

"I made the mistake of trusting a human. I should not have become so attached." I toss a pebble in the river and it disappears beneath the waves. "He chose another girl over me. Someone . . . prettier. I had not thought he could betray me so easily."

One never does.

"I am very glad," I say, unable to hide the tremor in my voice, "that I have you."

Always, sister, always.

I retrieve the message Ren hid in the palace, and I do not even pause by the fountain. A rose rests on the rim. Again. Is it for me or that other girl? A bitter taste settles in the back of my mouth and I flee the fountain and its happy little cherubs.

I shall not be distracted this time. I will do what I was created for.

I'll save those girls and stay away from Ren.

I have not ventured near the palace for the past few days, but tonight I feel bolder. Seeing Batu has lent me a measure of extra courage. Ren will not keep me from any facet of my mission, and Father says knowledge of the king and his council's plans will help.

The note I memorized said: *D must return to home base on the morrow.*

I cannot help wondering who or what D is, and where this home base lies, but deciphering messages is not my forte.

Rescuing damsels in distress, however, is.

With my razor-sharp focus, I arrive at the prison house in record time. In the shadows I close my eyes, letting my sense of smell inform me of the number of guards inside. I locate the fire in the hearth of the building next door, the sickly smell of the children in the prison, and the roses on the wind. The guards smell musky and earthy, sweat and fear sticking to their skin.

For a moment, I think I catch Ren's scent—like baking bread—but it fades before I can be sure. I shiver. He cannot invade my thoughts tonight. Nor ever again.

One guard is posted against the front door, nodding off. For several long breaths I watch him. He does not move an inch. With the slightest whisper of wings, I fly to the roof of the prison, move the shingles aside, and drop down through the hole in the roof.

The miasma filling the space hits me like a brick wall, but I push through it. The girls get sicker every day. The foul magic of the disease hangs in the air like a cloud of buzzing insects. Two guards peel off the wall and hurl themselves at me; I duck and sting them as I draw the vial of sleeping powder from my belt. The door to the prison bangs open, and more guards—many more than usual—pour through the doorway. The lone guard outside must have been meant to give me a false sense of security. I toss the vial into their midst and watch the plumes of smoky powder overwhelm half of them immediately. A handful resist longer than I expect and pounce toward me. Only two reach me on their feet, while the others succumb to the effects of Father's weapon. Hissing and with claws drawn, I sting the two remaining servants of the wizard. To my dismay, one manages to tear my cloak with his sword before he falls. I shall have to patch that tomorrow, but for now I turn my attention back to the girls.

I scan the room, searching for the bed next to the last one I emptied, and freeze.

There, in the bed nearest the door, is the girl who stole Ren.

I do not breathe for a full minute.

She's lovely, even with the pale cast over her looks. Her yellow curls fan out behind her head on the pillow, but her once-perfect face is now marred by a rash that creeps up her neck and over her cheeks, and her dainty hands have boils on the backs. Somehow, she still looks like an angel. Is this why Ren prefers her? She is fair and simple, while I am darkly complex.

At this moment, I understand what the word *hate* means. I hate this girl. I hate how Ren looked at her. I hate how she looked at him. I hate that I cannot stop imagining him showing her all the secrets of Bryre he showed to me.

But should I save her? That's the real question. I could tell Ren I rescued his new girl and he would be forever in my debt. She would be safe from the wizard and his tortures and poisons.

She would also be far away in a beautiful, safe kingdom. Far away from Ren.

I can't deny that temptation is strong. But if I leave her to the wizard, she'll be forever out of Ren's reach.

That temptation is stronger.

That would hurt Ren. If he does love her, he would be brokenhearted. I cannot bear to see Ren that way. I cannot stand the thought of him feeling pain for even so much as a second. He may not care for me, but he has taken up permanent residence in my heart whether I like it or not.

Despite his abandonment of me, I cannot act in such a manner that I know will cause Ren anguish.

I must save her.

Before I can change my mind, I collect my quarry and flee the prison as fast as I can.

The last thing I want to do is run into Ren with his new girl in my arms. I'm at the parapets in no time and then I fly home, my heart full of warring emotions—the satisfaction of knowing I have done the right thing, and despair at how completely I have lost Ren.

DAY FORTY-THREE

FATHER HAS INSTRUCTED ME NOT TO DISTURB THE GIRLS, BUT I CANNOT heed his words today. Not when that girl, my rival, sits up in the tower weeping. I hardly slept all night; every nerve in my body is aflame with curiosity and dislike.

A part of me needs to know who this girl is, who took Ren away from me so easily. She is prettier by far, but what else is there to sway him? I had not thought him so susceptible to those sorts of charms.

Mostly because I thought he was charmed with me.

But I was wrong.

While Father naps in his chair with Pippa curled in his lap, I tiptoe out of the cottage and head for the tower. The sun warms the patchwork skin of my arms, and I trace the lines between the sections with my finger.

The girl doesn't have strange skin like this. I thought there was something lovely about the many hues at first, but I have slowly begun to hate it. These pieces of skin would scare off a human like Ren. The tail and wings that prove so useful to me in my mission would be deemed hideous.

How is it possible that all the parts of me I value would be so disgusting to others?

The girl's cries echo across the yard. She must be standing by the window. Does she miss Bryre? Her home? Ren?

My claws spring out on their own accord and I clench my fists to nudge them back into place.

I miss Ren. I do not care whether she does.

I fly up the steps, stopping just outside the door of the room at the top. Dizziness surges over me. I will see what this girl is about. My tail is curled around my leg, my wings are flat against my back, and my cloak securely fastened. I should not scare her much.

When I thrust the door open, she scuttles away from the windowsill with a cry and grips the post of the bed with white knuckles.

My voice disappears. Something about her narrowed eyes strikes me dumb.

"You," she says. "Who . . . ?"

The telltale sound of the cottage door slamming shut rings out in the yard below. I do not have much time.

"How do you know Ren?" I demand.

"Ren . . ." she whispers. She steps back, confusion clouding her lovely face. The rash is gone, but she is still

172

pale from the wizard's sickness. She cannot be more than a year or two younger than I am.

Footsteps clomp on the stairs. Father is coming. How did he know I would go to her?

The girl's face twists. "You were in my dreams." She shudders. "You're a nightmare! And your eyes!"

I freeze while the blond girl who stole Ren shakes uncontrollably.

My eyes?

But I have my blue human ones on. Did this girl know the once-me?

The door bursts open. "Kym! What are you doing?"

The girl shrinks back against the wall. I whirl to face a very angry Father. "I'm sorry, I—"

He grabs my arm and drags me out of the room. "What have I told you about talking to the girls?"

"Not to do it," I say miserably. His grip on my arm hurts.

"That is right, and why is that?" His face is as red as my roses and his breathing labored as we stomp down the staircase.

"You do not want me to get attached to them." He is right, but he does not know that I am in no danger of getting attached to this one.

This girl is different. I do not think I like her very much. I saved her for Ren and . . . and she was not very nice to me.

And what did she mean, calling me a nightmare?

"No getting attached. We cannot keep them here for

long. It is too dangerous. The only place they are safe is Belladoma." We reach the ground floor of the tower and he spins me around to face him. "We cannot afford for anything to distract you from your mission, Kymera. Do you understand me?"

I cannot bear to look him in the eyes. "Yes, I understand." And I do—perfectly. I just cannot help being curious. Especially about her.

"Good, now do not do it again. I expect you to dose them regularly, but engaging them in idle chatter will only result in pain for you." Father sighs and places a soft hand on my cheek. "And you know how much I cannot stand to see you unhappy."

A coolness spreads over me, easing the burning anger in my heart. Why did I sneak in to see her? I hate letting Father down. Between Ren and Batu I've already done so much more than he knows! I must do better. For Father.

Ren and that girl are nothing to me.

Father—and saving Bryre from the wizard—are everything.

And Batu, well, he is dear to me too. I am determined to somehow sway the dragon to our cause. With a dragon on our side, the wizard's defeat would surely be quick.

I pat Father's arm as we cross the yard. The chickens squawk at us, no doubt hoping for more food.

"I promise, I will not disappoint you again. I will only go to the tower to sting them, nothing more."

He huffs, "That will do, my dear."

As I settle in by the fire to read, I realize two strange things. One, it never occurred to me to bring that girl roses, even though I have done so for every other girl I've rescued. Perhaps part of me didn't want to share anything at all with her, not even flowers.

And two, Father was so angry with me that he completely forgot to have me sting her back to sleep.

DAY FORTY-NINE

TONIGHT MY HEART WEIGHS ME DOWN AS I LEAVE OUR COTTAGE. RAIN pummeled the forest all day and now a thick mist coats the trees and paths. I can barely see my feet.

The last few nights I crept into the city along with the lengthening shadows, but I did not glimpse Ren at all. For a few seconds, I believed I caught his baking-bread scent on the cool night air, but it faded before I could trace him back to wherever he hid.

But I know he was in Bryre. He still left behind his notes in the palace like tantalizing, and confusing, breadcrumbs. The mysterious D has been an even more common theme in the messages than usual. *More girls sick. D was moved.* And then, *D is missing.* I am certain D is a person, though Father has suggested it could be anything from a person's name to a code standing in for defenses or who knows what else.

Who or whatever D is, Ren knows and Ren keeps the others informed.

My resolve to keep him out of my mind falters with every hour. It is practically impossible when he has become so entangled with my own mission. The other girl is gone, on her way to Belladoma. I am glad of it. Why shouldn't Ren care for me again? The desire to see him, hear him, smell him, laugh with him is stronger than I am.

Father keeps me hidden away in the cottage like the princess in my book was locked in her tower. And like her, I need something else. The part that is the girl I once was longs for a deeper, human connection.

Love is the word that pops to the forefront of my brain.

I roll it around, sounding it out in my mouth. I whisper it to the forest and it hovers there in the fog.

Love.

I am in love with Ren.

I can't help shivering.

And yet, I am angry. My heart is divided. I want to both hug him and rip him to shreds. Is this how humans feel all the time? A whirl of conflicting emotions tugging them in two directions? I do not think I could stand it. A wave of gratitude fills me. Father made sure I was not just a human. The animal parts he incorporated must spare me from the full brunt of these feelings.

The fog reaches all the way to the city walls. Once the guard patrols by this section of the parapets, I climb without hesitation. I must focus on rescuing the girls.

Forget Ren. Let him stay in your dreams where he belongs.

I run, skimming the shadows. The mist follows me into the city, too, wrapping every tree and house in fluffy clouds. Moisture clings to my skirts and tangles my hair, making me look as wild as I feel. I run faster.

I halt in my tracks, just outside the square with the fountain.

Bread baking and cinnamon fill my nostrils. Every part of me goes numb, from the top of my head to the tip of my tail.

He's here. Ren is here. At our fountain. Hope thrills me, spurring my frozen body into action.

I step cautiously into the square. Until Ren hears and glances up.

The expression in his eyes roots me to the spot.

Grief, whispers my mind.

His face is torment, but he tries to smile. I take a step closer. We're only ten feet apart.

"Kym," he says. "I thought you were gone." Warmth spreads throughout my body at the sound of my name on his tongue. He has not forgotten me after all.

I close the gap between us. "No, not gone."

"Where were you? You said you came here because you loved the city, but then you disappeared." I can't meet Ren's gaze for fear there will be an accusation there.

"My father," I say, latching onto the lie I told him before. "He has been sick. I haven't been able to sneak out again until now." I lean against the fountain, the silver and gold coins winking up at me from under the water. "Why are you so unhappy?"

I must know. It pains me to see his grief so tangible.

He stares into the fountain. He is not the same boy anymore. I miss that boy. I'd do anything to make Ren that boy again.

His fists clench and unclench. Then he slaps the edge of the fountain hard enough that I fear he will injure his hands. Humans are fragile.

"She's gone." Ren's voice is hoarse and throaty. The sound scratches my ears.

"Who?" My entire body goes cold. I believe I know the answer already.

His torso curls inward, as though someone has struck him in the stomach. I tentatively reach out my hand and place it on his shoulder, wishing to soak up his pain through my palm.

"Someone I was responsible for." He slaps the fountain again, making me jump. I've never seen him in such a state.

"She fell ill a few days ago. The people she was staying with put her in the hospital before I knew she was sick. They thought she'd be safe, but now she's gone. It is all my fault." He looks me square in the face and I shudder. A tear rolls down his cheek. I wipe it away before I can think better of it. His tear is warm and rolls off my finger into the fountain.

"What do you mean?" I ask.

"The king and the council—they instructed the hospital staff to keep the disappearances secret. It's bad enough that the demon wizard is sickening Bryre's girls, but letting on that he steals them from the quarantine ward too would cause mass panic. The city's full to the brim now because of the briar forcing people from their houses, so we don't even have anywhere else to hide them. All our attempts to keep them safe have failed, and now the wizard has taken *her*, too."

My breath catches in my throat. It is the girl I saw him with the other night and saved from the wizard's prison.

"I'm sorry." I want to say more, to tell Ren that I'm working to stop the wizard, that it's why I come to the city every night, that I saved his friend, but I bite my tongue. Father would be furious.

"All those girls, stolen." Ren puts his head in his hands as he leans over the fountain. "I should have warned the people she was staying with, but I didn't because of the council." He stares into the swirling waters. "I was responsible for her. I failed her."

I squeeze his shoulder. I hate this wizard. I want to rip his heart out with my bare teeth just like I ripped out that rabbit's throat when I was first training.

"Maybe she'll escape," I say.

"No one escapes."

The urge to tell him that is not true chokes me. I help them escape. That is why I live and breathe.

"What does she look like?" It kills me that he misses her so much, but I must know for certain whether it is the girl I saved.

"She has light hair and blue eyes. Almost as tall as me. She's always smiling." Clouds sweep over his face and I can guess at his thoughts. She's probably not smiling much right now.

"What is her name?"

"Delia."

The blood drains from my face. D . . . Delia. Could this be the mysterious D who was moved about so much in Ren's messages?

"Who is she?" Jealousy stirs within me even though she is gone.

"Someone important." Ren's face pinches. He straightens up and steps closer. My heart rises in my chest. "When you didn't come to the fountain, I was so worried. I thought the wizard must have taken you, too," he says.

I hang my head. "I am sorry. I should not have abandoned you for so long. Can you forgive me?"

Ren smiles, just a little, and it is like the dawn breaking. "There's nothing to forgive. I'm just happy you're here now." He takes my hand, sparking tingles down my fingers. "Can you stay a little while tonight? There's some people I'd like you to meet."

I breathe out with relief, and my heart tries to follow by leaping into my throat. "Yes, I can." More people? Who else would be up at this hour for Ren to introduce me to?

He leads me into an alley headed opposite the direction I usually go. "Where are we going?" I ask.

"Home," he says.

Home. Something balloons in my chest at that word, and my inner vision fills with a red-roofed cottage, a tower, and a rose garden. What does home mean to Ren? My breath quickens; I will soon find out.

Worry gnaws at me as we walk through the winding

streets and I unconsciously clutch my cloak more tightly around me. I have never been inside a human's house before, but we usually remove our cloaks when we enter our cottage. Will they think I am odd—or worse, suspect I'm in the wizard's thrall—if I keep mine closed?

I cannot risk removing it, nor should I risk going to Ren's home. If my tail slips out, or a single feather molts, it could give me away. But it's Ren, and refusing him anything is so very difficult. It has taken all my will not to tell him what I'm really doing in the city each night. Instead I wrap myself in lies even more tightly than my cloak. Tight enough to strangle.

Yet what worries me the most is whether Ren's family will like me. Will they think I am too dull looking for their son? Not normal enough? Not as good as Delia, for whom I'm sure they grieve, too? If they ever saw the true me, they would certainly not approve.

When we arrive at a small stone house, Ren slows. It is a low building, with red shutters and flowers in a white box hanging off the front window. They are not roses, but still quite pretty. It seems small at first, but it extends back from the street and must have several rooms. The gray stone walls have a warm, welcoming feel in the moonlight, and I am pleased to see Ren's home is not in shambles like many in Bryre. The vicious briar plant has not attacked his section of the city yet. A vegetable garden lies in one corner of the small yard, and flowered shrubbery lines the walk. Even here on the street the hint of cinnamon that always clings to Ren lingers.

"This is your home?" I ask.

He squeezes my hand and pulls me up the path to the front door. In mere moments, I'll meet Ren's family. My throat tightens and I mentally check my cloak fastenings, then flatten my wings closer to my back. My tail is so tightly wound around my thigh that I begin to lose feeling in that leg.

He pushes the door open and a blast of warmth and that wonderful bread-baking smell wash over me like sunshine. Someone in this house loves to bake. Voices chatter by a fire and it takes a moment for my eyes to adjust to the lighted candles. A woman stirs a pot of soup over the fire and waves at Ren as he enters. Her smile falters when she sees me.

My stomach drops into my feet. Could she see through my disguise so easily?

"Ren! What're you doing? Who is this?" she says.

"Mother, this is Kym." He points to me. "Kym, this is my mother."

She puts a hand on her hip and waggles the ladle at Ren. "You shouldn't have brought her here. You know how dangerous it is! It's bad enough you're scampering around the city after curfew to begin with! Now you're inviting guests over? After . . ." She swallows the end of the sentence like a rotten egg.

"Laura, calm down," a man's voice says from the chair by the fire. He has his back to us and I cannot see his face, but his graying hair peeks over the top. It is not long like Father's, but not close-cropped, either. For a second, I wonder if he's Ren's father, but then another man—younger than the first—steps out of the hallway and barrels toward Ren to give him a bear hug. They look so much alike, it is clear this is his true parent.

"Yes, Laura," Ren's father says. "We're all worried, but there's no need to be rude to our guest." He winks at me—just like Ren does—but with deep sadness etched in his face. This is where Ren gets his odd manners. "I'm Andrew," he says. I curtsy back like I've read girls are supposed to do in my fairy tales.

"See? She's all politeness."

Laura folds her arms. "It isn't safe for Bryre's girls to be out after curfew. Not with the epidemic."

"I am not from Bryre," I say, using the same excuse I gave Ren for my immunity to the wizard's disease.

"The wizard's curse can't hurt her, you see?" Ren says. I can't help noticing his demeanor has altered since the moment we entered this house. Does this place cheer him or does he hide the grief I saw at the fountain for the sake of his family?

Ren's mother narrows her eyes, then harrumphs and returns to her soup.

"It is a pleasure to meet you all," I say, still wondering who the gray-haired man is. Ren takes my hand again and leads me to a chair. I sit—as elegantly as I can manage—and watch in amusement as Ren throws a log on the fire. I've never seen anyone do that before. As I watch, the flames lick the wood. It's burning it. We never use wood at home. The flames simply come and go when they should.

"Kym." Ren draws my attention away from the

strangeness in the hearth. His eyes reflect the fire and my cheeks warm from that more than the fire itself. "This is Oliver. He's a guest, too."

The older man tilts his head in my direction and holds out his hand to shake. I clasp it, unable to escape the feeling of familiarity.

I look closer at his eyes. Shock ripples over me. This man, Oliver—he was in one of my visions showing me the roses in the palace garden. He looks much older now, but the resemblance is unmistakable.

So the images I see are not just appropriations of the present. How else can I explain this man's face in my head? The once-me, she knew him. Of that I have no doubt.

My stomach flips. That means the memory of her and Ren could be real, too.

Oliver frowns, continuing to hold my hand, and squints—have I done something wrong? Father taught me little of etiquette. He never intended for me to mix with humans. All I know, I've gleaned from my books.

He'd be furious if he knew where I was right now. The thought makes my palms sweaty and my hand slips out of the man's grasp. Up close, I can see he is not so much older than Ren's father after all; his hair has just gone gray earlier.

"What did you say your name is?" Oliver's face bears an odd expression.

"Kymera. Kym."

He repeats my name strangely, as though it leaves a bitter taste. I wrack my brain, trying to understand how I offended him.

"I don't recognize that name." He pauses and I hold my breath. "You remind me of someone. Your eyes, they're similar. It's—well, no matter. That someone is long gone. And you are here and have befriended our dear Ren." He tousles Ren's hair. A question stands on the tip of my tongue, ready to leap off into the conversation, but I bite it back.

Father has been quite clear. No one can know who I am. Apparently, not even me.

This man must have known me well if he can see the girl I was in my eyes. But perhaps it's just a trick of the light and Oliver is thinking of someone else.

Andrew joins us, passing around cheese and slices from a loaf of freshly baked bread. Ren tears into them and offers some to me. I take a bit of each, then hand them back.

"Thank you," I say, nibbling on the cheese. It is sharp and creamy, and the bread tastes exactly the way Ren always smells. Delicious. I can't keep my eyes off him. He tries to be happy, but underneath runs a current of despair. That girl, Delia. They all knew her and mourn her. Fear hovers in the air of this house, I can smell it.

I could allay all those fears. I could tell them Delia's safe. That I took her and sent her to the beautiful shining city of Belladoma.

But that would provoke questions, all of which would expose Father to the wizard's wrath. I can't betray him like that. Not even for Ren.

"Kym is new to the area," Ren says to Oliver. "She lives in a cottage outside the city."

Oliver raises an eyebrow at this. "Really? Where did

186

you come from, my dear?"

My breath hitches. I can't answer this line of questioning either. I must change the topic and fast. "Nowhere of consequence," I say. "Bryre is far finer than anywhere else I've been."

Ren's father laughs. "Well, you must've been to some run-down, rancid places."

Oliver gives him a stern look and he stops laughing at once. "Bryre was once the height of excellence and beauty. But I fear we have fallen on hard times."

"Oh yes, Ren told me about the castle and the thorns."

Ren winces and sinks down in his chair. I realize too late I shouldn't have mentioned that. His mother gasps and even his father frowns.

"Did he now?" Oliver says. "Showing her the seedy underbelly of the city, are you, boy?"

"Well, I, uh—"

"No!" I object, "not at all. While it's sad to see the palace in such a state, there's something lovely about it. Ren has shown me many beautiful things around the city, too. Like the palace garden. I just adored that. Roses are my favorite, and the king's are the best I've ever seen."

A light flashes in Oliver's eyes, but it extinguishes just as quickly. "Yes, the roses were one of Bryre's prized possessions. They're still kept up for . . . memory's sake."

This makes me more certain than ever that this man must be the palace gardener. "Whose memory?" I ask.

Everyone goes quiet. Andrew looks embarrassed and Ren himself squirms in his armchair. I regret asking.

Finally Oliver answers. "For the children who died at the hands of the wizard. My eldest daughter was one of them."

My body freezes from tail to nose. "I'm sorry, I should have guessed."

"It's all right, child. You're new to the city. One cannot expect you to know all our dirty secrets, even if Ren here is showing you the highlights."

Ren gazes into the fire, a sad, faraway look in his eyes. I know for a fact he thinks of Delia. I wonder if he looked that way about the once-me when she disappeared?

"I hate that bloody wizard," he says, hands balling into fists.

"Why don't we just find him and slit his throat?" My own hands clench over the arms of the chair as I watch Ren and Oliver's faces change with surprise. My outburst is no doubt an unusual one for a human girl, but I don't care. Between what the wizard did to Father and me, Batu and his clan, and now to poor, kind Oliver, I want to destroy him more than ever.

Oliver's face softens and he pats my taut fist. "I am afraid that is not possible. It is suicide to do such a thing."

My brow furrows. "What do you mean? When it comes down to it, the wizard is just a man, isn't he? Albeit a powerful one."

Ren's eyes widen. "You really don't know?"

I stiffen my back. I don't wish to seem naive and ignorant in front of Ren, least of all in front of his family. But then he squeezes my other hand and I melt. He has such a

188

strange hold on my emotions.

Oliver gives Ren a stern look. "It's all right. Not every city is as haunted as we are. Yes, the wizard is a man. And yes, he would die from a knife to the throat like any other. But wizards aren't feared and revered just because they can work spells. The magic lives inside them, it's a part of them. No wizard has ever been buried. When they die, the magic leaves, burning them up in the process."

"Why would that stop someone from killing him?"

"The person who kills the wizard would be incinerated, too."

My limbs go numb. Incinerated? Father never mentioned that. There must be some mistake.

"What if we shoot him with a longbow? Surely magic could not reach that far."

Oliver shakes his head. "Magic is canny. It has life and intelligence of its own. There's no hiding from it. That's why the wizard's cursed disease only attacks girls of this city and ignores you, along with our men and boys. Magic burns up the dead wizard's body because it seeks a new host. It will always choose the person who killed its master. But only a wizard could withstand an influx of magic like that. Anyone else would be overcome and perish in flames."

I shudder. "Only another wizard could kill ours? No one else?"

"Not anyone who wants to live to see another day. But yes, another wizard would stand a chance. Or some other magical creature strong enough to overpower him. A dragon, maybe. A nice griffin would do, but they haven't been seen near Bryre for decades. Unfortunately, good wizards, griffins, and dragons are all in short supply." Oliver leans back into his chair. His gray hair slips over his forehead. In some ways, Oliver reminds me of Father. Does Father know about this tricky business of how to kill a wizard? He knows all about the origin of wizards and dragons, so he should. But what if he doesn't and he tries to kill the evil man himself? I don't want my beloved father to die so horribly. Did he omit this detail so I would not try to stop him?

I try, just for a moment, to imagine what that would feel like. All that heat melting me into nothing at all.

Despite the horror that thought inspires, there is a way around it—Batu. I must redouble my efforts to convince him to help. Father and I may not be able to kill the wizard after all, but Batu can.

"Even a good wizard, if such a thing existed, would demand too high a price," Ren says, snorting with derision. "That's what got us into this mess in the first place."

"What do you mean?" I am suddenly curious. Father has told me nothing of this part.

Oliver shakes his head. "Ren, she doesn't need to know every detail . . ."

"We can trust her," he says. Heat lights up my face. "I trust her. Tell her the story."

"Ah, to be young again." Oliver fondly ruffles Ren's hair. "All right. I'll give her the condensed version. Not long ago, the king of Bryre was in a fix. Another king from a distant city was rumored to be marching on Bryre, set to take it over by force. We are a peaceful people. War is not in our blood. We have guards, but they would be no match for an entire army of trained soldiers and mercenaries."

"I wish I'd been old enough, I would have fought them," Ren says.

"I'm sure you would've fought well," Oliver says, "But it never came to blows. A man appeared at the palace gates one morning, claiming he could make the warmongers go away forever. The king and queen were desperate. The man said he'd only name his price when he was successful. It sounded fair to them at the time. As they discovered, the man was a wizard and he put warding charms in place all over the city. No person intending to kill or harm our citizens could enter. To this day, the spells hold."

"How does the wizard operate in the city? How does he steal the girls?"

Oliver spreads his palms out. "I wish I knew. All we have are guesses. Either he has spies here in Bryre or the charms don't keep him out, since he made them. Magic is as tricky and fickle as the wizards who wield it."

Ren scoffs. "Now that's an understatement if I ever heard one."

"What happened next?" I ask.

"Once the rival king discovered an invisible wall of magic blocked his path into the city and could find no chink in Bryre's armor, his army retreated. The king and his army made a second attempt six years later, but the spell was still too strong. We haven't heard from them since."

"That's a good thing, isn't it?"

"Oh yes, it is." Oliver nods.

"What went wrong?"

"The price. There's always a price." Oliver studies his hands miserably. When the silence grows long enough that I'm ready to break it, he speaks again. "He wanted the king's firstborn child. A daughter. She was three years old at the time. The king and queen refused."

I gasp as confusion fills me. "Did he want to marry her?" That is the only real use of princesses in my fairy tales.

Oliver shudders. "No, the blood of a royal firstborn is the key component to a spell that could give him power over all the magic in the realm. Dark magic. The king and queen didn't suspect until then that he practiced anything other than white magic. They were terribly wrong." Another long pause passes, which makes me nervous. "Needless to say, the wizard didn't take the king's refusal well. He stormed out of the city, swearing to return and take his revenge. Ten years passed and the royal family grew comfortable within their warded walls. The princess grew up into a lovely, though sheltered, young girl. One day, rumors began of the wizard's return. The king and queen did everything they could to protect their daughter, to keep her hidden away in the palace. But the wizard found a loophole to his own spells. He returned to the palace to claim the princess who was rightfully his according to the blind, yet binding, deal the king and queen had made. The guards were no match for his tricks. Nor was the queen. When it came down to it, no one could stop him. The deal had been sealed by magic and his only intent was to take what was rightfully his. He killed the girl in the palace and then they disappeared in a burst of darkness. There wasn't even a body to bury."

Horror rolls over me in waves. What an awful thing. To deprive a father of his beloved daughter. Oliver, with his pained expression, reminds me so much of my own father, that I wish to throw my arms around his neck and squeeze the sadness out of him. But I resist for fear of appearing unseemly.

"Did the wizard's spell finally work? Does he truly rule all the magic in the land now?" I ask.

"Not exactly," Oliver says. "The spell loses potency if the royal firstborn has matured. He may have drawn some power from murdering the princess, but nothing like he would have if he had done it when she was a mere babe. The more cruel and abhorrent the act, the more it feeds the dark magic." He gazes into the fire. "No, instead he bided his time, scraping as much magic from the realm as he could the hard way—killing every magical creature he could find, stealing every potion and amulet he could track down. There were precious few hybrids left at the time; now they are extinct."

"What a horrid creature," is all I can say.

"Now he is back for the rest of the girls," Andrew says.

The silence that follows is heavy. Even Laura stops her fussing by the fire. I can almost taste the salty sadness in the air.

"I'm afraid it's long past time for me to retire." Oliver stands up from his armchair. He suddenly looks much older than he is. "My dear girl, it was a pleasure to meet you. Do take good care of Ren and keep him out of trouble, will you? And, please"—he squeezes my hand—"be very careful if you must be out in Bryre at night. The curfew is in place for a reason."

"I will," I say.

Oliver pats Ren's shoulder and bows to the others and me. "Good night."

"It is getting to be time for you to go to bed, too, Ren," Laura says with a meaningful glance in my direction.

"Of course it is," I say, rising. "I must go home, anyway."

"So soon?" Ren scowls at his mother, then gives me a pleading look. "Can't you stay a little longer?"

"No, she can't," Laura interrupts, waggling that ladle again. I suspect she is not one to be trifled with.

Grumbling, Ren walks me to the door. "I'm going to see her to the gates, and I'll come straight back, Mama."

"You better. I know how long that takes, so no dawdling, you hear me?"

"Yes, Mama."

As soon as we're alone, I turn to Ren with a question spilling off my lips.

"What if there was a way to kill the wizard? What if we could find a good wizard or a dragon to help us?"

Ren stares at me for a moment and frowns. "Frankly, I don't believe there ever have been good wizards. All that power in one person? I can't imagine anyone wouldn't be corrupted. It isn't natural." His fists clench at his sides. "And dragons, well, they're just a myth. Some of the older folks in Bryre swear they were real once, but I'm not convinced."

If only I could persuade Batu to face the wizard. "But what if there are?"

Ren laughs. "You're a strange one." He stops when he sees the expression on my face. "You're not serious, are you?"

I force a smile. "Of course I'm joking." I head back to the road, but Ren holds on to my wrist, turning me to face him.

"You are, aren't you?" He looks so confused, I wish I hadn't asked the question. I'm such a fool.

"Yes," I say. He still doesn't let go of me.

"Have you seen something out of the ordinary?" A mix of hope and fear fills his brown eyes. My heart takes a seat in my throat.

"No, never," I lie. "Just the things you have shown me."

I see many extraordinary things every day, but I cannot tell him about Batu or Father or his laboratory. That I know. Something in the back of my brain screams it. *Do not tell.*

Ren breathes out and releases his grip. "Well, good. You threw me off for a second there. Don't do that."

I shrug, trying to pretend my stupid curiosity was nothing but a joke. "Sorry, I didn't mean to scare you."

"No need to worry. It's just that . . . the people of Bryre don't like magic users. And when we supposedly had dragons around, we didn't like them much either."

My face pales. Father told me people could confuse his science for magic. Is that why he doesn't live in the city?

"I understand," I say.

"Sorry, I've been raised to be wary. You wouldn't know that since you're not from Bryre," Ren says. "May I walk you to the fountain?"

I take his hand. "Yes, please. Thank you for showing me your home. You have a lovely family."

"I'm just glad you showed up." Together, we walk the streets hand in hand under the moonlight. An idea has been niggling at the back of my brain all evening, ever since Ren mentioned the hospital. Maybe I can stop the wizard, maybe even prevent him from getting the girls at all. From causing such grief as he's inflicted on Ren.

When we reach the fountain again, I can contain my curiosity no longer. "Where is this hospital you mentioned earlier? The one the wizard takes the girls from?"

Ren looks at me askance. "You haven't seen the hospital?"

I shake my head.

"I thought you would have by now. You always seem to be coming or going from that direction."

"Where is it?"

Ren points down the alley I take each night to the wizard's prison. A knot of fear twists in my stomach. That can't be right. I know that path too well.

"How far?" My voice cracks. Air no longer passes through my lungs correctly.

Ren's brow furrows; he obviously doesn't understand my questions. I barely understand them myself. "A couple blocks. It's the square building on the right."

The world stops like a door caught midswing on its

hinges. Blood throbs in my ears, blocking out the night sounds.

Suddenly I'm desperate to get out of here. All I can think of is the girls. What if the wizard isn't stealing them this time? What if it's me? Just me?

A sick feeling threads its way through my innards. Father couldn't have known about this, could he? Everything feels upside down and inside out.

"I must go. My father will wonder where I am." My tail and wings quiver beneath my cloak, aching to be free and release this awful tension. I can't keep them hidden much longer.

Ren places his hand over mine. "Can you stay, just for a minute?"

Oh no. How can I leave with him staring at me in such a manner? I focus on breathing in and out as we examine the moon's fuzzy reflection in the fountain and the fog swirling around our feet. Emotions spin in my chest and I feel as though I will burst at any second.

I barely last a full minute.

"I must go, I'm sorry." With one quick squeeze of his hand, I turn to flee, but he holds it tight.

"Please, Kym, stay." Ren's face falls. "I've missed you." His grip is warm and welcoming, but I rip my hand away nonetheless.

"Your mother will be getting worried. So will my father." I must get away before I explode. Unable to form any more words, I spin on my heels and run.

"Kym! Wait!" Ren's voice follows me down the alley

and I duck into an offshoot, then another, hoping to lose him. His feet fall behind me, but I can still smell the cinnamon that clings to his clothes.

Faster, must run faster. Another alley. When I know he can't see me, I leap up to the nearest rooftop and scramble across the buildings instead. The fog will hide me.

Must keep running.

Father will know what to make of this information about the hospital. If he has made a mistake—or worse, if I misunderstood his directions—he will correct our path. He will know what to do.

But what, says a voice in the back of my mind, *if he doesn't? What if he misled you?* I squash it down with all my might, forcing it away with memories of Father's kindness and care.

No, Father would never do that. Unless . . . unless he has somehow fallen under the thrall of the wizard. But I can't believe that. Everything else he has done proves he is working against that horrible man. Doesn't it?

A night without a rescue would normally be inexcusable, but I must be certain we have not made a terrible mistake. I cannot remove another girl from Bryre until I have spoken to Father.

With the fog, I need higher ground to get my bearings. I vault to the roof of the tall building next to me and take in the city. I fled west from Ren; going east should bring me back to the fountain. As I scan the city, I glimpse the tip of a happy cherub in the distance.

198

I take off, skimming over the roofs, and wing my way toward home and answers.

"Father, Father, wake up," I say, shaking his shoulder. The edges of my voice crackle in the sleepy silence of his bedroom. He finally stirs.

"Hmm? What?" He bolts up when he sees my face. "Kym, what on earth is the matter? You look as though you have seen death himself!"

I burst into tears. Father puts his arms around me. "My dear, what has happened? Tell me!"

I pull away and sit on the edge off the bed. Father's nightcap is askew atop his alarmed face. He does not look like someone who would carry out the wizard's plans, unwittingly or otherwise. He looks like my kind, and very worried father.

How do I even begin?

"I think we've made a horrible mistake."

Father's jaw drops, but I press on, terrified that if I don't get it all out now, I will never find the right words. "The prison on the map—I do not think it is really a prison after all. I think—I think it is a hospital. Bryre's hospital. The wizard is not taking the girls this time, it's just us. Just me."

I stare at the floorboards, my pulse stuttering in my ears. If Father is involved, I fear he will be furious. If he is not, he will be disappointed in me for not realizing this earlier.

When he finally speaks, Father's voice is low and soothing. "Kym, what makes you think that?"

My breath falters inside my chest. I must not tell Father about Ren. "I—I overheard people talking about the hospital," I lie, trembling. "They were near it and pointed to the prison, calling it the hospital. Could we have the wrong place? Is it possible?"

Father takes my face in both his hands. A cool, calm feeling blooms and spreads out through my limbs. "No, my dear, it is not possible. The place I directed you to is not the hospital; it is undeniably the wizard's prison. He takes the girls and we free them. That is how it has always been. Trust me."

I do. I trust Father completely. What was I so worried about earlier that I abandoned Ren in such a manner? The reason is out of reach now, slipping further away every second.

"Now, get some sleep and forget all about the hospital."

Father's palms are suddenly warm against my cheeks. Exhaustion consumes me. "The what?" I say, trying to hold on to the conversation.

"Exactly." He smiles. "Everything will be clearer in the morning."

He releases me and I stumble toward my room. Yes, Father is right. I must sleep. I have worn myself out.

Tomorrow is a new day. Tomorrow everything will make sense.

DAY FIFTY-ONE

THE NIGHT I SPENT WITH REN'S FAMILY HAS TROUBLED ME FOR DAYS.
That man—Oliver—is older and grayer, but is undoubtedly
the same man I saw in a vision of the palace rose garden.

The once-me knew him, but who was he to me? A gardener I befriended who showed off the roses? When I close
my eyes, I can still feel the trust and warmth of that memory, and I can't helping thinking there's more to it.

I have remained in my bed, staring at the sun peeking
through my curtains far too long today with these questions
that plague me. Above all else, one thing worries me most.

Father has not been in any of these visions.

Ren, Oliver, the woman in blue, and the little blond
girl—but no Father.

He assures me that these are not memories, only a

confusion of my subconscious mind grappling with shattered pieces and merging them with the present. Yet every one I have unnerves me more.

When I finally enter the kitchen, Father closes his book with a sigh. "My dear girl, what is wrong? Do you feel all right?"

I curse these terrible musings that show so easily on my face. I do not wish to trouble him, but I've never been good at concealing my emotions.

"Yes, I'm quite well." I toy with a crust of bread. My stomach flutters with confusion. I'm not sure I can keep any food down right now. "It's just . . ." How can I phrase this so he does not suspect I've been talking to the humans? Or that I'm lending any credence to the visions? I certainly can't tell him I've met some of the people in them. "Sometimes I hear things and see things. When I am out in the city. They do not always match what I've learned from you." I tear a piece off the bread with my teeth.

His eyes narrow. "Have you spoken to anyone in the city?"

"No! No, of course not." There's that sour feeling in the pit of my stomach again. I drop the bread on the floor. Pippa swoops in, snatches it, and flies off with her prize to her nest in the rafters.

"What distressed you?"

I fiddle with a loose thread on my skirt. "Well, I saw a woman through a kitchen window. As I passed, she . . . she put a piece of wood on the fire. I did not understand. I have never seen you do that." Nor have my visions shown anyone doing the things Father does. No merging animals together, no healing with a single draught, or grinding powders that make people fall asleep.

He laughs. "My dear, there is more than one way to build a fire. Mine may be a little different, but it is no reason to be upset." He places a hand on my cheek and suddenly all my fears about the fire and science and magic melt away. His touch is always calming. It's silly of me to question how he builds a fire.

"Is there something else?"

"Yes. A few weeks ago I heard two women talking about you."

He tenses and I wonder why. Could he know these women?

"From what they said, it sounded as though you once knew the king. Did you?"

He sighs. "Yes, once upon a time, I did."

I'd expected he would deny it. That he'd say it was a misunderstanding. "Why didn't you tell me?"

"My dear, I am afraid King Oliver and I did not part on good terms."

I start at the mention of the king's name. Oliver. The man staying with Ren and his family has the same name. Could the king really be hiding by Ren's hearth? It would explain his forlorn expression when he spoke of the king's plight.

My heart sinks a little. Ren doesn't trust me enough to tell me who Oliver really is.

But how could I have known the king well enough for

him to show me roses in the palace garden? Perhaps Father is right; my mind is only playing cruel tricks on me.

"We did not see eye to eye in regard to the business with the wizard and I may have said some unpleasant things to the man." Father runs a hand through his silver hair. "It is not something I am proud of, and why I do not set in foot in Bryre anymore. That is why I did not tell you. You ask so many questions that I could not very well tell you I know the king and then not tell you why we are not working with him."

I take Father's hand. "I understand. But I'm sure if you just went and talked to King Oliver, he would forgive you. We could accomplish even more together."

He drops my hand. "It is out of the question. You do not know what you are suggesting."

I remember Oliver's kind face, warm like Ren's but lined like Father's, too. I know exactly what I suggest.

"Why? Did he want to do something you did not? Or was it the other way around?"

"I am finished speaking on this matter. Is there anything else bothering you?" Father's face transforms to a hardened pallor. His falling out with the king must've been grave for him to get so upset about a mere question or two.

I blush. "Yes, Father." So much bothers me that I can hardly find the words.

He groans and leans back in his chair with folded arms.

"Sometimes people talk about magic." I hesitate—this one troubles me most. "I hear that we can't kill the wizard if we want to live. That whoever kills one will be burned up by the magic that's released. Unless they're a dragon or another wizard." I twist my hands together in my skirts. "But how can that be? Didn't you create me to kill him? That has always been our plan, hasn't it?"

Father reaches out to touch my face again, running his thumb over my chin. A wave of calm washes over me. "Oh, Kymera, I never meant for you to kill the wizard. I have yet to find a safe way to do it. I created you to stop him. There's a difference. Freeing those girls and getting them away from him, that is how we will stop the wizard."

Relief floods my limbs. I don't have to worry. Father always tells the truth. It makes much more sense now.

Except that Father seems as troubled as I did a few minutes ago. I squeeze his hand as I pull it away from my face.

"Are you sure there are no more dragons like the ones in my books?"

"Not anymore. The wizards have hunted them all down for their magic. Sometimes one hears rumors, but that is all nowadays. Why do you ask?"

Heat creeps around my shoulders and onto my neck, like it will burn me up just for thinking of the words crossing my tongue. I have no choice but to keep Batu secret. "I just wondered. I wish, very much, to meet a dragon. There are not many of them, and there are even less of me."

Father brushes my hair away from my face as I toy with my fingernails. If I look him in the eye, he will know I'm hiding something from him.

"That just makes you special," he says.

"Sometimes, I wish I was not so special." Sometimes,

I wish I was still the once-me girl. Normal, and loved by friends and family, not the creature who hides in the forest and skulks through the city at night. And yet at the same time, I am so grateful that I am able to help these girls, as no one was able to help the once-me.

He considers me with raised eyebrows. "My dear, I think we need to lay out some new ground rules for your visits into the city. If you're overhearing that much, wanting to mix with humans that much, you must be straying from the route I planned. It will not take you near any of the public houses or other places where large groups could be overheard." He points his finger. "You have been going off on your own and exploring Bryre."

The skin from my skull to tail turns red. I stare at the floor. "Yes, Father. I have."

He rises from his chair, trembling with pent-up anger. "It must stop immediately. Do you understand?"

I nod, unable to meet his eyes. The pounding in my chest reverberates in my ears.

He takes my chin again and tilts my head up, forcing me to look in his face. I flinch. "Are you certain? If the humans find out about you, it will ruin everything."

His words send prickling shivers down my spine. Does he know what I've really been doing? Could he?

"Answer me!"

The fury in his voice makes me jump in my seat, while guilt and fear flood my veins. "Yes, yes, I understand. I will not do it again. I promise. I will follow your directions to the letter." I clutch my quivering hands together in my lap so Father cannot see them.

"You had better. If not, you will doom every one of those girls in the prison. Not to mention yourself." He storms out of the house before I can even attempt to utter an apology.

If I do as I have just promised, it means I can't go anywhere with Ren. Except to the fountain. That's on Father's route. I can only meet Ren there.

I throw up my hands, covering my face, as I rise from my chair. I should not meet Ren at all. But I will. I can't help myself.

I run to the door, watching Father's receding figure as he marches to the tower and his laboratory. I can't help wondering whether I have already ruined everything with my actions. If only I had never strayed from my path and never bothered with Ren.

But most of all I worry that too many things don't add up. What if Father is wrong? About the humans, about me, and about my memories?

DAY FIFTY-THREE

BETWEEN THE VISIONS, WHAT REN AND OLIVER SAID ABOUT KILLING wizards, and the contradictions from Father, my head is a jumbled mess. I don't know what to think anymore. Perhaps they're all misled and the truth lies somewhere in between?

Despite my promise to Father, I enter the city through a different route tonight. Bryre is a haunted place, and I have not yet ferreted out all its secrets. Ren has told me much, but even he can't know the whole truth. I am certain more remains to be discovered that could help us, and perhaps could help me remember my past.

This part of the city has not yet been taken by the briars, but when I land on the highest rooftop in this section, I can see it's on its way here. Slowly but surely, the creeping vines move. Every night, I check their progress, and every night, I'm disturbed to see another building's foundation uprooted, or another room in the palace turned to rubble.

Voices carry on the wind. Women. And men's voices like Father's, too.

Heat flashes over my face. These voices are animated and I think they might be arguing. They come to me from a long, squat building at the end of the alley. The windows are dark and the roof sags in places. I hop down from my perch and creep closer. Perhaps the curfew only applies to children?

Curious, I lean against the side of the building, just beneath the window.

"You don't even know if that's true," says a man's voice. "Leave it alone and fetch me another ale, will ya?"

A woman snorts. "I have it on good authority from my cousin, a nurse at the quarantine hospital. Every morning when she gets to work, another girl has vanished. The guards wake up groggy with no memory of the night before. They're either dying or someone takes them. Either way, the hospital is hushing it up."

"It's that beast on the road," a man says, but his words bleed together and it's difficult to make them out. "That girl . . . with the tail and fangs . . . and . . ." A clatter and snickers follow his words, but my heart grows cold. On the last day of my training, I stung a man. Could this be him?

"Why don't ya just have a seat in that corner, William," the woman says. "Sleep it all off, boy."

More people talk at once, but I pick out pieces of what they say.

"It's the wizard again, Marta, you can count on it," a third man says.

"Well, what are you boys going to do about it, eh? Just let him take our girls?" the woman answers.

"If we could find him, we'd string him up for the crows." Several male voices echo this sentiment, then fade to rumblings.

"I think it's something different," interrupts another man. "When I was over the mountains for business these past few weeks, the people in the village at the foothills spoke of men who deal in live goods."

"What are you talking about?" snaps the woman.

"Human goods," the man says.

The room goes silent.

Human goods? What on earth is that?

"Slaves?" the woman finally whispers.

"Exactly. It's different this time. Not like what the wizard did before. Something's changed. I stake my money on traders. And I'd bet they're living among us."

"Jonah Barry, that's ridiculous. No one in this city would do that. Except maybe Jimmy Hill, but only if he was real drunk and desperate for coin. Besides, these are peaceful times. Who would he sell them to?"

Several voices speak at once, rising into an indecipherable cacophony. I press my hands to my ears, not wanting to hear any more. Their conversation has made me uneasy, something in their words picking at a memory that refuses to shake loose.

I flee into the shadows, wishing only for comfort, but

there is none to be had.

The wizard attacks from all sides. He will ruin the city one way or the other. And he can't be killed by anyone other than another wizard. At least not anyone who wishes to live.

I still don't understand why Father didn't tell me about that. He claims it's because he does not want me to take such a risk, but why did he give me the tools to stun, to tear, and to kill? Why did he teach me how to hunt and be stealthy if not to destroy our enemy?

The night breeze picks up, toying with my cloak and a lock of my black hair. Ren waits for me by our fountain. I'm dying to go to him. But I don't think I will tonight. My head is too muddled and I never can think straight around the boy who sneaks me roses from the king's personal garden.

Tonight, I'll rescue another girl and return home. It's better this way. But just for tonight.

I tackle the guards in the prison earlier than usual, and leave with a girl with unruly brown curls as fast as I can. I worry about the guards; do they have families too? How willing are they in their aid of the wizard? The prison has always made me uncomfortable, but it is getting worse. Just entering the building makes my stomach flip in all sorts of unpleasant ways. Something about that place niggles at the back of my mind, something I should know, but I can't remember what it is, or even why I feel this way.

Carrying my burden, I alight in an alley by the cherub fountain and prepare to run home.

"What're you doing?"

Cold dread pierces my heart and the smell of baking bread roots me to the spot.

No. Not Ren. Not here, not *now*.

I clutch the unconscious girl close to my chest and do not turn. He can't see me like this. Instinct roils in my gut—do I fly or sting him before he discovers what I am about? If he knew I took Delia from the city, Ren would hate me. If he sees what's in my arms, he just might make that assumption. I did it to save her, but he misses her enough that I doubt he'd understand.

Before I decide, he chooses for me. He circles around; turning away again will only make it too obvious.

"What—?" He stops midsentence, staring at the girl's hair spilling out of my cloak. I can guess the thoughts that must be going through his head.

"It's not what you think," I squeak. Every muscle in my body is strung as tight as a bow. I should flee. Now.

He brushes my cloak away to reveal the girl's face. He jumps back, shuddering. Horror creeps over his face, changing his warm features into a cold expression. "What in Bryre are you doing with the miller's daughter?"

My cheeks redden and I cling to the girl tighter. Of course he knows her. He probably knows them all.

Just like he probably knew me.

"I swear on my life. It's not what you think."

"You." He points. "You work for the wizard."

"No!" I cry. "I hate the wizard. He took everything from me. I work against him. I am saving her!"

Ren shakes his head and paces back and forth between the alley walls, gulping ragged breaths. "No, only the wizard takes the girls."

Ice forms at the base of my spine, chilling me inside and out. I am nothing like the wizard. How could he even think that? "Ren, please."

Realization dawns, spreading over every inch of his exposed skin in a furious red. "You took Delia," he whispers.

I can't answer. I did take her, but not in the way he thinks. The awful cold feeling crawls into my chest and curls up under my heart. There is no getting out of this. I cannot fully explain without betraying Father.

He grabs my arm and squeezes. "Where is she?"

I try to shake him off, but he's stronger than I expect. Something frightening burns in his eyes. My arm begins to ache. The terror welling up inside has me shivering uncontrollably.

"I saved her life," I say. "And I'm saving this girl, too. Now let me go."

When he releases my arm and lunges for the girl, the green scales of my tail flash in a blinding arc. He staggers backward, fear and hatred twisting his once kind face. For a moment, his usual scent transforms to that of burned toast. Then Ren is on the ground, clutching his chest. I can only stare, horrified at what I've done—again—as the fire in his eyes flickers out.

Footsteps and voices echo from the far end of the alley. Someone heard us arguing.

I leap up to the rooftops, skimming along until I reach the walls and can fly off without fear of being seen by human eyes.

But the guilt of what I've done to Ren, and the lingering fear of something *wrong*, follows me all the way home.

DAY FIFTY-FOUR

THE SUN WAKES ME, BUT I'M COLD WITH CONFUSION AND TROUBLED dreams. Nothing makes sense anymore. Ren despises me. I can't believe I stung him again. I wish there was a way to make him understand we're saving the girls, not hurting them.

I roll out of bed, my legs like jelly. I must tell Father about Ren and beg his forgiveness. Perhaps he'll have an idea on how to convince Ren our mission is a good one. I'm sure he'd want to help if he understood. He hates the wizard as much as we do.

If only I could tell Father about Batu, my rock dragon, but I push that thought aside. Even if it weren't impossible due to the blood bond, my friendship with a dragon is not something that would compromise our mission. Ren's awareness, left unchecked, definitely could.

I tiptoe into the cottage proper, but Father is not in his usual spot by the fire.

Pippa whines in the corner, begging to be let outside. She loves to chase the chickens. I open the door and she zooms into the yard. I wander after her, but Father is not outside, either. He must be working in his laboratory. The tower door creaks open at my touch, but no other sounds present themselves. I pry open the trapdoor with my claws and climb down the stairs. The room is empty and dark. Has he gone out for a walk? I'll have to wait for him to return.

I shiver from the chill of the boxes Father keeps down here. There are so many more now that it makes the room colder than I recall. What does he keep in them all? Is he preparing an army of goat-footed chickens to defeat the wizard? The locked box comes to mind. I can't be sure what I saw, but it was very strange. Curious, I crack the lid of the nearest one—more chickens waiting to be returned to life. The next contains a large owl; its beady, empty eyes glare back and I quickly shut the lid. The next has the oddest thing yet—huge curved claws. Like a giant version of my own.

I approach a fourth box, the one in the same place the locked cold box once was. My palms are sweaty, and I wipe them on my dress. I have no reason to fear this box. It is only more parts for Father's creations.

It could not be anything else.

This does nothing to calm me, and my heart beats a

staccato rhythm in my chest. I place my hands on the top of the cold box and thrust it open. I yelp, clapping my hands over my mouth.

The sickly girl whose death I hastened with my venom lies inside. Her hands are crossed over her chest as though she's trying to keep warm in her sleep. It *was* a hand I saw slip out of the cold box. Panic rushes over me. Father said he sent her off with Darrell to be buried in Belladoma. How did she get back here? Did Darrell return her for some unfathomable reason?

More important, why didn't Father tell me?

Another body comes to my mind. That faun Pippa uncovered beneath my garden. A chill slinks from the crown of my head to the tip of my tail. Was this girl here all along? I know why he kept his faun friend's body, but why would he keep hers? He keeps only bodies for parts in the boxes. . . .

What about mine, when he first found it? Did he keep me in a cold box once, too?

"Kymera?" Father's voice echoes down the stair, and my heart lurches into my throat. My palms continue to sweat in spite of the temperature as I drop the lid on the girl's cold-box casket.

"Down here, Father," I say, keeping my voice light. I'm desperate to ask about the girl, but fear gnaws at my gut. Father didn't want me to know. If he had, he would've told me. He kept it from me for a reason.

But what could that reason be?

"What are you doing?" He frowns. I slide my blue eyes into place and give him a shaky grin.

"Looking for you. I must speak with you." Despite the shock of finding the girl, I have not forgotten why I sought him in the first place.

"Of course, my dear. Let us go sit by the fire." He takes my arm and begins to lead me up the stairs. Does he not want me in his laboratory? I feel much less welcome now than the time I watched him make a new chicken.

"Wait," I say, pulling my arm out of his grasp. I take a deep breath and brace for Father's anger. "I opened the cold boxes. I saw *her*. Why is that girl who died still here? Why didn't you tell me?"

For one second, Father's face slips into an angry mask, but it's gone before I even blink. "You should not play down here. There are dangerous, powerful things. I would not wish you to be hurt accidentally." His cool fingers wrap around my shoulder, radiating numbness toward my head. "The girl is only here in case you need spare parts. But you will forget all about that."

"But I . . ." I struggle to hold on to the thread of conversation, but it slips from my mind like an eel through the river. What was I so concerned about a moment ago? I glance back down the stairs as Father leads me out of the tower. The usual boxes, stone table, and shelves filled with an array of gruesome jars look back, just as they ought.

The unsettling feeling of something missing haunts every step I take away from the laboratory. I clench my hands in frustration, but Father won't let me out of his grasp. If I could just go back down those stairs I might remember why.

When we're settled in our usual chairs, Father clears his throat. "Now, what did you wish to speak to me about?"

I may not remember why I was upset in the laboratory, but I do know why I was looking for Father: to tell him about Ren. My hands are clasped so tightly in my lap that the tips of my fingers turn white.

"I have something to confess," I begin. "You will not like it."

Father raises an eyebrow. "That is not an auspicious beginning."

I swallow. "I spoke to that boy. Many times."

Father's face pales, then reddens like my roses. "You what?" His hands grip the arms of his chair hard enough that I fear he will rip out the stuffing. "You disobeyed me?"

My face matches his. "I'm sorry, Father. I didn't intend to disobey you, but he was persistent and I was curious. I couldn't help it. I have no one to talk to when I go into Bryre."

I have no one to talk to at all but you, I think, but refrain from saying. Father would keep me locked away like the fairy-tale princess trapped in her tower, alone and unaware of the outside world. But like her, I couldn't resist the desire to break free.

"You do not talk to the people of Bryre because you are supposed to be sneaking their girls out of the city!" Father leaps up and begins to pace.

This does not bode well. He hasn't even heard the worst of it.

"There's more."

219

He spins, eyes blazing, and I shrink back into my chair. Even Pippa cowers under the table. Neither of us has ever witnessed Father in such a state. "What did you do?" he says.

"I was only doing as you instructed last night, as I do every night. I snuck into the prison and took one of the girls with me. Ren must've been nearby because—"

"Ren? *Ren?* You know his name?"

I blush deeper, though I didn't think it possible. "And he knows mine," I whisper. Father throws his hands up, grumbling. He resumes stomping around the room.

"On my way out of the city, he found me and saw the girl." I pause, remembering the confused, horrified expression on Ren's face. "He didn't understand what I was doing and I couldn't explain. I stung him." I grip the bottom of my chair, steeling myself in the face of Father's fury. "I want—I need—to tell him everything. What we do, what I am, everything."

Father grasps my shoulders and shakes me until my teeth rattle. "Are you out of your bloody mind, girl? Tell him?"

"He will understand!" I manage to spit out. "He will help us if he knows! He hates the wizard as much as we do."

"Oh, I am sure he does." Father snorts. "He is just a stupid boy. He cannot help us."

I bristle at his assessment of Ren. "He's no such thing. He's smart and sneaky. The king trusts him to carry secret messages to his advisers!" I leave out the fact that Ren also introduced me to his family and possibly the king himself.

"That is true." Father stops pacing and scratches his

chin. "He trusts you, then? You might redeem yourself yet."

Hope surges in my chest. Might I have both Father and Ren? "How? What can I do?"

Father shrugs. "You will bring him back here on your next trip to the city. I will be the judge of whether or not he truly works for the king."

"You want me to bring him here? I doubt he'll come with me. Our last meeting did not go well."

He laughs and it chills me. "Kym, all you have to do is sting him. I will interrogate him and find out what he knows about the wizard, the king, and any plans he may be privy to."

My lungs stop working. "You want me to put him to sleep?" Panic surges where hope flamed moments before. I don't want to sting him again—I already feel terrible about the times I did. "You won't send him away to Belladoma, will you?" I can't fathom Ren being that far away.

"Of course. You cannot believe he will want to stay near you once he discovers what you are, can you?"

I can. I do. Of all people, I need Ren to believe in me, whatever form I may take. It is the secret wish of my heart that I've hardly dared to utter. My face blanches.

"You do?" He takes my chin in his hand, harder than usual. "How many times must I tell you, Kymera: No human will ever trust you. Accept you. Or love you. Not like I do. I am the only one because I made you. They would kill you as soon as look at you."

I wrest my chin out of his grip. "Ren would not. He's upset because he saw me taking that child, but once he

221

knows everything he'll understand. I know he will! He will help, because I'm certain he has nothing to do with that wizard!"

I stand, every limb quivering.

Father folds his arms and stares deep into my eyes. "No, Kym. He will not understand. He will hate you. He already hates you."

"No!" I scream, kicking over the chair and scaring any of Pippa's remaining wits right out of her head.

Then I do the one thing I can.

Run.

The only thought filling my mind is how much I don't want to be near Father. How much I crave Ren's company. Heedless of the daylight and Father's objections, I throw myself into the hedge path.

The air is cooler here, but my entire body is aflame with misgivings. Father can't be right. Ren does not hate me. He can't hate me! I love him. I'll do anything to redeem myself in his eyes.

I'll explain everything. I'll apologize for taking so long to tell him. He'll understand.

He has to.

I'll confess that I rescued Delia. I wish I hadn't given her to Darrell to bring to Belladoma. I should've taken her to Ren instead. But I allowed jealousy to cloud my vision and made the wrong choice. Still, Ren should be relieved she's safe and in a happy place. He won't have to worry anymore even if he misses her. Perhaps we can visit her someday.

Hope buoys me as I break free of the hedge and enter the forest proper. I pull back my cloak and flutter my way between the trees. When the road comes into view, I clutch my cloak around my body, pulling the hood up over my head, and wind my tail around my thigh. No one can stop me from finding Ren. Not Father, not the city guards.

I wish I could fly, but I can't take the risk in the daytime.

The sun is high and sweat trickles down my spine as I pass other travelers. I barely give them a second glance. My thoughts have one focus.

By the time I near the gates, I realize I may have trouble getting into Bryre. The guards appear to be stopping everyone. Surely I will not be an exception. I veer into the woods and wind my way toward the wall nearest the forest edge. Closing my eyes, I listen for sounds of the guards on the parapet above. A dull roar echoes somewhere out of reach. When the nearest guard passes out of range, I climb up the stones using my claws. I must be stealthier now than at night. I reach the top and leap into the nearest tree. The whole city is alive with motion. I'm not sure what to make of it.

This is very different from the quiet, sleeping city I've grown to love.

I'll have to find my way to Ren. To apologize, to explain. I must see him.

I drop out of the tree and crouch on all fours in the yard of a house. A young boy watches me with wide eyes through the back window.

"Mama, look!" The child points and I freeze. "There's a girl in our yard!"

I burst into the streets and hit a wall of people. There are so many. Young, old, in between. The colors of their clothes swirl around me in streaks of reds, blues, greens, and browns.

All of them are talking or moving or making noise. So much noise! I've never heard this much at one time before. This is the dull roar I noticed in the forest, realized as a true cacophony. I slap my hands over my ears and crumple to the cobblestones. It's so loud that it hurts. I can't stand it. I wish I could curl up and dissolve into the ground.

Instead a woman trips over me, her foot catching on my rib and robbing me of my breath.

"What're you doing, missy?" Hers is not the calm tone Father uses. It's gruff and . . . irritated. That's the word. She's unhappy with me for blocking her path. I crawl to the side amid curious gazes as she *harrumphs* and passes.

So much happens all at once here, it's a wonder the humans can stand it. I want to go back to the forest, to the quiet peace and low chitters of animals. My eardrums are ready to explode.

But I must find Ren.

I stagger to my feet and stumble into the crowd. They push and I shove back.

"Hey!"

"Watch it!"

I reach a break in the throng and pause to catch my breath. A rib throbs in my chest. I have no idea where I am. I didn't have time to take Father's map. The crowd turned me around. I'm dying to fly out of here, if only to get fresh air and solitude.

But I came here for Ren and I'm not leaving until I find him. Tears prick at my eyes, but I blink them back.

The ground rumbles and I flatten my body against the nearest building. No comforting shadows to hide in now. A rectangular formation of men with swords on their belts marches down the street. They don't glance at me or any of the people milling around. They're full of purpose and motion.

That's what I need to do. Move purposefully. I take a deep, steadying breath and step out into the street again, following the guards. They know where they're going, and the people part to let them pass, filling in the space immediately after. Following them is not as easy as I'd hoped. It's like swimming upstream. I must get through this. My hands sweat and I can barely hold my cloak shut. My hood slips off my head every few minutes and I pause to adjust it, only to be jostled by the next cart or person. Walking through so many sweating humans makes me feel dirty and nauseous.

By the time I catch up to the guards, my body trembles and I'm sure I will vomit.

"Kym!"

We've reached the little square with the fountain. Our fountain. Ren sits on the opposite rim and waves. He isn't

225

angry. I'm so relieved, I could cry.

Before I can run toward him, a small voice chills me to the core.

"Mama, what's that?"

A little girl points at me. Her mother gasps.

I'm dizzy. I'm such a fool. My skin is slick with sweat— my tail slipped down my leg and now peeks out from beneath my cloak. In all the confusion I hadn't noticed.

Father will be even angrier with me now.

I whirl back to Ren. His waving slows and he tilts his head, confused. No sign of last night's fury mars his face. Has he already forgiven me?

Hands grab me from behind, ripping my cloak. Air cools my wings in a shocking rush.

"Monster!" cry the two women clutching my cloak.

"No," I murmur, pressing my hands to my ears. I'm not a monster. The wizard is a monster. I'm a hybrid. I'm here to save these people from the wizard.

"Monster! Monster!" The cry catches fire through the crowd and all eyes stare at me. Hands shackle my wrists. "Monster! Burn her!"

Burn? Oh Father, how wrong I was! They're as horrid as you claimed!

"No!" I scream, spinning to shake off my captors. I sting two men with my tail in the process, and they drop like coins into the fountain. The tears can't be held back now. I gaze one last time at Ren. Shock covers his warm face. Disbelief fills his wonderful brown eyes.

Even he thinks I'm a monster.

Instinct is all I am, all I can feel. All that matters.

I spread my wings to their full length, preparing to take off and leave the screeching mass of people—and Ren—far behind.

But before I can reach the safety of the air, something hard connects with the back of my head and everything slips away into black.

DAY FIFTY-FIVE

MY HEAD RESTS ON SOMETHING THAT PRICKLES MY CHEEK. WHEN I JOLT up, the something sticks to it. I pull it off my face—hay. I'm in a dark room with one door and an earthen floor haphazardly dotted with bits of hay.

They caught me. I wasn't careful enough, I didn't heed Father's warnings well enough. I let my guard down, and now I'm here. Wherever that may be.

How long have I been unconscious? If a day has passed, Father will worry. If it's more than that, he will be beside himself. I was so stupid! How could I let myself be caught?

And what must Ren think of me? Finding out what I am in such a manner? I ache to explain myself to him.

I rest my head on the floor, letting the cold seep into my skin and temper the flush in my cheeks. The back of my head is sore, but I don't have time to worry about that. I must escape. I must save the girls. Or all Father's work will be for nothing.

My hand flies to my throat. The black ribbon choker Father gave me remains around my neck. My sleeves are long enough to cover my patchwork arms, too. They may not have seen my bolts. Or my multicolored skin. There's hope I might be able to convince them I'm just a hybrid. A creature that they think died out a long time ago.

Short of ripping my way through the humans, what else can I do? Hurting them is not an option. Maybe I can convince them to let me go.

A hundred maybes and what ifs flutter through my brain.

The knob on my cell door jiggles and creaks. I'm on my feet in two seconds flat. This is better. When the guard comes in, I will overpower him—that should be easy if it's only one—and return to Father as fast as I can. It doesn't matter if the city folk see me fly; they already know about my wings. I only hope they have not connected me to Father. He said they did not trust his science. If they discover he created me . . .

Another jiggle and the door slowly opens. I wait behind it, ready to pounce.

Ren's head pokes into the room. My breath catches in my throat. I retract my claws and wind my tail around my leg.

"Kym," he says as he sees me standing behind the door, frozen in surprise.

The world halts on its axis. Neither of us can move. Neither of us dares to breathe. I'm so terrified, I can't even tremble.

Is he here to kill me? Have they charged him with that task?

"You're all right." He lowers his voice as he shuts the door behind him and the earth moves again. "Look, the citizens think you're the one taking their girls."

My face blooms red. I can't meet his eyes. He keeps his distance on the other side of the small room. Fear hovers in the air between us, threatening to engulf us both.

"I don't understand this." He gestures to my wings, wincing. "But I can't believe you'd hurt anyone. I really thought I knew you." His expression crumples in confusion.

I'm speechless. Ren speaks as though he has no memory of the night he caught me taking a girl—as though he never saw me doing exactly what the city folk fear. How is that possible? The expression on his face when he caught me flashes through my mind and I cringe. No, if he remembered, he wouldn't defend me.

The question is: why doesn't he remember?

"Kym, please, say something?"

I want desperately to ask him about the last time we spoke, but I hold my tongue. "How long have I been here?" I say instead.

"A day and a half." He shifts his weight to his other foot uneasily.

"They let you in?" I confess, I would have thought I'd be better guarded than that.

230

Ren gives a wry laugh and folds his arms over his chest. "I waited until it got dark and then tricked my way in. I heard them talking earlier in the square. I . . . I can't let them do . . . what they want to do to you."

Tiny shards of ice needle over my skin. "What? What do they want to do?"

Ren looks away. "It doesn't matter. I'm getting you out. You'll be safe."

The cries of the crowd return to me: *Monster! Burn her! Burn the monster!*

"They want to burn me," I whisper. Father was right. Why did I ever doubt him? If he was right about them, could he be right about Ren? If I remind him of what I've done, that I rescue the girls, will he want to burn me too? Or should I take his memory loss as a reprieve and keep up my lies?

"They won't. But I have to ask you something first." Ren pauses, gripping his elbows so tightly his fingers turn bone white. "What are you?"

The spark of fear hovering in his eyes makes my heart sink. He may not remember the other night, but I have lost him nonetheless.

My brain latches onto the answer I've prepared to tell him if he ever accidentally saw my true form.

"Where I'm from, there are still hybrids. I know you don't believe they exist anymore, but you're wrong. I'm proof."

Ren's eyes widen. "But where?"

"I cannot tell you." This is where I stumble a bit. I've

never gotten this far in my daydreams. "For their protection, you know."

Ren runs his fingers through his hair and shakes his head. "I guess I can't blame you for wanting to keep your family's location a secret. Not after this."

An uncomfortable silence fills the room.

"But why have you been coming to Bryre?" Ren finally asks.

"Curiosity, that part was always true," I say. "I couldn't help wanting to know more about humans, and couldn't pass up the opportunity to discover Bryre with you. If you recall, I did try to avoid you at first."

He smiles sadly. "I was quite insistent on knowing you, wasn't I?"

All I can do is swallow down the lump forming in my throat.

Ren moves toward the door, then holds something out to me. "Here, you'll need this."

My cloak. I hadn't even noticed he carried it before. "Thank you," I say, throwing it around my shoulders.

"Come on, I'll get you out of here."

We tiptoe from the room. In the hall beyond, a guard slumps over a table. I give Ren a questioning look and he answers with a smirk. "A bottle of rum laced with a strong sleeping tonic. Works every time."

He leads me down several passages and eventually out into the welcoming darkness. It feels like I am coming home. Bryre was not familiar to me at all in the daylight.

"Go," he says, "run."

I can hold my peace no longer. "Ren, why are you doing this? Why don't you hate me like everyone else in Bryre?" My face is suddenly hot and my eyes sting. I don't breathe until he answers.

"Because I know you."

Pressure builds behind my eyes, making them burn. "Don't I frighten you?"

He laughs unsteadily. "Honestly? Yes. But I can't blame you for hiding it. I'd have done the same thing if I were you."

Confusion makes my head ache. "But what about—"

"Shh! Someone's coming!" he whispers. "Go! Now!" He shoves me into the alley and I run away fast and willingly. I'm followed only by my lingering questions.

DAY FIFTY-SIX

FATHER MUST BE WORRIED SICK. I FEEL TERRIBLE THAT I DOUBTED HIM, and have strayed so far from my path. But I cannot return home. Not yet. I cannot escape the uneasiness I feel at the thought of Father sending Ren away. Sometimes I wonder if Father is a little misguided. If he might be wrong.

Yet he was right about the people of Bryre—they do fear me, hate me.

I find my way to the river in the wee hours of the morning, and I kick my legs in the water, watching the early-morning sun glint off it, and hope that Batu appears. He is the only one who expects me to be . . . just me. In that, I will not disappoint. Not like I've disappointed Father and Ren. Their saddened faces haunt me despite the flowers and greenery on the riverbank.

My mind keeps wandering back to Ren and his inexplicable forgiveness. What could have happened? Does the wizard have him under a spell? But why would the wizard have him forget what I did? Unless that wasn't the only memory he lost . . .

A terrible thought blindsides me.

Ren didn't remember anything the first time I stung him either, and now, after I stung him a second time, his memory is clouded again. The girls never remember me or how they get to our cottage. The guards always seem shocked when they see my monstrous form, even if I've stung them several nights in a row.

It's me.

My sting is the only connection between all those things. The venom—it doesn't just put people to sleep—it must make them forget, too. I shiver. Why did Father never tell me this? Does he even know or is this an unforeseen side effect?

I dig my hands into the mossy bank in frustration. What can I do about it? Nothing. I can do nothing to change what I am, and it would seem that is a part of me, too.

I smell my dragon before I see him—the dank, metal-tinged scent is unmistakable. He is as glorious as ever as he materializes. Shimmering scales, refracting the sunlight like tiny prisms, and huge leathery wings flapping as he gets his bearings. Golden eyes above his regal snout gaze down at me with affection.

I don't understand how dragons travel, but I love to watch the effects. Surely, not all magic can be evil if dragons are made of it.

Sister. He puffs in my direction, lowering his snout to my level.

"I am glad you found me today," I whisper. "The people of Bryre hate me."

Ah, the humans do tend to fear that which they do not understand.

"That is what Father said," I say miserably. "But I thought he was wrong. We save the girls from the wizard, but the king's messenger, a friend, caught me in the city. Father told me to bring him home so we could find out what the king knows about the wizard's movements, but then he would send him far away from Bryre. I couldn't bear that, so I went into Bryre during the day to find my friend, and . . ." The tears spring forth and my voice is lost.

And you were caught by the humans.

I can only nod. Batu nuzzles me with his snout in reassurance.

You escaped?

"Yes, my friend helped me. He doesn't remember the night before."

Batu snorts, seeming to consider my words. *That is very strange.* If I didn't know any better, I might think Batu frowns, but he says nothing more. The revelation about my venom is still so fresh I can hardly believe it, so I keep it to myself. For now.

I settle back on the riverbank, watching the patterns of

236

the swirling water. "I must return home, but I can't shake the feeling that . . . well, I don't know what it is. This bad feeling every time I think of home."

Perhaps you should heed it. Your unconscious mind may know more than you realize.

Something hides between the spaces of the dragon's words. A brief flush of fear and anxiety that is not my own washes over me. It lingers longer than I'd like.

"I cannot abandon Father. I am all he has left, and he sacrificed so much for me. I will have to face him again. I miss him."

Batu huffs an earthy breath in understanding. *That is not your only home. I would open my nest to you, if you need it, sister.*

"Thank you."

Have you considered that this sense of foreboding may have to do with your father? You would be returning to him, after all.

"My father?" I say, swallowing down the unexpected burst of discomfort that accompanies that suggestion.

Has he been acting strangely lately? Could he be in the wizard's thrall? Your animal senses might pick up on that in a way your human eyes cannot.

"There is no one less likely to be under the wizard's thrall than my father. He never ventures near Bryre, and only leaves occasionally for the traveling markets." While I say this with all the certainty I can muster, I can't help thinking that Father has been more short-tempered with me lately than usual. And more secretive than ever. I can't deny that the unpleasant sense of something wrong has been nipping at my heels. The discovery that my venom steals

237

memories is only making it worse. Father is so careful and smart that he must have known. The fact that he kept it from me troubles me deeply.

Before Batu can respond, an awful wail pierces the forest. I am on my feet in seconds.

I must leave. The dragon begins to shimmer and fade. *Good-bye, sister.*

I fly through the forest in the direction of the sound. It continues, a terrible keening. When I hear shouts from the road join it, I freeze between the trees, terrified I've been spotted. But it is not the sight of me that makes them yell. Something's being carried to the city gates in a simple wooden cart. A small, limp foot hangs off the back. My heart ricochets in my chest.

Someone died.

But who could it be? Has the wizard, thwarted by our efforts, exacted a new and terrible form of revenge?

I *must* know.

This could directly affect our mission; nothing less could possibly inspire me to return to Bryre in daylight.

Instead of using the road as I did the day before, I hide in the trees and keep close to the shadows. It's the long way but I don't want anyone to recognize me. I'll have to find places to hide in the city. Luckily, I've seen many on my nightly excursions.

An invisible vise around my ribs hitches tighter with every step I take. Returning to Bryre is not something I relish. All those hands grabbing and mouths screaming—so much noise! But something is wrong, and nightfall is much too far away.

When I reach the city walls, I remain in the trees until the guards pass. I scale the walls and drop silently into the bushes below. A crowd of people meet the cart at the gate, and I follow their wailing until they stop in a large square before the palace gates. The wrought iron curls against the blue sky. The tops of the hedges peek over the walls, and the scent of roses wafts over my hiding spot in a shadowed alley. I sneak a look around the corner, and the crowd's words begin to make sense.

"Murderer!"

The crowd chants as a tradesman carries the limp body up to a platform in the middle of the square and a woman throws herself on the girl, keening and pounding the planks.

Mother. That's her mother.

Did my mother love me like that?

Shock jolts through me as I catch sight of the dead girl's face. It's the girl I killed with my venom.

Her poor mother. How did the girl get here? I—

Something slams at the edges of my vision, forcing me to my knees. It is out of reach, but it fills me with the same uneasiness that has trailed me for the last few days. A buzzing rings in my ears as I struggle to push past it to the memory that wants to return. Some other part of me, locked away, is filled with a desperate need to break through—and seeing that girl's face triggered it.

Did I know her? Have I seen her somewhere else?

239

A small hand, reaching over the edge of a box . . .

I grasp for more, but the image flits away, frightened by the truth that still can't get through. Where was that? From my past or more recently? And if it is recent, why can't I remember it? It almost looks like . . .

One of Father's cold boxes.

The block in my mind shatters, searing my skull with ice and chilling me down to my very marrow.

The girl lies in the cold box, still as death, arms folded across her chest. Frost coats her skin in a thin, glittering sheen. The fear I felt when I saw her skitters over my arms and legs and digs its roots into my heart.

Why did Father keep her?

Why did I forget?

And how could the city folk have found her when she was in Father's tower?

Has the wizard found us or is Father hiding many more things from me than just this girl? The fear in my heart twists at this thought and I shove it down. Father loves me. And he loves this city. He has nothing to gain by enraging the city folk and blaming me.

But the wizard would. First the questionable effects of my sting on memories, and now this girl . . . I cannot decide what to think. If the wizard has enchanted Father, we are lost.

My eyes burn, but I can't look away as the father pulls the mother off their dead child. Father lost my mother, too. He would never do anything to make another parent feel that way, would he? Their twisting expressions stab my heart. The man clutches her to his chest like he is afraid of losing her, too. The mob swells in noise.

"The beast is in league with the wizard!"

"The beast is a murderer!"

The beast. That's what they think I am. They believe I work for the wizard. Me! Who was murdered by the wizard before Father brought me back to life. The chanting of "murderer" grows louder with each passing second. I clamp my hands over my ears and fold over in the alley's corner. I am responsible for that girl's death, but it was an accident. I can't fathom why Father kept her. If I'd known she was too weak, I never would've stung her. I only want to help these people, and now they hate me.

Father's right; humans are strange, fickle creatures. I'm glad I'm no longer one of them.

When the noise in the square dies down to a dull roar, I relax the death grip on my head. A man speaks over the crowd. I poke my head around the corner—who managed to quiet the angry mob?

A familiar gray-haired man stands on the platform, framed by the palace in the background.

Oliver. He wears a crown. He really is the king.

My heart aches even more for Bryre's plight. The story he told—that was his daughter, his wife, who died by the wizard's hand. I nearly forgot about that after I told Father I overheard things. I wish I'd been here to help them both.

"Please," Oliver says, raising a hand in the air. "Please, calm down. This is a horrible and unfortunate event. I know exactly what you're feeling right now."

"Murderer! Kill the murderer! Kill her accomplice!"

"Stop!" Oliver shouts, but it has little effect. "More blood will not solve this. Let's break this vicious cycle of death and retribution. Bury our dead and stay the higher ground."

"Find the creature and kill her!" yell several voices in the crowd. "Kill the murderer! Kill her accomplice!" I clap my hands over my ears again to block out the awful refrain as it echoes through the city. I tremble. Accomplice? Have they figured out I belong to Father? I may have powers they don't, but I'm afraid. They want my head. They'll kill me if they find me.

They'll kill Father if they discover he made me.

Whatever he may have hidden from me, whatever he may have done unwittingly or otherwise, he is still my father.

"We've found the beast's accomplice!" a voice shouts from the crowd. The crowd parts as two men drag a wriggling person between them.

When they shove Ren to the ground, my heart nearly stops.

"What?" Oliver says, his face going white.

One man—who I recognize as the guard Ren put to sleep—steps forward, pointing his finger and sneering. "That boy gave me a sleeping draught in a bottle of rum. Said it was a gift from the king and his council for watching over the monster. When I finally woke, the beast had escaped and my keys were in the wrong pocket."

My breakfast threatens to come up. Stupid, stupid Ren.

Why did he do that? He took such a foolish risk to help me. He must think he'll get leniency because Oliver is fond of him. I doubt the grumbling crowd will allow any fondness the king has to dull their bloodlust.

"Ren, please tell me you didn't." A warning tone slips into Oliver's voice.

Ren rises to his feet and sticks his chin out. "I did. She isn't responsible for the girls who've gone missing. And she didn't kill this girl, either."

"Oh, Ren, how could you?" Oliver whispers, barely audible over the thrum of the crowd.

"I know her. She may not be like us, but that doesn't mean she's a monster."

The mob pays Ren no heed. "You helped the murderer!"

"You let the beast escape!"

He struggles with the guard holding his arms behind his back. "She is not the murderer—it's the wizard! Can't you see that?"

"Ren," Oliver says, "you are only making things worse."

"No! They're fools if they can't see what's right in front of them." He turns toward them again. "The wizard is back, we all know it! Killing her won't solve a thing."

My heart constricts as the mob descends. I thrill to know Ren believes in me, but I'm ashamed that he's only half right, and that it's only because he doesn't remember. I did kill that girl. Just not the rest. Ren disappears in the masses as they cart him off down the street. Where are they taking him?

Oliver sags on the edge of the platform as the crowd disperses, leaving him and a handful of guards behind.

I shudder. Something awful is about to happen to Ren. Something Oliver—even as king—is powerless to stop.

No. They will not harm my Ren. If Oliver can't save him, I will.

When the noise of the crowd begins to fade, I creep into the alleyways. I close my eyes as I run, orienting on the sound of the crowd. All those voices. So much anger, hate.

All the blame they want to place on me focused on Ren.

My blood roils at the thought, claws aching to rip apart the fools who don't understand that the problem is not us; it's that blasted wizard. Who else would go around killing girls?

Ren's right; they're afraid. Can I blame them for that? Perhaps not, but I will blame them if they harm a hair on Ren's head.

Determination spurs my feet to move faster and soon the crowd is close. Their steps make the ground quiver and my ears burn with noise.

"Hang the traitor!" cries a voice. Then another. Soon the whole crowd chants the refrain. "Hang him!"

If only I had many tails with barbs, I could sting them all and silence them long enough to get Ren away.

A low whine slips out between my teeth. Instinct rears its head and I have to squash it down. Fight and flight are not real options. Saving Ren is the only one.

I crouch down within the alley shadows, close to the wall. The crowd lies around the corner with Ren. I hear the creak of wood and the rustle of what I guess is rope. What on earth are they doing?

I close my eyes and take a deep breath. And another. The ache in my hands retreats. I open my eyes to peek around the corner. The crowd surrounds a wooden platform with a high crossbar. A rope with a loop at one end hangs from the bar.

I puzzle at the contraption, but I can make no sense of it. I only know it will not do anything good for Ren.

I loosen my cloak, stretching my wings and tail. They've already seen me as I am; I have no reason to hide it now. Besides, my wings need to be as free as possible.

A man drags Ren onto the platform while he struggles. His face is the color of the ash in his fireplace.

As the man places the rope around Ren's neck, I begin to understand what the contraption does. It will snap his neck in half. He will not survive it.

Panic sends me airborne. I ride the air current over the people, flapping my wings wide, and swoop down to the platform. Ren's startled face goes through several expressions, none of which I can make sense of now. My claws slice the rope from his neck—the crowd gasps—and I wrap my arms around his waist and take us both into the air.

Shouts follow, and the whistle of arrows. It is not easy flying with one so much taller and more unwieldy than the girls, but adrenaline fuels me to dodge and weave until we're clear.

Ren clings to me, eyes squeezed shut as we soar out of

the city. For the first time, his arms encircle me, but for all the wrong reasons. He is so close, and so warm, his fingers burning through the fabric of my dress. He is all I can smell, his quick shallow breaths all I can hear. Despite his height, I am keenly aware of how fragile he is. He hasn't said a word, but he shivers. Perhaps he is afraid of heights? Humans weren't meant to fly, not like me. We're over the deep forest, far enough from the angry mob to alight safely. If not for my aching limbs, I'd fly with Ren forever.

I land and set him on his feet, immediately regretting the loss of his warmth. He still shakes and I can't fathom what the expression on his face means. I've never seen this before. At least, not in this life. The once-me girl might have recognized it in an instant.

I simply stand before him, my insides quivering as much as he does on the outside. I don't know what to say, even though I'm filled with jumbled words. I have to look away. Staring only makes it harder to think.

I'm not what he thought I was. I pretended too long and now it's too late to fix it. After rescuing him, I can't help being painfully aware at how very human he is—and how very much I am not.

Yes, I love Ren. And it is quite possibly the most foolish thing I've ever done.

I betrayed him by stealing his memories. If I'd realized my sting could do that, I would never have stung anyone at all. Especially Ren.

I glance his way again—the strange expression remains.

He steps toward me and takes my hand. Sparks flitter up my arms.

Another step. My stomach seems to want to fly away of its own accord.

He grins. I adore that grin more than anything else on this earth.

Regret pinches me as I think of Father. He'll never approve of this.

"Thank you," he says, squeezing my fingers. "I knew you were good. No matter what the city folk say. I knew it. I knew you."

I want to bask in his smile, but I'm still troubled. "You're not bothered by what I am?"

"It will take some getting used to." He runs a finger over the edge of my left wing. "But who you are is all that really matters. You're not the sort of person who'd steal girls from the sick house in the middle of the night like the wizard."

I stiffen. Ice creeps over my body, chilling me from the inside out. If I hadn't stolen his memory of that night, he wouldn't feel this way. He was devastated by his friend's disappearance.

I pull my hand away and he frowns. "What's wrong, Kym?"

Oh goodness, that look in his eyes. How can I tell him what I did when he's looking at me that way? In spite of everything I am?

"I must go. And you have to go, too, before they find

you." I push him back with one hand. "You must hide."

"Don't worry, I've got plenty of hiding places no one knows about. I'll be safe. No one will see me unless I want them to."

I've lost the ability to speak. I swallow in vain and run into the forest.

"Kym! Wait!" His footfalls patter after me for a few minutes, then cease. He knows he can't catch me if I don't want to be caught.

But I'm afraid. I fear that he is wrong.

He doesn't know me at all.

DAY FIFTY-SEVEN

BIRDS CHIRP ABOVE ME AS SUNBEAMS SLANT BETWEEN THE BRANCHES.
The trees and bushes are full of life, but I am dull and heavy.

I am not even hungry, despite my predator instincts.

I've wandered through the forest all night, not ready to return to Father's house, not even with the dawn of a new day. My thoughts are too conflicted. Father is always good to me. He sacrificed so much for me in life and now even in death and second life.

Yet so many things don't make sense. Things that don't cast Father in the same light in which I've always viewed him. Things that I would've thought he'd find abhorrent. Stealing memories when his daughter is deprived of hers? Leaving that girl on the road for an already grief-stricken city to find?

I fear the wizard is closer than we thought.

To make matters worse, now the city folk know what I am. They've seen me in my full form. Soon they'll figure out I belong to Father and they'll come for him. Despite the cover story I told Ren, I imagine he has already guessed at the truth.

Ren. Who doesn't recall he caught me taking that other girl from the city, nor that I stung him. Can I hope he'll forgive me for taking his memory? If he can see past the strangeness of my body, perhaps he can see past that, too?

If I ever see Ren again, I will tell him the truth about Delia. Father might not allow me near the city anymore after my antics the last couple of days. But I already miss Ren.

When I tire of wandering in circles, I leap onto the lowest branch of a large fir tree. I burrow into the nook between tree and branch and let tears roll down my face uninhibited.

The truth is, I have no idea what I should do. I thought I knew right from wrong, but everything has turned on its head.

I need Father. I need Ren. And I can't have both.

I'll do everything in my power to protect each of them in whatever way I can. Which means I must return to Father and confess what happened yesterday, why I didn't return. He must be mad with worry, but I regret none of it. I'd do it again in a heartbeat.

And I need answers from Father—about that girl, and about exactly what my venom does to those I sting. There can be no more secrets between us.

If he cannot give me answers, I'll know the wizard has him in his thrall. I'll have to beg Batu to help me find a way to release him from it.

And I'll destroy that wizard, once and for all.

I wipe my face with my sleeve, then lean my head back against the rough bark of the tree. I love the smell of fir trees, spicy and sharp.

Something crashes through the brush.

"Kym! Kymera!"

I flutter down from my perch. "Ren, what are you doing here?"

He bends over, hands on his knees, gasping. Fear fills his eyes and I recoil. Is he afraid of me now?

"Run. Hide. They're coming." He heaves another breath. I rest my hand on his shoulder.

"Who is coming?"

"Everyone. The entire city. Pitchforks, torches. They're hunting you. If they can't find you, they'll burn you out of the forest."

Father.

My claws snap into place and my eyes change to cat's irises.

"Thank you for warning me," I say. "I will go."

Ren latches onto my hand like a vise. "I'm coming with you."

My resolve to go to Father falters. I could run away with Ren right now. Far away where no one, wizard or angry citizen, could find us.

But I can't leave Father. No matter what he may have done since, he didn't leave me behind, not even when I died.

And Ren doesn't remember what I did. I can't just pretend it never happened, however much I want to.

"No, go in the opposite direction. Flee the forest, hide."

"I'm not leaving you."

Tears burn in my eyes. Cats must not be accustomed to crying. "You don't understand. I did something bad. It will make you unhappy."

Ren drops my hand like I stung him. "What are you talking about?"

"What I told you before, about my parents? It wasn't true. I'm not a real hybrid."

A puzzled look fills his eyes.

"My father made me like this. He and I have been working against the wizard." I flap my wings for effect. "He discovered where the wizard hides the girls in Bryre, and I rescue one every night. You found me taking a girl once. Do you remember at all?"

Ren stumbles backward.

"I don't remember. I don't understand. If you're saving the girls, why have none of them come home?"

"We send them to a safe place, but that's not important. This is: I found Delia and saved her. She's safe, but I sent her away from you because I thought"—my face reddens—"I thought you were sweet on her. I was jealous. I'm sorry. I never meant to hurt you."

I'm out of breath from speaking so fast. Every muscle tenses as I wait for Ren to respond. His face goes through several changes as he digests the information.

"You took Delia?" His hands ball into fists.

I nod. "From the wizard. I saved her, but to do that we had to send her away."

"Do you have any idea what you've done?"

"I am sorry, I—"

"Delia is Oliver's daughter," he says through clenched teeth. "She's the sole heir to Bryre's throne since her older sister was murdered by the wizard."

Horror curls around me like a cloak of ice. "She's a princess?" Everything makes sense. Ren is the king's page boy. He delivers messages for him. Of course, he would be charged with delivering his daughter, too. That explains why the D for Delia was so prominently featured in those messages—they were concealing her from the wizard.

Jealousy is a very stupid thing. It only leaves the bitterest taste behind—regret. One foolish choice and I've hurt far more people than I imagined.

"Where did you take her?" His voice cracks.

I've told him this much, I may as well tell him everything. "Belladoma. Father says it's wonderful there. I know she is—"

"Belladoma?" he whispers as he sinks to the dirt path, wrapping his arms around his head. "Belladoma?"

The ground is tugged out from under me and I hover weightless and wingless over an abyss. Something is terribly wrong. Belladoma should have comforted Ren. Instead, it crushed him.

"What's wrong with Belladoma?" I ask, struggling to

keep the panic out of my voice.

His eyes fill with shock and anger. "Belladoma is the rival city that attacked Bryre. That the wizard protected us from. Are you really that stupid, Kym?" He spits as though saying my name leaves a bad taste in his mouth.

I can't breathe. "That cannot be," I whisper.

Ren stands, shaking as though he's about to explode. He gazes at me as though seeing me for the first time. Shock. Amazement. Revulsion.

"You're a monster," he growls. "And only a wizard can create a monster."

It takes everything I have not to sting Ren to shut him up. So he can't say those awful words. So I can't hear them. Instead I run blindly through the forest.

It is not true. It can't be true. Father is a victim of the wizard, and if he's enchanted, more so now than ever. How could Ren even suggest he's the wizard himself?

Tears pour over my cheeks. Nothing can hold them back. Ren hates me. Father will hate me for telling him.

Ren's words repeat in my head. I can't make them stop. *You're a monster, and only a wizard can create a monster.*

I shove another branch out of my way; it snaps off the tree, raining leaves onto the path.

How can Ren's words be true? Yes, Father made me, but that doesn't make him a wizard. Father is a scientist.

I pause in my flight to catch my breath next to a birch tree. I lean my back against it. The trouble is, Ren's words have put a name to the gnawing uneasiness that's been slowly growing for some time. The fear whispering in the back of my head that something is wrong with Father and his behavior.

But if Father is the wizard and not just enchanted, why would he bring back his own daughter while killing the others? What really happens to the girls after Darrell carts them off?

No, Father is not like that. He can't be the wizard. Ren is wrong.

I double over as though I've been punched in the stomach, clutching my aching head.

Flashing images burn in front of my eyes. Roses. Sculptured hedges. The parquet dance floor of the castle. Sun sparkling on all of them.

Laughter fills my ears and the smell of roses fills my nose.

I stumble forward and hit the ground, trembling.

Why do these images in my head plague me? I've only seen these things by moonbeam and shadow. They don't belong to me.

But they might belong to *her*. Who was I really? And why won't Father tell me more about my past?

I must find Father. Warn him of the people coming to find us. He must answer all these troubling questions and put the poisonous doubts to rest.

I manage to regain my shaky footing. The scent of roses lingers in my senses, though there are none here. I shiver.

Home.

I fly as fast as I can.

I alight in the yard—startling the goat-chickens—and run for the front door.

"Father!"

My hands shake as I tear through the cottage.

"Father!"

Noise comes from his room. He bursts around the corner. "Kymera! Where have you been?"

I throw myself into his arms. Stunned, he hugs me and pats my back.

"What is wrong? What happened? I've been looking for you ever since you ran out on me the other day!"

I clutch his shirt and bury my face into it. I wish I'd listened to Father. I never should have spoken to Ren in the first place. Then none of these fears would plague me.

But the doubt Ren planted in my mind continues to thrust its way forward. There's no way to unhear what he said. No way to unknow what I've discovered. But first we must get to safety.

"They're coming for us, Father. We must flee!"

He looks at me askance. "What on earth are you on about, child? We are well hidden in the forest behind our hedges. No one can find us."

"People from Bryre. They have torches and they want to burn us out!"

He grows still. "Why would they want to do that?"

"Because I disobeyed you." My voices wobbles. I need answers, but I must be careful. Telling him everything is more likely to inspire discussion than accusing him.

"Kymera, sometimes you are such a fool. We are

protected here. They cannot burn us unless they get inside the grounds, and unless you led them here yourself, they will not find us." Father sits me down in my favorite chair by the fire. Pippa skitters away from Father's stomping feet. "Now, tell me everything." His gaze burns into me as though he examines the contents of my thoughts. The idea is more than unsettling.

Father seems certain we're safe, but worry gnaws at me. I have seen for myself how determined the city folk are. "I went into the city. I got caught in the crowd and my cloak came off. I tried to get away, but they captured me. Ren helped me out of the prison. He's close to the king so he must have assumed he'd get away with it." As I wipe my eyes with my sleeve, I can't help noticing how hard Father clasps the arms of his chair. His knuckles are white.

"What did you do, Kym?" he says in soft voice.

"At first I just fled. But then I heard a horrible noise, wailing and crying. They'd found that girl who died from my sting. They blamed me. The crowd had already taken Ren. They were going to kill him for helping me. But I . . . I saved him. I flew down and grabbed him and left him in the forest." My face reddens as memories of flying with Ren rush to the front of my mind. That will never happen again, but it's one of the best memories of my short life.

"You are an idiot, girl! You revealed yourself to the entire city? And took one of their own right out from under their noses? Do you want us to fail?"

Father scowls as though he wishes to break me in half. I sink lower into my chair.

"Of course not, Father. But I couldn't let Ren die." I twist my hands in my skirts. "I think I love him."

This earns a derisive snort. "Love him? You know nothing of love. Do not be ridiculous." He shakes his head and his silver hair flies back and forth. "This is why I told you to stay away from the humans. They are too fragile and silly. That boy has confused you."

I bristle. "It's not ridiculous. It's true. I do. I think he did, too. At least as much as he could love a creature like me. I don't know why he helped me, but it was the bravest thing I've ever seen."

I try to swallow, but find my throat has gone numb. My next question sinks into the tip of my tongue, terrified to be out in the world.

But ask it I must.

"Father, the venom in my sting, does it do more than put people to sleep? Ren caught me with a girl, yet when I saw him next, he had no recollection of it at all. And the girls, they never remember me the next day. The guards are always so shocked by my entrance."

Father's eyes shine with a cold, hard light. "Yes, Kymera, that is the only reason why he helped you escape. He truly remembers nothing of seeing you with the girl. Your venom takes away their memories temporarily, up to about an hour before you sting them. That powder I gave you does the very same. You should be grateful for it. Why else do you think you've had such success sneaking in and out of the city?"

I grow cold. "Why have you never told me this?"

"Because I was afraid you would take it personally and

258

refuse to use the barb since most of your own memories are missing."

He is right. I'm not happy about that. But is that the only reason he concealed it? "But how did you make the venom do that?" I've never heard nor read anything about venom that could do such a thing.

Father smiles tightly. "You do not need to worry about that."

"But I *am* worried. The things people say worry me, too." I toy with the end of my tail, studying the barb for the millionth time. "And that isn't the worst of it. That girl's body, the one my sting killed, I found her in one of your cold boxes. Why was she still here? Why did you keep her? And how did she get on the road?" I twist my hands together, mirroring the knots in my stomach. "Father, I am afraid the wizard got hold of her body. How else could they have found her on the road? We must strengthen our defenses around the cottage or he might come after us next!" Tendrils of fear wrap around me.

Father frowns. "The girl was potentially contagious. Belladoma wouldn't take her corpse, so I put her in my cold box until I had time to bury her." He leans forward. "I didn't tell you, because I saw no need to upset you. The wizard must have discovered where I buried her and left her in the road for the city dwellers to find."

Relief trickles in and releases some of the tightness in my chest. Father has answers for all my fears. Perhaps he is not enchanted after all. "The wizard must be close, and watching us to have found her so quickly."

"That is a grave concern indeed. But do not worry, I will take care of it. We are safe here."

"What will you do?"

Father scowls. "I said do not worry about it."

I recoil at the harshness in his words, but I press on. "There is more."

"Kymera . . ."

The scales on my tail are duller than usual, reflecting my mood. "I told Ren everything. One of those girls was his charge, the youngest princess. Did you know there was a younger one the wizard didn't get? I had no idea who she was when I took her, but I've felt guilty ever since." My eyes are glued to the wooden slats in the floor. "I told him our plans. That we rescue the girls and send them to a better place. He didn't believe me." My voice cracks.

The fire flares in the hearth, flames leaping up and licking the iron kettle. "You told him." It is not a question and doesn't require an answer, but the intensity in Father's voice frightens me. The wooden arm of his chair cracks under his tightly squeezing fingers.

"What did he say?"

I swallow, desperate to clear the sand filling my throat. "He said Belladoma tried to attack Bryre years ago. He said I'm a monster. And only a wizard can make a monster." Tears threaten again, but I hold them in.

"So this boy knows everything, does he? In that case, you have sealed his fate. I shall have to take care of him."

Tingling flashes of ice prick every inch of my skin. "What do you mean?" I whisper.

"He cannot be allowed to tell anyone what he knows." Father stands and places a hand on my shoulder. A brush of cool seeps into my arm before I shove his hand away. Right now I need answers, not comfort.

"Why? If he's wrong, it should be easy to prove." A horrible sick feeling wells up in my gut, buoyed by the weight of too many easily answered questions. "Father, tell me he's wrong."

A pleading edge creeps into my voice. Ren must be mistaken. We have been saving the girls. But every nerve in my body screams that something is terribly wrong with Father's behavior.

He considers me for a long moment, then paces the area before the hearth. The fire jumps each time he passes.

I can't move. I can't even breathe. The fire in Ren's hearth did not behave like that.

And despite Father's easy answers, no animal I've read about can erase memories with a single sting.

Memories flood over me. Father pressing his hand to Darrell's arm, the angry man calming. He did the same to the girls on occasion. The flames of our cooking fire burning without wood. The always full sack of feed. The chickens with goat legs.

Me.

Why me?

Why do I have visions of the palace in my head and none of Father?

Why Belladoma?

The awful truth threatens to crush me into the ground.

Why else would Father want to silence Ren so thoroughly?

"It's true." The words choke from my mouth before I can bite them back. "You are the wizard." Terror marches over every inch of my body like an army of tiny ants.

Father stops in front of the hearth wearing the strangest look on his face. The flames are so high now, they leap into the chimney. A slow chuckle rumbles in his chest. The rumble grows into an outright guffaw, manic in its intensity.

This terrifies me far more than his angry outbursts.

He stops laughing long enough to speak. "Yes, I am the wizard they all whisper about in Bryre. Why do you think I never go into the city?" He taps his head. "Because I cannot. I set up the warding charms to prevent anyone who would do the city harm from entering. That is where you came in. You were perfect."

Horror rolls over me in hot and cold waves. I wobble to my feet, claws and tail taut with tension. "What do you mean?"

"You were naive and innocent. Not to mention absolutely certain you were aiding the city and its people."

Dizziness threatens to overwhelm me. "Belladoma really is the city that attacked Bryre?"

He nods. "Fitting, is it not? Sending Bryre's girls off to its enemy." He chortles again and I shudder. Even now, I cannot quite grasp that the Father I loved is nothing like I thought.

"Who am I? Who was I really? Before." I sputter. Am I really his daughter or is everything he's ever told me a lie? I wait while he considers his answer, praying he says anything but what I fear most.

"Your name was Rosabel." He draws near, but I match him in my retreat, step for step. "You were a princess. My princess."

A leaden weight presses on my chest. It's an ache I fear will never subside. My worst fear realized. I'm the king's daughter. Oliver's daughter, returned in a different, monstrous body. My true father would despise me as I am now.

Delia. I gave my own sister over to Bryre's enemies. My legs wobble and I reach out to the wall for support. I am as horrible as Ren believes.

"Why did you lie to me?" Fury cracks my voice.

Father looks affronted. "I did not lie. They promised you to me. But they lied." His face softens. "I only claimed what I rightfully earned. They made a binding deal. You were supposed to be mine."

He sneers. "They said they would give anything for help defending Bryre, but when I came to claim Princess Rosabel, they balked." He folds his arms across his chest as his eyes narrow. "They offered me money, jewels, a title—everything but the one thing I wanted. They threw me out of the palace like I was garbage they could just dispose of. Well, they were quite mistaken." He throws his hands in the air dismissively. "Besides, Queen Aria should have known better. I was her suitor once when she was just a princess. I wooed her, offered her everything—even tried to give her that choker you wear. But she refused me and chose Oliver. You should have been *my* daughter. It would have been so much simpler if she had chosen me instead."

Rage twists my heart at these revelations and makes my head throb, but something more troubles me. "If the king and queen refused you, then how did I die? What happened?"

"Years later, I returned in a final attempt to reason with the king and queen. The wards did not affect me then because of the bargain. My intention was not to hurt, but to collect what was owed me. The guards tried to throw me out again, but this time I had had ten years to prepare. I incinerated them. Aria tried to block my path to the princess. I killed her, but Rosabel got in the way. Offering to go with me willingly, of all things, if I would leave her family alone. I killed her, too. I took her body and disappeared."

My back is flat against the wall of the cottage. I stare at Father, unable to comprehend what he's done. What I've done.

"But if you got the princess, why did you take all those other girls? What did they do to you?"

Father smiles horribly. "Why, Kymera, where do you think I got the parts to bring you back?"

My heart stutters in my chest. "What?" I whisper.

"Each time I tried to bring you back and failed, the magic burned off another piece of you. There is always a price for magic. I tried so many times that I had to replace everything but your head. It was simple work to pick them off the road on the way to the markets in the east and north, at least until the fool king instituted a curfew and quarantined the girls. After you were reborn, charging you with taking more girls from Bryre made my revenge even sweeter."

Nausea creeps up from my toes, weakening my knees. All this time I was certain I'd find the wizard and punish him for what he did to my family, and I've been living with him all along.

I'm the truly monstrous one. I did his dirty work without question. I'm a living quilt of every girl he killed.

Bile tickles my throat, but I shove it down. I can't stay in this house another instant. I can't stand to be near Father. I should want to kill him. But I can't yet reconcile the man I loved with the monster inside him. It doesn't make sense. I press my palms to my eyes to hold in the tears.

I've done so many awful things. But there's one place where I draw the line.

I will not shed another tear for Father.

Barnabas, rather. I must stop thinking of him as my father. He's an impostor.

So am I. Playing around in someone else's body. The girl the king recognized in my eyes is long dead. Irretrievable.

Or is she? Is there a spell that can undo what was done? Return my memories to me in full instead of shattered pieces? Barnabas said he could do nothing, but he had every reason to lie.

I pull my hands away from my eyes and as I do, Barnabas reaches for me. He holds out his hand for me to take and smiles as he used to do. Something inside me tears in two.

His hand doesn't slow its pace. I recoil. He takes a step toward me.

"Now, Kymera. Do not be afraid. Father will make everything all right." He reaches for my cheek. I cringe, and slap his hand away.

"You lied. You never even sent that girl off with Darrell, did you? You kept her here. Then you put her on the road for them to find. Why?"

"My dear, it was only to teach you a lesson. You can never trust humans. You weren't taking my word for it; you needed proof. I provided it."

He reaches for me again and a memory thrusts itself forward. Father holding Darrell's arm firmly. Darrell growing calm. And having no recollection of meeting me the next time we met when I was safely ensconced in my cloak.

I stumble backward.

Barnabas didn't just calm Darrell. He erased his memory.

Something unpleasant glints in his eyes. He's going to do the same to me.

My throat closes with panic. Has he done this before? How many times have I discovered his treachery only to have my memories wiped away? Is that why he put his hand on my shoulder after I told him about Ren? Is this why I had such trouble remembering the girl in the cold box? Why I have so few memories of my former life?

"Don't touch me," I squeak as I slink back along the walls.

He hesitates. "My daughter, I only wish to comfort you."

I inch closer to the fire. Pippa skitters off to a far corner. "No, you want to take away my memories." He'd take everything. My time in the city, the things Ren told me.

Even with the pain they've brought, I cherish these memories. They're the only real things I have.

Batu. My rock dragon. Thank heavens I could never tell Father about him!

He matches me step for step as though we're dancing in a slow, strange pattern. "But wouldn't that make you feel better? I can take away your pain."

I shudder. "I'll keep my pain and my thoughts to myself," I growl. My animal instinct rears its head. I'm cornered. I need to get out of this house.

Without warning, Barnabas lunges. Instinct takes over. I wrench away, whirling around to strike him in the chest with my tail.

He staggers from the blow, but doesn't fall asleep as the others always do. He sways and reaches for me again, tearing off my cloak in the process.

I run.

DAY FIFTY-EIGHT

LAST NIGHT, I STAYED IN THE WOODS. THE CITY FOLK CREPT THROUGH the forest with burning torches, hunting for me, just as Ren said they would. I hid in the trees, flattened against the trunks with branches wrapped around me. Most of the men retreated once darkness fell, but a few determined hunters never rested. And so neither did I.

Despite how much I would've welcomed Batu's comforting presence, I stayed away from the river. Summoning my dragon into the open when the woods were crawling with people ready for an excuse to kill and burn seemed a very bad idea indeed.

Now in the morning light, as the city folk return full force, buzzing with hatred, I know I have to go back to the cottage I shared with my false father. I need my cloak and a change of clothes. Then I'll run far away and never return.

I barely touch my feet to the forest path, when brush breaks behind me. I fly behind the nearest tree, holding my breath and making my body as compact as possible. The whole forest reeks of humans. That and the lack of sleep are making it difficult for me to distinguish where they are.

The heat of their torches reaches into the trees as the men tromp by my hiding spot.

"Hold on!" one man shouts. I suck in the breath I was letting out, heart throbbing.

"What is it, John?" another voice says.

"Look here, the branches are all broken in this direction—the monster may have gone this way. Deeper forest lies in that direction."

The footsteps resume, but to my relief they move away from the tree I hide behind.

I must get out of Bryre. I rest my head in my hands and tears slip through my fingers.

The only real chance I have at life is away from everything and everyone I know. I wipe my eyes and listen for people. The cottage I shared with Barnabas is not far, but I'll need to hurry. And hope Barnabas is not at home.

A few minutes later, I reach the hedge and slip through, coming out near my rose garden.

I stumble with shock. My rose bushes are torn up. Destroyed. Petals and thorns and leaves litter the yard as though some wild force shredded them to pieces. Goat-chickens peck and paw through the wreckage.

I drift closer. It's not just thorns and leaves—there are

bones. Huge wings, claws of all sizes, and hooves poke out of the soil amid other limbs and bones and parts for which I have no name. They take shapes before my eyes. Something like the hybrids in the castle topiary, or in the laboratory under the tower. These are plied together, but not quite as sturdily. Not quite as naturally.

Magic. Barnabas's magic.

And then one important, gruesome fact lurches to the forefront of my brain: not one of the skeletons has a head.

Horror drops me to my knees. I hardly gave that skeleton Pippa dug up weeks ago a second thought. Barnabas explained it away so thoroughly.

But now I understand. It was just another lie.

These are my old bodies. His first attempts at making me into a monster. These are pieces of me that Barnabas couldn't quite get to fit. But he always kept my head, moving it from one discarded body to another, and replacing the parts of it that the magic burned off. But by the time he succeeded all that was left were my brain and eyes.

I loved this garden and now it is gone. The rest of the yard and house remain untouched; Barnabas must have destroyed it to get to me. To show me just how little human remains of me.

A larger flash of red catches my eye in the far corner, hidden behind another shrub. One last rose. I snatch it greedily, then sneak into my room through the window. I can't smell Barnabas anywhere. I wonder if he took my warning about the city dwellers to heart and ran away after he ruined my roses.

It takes me no time at all to pack a few things. Pippa whines and sticks her nose into my room. She allows me to scratch her ears. I might actually miss her.

A door slams at the front of the house.

I stiffen and secure my satchel around my body, then fly out the window. I have a few things I must do before I leave forever.

I sneak out of the hedge and wind my way through the thick woods, desperate to reach Ren. I don't believe he'll ever forgive me, but I can't leave without saying good-bye. My last red rose is tucked into the belt around my waist. Barnabas may have destroyed everything I loved—even if I can't remember most of it—but I destroyed the friendship Ren and I might have had. I went so far as to steal my own sister in a fit of senseless jealousy. Thanks to Batu, I'm beginning to understand what the word *sister* means, but I fear I have a way to go. A strange sensation wells up inside me each time I think it. But even now that monstrous jealous feeling grumbles in my chest. Yes, I'm still jealous of her. I envy her ability to love and be loved freely, even though she's no longer free. And I envy Ren's devotion to her. No one will ever be that devoted to me.

Except Delia is probably dead now. They're all probably dead. That's what happened to those who were taken before Barnabas brought me back to life. What use could they possibly be alive?

The conversation I overheard at the inn many nights ago springs to mind. Something about rumors of trading live goods. Surely, the man was talking about Darrell.

Slaves. I can't decide which is worse.

Either way, it is entirely my fault.

Only a few yards from the hedge, I round a tree and come face-to-face with a handful of men. All hold torches and knives and spears. Time slows for a brief moment as our eyes meet and tighten. I leap into the air and fly up, up, up. They can't touch me if I'm high enough.

Below me, shouts ring out as they try to follow my path.

Then they stop. My keen ears can still hear the voices when they pick back up again. "It's a hedge in the woods!" More voices join the fray. "And a house! Little monsters in the yard! It's the beast's! Burn it! Burn it!"

A chill slithers over my body, scales to feathers.

When I left a few minutes ago, Barnabas had just returned to the cottage. He must be inside it still. If they burn it, he'll die, and if the whole mob is involved in burning down his cottage, the backlash of magic might just kill them all. They're so crazed in their chase, they haven't stopped to consider the danger they're walking into.

I've wronged Bryre enough. Letting their citizens die is unthinkable, no matter the repercussions for me.

But it kills me that helping them means helping Barnabas.

Fire already eats away at the hedge when I reach our yard and cottage. Men run amok, setting ablaze everything in sight, chasing and being chased by the goat-footed chickens. Smoke taints the air and clings to my nose and skin.

Orange flames lick the sides of the cottage and roof. The heat is searing even from yards away. A downed tree trunk has been placed before the tower door. Screams and hisses and bangs ring inside it. Barnabas must've been in his laboratory when they found the hedge.

With all the confusion, no one notices me yet. I circle the tower, frantically grasping for a plan. Barnabas will decimate the city folk when he gets out. I must reach him first.

The roof creaks and moans. Sparks pop. Instinct warns me to flee, to get as far from the fire as I can.

I swallow it down and head for the front of the tower.

Crack.

The roof collapses and a yelp leaps from my mouth. Stone and wood fly every which way and I dodge them in the air.

Barnabas can't die at their hands. I must prevent it.

I fly up and over the broken tower for a better look. A leg juts out beneath a wooden crossbeam. And I see a slant of bloody forehead.

I use my wings to keep the smoke and flames at bay as I pull the beam off Barnabas's body and drag him out.

"The monster!" The shout echoes across the yard, shattering all hope of a stealthy escape.

Every man runs toward me, knives, swords, and torches high.

I heave Barnabas up, winding my tail around his neck just in case he wakes, then rise into the air. He is much heavier than the girls were, making flying difficult. I struggle to stay airborne as the men swing their weapons and fire at my feet. The bottom of my right foot is burned, but I continue on despite the pain. Finally, I catch a blessed gust of wind and it lifts me up and over the hedge. I wing my way over the forest—much of it burning now—toward a ravine that cuts an unexpected swath in the ground. I've skirted it often on my trips to the river. I set him down at the very bottom. I'll leave Barnabas there. The walls of the ravine are steep, impossible to scale without a rope. He won't have an easy time getting out. The city folk will be safe from him, at least for a little while.

I can't help studying him for a moment. He looks peaceful asleep like this, even with the burns and ash marring his skin. Inside, he's nothing but evil.

I was such a fool to believe Barnabas was my devoted father. No shred of goodness lives in that cold heart.

Everything I know is based on what I learned from him. How to speak, think, act. No wonder the city folk will never accept me. I'm still discovering the depths of his lies.

I finally understand. The monster in this story is me.

I am the abomination.

I am monstrous.

And the man who made me is even worse.

It would be so easy to kill him now and be done with it. My claws snap out, and my tail coils around his neck. He may be a wizard, but he is still made of flesh and bone. His black heart is still human.

One squeeze of my tail and I could crush his windpipe. Snap his neck. Remove any chance he might ever terrorize another city.

He did more than just deceive me. He tore me from my

true family—from Oliver, and Ren, and the mother whose face I still cannot glimpse in my memories.

He killed my mother. He killed *me*.

He murdered who knows how many other girls and hybrids and animals in pursuit of crafting the creature I've become.

He took everything that made me human and transformed me into this mockery of my former self. A mishmash of parts, designed to do his bidding.

No one should hate him more than me. Surely killing him would be serving justice.

But there is a price.

I will not survive it. Killing Barnabas means killing myself. Being incinerated by magic.

I would never see Batu or Ren or Oliver again. No more sunrises or sunsets. No more roses.

Tears stream over my cheeks. Death is final. There is no turning back from that.

Barnabas shudders and coughs. I'm startled, and my tail recoils on instinct.

I can't do it.

Panic lifts me up and I fly out of the ravine, settling back onto the forest floor.

I blink back tears and run deeper into the forest, away from the fires. I have not forgotten what I set out to do this morning. I must find Ren and say good-bye, no matter how much he hates me. But now that the forest is on fire, I must find Batu, and warn him of the very real danger.

I take a circuitous route to the river in case I'm followed.

Many times, I soar above the trees to see who or what might be lurking near. I skirt several search parties this way. When the coast is clear enough, I settle down on a boulder near the river that I have never seen there before. I smile, certain it is Batu. The dank metallic scent gives him away. He must have been looking for me.

"Brother dragon," I whisper, and the rock begins to transform. Snout materializes first, then shimmering wings flap away from the stone. Soon he stands on his haunches at full height.

Sister. You have been all over the forest this day. Your scent is so strong, it made me curious.

"There are men in the forest, Batu. They're burning it." I glance at the trees on the far side of the river. Smoke curls out of the woods like dark, murky fog. "It hasn't reached this side of the forest yet, but it might. You must flee."

Men are foolish. But do not worry, sister, the flames will not reach me in my lair. I am more worried about you.

"You don't understand. They're burning the woods to flush out the wizard." I wonder for a moment whether the revelation I was made by the wizard will make Batu hate me, too, but I cannot keep that from my dragon brother. "And me. They're also after me. I am not what you think I am."

What are you?

My fists clench at my sides. "The wizard . . . he's the man I thought was my father. He lied to me. He destroyed my life."

The dragon rears his head back, eyes narrowing. My

heart sinks into my feet, but he presses his snout against my middle and inhales.

So that is why you smell of magic.

I shake my head, ashamed. "I had no idea. He told me he was a scientist. And I did awful things because of it." I was a fool to believe him, but what else was I to do? All I knew was from him. He ensured all my knowledge supported the lies he told.

Wizards are the most deceitful of creatures. I am grieved to hear he pretended to be someone so close to you. I know how much you loved your false father.

"I was so wrong, about so many things. Now he's here in the forest, and I'm afraid he will find you."

Batu shrinks back and shimmers, like he does when he's about to fade. My hand on his snout tingles.

"Wait!" I say. "Come with me."

Where are you going? I dare not stray far. Travel would leave me exposed, and easier for the wizard to find.

My heart sinks. "I don't know where exactly. Just . . . not here. Somewhere far from Bryre and anyone who might have known the girl I was before. I do not wish to cause any more pain."

I have told you before, my nest is yours, if you wish it. The mountain will keep us safe.

For a long moment, I consider Batu's offer. He may not be my human family, but he is the closest thing I have, the sole creature left on this earth who can understand me.

But if I stay, can I remain hidden? Can I hide so close to

Bryre and resist the temptation to seek out Ren again? Or the city and its palace and fountains and roses? I'd be putting Batu at risk, and that I could not bear.

"I wish I could," I say, tears welling up in my eyes. "But I can't stand to be this close to my city. It would call to me every day, but going back would be too dangerous, for me and for you. I can't risk it. If the wizard found me here again, he could remove my memories, make me forget everything I've done, what I am, even you." I sigh. "No, the only safe place for me is as far away as I can fly."

Batu nuzzles his snout in my shoulder. *I am sorry to hear it. But I understand. If you ever return, come to the river, and I will find you again.*

I wait in the forest just outside the city until almost midnight, playing a dangerous game of hide-and-seek with Bryre's men. But when the moon is finally high enough, I creep over the parapets.

My feet know the way and I stand in a garden, just below Ren's window, before I can reel in my fluttering thoughts. His scent led me here, but I'm surprised to find him at home in bed instead of hiding in a secret nook. Perhaps the best hiding places really are the ones in plain sight.

Of course, it doesn't hurt that the people who wished to punish him most are out in the forest hunting me.

I pop open the window and slither inside. Moonlight paints his room in silver. I pull my book of fairy tales out of my satchel and lay it on the table next to his bed. It overflows with the dried roses he gave me when he believed

I was someone else. I do not feel right keeping them any longer. Then I place my last rose on the pillow beside him and pause.

This is the last time I'll ever see Ren.

Something wrenches inside me and I stare harder at his face, as if to imprint his image upon my eyes forever.

This wonderful boy, with his curly brown hair and warm brown eyes, hates me. With very good reason.

If only I'd realized sooner that I'm the monster.

I must leave, but my body refuses to move. My need for him has become a physical one. Like breathing or flying.

He hates me.

Just the thought is crippling. I must keep reminding myself of it or I'll never leave his room. I'll never leave alive.

He hates me. If he wakes, he or his family will kill me.

Each word has a jagged edge.

My feet budge at last. I take one final look and creep back outside.

The forest still burns, though now the men take measures to put it out. When I alight on the road beyond, my vision is blurred and my throat sore from inhaling the smoke. I no longer care who sees me fly. Why bother? Ren knows. The citizens fear me and now that the forest burns, they've gone running back to Bryre. Scaring travelers and children is what Barnabas created me to do.

What pains me most is that even though Barnabas is evil incarnate, I couldn't kill him when I had the chance. I can't kill a wizard, let alone the man who's the only father I've ever known. Even though he made me to be a killer.

I'm a foolish creature!

I head for the green hills and wooded mountains beyond the cottage I once called home. I hear the sounds of travelers, wheels over gravel and whinnying horses, but I don't care. My pack is secured between my wings, and my cloak rests beneath it. The full range of my monstrosity is in clear view for all to see, gawk at, and despise.

A sharp pain ricochets through my skull—

DAY FIFTY-NINE

MY NOSE REGISTERS THE SMELL BEFORE I OPEN MY EYES. WHEN I DO, I
skitter back and meet cold metal bars.

Caged.

"Well now," a familiar voice says, "what have we here?"
Darrell's wicked laugh reverberates in my head.

I'm in the same caged wagon that transported the girls.

The animal in me rages. I growl, baring my teeth, and
he jumps. The moon is far enough across the sky that it must
be nearly dawn. How long was I unconscious?

"None of that, girl. You can't get through them bars.
Not even your claws can cut through steel." He leers and I
hiss again. My tail whips between the bars, but he stumbles
back before I hit him.

"Don't bother. You can't hurt me."

I frown. What can he mean?

"Do you really think Barnabas is stupid enough to create a beast like you and not take precautions?"

"Precautions?" I whisper hoarsely.

"He made a serum that nullifies your poison. You won't do any more damage than a pinprick."

Shock holds me in an iron grip. I have no defenses against this man. I'm helpless. Barnabas knew this day would come.

I was so stupid, asking him when I could go to the happy place we supposedly sent the girls. When he told me in good time, he meant it. I scream and pound my fists on the floor of the cage, needing some outlet for my fury.

"Ah, yes. You will fetch a fine price, missy." Darrell winks at me through the bars. I stumble back as understanding overwhelms me. They sold the girls I stole, and now he will sell me, too.

"How long have you known what I am?"

"Long enough to realize how much you would be worth. It is so rare to capture a beast such as yourself alive." He grins, revealing yellowed teeth. "Barnabas is a tricky one, but once I remembered what you are, I renegotiated my reward for ferrying the girls. He knew he'd have to dispose of you eventually, and we worked out a mutually beneficial arrangement."

As Darrell covers my cage with a thick tarp and mounts the front of the wagon, I shiver in spite of the warmth in the air.

I will suffer the same fate as my own victims.

From the six-inch-wide hole I made in the tarp, I've seen more of the country in which I live in one day of travel than in all the rest of my short life. So much green. Trees of all shapes and sizes, some with sharp pointy leaves and others with long dangling branches I wish I could reach out and touch.

But I cannot.

I can't even broach the locks on the outside of my cage. Darrell, that tricky beast of a man, placed several of them on the bars, but none will open to the needling of my claws. Barnabas must've spelled them when Darrell was transporting the girls. The key is the only thing that will open them.

Darrell drives the cart up steep ravines that I can't believe we manage to pass, and past waterfalls with high cascades. In the distance lies another range of mountains covered with scrubby purple brush. They're aflame with colors in the dying light. I'll never get to touch any of these. Smell them up close. Befriend the animals scurrying in the undergrowth.

I'll be sold.

I've become that princess from the tower who escaped and found the world to be a far more dangerous place than she had ever dreamed.

Darrell hummed to himself all day. Every once in a while he glances at me, winks, then cackles to himself. Each time he does this my claws slip out, useless.

As the day wanes, I lie on the floor of my prison. The food Darrell shoved through the bars at midday remains uneaten, spilled on the floor at my feet. The feral hunger I used to feel before every meal has ceased in the face of my grief. I only want to watch the sun slip over the mountains, disappearing an inch at a time in a blaze of color and light.

This is the time of day when I would sneak into the city, filled with purpose—to save another girl, to see Ren. I wish what Father—no, Barnabas—told me was true. That I really was a hero, not the beast terrorizing the city. The stars twinkle down above the tarp covering my prison, silent witnesses to every awful thing I've done.

When the cart finally stops, Darrell bangs a spoon on the bars.

"Get up. Eat, you stupid girl. I can't deliver you half mad from starvation." He shoves another moldy lump of bread through the bars.

I hiss at him. Right now, the only thing I hunger for is his blood.

I curl on my side. The mountains are clearer that way. Darrell shuffles items on and off the top of the cart as he makes camp for the night. I have found no nook or cranny I can use to escape from this cage.

I've made up my mind. The second Darrell opens the door to deliver me to the slavers or whoever it may turn out to be, I'll tear him to pieces. I've never killed a human before. But I'm confident my feral instincts will guide me well.

Those parts that separate me from the other girls of Bryre will be what saves me.

DAY SIXTY-ONE

I AM NOT CERTAIN HOW MUCH TIME PASSES. AT LEAST TWO SUNSETS, I believe. I spend my time focusing on the one thing I still want: my memories. I replay the visions I've seen in my head, clinging to the faint feeling that I was once loved. That, once, I belonged somewhere.

I was the crown princess. Oliver's daughter, Delia's sister, and Ren's friend. I knew them, loved them, but they would never want to know me as I am now.

Once, I had everything I've longed for. Barnabas stole it from me.

But something in what Darrell said gives me hope— Barnabas removed his memory of me, but eventually it came back. Whatever the spell is, it holds only for so long. Bit by precious bit, more memories rise to the surface now that I'm away from Barnabas and his memory-erasing touch. Now I have all the time in the world to focus solely on retrieving them. My mother reading me a story. I still cannot see her face, but I hear her voice, the warmth in it. This vision comes with a sense of comfort, love, and quiet joy I've never known since.

In another I tend a small garden surrounded by high hedges, unlike the others I've seen at the palace. It's a mishmash of plants—roses, of course, alongside sunflowers, begonias, and lilies. There are several others I cannot name, but I delight in the look of them. I water each one from an old tin watering can, and pull up the weeds with care. Rosabel loved this garden. I wonder what happened to it?

I cling to each memory, growing fonder of them by the hour, wrapping them around me like a warm blanket. The whispers of the past sing me to sleep.

In the predawn hours, the quiet patter of feet tiptoeing up a rocky path rouses me. Someone approaches our camp. I peek out the hole in the tarp, hoping the person or creature comes into view. For a fleeting moment I consider screaming for help, but I brush that aside.

Anyone who saw me would think Darrell was well within his rights to take me as far from their country as possible. They'd probably applaud him. They might even help.

In the half-light, a shadow creeps past the dull embers of the campfire toward Darrell. My lungs tighten. What if it's a robber and they kill him and steal me? I might be able to defend myself against that sort of men. They wouldn't have the antidote to my poison barb.

The figure leans over Darrell, but I can't see what it does to his sleeping body.

Thwack.

Darrell cries out for a brief second; then all is silent. It is a robber, I'm sure of it.

The person drags Darrell's body toward my cage, probably intending to stuff him inside. I crawl back under my blanket, feigning sleep, though my claws slide into place and my legs prepare to pounce. Every nerve is a live wire. This is my chance to escape. The sound of keys jingling reaches my ears, and then the interloper tugs off the tarp covering my cage. I risk a peek with one eye.

The hood of his cloak has slipped.

Ren.

The emotions swirling inside form a vise around my chest. I can't breathe. I can hardly think.

He turns the key in the lock and yanks the door open.

"Hello?" he says, putting a hand on my shoulder and shaking me gently.

Just like he would any other captive girl.

The fight slips out of my body. The cage door is open and I've deceived Ren long enough. I sit up slowly, pulling my cloak around my shoulders and letting the blanket that hid me fall to the floor.

Ren recoils.

I hate the expression on his face. Terror. Disgust. He can't stand to look at my monstrous body, half creature, half girl. He must be revolted by how many nights he spent holding my hand. A tear trails down my cheek. I miss him so much; it's clear I'm the last person he hoped to find in this cage.

We remain still for a moment, eyes locked and wary. Ren doesn't budge. I dash out of the cage, breaking the standoff first. I can't bear to see the hate in his eyes anymore, and it's such a relief to stretch my wings again.

"I'm sorry, Ren." I have to say it. Even though it's futile. Even though it will mean nothing to him, it means everything to me.

He grunts and stomps out of the cage behind me. "Don't bother. I don't want to hear it. If I'd known it was you in there, I'd never have let you out. Don't you dare try anything. If your tail moves an inch in my direction, I'll cut it off." He points to the scabbard at his belt. He must've taken a sword from the palace. I've never seen him armed like that before.

"I would never—" I start to say but think better of it. Because in truth, I did.

He doesn't take his eyes off me as he drags Darrell closer to the cage.

He's afraid. I stare up at the night sky for a few seconds to keep tears from falling. I don't want Ren to see me cry.

He struggles with Darrell's limp form as he attempts to put him in the cage. When I move to grab the man's legs, Ren flinches. I hold my hands up. "I just want to help."

He shrugs. "Suit yourself."

I lift Darrell's feet and we throw him inside, locking the bars behind him. Satisfaction warms me, but doesn't dull the sharp desire for revenge. Darrell was an all too willing participant in the girls' forced slavery; he deserves this more than I do.

Ren wipes the dirt from his hands on his cloak, then pokes at the embers of last night's fire. I can't stand the awkwardness between us.

"Why are you here, Ren?"

"I'm not here to rescue you, if that's what you're asking."

My face turns pink. "No, I didn't think you were."

"Good." He scuffs the embers with the sole of his shoe. "I'm going after Delia. She was my responsibility. Some men in the tavern spoke of a man transporting live goods to Belladoma that he kept tightly under wraps. I figured it was the best shot I had, and that maybe I could find the other girls, too. They described this man exactly." His eyes blaze. He's angry at everyone and everything and—most of all—me.

Perhaps this is my chance to set things right. And find out whether my sister still lives.

"I'll help you."

Ren scoffs. "I doubt that. You're probably in league with him." He nods at the cart. "You could be pretending. Maybe you're a trap. I don't know!" He throws his hands up and sits on a tree stump. The sun is gaining ground, tingeing the world with red and gold, including Ren's hair.

"I'm not with him, but I do know him. This man's name is Darrell and he attacked me on the road. He intended to sell me." My voices lowers. "Just like the other girls. Said I'd fetch a fine price." I sit by the dead fire pit, across from Ren. "I'll help you. This is my fault. I'll make things right, whether you like it or not."

He snorts. "Wonderful. I've got the monstress on my side."

"I've always been on your side. Unfortunately, I was deceived by the person I thought was my father." My face burns again. I'm ashamed of my blindness. But Father was all I knew. What else was I supposed to do? What would anyone else do in my place?

"You should've known. Somehow." His face twists. "Fine, you can help. But I'm in charge. This is my quest."

"Thank you." A smile of relief tugs at the corners of my lips, but I suppress it. It might make him angry again. "What are you going to do with Darrell? Leave him to rot?" I rather like that idea, but Ren shakes his head.

"Not yet. I need to know who he sells the girls to and where they are now. Unless you have that information?" He looks at me skeptically. He will never trust me again. If I were him, I wouldn't.

"I only know what my fa—" I stop myself from using that word. Barnabas doesn't deserve it, and it's an insult to Oliver. "What Barnabas told me about Belladoma, and there's no guarantee it's true."

Ren picks apart a leaf, bit by bit. He may as well be tearing up my heart. "It's a start. What did he tell you?"

"He said that Belladoma is a city over the mountains"—I point to the purple crests in the distance—"and that the girls are well loved and cared for. He told me the city is filled with gardens and fountains and every pleasure they could want, but I doubt that now."

"I think that's a safe bet." Ren says. "At least we know what direction to go. Darrell's path confirms he was headed toward Belladoma."

My face brightens. That's the first positive thing he's said since he arrived.

"When he wakes up, you can help me convince him to spill the exact whereabouts of the girls in that city."

I frown. "How? I doubt he'll tell me any faster than he'll tell you."

Ren laughs bitterly. "Barnabas only taught you what he needed you to know, didn't he? We'll have to torture him. Simple as that. With your claws and that tail, you were made for it."

"Torture?" The word circles around my brain. To inflict pain. "You want me to hurt him until he tells us what we need to know."

Ren doesn't answer. He doesn't have to.

I've already hurt so many. Do I really want to hurt another person?

Darrell would have killed me without a moment's hesitation if it served his purpose. I was just more valuable to him alive.

If hurting him will help me reclaim my sister and Ren's good graces, I'll do it. I'll do anything.

When Darrell regains consciousness, we're prepared. He yells and curses at us for a full five minutes before he calms down enough to listen. He almost knocks the cart over in the process.

When Ren rattles the bars of the cage, Darrell ceases his hysterics.

"Who the hell are you, boy?" A jeer crosses Darrell's face. "Do you fancy the monster girl?"

My skin warms. Ren scowls at the suggestion and that only makes me blush harder.

"I'm here to find out where you take the girls."

Darrell snickers. "Well, I'm not gonna just tell you that, now am I? I'll be needing some compensation for my assistance." He holds out his palm and waggles his fingers.

Ren slams the hilt of the sword against the bars. "You're in no position to bargain. We've got you locked up. We can starve you out if we have to."

"I don't think you'll be doing that. There's far too many travelers on this road. I expect we'll see some merchant friends of mine any hour now."

Ren's face turns white. Waiting Darrell out isn't an option. And we can't expect him to help us out of the goodness of his heart.

Which leaves one choice.

I step forward, wrapping my clawed fingers around the bars. Darrell flinches. Good, I still scare him.

"You'll tell us where you took the girls. All of them."

"Not likely." He scoots to the far side of the cage, but he can't evade my tail as it winds through the bars and curls around his middle and neck. He gasps and struggles, but I squeeze harder. I may not be able to sting him, but I can choke him.

I yank him toward me until he is pressed up against the

cage, close enough that I can smell the rabbit he had for dinner stuck between his teeth.

"You'll tell us where you took the girls. Or I'll carve the information out of your skull." I tap his temple and a bead of blood forms, then rolls down his face. "Or I could just squeeze it out of you." I tighten the noose of my tail and and he claws at it. "Your choice."

"You wouldn't," he chokes out.

He's testing me. A part of me abhors this, but I must do it for Ren. And for me. I squeeze harder. And harder. He sputters. Gags. The skin on his face takes on a blue shade. I have to look away, but I keep squeezing.

When he manages to nod in agreement, I loosen my hold. He coughs for several seconds and lies still on the floor of the cage, breathing laboriously. Ren must be disgusted by my cruelty. But he was right. It had to be done. If we don't stop Barnabas and Darrell, some other naive hybrid Barnabas creates will be handing over the girls of the city.

I will stop them.

"I take them to King Ensel of Belladoma." He spits up blood. I wonder if I crushed any of his ribs. I hope so.

Ren pales. "What does he want with them?"

Darrell grimaces, as though he'd like to smile but is in too much pain. "What do you think? Haven't you heard the rumors?"

Ren gasps as understanding dawns on his face. He jabs the point of the sword at Darrell's shoulder, stopping just short of puncturing skin. "You sold them to be fed to the Sonzeeki?"

293

Darrell holds up his hands. "This was Barnabas's brilliant plan. He just cut me in on the deal. He pays handsomely, and I'm in it for the money. Besides, I'd be a fool to refuse a wizard anything. No, he's up to something else. For him it's personal." He glances at me. "So was killing you."

Ren paces before the cage. "All those girls, some so young. And Delia!"

"What is a Sonzeeki?" I ask, bewildered by their conversation.

Ren turns on me with fiery eyes. "Don't you know anything? Belladoma has no flowers or fountains. It's a city of mercenaries and traders. Their idiot king managed to enrage an ancient sea creature that lives below the city's cliffs. If he doesn't send a young girl off the cliff at the apex of each full moon, the Sonzeeki floods the city. It's why Ensel tried to take over Bryre in the first place and began this whole nightmare with the wizard." He smacks his hand against a nearby tree, then shakes off the sting. Darrell chortles and is rewarded with a blow from the hilt of Ren's sword.

"You." Ren points and marches toward me. "This is all your fault."

I stare at the ground, bits of grass poking through the soil. "I know," I say.

Ren halts. He didn't expect me to agree. He ought to know me better by now. I'm almost disappointed.

Resolve courses through me, washing away my sadness and self-pity. Yes, this is my fault. But I will fix it. Somehow, I'll find a way to make Barnabas and Ensel and

Darrell and anyone else who aided them rue the day they ever heard of Bryre.

I straighten my back and head for the horse pulling the cart. It whinnies and nuzzles my neck as I unfasten the reins.

"What are you doing?"

"Here." I offer the reins to him. "We're going to Belladoma. We're getting Delia and the rest of those girls back."

DAY SIXTY-TWO

I LIE NEAR THE EMBERS OF THE FIRE, GAZING UP AT THE STARS LINGERING in the early-morning hours.

Ren hasn't spoken a word to me since I announced my plan. But he did come along after we rolled the cart behind a grove of trees and covered it with the tarp. The longer Darrell stays hidden and stuck, the better for us. If he gets out, he will probably go looking for Barnabas.

I shiver. The last thing we need is for the wizard to come after us. He may already be on our trail.

Ren slumbers, curled up in a blanket we snatched from Darrell. He looks cold and scared and I just want to wrap my arms around him and tell him everything will be all right.

But touching him is out of the question. He flinched when our hands brushed together while I handed him the rabbit I cooked last night.

I disgust him.

I don't belong in Bryre. I don't belong in Belladoma either, though Ren might think so. I don't belong with Barnabas, my pretend father, nor Oliver, the real father of the once-me, Rosabel.

I don't belong anywhere.

Ren yawns. I roll onto my back. It would not do for him to catch me gawking. The sun is up now, pushing the last vestiges of starlight from the sky. Neither of us knows how far Belladoma is, but we ought to get going. Darrell used to make the round trip in a few days, so I'm sure we'll reach it soon.

What worries me most is how we'll get the girls out of the castle. Even if we can find a way inside and reach them, they won't go anywhere with the monster who brought them to Belladoma in the first place. And I'm sure I'll need to use all my parts to the fullest to ensure their escape.

Somehow, I will have to convince them I'm on their side. I don't expect it will be easy.

Ren rises and heads into the woods without a backward glance. He pretends I don't exist. He can ignore me as much as he likes; I will help him no matter what he says.

He's changed since Delia disappeared. Lines mar his warm face, giving him a drawn and sullen appearance. His eyes are still bright, but now with thoughts of vengeance instead of mischief.

That is my fault.

After Rosabel—I—died, he must have taken more

responsibility for Delia. Now he's lost them both.

As I put the gear we stole from Darrell together, a thought freezes me. Did Barnabas send Rosabel to Belladoma? Is that where I truly died? He never did say where he took my body when we disappeared from the palace. In light of all the lies he told, his assertion that I died instantly is dubious at best. I shudder despite the warmth of my cloak.

Ren returns, pulling a piece of jerky from his pocket. He chews while he mounts the horse and takes off along the path.

I do my best to keep up with him, but he spurs the horse to move faster every time I get close.

He leaves me with little choice. I will have to fly to keep pace with him. I stretch my wings and take off. I love flying, but I fear I only reinforce the monster in me in Ren's eyes by doing so.

He still will not look my way.

"Ren."

Nothing. Not even a quirk of the lips or twitch of the eyes. He remains silent, studying the road ahead while I flap my wings beside him and the mare. I veer into the horse's path. It whinnies and rears, jostling Ren about in the saddle.

I hold out my hands imploringly. "You must talk to me. We need a plan."

He tries to guide the horse, now back under his control, around me. I swerve into his path again.

"If we don't work together, we'll never succeed."

That, at least, earns me a fierce scowl.

"It's true and you know it. We need each other to do

this. Otherwise, we'll fail."

He urges the horse onward.

"We'll fail Delia."

He circles the horse, his once warm face cold. "Fine. What do you want me to say? I'm thrilled I have to work with a monster to get the princess back from an evil king in his disgusting, squalid city?"

I sigh. "I understand you hate me. But I'm doing this for me just as much as for you or any of those girls."

"For you? What stake do you have in this?"

My heart sinks into my feet. He has no idea who I am. Will he even believe me? A small part of me had hoped he might figure it out on his own. I take a deep breath. "The wizard killed me. I was once a girl from Bryre."

Ren snorts. "What was your name?" He folds his arms over his chest, clutching the reins with white knuckles.

I steel my nerves. He can't possibly hate me any more than he already does, though that is a small consolation.

"Rosabel."

He nearly falls off his horse.

"Liar!" He whips the mare and she rears, then lunges ahead. I fly after them, weighed down by fear that any ounce of the trust he had in me may have vanished.

"I'm not a liar. Why do you think I seemed familiar when we first met? Why did Oliver recognize my eyes?" Ren turns the horse to face me.

"Stop!"

"Because my eyes belonged to Rosabel."

"Stop it!" The mare stamps her feet. The threatening

tone of Ren's voice frightens her. I regret telling him, but it's too late now.

"I know the rest of me doesn't look like Rosabel. But her brain and her eyes are mine. Sometimes I catch a glimpse of her memories, too." I take a tentative step closer. The expression on Ren's face is unreadable. "That must be how I knew I could trust you, despite Barnabas's attempts to instill a mistrust of all humans in me. You knew Rosabel well, didn't you?"

"She was a lovely, kind girl. You're nothing like her. She'd never help the wizard. She'd do anything to protect Bryre." He spits.

"Which is what Barnabas convinced me I was doing! Saving Bryre's children from the wizard." I wring my hands, feeling awful and indignant all at once. "You must understand, Barnabas was all I knew. He brought me back to life and suppressed my memories with his magic. I had no way of knowing what he told me was a lie. Not until I met you did I begin to question. Now I question everything."

"I don't have to understand anything." Ren heads down the path again, this time at a more reasonable pace. He's angry, that much is clear, but perhaps I've gotten through to him a little bit. At least I tried.

He trots silently and I walk beside him for another half hour before Ren gives in and speaks. "Did you really believe what Barnabas told you about Belladoma? That it was a paradise?"

I grimace. "I did. He made it sound like the most beautiful place in the world. I begged him to let me go there when our task was complete." My face darkens. "He said he'd be happy to take me to Belladoma as a reward. He meant it, too, just not in the way I thought."

Ren grunts. "Belladoma is nothing like that. My grandfather used to trade with them years ago when Bryre and Belladoma weren't enemies. King Ensel was just a baby. His father was a kinder man. Perhaps it was beautiful then." He pauses. "Anyway, my grandfather once told me about an entrance to the city that didn't pass through the main gates. He used it when he was in a hurry and didn't feel like getting accosted by the guards or waiting in line. Catacombs carved into the cliff run beneath the city. Belladoma overlooks the ocean, so the only ways in are through the main gates or to find the entrance to the catacombs."

Ocean. A vast body of water. Salty. I can't picture it, but the air around us has taken on a saltier quality. We must be close.

"I've never heard of the ocean until now," I muse. "Barnabas never told me about that part."

Ren shakes his head. "Belladoma is famous for its location and its ravenous sea monster. The latter is why King Ensel has quite the penchant for throwing people off the cliff when he tires of them. His courtiers are notorious for their short life spans."

"Then why would anyone want to be his courtier?"

"Because their families are the only ones in the city who eat on a regular basis. He only allows one hundred of them. In order to get the position, someone needs to be thrown off that cliff."

This is where I sent those poor girls. "That's insane."

Ren nods. "It is. The rest of the city is stricken by poverty. People will do incredible things to feed themselves and their children. To the king it's all a game." His face pales. "Now Delia and the other girls are part of the game, too."

The thought chills me. He is right, of course. I must stop it.

"Anyway, if we can find the entrance to the catacombs, we could get into the city unnoticed and decide how to proceed from there. My grandfather said the entrance was at the base of two huge trees twining around each other, in the woods outside the perimeter of the city walls."

"Perfect. There can't be many trees like that."

Ren says nothing, only rides onward.

DAY SIXTY-THREE

WE FOUND THE TWIN TREES LAST NIGHT, HUDDLED TOGETHER LIKE TWO children trying to keep warm on a cold winter's night. The hollow looks like an animal den, but the stairs just inside the entrance reveal its true purpose.

We enter the catacombs shortly before dawn. The guards who line the high ramparts don't see us under the cover of the morning fog. Water drips around us, and the drab stone floors are slick beneath our feet. My tail is tense and ready. Ren leads. He claims he knows where this tunnel will take us, and I don't see much of a choice but to believe him. Walking in the front gate would not be a good idea. As we gathered from a caravan of traders we eavesdropped on last night, the city is closed to all outsiders except those known to King Ensel. They were turned away at the gates, and none too happy about it.

King Ensel is preparing for war and fears his enemy will learn of his plans. The "enemy" must be Bryre. If we want any chance of getting close to the castle, let alone inside, we have to take the sneaky route.

We walk in silence through the winding dark and shadowed damp for some time, until Ren signals for me to stop.

"Wait here. I'll be right back."

I frown as he jogs ahead, but remain where I stand. He returns quickly.

"We'll need to camp out here for a while. The exit is a few yards ahead of us, but we're bound to get caught if we go out in broad daylight. It lets out in the middle of the square and, if it's anything like Bryre, it'll be filled with people until late afternoon. When they start to go home to their families, we can leave."

I settle on the damp floor of the tunnel and lean my head against the wall.

"That's a good plan." I can't deny it even though I wish we could act now. I hate waiting. "Have you thought about what we will do once we're in the city proper?"

Ren shrugs. "A little."

"Really?" I say, surprised. "It's all I can think about." I stretch my legs out in front of me. "I have an idea. But first I need to know more about this sea creature. What is it? Why is it ravaging the city?"

Ren settles down across from me on a patch of semidry rock. "They call it the Sonzeeki. It's an ancient creature, a relic of a time long past. They say it has a huge impenetrable shell, like a turtle's, but a hundred times larger. It has tentacles that can rip a ship in half, and a beak sharp enough to pierce any armor."

"It sounds ferocious."

Ren laughs bitterly. "Yes, and ravenous. If it isn't fed a girl on the full moon, it spins and spins in its underwater lair until the water rises and floods the catacombs and city streets. And it will only go back beneath the cliffs if it's a girl that's offered. Ensel could toss all the boys and adults he wants over, and the beast would still flood the city."

I remember the time I fell in the river and nearly drowned. I don't want to imagine the streets and homes filling with rising seawater, but now I can think of nothing else. My stomach turns. "What could Ensel have done to anger such a creature?"

Ren pulls an apple from his pack and tosses it back and forth between his hands. "I have only heard the rumors. Some say Ensel woke the beast from its thousand-year hibernation. Others say he stole something from it, and the beast wants it back. I don't think anyone really knows for certain. It wasn't terrorizing the city in my grandfather's day, that's for sure. But whatever happened, it's here now."

"And we have to get Bryre's girls away from it." I pull my cloak closer to fend off the damp chill that permeates the catacombs. It helps only a little.

"So what is this idea of yours?" Ren asks. "How do you propose we get them out?"

I grimace. I am not looking forward to this, but without knowing the layout of the palace ahead of time I believe it is our best shot.

"They need a meal for their monster. So we bring them one."

Ren tightens his hold on the leash around my neck. My choker now acts as a makeshift collar. It has lost a measure of its value now that I know it was only a trifle Barnabas bought for my mother, not something she ever actually wore. But it keeps my bolts hidden and that is what matters now. Ren pulls harder and I stumble forward as we walk up the cracked steps of the castle. He enjoys this a little more than he should. Though I can't blame him. If I had Darrell on a leash like this, I wouldn't be gentle either.

We reach the gates and Ren marches right up to the burly guard posted out front. The murmurs of several other men inside the nearby guardhouse reach my ears. Ren doesn't even flinch as the man towers over him and scowls.

"What do you want, boy?" The man jerks his head in my direction. "Who's she?"

"An offering for the beast. I'm here to deliver it. Personally."

The guard studies us, his expression growing more dubious by the second. "What do you want in return for the girl?"

"I'll discuss that with the king." Ren's hard face doesn't budge an inch.

The guard grunts and takes a step closer to Ren until

they're toe to toe. He's at least a full head taller. "Really?" A handful of guards wander out of the guardhouse behind him. Each one is just as big and mean looking as the first. Their uniforms are a dingy gray, stained with what I suspect is ale and the remnants of suppers past.

Ren holds his ground. If I wasn't supposed to be his captive—and he didn't hate me so much—I'd hug him. Instead, I keep my mouth shut and my eyes on the ground.

"Yes." Ren stands stock still. Not a single muscle twitches. I hold my breath.

The guard laughs, and those behind him join in. "You're nuts. The king'll love you." He claps Ren on the back, then opens the gate. "Go on in, boy. Hope you make it out again."

Ren strides through the gate, yanking me after him. I stumble, but recover, taking care not to let my wings or tail poke out from beneath my cloak. My neck is sore. I hadn't anticipated Ren would take his role so far.

We pad up the cold stone walkway toward the palace. The low rumble of many voices thrums from inside the walls of the building, but only we and the guards remain outside. It's a gray monstrosity, set on a cliff overlooking a vast ocean.

I can't fathom being engulfed in all that water and depth. Hopefully, I'll never have to. My one excursion into the river was more than enough for me. And I do not have Batu here to drag me out this time.

My heart trembles. I hope he is far from Bryre now, and far from the wizard. I need my dragon brother to be safe.

Unlike Bryre's palace, Belladoma's has no garden, no exquisite hedges. Pools of rainwater and marsh dot the overgrown grassy landscape leading to the palace doors. The occasional naked tree sticks out of the ground. No one loves this place. It looks as though it has been flooded with salty seawater again and again. Not much will grow here, not without an infusion of fresh water and loam. How can people live here? If this palace, on the highest ground in the city, has been flooded enough to inflict this level of damage, how much worse must it be for the commoners? I shudder. Small wonder they so readily turn a blind eye to what Ensel does to some other city's girls.

The building is tall and imposing, but the opposite of Bryre in every other way. My home city's palace has a marble facade and interior; Belladoma's is a gray, rotting limestone that seems to shift and shudder in the wind. Everything about Belladoma spells cold. Bleak. Lonely. Death.

Horror crawls over me like a hundred tiny spiders. This unfeeling place, with its wretched citizens and monster lurking in the deep, is where I sent Bryre's girls.

Ren pushes me up the stairs. Are the guards watching anymore? I doubt it. My heart sinks even further. The damage I've done to our friendship is irreparable, even if we do rescue the girls. It makes no difference who I was in the past.

What I've done in this life is all that matters.

I wish my sister's name and face could evoke the same possessive emotions in me that they do in Ren. He knows Delia, cares for her in a way I can't yet. Only if all my stolen memories can be found. They are beginning to come back, but not fast enough. I believe the blond child I saw once may be her, but thus far that is the sole appearance she has made in my visions.

Another guard waits at the front door and he eyes us with amusement. This one is scrawny compared to the guards at the gate, but he is still larger than Ren and me put together.

"I'm bringing her to the king for the Sonzeeki," Ren says with a gruff tone that makes me shiver. Even worse is the guard's grin as he nods.

He opens the door. "The throne room is straight down the hall." The guard's eyes burn into my back as Ren marches me down the corridor. Why do these guards aid this evil king? There is no wizard here to keep them in thrall. The castle is overflowing with evil hearts.

The inside is just as bleak as the grounds. Gray stone and not much else. That is, until we get to the section of the palace where the king lives.

At least, I assume it is where he lives, because it's the only part that resembles a home. These walls have rich tapestries with gold threads and suits of armor in every corner. Vases on fancy tables and statues made of exotic marble line the long hall. The silver sconces shine brighter. People in fine clothing mingle, and drably clothed servants scuttle out of their way. The courtiers eye us with curiosity, and I can sense them shadowing us down the hall. When the room at the end comes into view, my breath halts.

This is what I imagine Bryre once looked like. When

the king and queen and Delia and the once-me still lived there. When it was not being torn apart by a ruthless plant. When I was not yet a monster.

Gold and silver fill the view through the half-open door. The parquet floor gleams a rich mahogany. Brightly colored silk skirts sweep across it.

Only when Ren tugs on my leash do I realize I've stopped to stare.

"It's beautiful," I whisper. Ren just glares ahead. A woman titters behind us, and other voices join in. My cheeks burn, and I remind myself to stay silent.

We reach the edge of the entrance but remain in the shadows. I can't help marveling at the splendor here and the squalor outside this hall. It's as though the king has built up just enough for himself—and his courtiers—and can't be bothered with what lies outside his doors.

"You must want an audience with His Majesty, yes?" says an imposing man who materializes in front of us. He's dressed in a white silk tunic edged with gold brocade and a fine matching cloak. It sets off his black hair—and the sword at his hip.

"We do," Ren says, his hold on my lead tightening.

The man smiles, but no mirth lies behind it. Something in his eyes and manner feels predatory, setting my instincts on edge. "Then come with me."

Ren plunges after the man into the ballroom and the multicolored throng. I follow before he can yank my leash again. The courtiers from the hallway enter as well, making our procession feel formal. The crowd hushes and parts.

Whispers swirl around us like fog. The dance ceases and the musicians set aside their instruments. A portly man on the black marble throne studies us with a displeased expression.

We interrupted his entertainment. My heart rises into my throat as we march closer. We walk only yards, but it feels like miles. I wilt under the king's withering stare, but Ren seems unaffected.

The man in white halts in front of the throne. The king is an odd-looking man. All nose and ears and pasty jowls.

"Your Majesty," the man says, bowing low. "These children wish an audience with you." The hushed crowd is broken by laughter that's just as quickly snuffed out by a sharp glance from the king.

"Who the devil are you, boy?" The king sneers at Ren and the courtiers titter.

"My name is Rendall."

The king grunts, then gestures at me with increasing annoyance. "Who is this?"

"An offering. For the Sonzeeki."

I shudder involuntarily as the king strokes his chin, considering Ren's offer. My skin grows cold and clammy, and I send reminders to my claws to remain in place. Any of my nonhuman parts would reveal me to the king in the worst possible way.

He'd know I'm a monster. No doubt, a man like him would have unpleasant uses for me.

"Where did you find this one?" His eyes are cold, beady little things. I can't keep the defiance out of my face.

"Bryre," says Ren. A hush falls over the room.

"Really?" The king's eyes are alight with keen interest. "Are you certain?"

Ren snorts. "Of course. I took her from the city myself a few days ago."

"What is it you ask in return?" Ensel's eyes narrow.

Ren swallows. The first hint of nervousness. I don't understand. We practiced what he'd say many times over the course of the day spent in the tunnels.

"A trade. For another of the girls you have captive."

My eyes widen. This is not what we planned. He was supposed to say one hundred gold coins so he could buy us bigger transport and supplies while I worked on getting the girls out unseen.

The pit of my stomach sours. Ren only wants to save Delia. And he definitely doesn't care about what happens to me.

He is not acting anymore. He really will trade me for my human sister. Panic slices through my chest on the knife of Ren's betrayal.

The king gestures to a lackey in a gray tunic. He disappears down a hallway behind the throne.

"One of my girls, eh?" The king laughs and it sets my nerves on edge. "You drive a hard bargain, but I'll consider it."

The girls file into the room. There are so many. Did I really take them all?

When Delia walks in, Ren's face lights up.

"Which girl do you want?" Ensel asks with a touch of amusement. I'd like to strangle it out of him. "You must be sweet on one of them, yes?"

Ren pretends to consider each for a few minutes, walking up and down the line as though he were picking a dance partner, not the girl whose life he's about to save.

"Her." He points at Delia. She doesn't glance up, but a deep blush creeps up the side of her neck and ears. She knows better than to reveal she recognizes him. My heart breaks for her. How awful has her life been here?

"An excellent choice." The king laughs again, with an edge that sets off warning bells in my brain. "Albin?"

He waves a hand, and the man in the white tunic shoves Ren to the ground. Ren still holds my lead and I tumble after him. The gray-clad lackey hustles the girls away as Ensel grins.

"That's better. On the floor groveling where you belong. Did you really think I'd make a trade? Idiot. I always need more food for my pet. But thank you for choosing who will go over the cliff next. You can have a nice stay in our dungeon."

The guards tie up my wrists and Ren's. The same lackey that ferried the girls returns and drags me down the hallway. My last glimpse of Ren is him being pulled, kicking and screaming, out of the grand hall down a dismal corridor.

Terror courses through my veins. We've failed before we've even begun.

The lackey brings me down a corridor behind the throne room. Then he turns down another until we reach a guarded room in the middle. He shoves me inside and bolts the door behind me.

I am in more trouble than I could have imagined. Ren was ready to trade me for my sister. He would have left all these girls here to die. How could he do that? That is not the Ren I grew to love. I cannot make sense of it, nor can I shake the expanding hollowness in my chest.

The room is an odd mix of squalor and finery, just like the rest of the castle. The walls and floor are stone, but the beds are covered by silk sheets and jewel-toned pillows.

One of the girls helps me up. She has the long dark curls I once tried to emulate. She stops and stares, her hands jerking back to her sides like she touched a burning coal.

She recognizes me. Panic surges in my chest.

She backs away with a confused expression, as I sit on an empty bed filled with straw. I draw my cloak closer. The girls, more than thirty of them, huddle on straw pallets like mine. A few of them chew on what I imagine is stale bread and cheese from a tarnished silver platter set on the floor. I single Delia out right away. She is with a group of several others who whisper, sending fearful glances at me. They know something is different about me. That I am unnatural. These girls don't trust me. They hate me.

Still, I must find a way to allay their fears and rescue them.

I've been fretting all day over how to free the girls. In every scenario I dream up, it all comes down to one major hurdle: getting them to trust me.

Not an easy challenge to overcome. Even if my poison does make them forget temporarily, my deeds have left an imprint on the girls. I'd bet the memories of several have returned in full, judging by the looks they send my way.

These girls aren't likely to follow the one whose face is the last thing they saw before waking here.

As I rise from the bed, a girl with light-brown hair and freckles flinches and almost drops her crust. I hold out my hands, palms out.

"Hello," I say. "My name is Kymera." They stare back, mouths agape. Delia, I notice, won't even look at me. My stomach turns. Not an auspicious start. I try again.

"I see some of you remember me." I smile, but a different girl flinches. "I'm not here to hurt you."

One with dark-brown hair steps forward, arms crossed over her chest. I recognize her as the girl who tried to escape and ran afoul of the goat-footed chickens. A handful of scars still dot her forearms. "Why are you here? To take us somewhere worse?" Her blue eyes blaze with unfiltered hatred. It is more terrible than any blow. I swallow hard, knowing full well no words can undo my horrid deeds.

"I'm here to take you home."

A deathly quiet hovers in the air. Delia finally turns her gaze to me, but the expression on her face is hopeless. No one breathes. I can see no one believes me. Heaviness descends on my shoulders. What if this doesn't work? What if we all die here?

"I'm serious. I can help."

The brave girl speaks up again. "How? What can you do against King Ensel?"

Dread billows in my chest. I knew this moment would come eventually. It will either convince the girls or make them despise me even more.

I did everything out of love—misguided as it was—and all I can expect in return is hate. The irony leaves a bitter taste on my tongue.

"Many things," I say. "I have . . . gifts. They will aid me in getting you out."

The girl's eyes narrow, while the others murmur behind her. "What gifts? Is this a trick?"

"I will show you, but be warned—it may shock you. Please, try not to scream. I don't want to alert the guards."

The girls take several steps back. The brave one's eyes don't leave me for a second. Her hatred burns into my heart like a scalding flame.

I throw off my cloak.

My cramped wings spread wide, and my tail peeks around my thigh. Two girls faint. The rest gawk.

"You!" cries Delia, pointing an accusing finger at me. "You're the monster who haunts our dreams! You stole us!"

I swallow my despair. My own sister hates me. "Yes, I did. And I will steal you back if you'll let me." I flutter forward, wishing to reassure her. A couple are brave like the dark-haired girl and don't flinch, but Delia and the rest tremble against the wall with terror.

"What are you?" cries the girl who challenged me. She positions herself in front of the others. I admire this girl's willingness to protect them. All I ever wanted to do for these girls was the very same. Perhaps in another life, we'd have been friends.

"I was made for the purpose of stealing you from Bryre.

I'm so sorry. I was deceived. I was told I was saving you. Now that I know it was all backwards, I'm determined to right my wrongs."

The girls look skeptical—most of them downright terrified.

"I am here to help you escape, but I need your assistance. I need to know more about this palace, this room. When Ensel will feed the Sonzeeki again."

The brave girl swallows hard, greener than a few moments ago. "If we get caught, Ensel will toss us all off the cliff, whether it's time or not." A whisper rolls through the huddled crowd of girls.

"I won't let that happen."

"Right. Just like you saved us before." The brave girl straightens her back. "We don't need your help. We'll find our own way."

My heart sinks into my tail. "Wait—"

"Don't bother," she says. "I remember you. My brother is alone in Bryre because of what you've done. You're as evil as the wizard."

I am too stunned to speak as the dark-haired girl herds the others to the far side of the large room. They refuse to say a word to me for the rest of the night.

DAY SIXTY-FOUR

I WAKE GROGGY AND DISORIENTED. I SIT UP, RUBBING MY SORE BACK. I AM alone in my corner of the large room. The other girls remain as far from me as possible.

I've made no progress whatsoever. Every attempt to convince them I'm here to help has been ignored or vehemently brushed aside.

Frustration has made for a sleepless night. We must work together if we are to escape. My strength, flight, claws, and night vision will leave us stumbling in the dark without their knowledge of the palace and its routines. But I cannot force their trust. I cannot squeeze it out of them like I did information from Darrell.

No, their trust will have to be earned, but I haven't the faintest idea how.

Our time is spent in isolation. A few guards came by to bring us the meager leftovers from Ensel's banquets. I haven't eaten much. Despite the hunger that claws at my gut, I have no wish to tussle with the other girls over scraps. They are thinner than they ought to be—some dangerously so—and need all the food they can get.

This is what I condemned these girls to suffer.

Not all the girls remember me yet, as the venom wears off more slowly for some, but I remember every one of them. The girl with the straight, dark-brown hair who escaped Barnabas's tower and caused a ruckus in the yard. The red-haired one from that same night. Delia, with her dainty hands, bright hair, and flushed cheeks, now thin and pale from malnourishment. I wish my heart would leap with recognition at her face, but it doesn't. But now that I know the truth, I feel fiercely protective of her. Then there's the small child whose gold curls framing her face are unforgettable, though they are dull and limp now. She's the first one I took from Bryre. She threw away my roses. She missed her mother.

I steel myself to try once again to talk to the dark-haired girl. From her conversations with the others, I've learned her name is Greta. It suits her; her name sounds as fierce and determined as she is.

But before I can stand, the door to our prison flies open. A host of guards headed by Albin, the man in the gold-trimmed white tunic, stands in the doorway. The girls recoil.

The man smiles, but there is no mirth behind it. "Come along, girls. King Ensel has requested our new guest be given the grand tour."

All eyes turn to me, and I'm grateful my cloak is around me. I showed these girls my real form, but this man does not know. I pray they don't give me away.

The guards tie our wrists together with harsh rope, then lead us out into the hallway. Finally, I will see some of this palace, and can form a real plan even if the girls won't help me. The guards don't take us back the way we came through the throne room. Instead we go right down a long hallway. The stone floor beneath my feet is rough, and several stones are loose. Delia walks in front of me and falls victim to the loose flooring. I help her up, but she cringes when my hand touches her elbow. The only thanks I get is a backward, fear-filled glance.

We're marched up a narrow stairwell. We pass landing after landing without pause; the climb feels interminable. Greta picks up the small girl with once-gold curls because she is too tired to keep going. I wonder how we'll get back down.

Or if we will go back down at all.

Finally we reach the top. It opens into a large circular room with stone walls and long window slits that open onto the fresh salty air. We shuffle in. From the looks on the girls' faces, this is not the first time they've been up here.

Several of King Ensel's men stand around the room, and I'm startled to see the king himself here too. He clearly isn't accustomed to much exercise, how could he have—

A hidden passage. There must be hidden passages in Belladoma like there were in Bryre. Hope billows in my chest, but I keep my face placid so it doesn't show. The passage must not be too strenuous; otherwise King Ensel couldn't climb it all the way up here.

The seed of a plan sprouts in my mind.

Ensel clasps his hands together. "Girls, as you know, we had a visitor yesterday. A boy suffering from the ridiculous notion he could arrange a trade." At a sign from Ensel, Albin steps forward and grabs ahold of Delia.

I stifle the scream in my throat. This is my sister. I will save them all, but, most importantly, her.

Delia doesn't look up. She keeps her eyes on the floor, her body trembling. She grew up in Bryre's palace; though she is no stranger to fear, she has never known treatment quite like this.

"This girl," Ensel continues, "is apparently special." Albin yanks Delia's hair, forcing her to look up. Her eyes shine with unshed tears. "What is so special about you, my dear? Is that boy your brother? Your betrothed?" His eyes narrow. "Or is it something else?"

Horror creeps over me. Ensel can't discover she's Bryre's only living heir. She would be a valuable prize for the man who hates that city. Who knows what he'd do? Ransom her? Kill her outright so Bryre inevitably falls to ruin?

"I am not special, Your Majesty," Delia whispers. Terror quivers in her voice. I can smell the fear in this room, rolling off the girls in waves.

"I do not believe you," Ensel sneers. This time Albin drags Delia over to one of the long windows. My stomach turns. The man holds her up to the window by her hair and the back of her gown. She screams at first but then goes utterly still. Her head is out the window, with nothing but the sheer drop onto the cliffs and the ocean below.

"Does this ring any bells for you, girl? Any idea why you are special now?" Ensel taunts.

I can stand it no longer. I've been working at the knots holding my wrists together since we started up the stairs, and now they're loose enough to move my hands. I leap forward to wrench Delia away from the white-clad guard. Albin is so stunned by my behavior that I have Delia away from the window and back with the other girls in a matter of seconds.

He advances toward me, growling and pulling out his sword. If I defend myself, I will have to show my hand, my beastliness, ruining our chance to escape.

A deep, throaty laugh ricochets off the walls of the high tower room, vaulting my heart into my throat. Albin halts, and looks back at his king.

"How poetic. That boy condemned you to death to save that little thing, and yet you put your own neck on the line for her?" He laughs again, but stops as suddenly as he started. With a nod to his guards, he says, "Take them back. My Sonzeeki will eat very well on the next full moon." His eyes meet mine, then travel to Delia. "He will have two meals. Hopefully, he will find them satisfying."

I stumble down the narrow stairwell after the other girls, numb from head to tail. I sneak a look back in time to see the king and several guards disappearing into the floor. I was right. There are passages here.

Now I just have to find them. Before the next full moon.

We are forced back to our prison chamber and each of us is unceremoniously shoved inside as they cut the ropes around our wrists. The door clicks behind us, and I settle on my cot to think.

"Thank you," a soft voice says, startling me. Delia stands about five feet away, hovering like a frightened bird.

"You're welcome," I say, but when I get to my feet she moves back. We're making progress, but I terrify her still. Part of me longs to tell her I'm her older sister brought back to life, but how could I prove such a thing when my memories of her are so ill formed? I've tried so hard to remember, and bits and pieces have surfaced, but not enough to prove it beyond doubt. I would lose any chance of the girls ever trusting me.

I may not recall what I felt for Delia before as her sister, but I'm growing strangely fond of the girl. She is innocent, and the way she helps look after the younger girls is rather sweet. I understand better why Ren was desperate to see her freed. I must protect her. Even if she hates me.

Now she casts her eyes at the floor and turns away. I'm close enough to grab her arm, but really, miles stand between us. I have more in common with my dragon brother than I do with my sister.

Several of the girls come forward, and Greta positions herself in front of Delia with folded arms. "What you did back there, that was . . . good of you."

The girl with long black curls interrupts. "Why did you do it? What do you have to gain from helping us?"

My mouth drops open. "Why?" I echo. I hardly thought about it at the time; I simply acted. "I—I couldn't let them harm her. I told you, I am here to free you. All I wish to gain is our freedom."

Greta eyes me appraisingly, but the black-haired girl next to her looks dubious.

"Why didn't you give me away to them? Tell them I am a monster?" I ask.

"It wasn't in our best interest," Greta says, shifting her weight from foot to foot.

A fragile hope springs to life in my heart. "Does this mean you will work with me to escape?"

She frowns. "It won't be easy, and if we fail, we're all dead."

"If we do not try, we are all dead anyway," I say.

Greta smiles wryly. "We will have to take care not to get caught."

I stretch out my hand. "Excellent."

She hesitates, then shakes it. "I'm Greta." She nudges the black-haired girl forward. "This is Bree."

The girl frowns, but takes my offered hand. "I can't say I trust you, but every other attempt we've made to leave has failed. I suppose we don't have much of a choice but to try this, too."

A tall girl with pale blue eyes and hair so blond it's nearly white shakes my hand next. She rolls her eyes as Bree walks away. "I'm Mildred. You can call me Millie. Don't mind her. She was just as rude in Bryre. Always thought she was above everyone else because her parents have lots of money.

324

But money is worthless when it comes to the wizard, or that beast outside."

"That must be a hard truth to swallow," I say.

"As hard as a porcupine," Millie says. "But I'm glad you're here, and that you're on our side. The ocean terrifies me, even without the Sonzeeki. I just want to go home."

The red-haired girl I stole the night Greta got loose in the yard is called Fay, and she views my hand with wide green eyes.

"Your claws," she whispers. "They don't just pop out, do they? How do they work?"

I laugh uneasily. "No, they only extend when I need them to. They came from a large cat and were fused into my fingertips. You are in no danger from them, I promise." I shake her hand extra gently, though she still looks skittish when she walks away.

Greta continues to introduce the other girls, many of whom still cower. Anna, a girl with brown hair and eyes, refuses to shake my hand or even come near me. Hazel simply waves in my direction. She twists her light-brown hair nervously in her fingers. There are so many it is over-whelming. I may not remember all their names, but that is not important. All that matters is that I bring them home. People in Bryre love them and miss them.

One of the youngest girls, the one with the gold curls, sneaks up behind Greta, sucking on her thumb. She stud-ies me with wide-eyed curiosity. I smile at her, and to my shock, she smiles back. The only person who has ever smiled at me without my cloak is Barnabas. My heart clenches at the thought of his name. I shouldn't miss him, but a tiny part of me does. Even though it was all a lie. He loved that I was so easy to use, that is all.

The little girl steps out from behind Greta, and reaches her free hand toward my wings. "You have pretty feathers."

I have always thought the deep ebony color of my wings lovely, but no one, not even Barnabas, has told me they agree. "Thank you," I say to the girl.

"May I . . . may I touch one?" She squints up at me, still sucking on her thumb.

"I suppose so. What is your name?"

"Emmy," she murmurs. She gently strokes the bottom of my left wing while Greta looks on with a mix of wariness and amusement.

"So, what's your plan?" Greta asks. "You do have a plan?"

"The start of one, yes, but I need your help."

"We've learned a few things while we've been here that may be useful," Greta says. "I have been trying to get out of here since the day I arrived. I've been marched to the dungeons enough times that I know many of these halls by heart. But we'll have to hurry—the next full moon is only a few days away." She takes me by the arm and leads me to the nest of pillows in the corner as several girls join us. My claws nearly slip out, I am so overwhelmed by her sudden acceptance. No one touches me so freely when they know what I am. Even little Emmy had to ask first.

Yes, I like this Greta very much indeed.

DAY SEVENTY

TONIGHT IS THE FULL MOON. IT'S TIME TO PUT OUR PLAN IN MOTION.

The girls are not perceived as a threat. Only a handful of guards accompany them to the tower room each month. We will rebel against the guards and flee through the escape tunnel I spied Ensel using. It's risky, but it's our best chance of success.

The girls have pooled their knowledge of the castle and I have drawn out a crude map using a piece of curtain and hunk of charcoal from the fireplace. We are located in the main level of the palace, far in the back. The only way in and out of our room is the single heavy door, guarded by two soldiers. Our window overlooks the steep drop into the ocean, the salty scent so constant I hardly notice it anymore. This level also contains the public areas—the throne room, the dining hall, and sitting rooms, while the level above is for the king's private chambers. If the man had any family they would live there too, but from what we can glean, the second floor is not well inhabited.

On each side of the castle is a high tower—the one we climbed sits directly over the cliff face, and another on the other side is more inland. That is the entrance to the dungeons, and where most of the guards congregate. Below the tower is a basement level with the kitchen and servants' quarters. And below that are the dungeons themselves.

True to her word, Greta has been most helpful in mapping many sections of the castle, especially the dungeons and guardhouse. I'm lucky she was sick when I stole her from the hospital. She would've put up a serious fight under any other circumstances.

Bree and Millie were also quite observant when they were brought to the palace. Darrell took Bree through the servants' quarters and Millie through the kitchens. There are still some gaps in my map, but I feel confident we've pieced together as much as we can. I only hope it is enough.

The guards talk when they change shifts outside our door, assuming we can't hear through the thick stone walls. The girls wouldn't, of course, but my ears have picked up many things—feasts the king has planned, how little of those feasts he shares with his guards, and the irritating fool of a boy in the dungeon who spurns all food spared for him but water and bread.

Spending this time with the girls I ripped away from

their homes has convinced me there is something else I must do besides freeing them.

I must help Ren escape too.

If they can forgive me enough to put their lives in my hands, surely I can forgive him for betraying my trust. Did I not betray him first? How could I expect him to act any differently? He has paid the price for his foolishness. I care too much to leave him behind. Rosabel would never leave him to rot in a cell, and neither can I.

When the sun passes the midpoint of the sky, it's time for me to rescue Ren. My first duty is to free the girls from the castle, but I need his help. He can reach the town and at least secure a donkey to help the smaller girls move quickly when we reach the forest. The only entrance to the passageways that we've identified is in the tower, and it is far too risky to sneak thirty girls that distance. We're prepared to overwhelm the handful of guards that take us to the tower, and flee from there. Ren must be clear of the castle before we make our escape, but not so far in advance that anyone will suspect our plot.

"You're mad," Greta says. Millie nods agreement beside her, pale hair falling over her shoulder as we finish tying the bed sheets together into a makeshift rope. "If you get caught, the rest of our plans will go up in smoke." She folds her arms across her chest. Greta and the girls will still make their attempt without me if I do not return in time, but we all know that their chances are far better if I am with them.

"I will not get caught. I've told you: if Ren is free, he can help us. And I can incapacitate some of the guards while

I'm at it." While they've seen my full form, I haven't told them my tail can cause a man to sleep, for fear it may be a bitter subject. I'm not worried about the guards when it's only Ren and me. In fact, I have every intention of putting as many guards as possible to sleep. The fewer who are awake when we go up to that tower, the easier our escape will be.

"Is Ren really worth the risk?" Bree chimes in, scowling. Several of the girls knew of him because everyone did. He was the king's messenger. "Besides, King Oliver must have an idea where he went. Someone will come for him eventually."

I finish coiling the rope and tie one end to the door handle. A heavy steel bolt lies across the door to our room. Even if I could pick the lock, I couldn't get out without making a terrible noise and drawing far too much attention. Flying out the window and circling the palace might also be seen by unwanted eyes.

Scaling the castle walls, however, would be much less expected.

"That is true. But by then it might be too late. I wasn't always like this," I say, gesturing to my wings and tail. "Once I was a human girl, and Ren was . . . he was a dear friend. I have to try."

Part of me wishes to tell them I was Princess Rosabel, but I fear Delia's reaction. She's so skittish, she can barely stand to look at me. But ever since we mentioned Ren, she's been hovering nearby listening to our conversation.

"Ren can help us. I know it. He's a good friend, and

very smart." Delia gives me the briefest of smiles, but it is enough to fuel my resolve. In this, and this alone, she and I are on exactly the same page.

"Smart enough to land himself in the dungeons," Bree mutters. Delia's face falls.

Greta sighs. "Fine. Just promise you'll be back by sundown, Kym. If you're missing when the guards arrive, Ensel may decide to throw us all off the cliff."

I squeeze her arm. "You have my word."

Tucking my cloak behind my wings, I tie the loose end of the rope around my waist and hop onto the window ledge. The height is dizzying. It must be the cliff. I've never felt this way while flying before. The water below is dark and frothy, so unlike the clear rushing river water I'm accustomed to.

So much water. So vast.

It crashes against the cliff below in angry waves that grow higher with every turn. The beast lurks in those depths. I wonder if it's as big as Batu. I suspect it cannot be half so kind.

I take a deep breath, shoving down the pang in my heart when I think of my dragon brother. He is too far away to help me now. The castle is set on a hill, so the lowest levels sit below ground in the front of the building and have windows looking out over the water in the back. I only have to climb down for a few feet, then sneak back in one of the windows and make my way to the dungeons. For Ren.

I lower myself down. Immediately, the wind buffets me against the wall, yanking my hair out of my thick braid and tossing it back into my eyes. Clinging to the rope, I work my way down the limestone walls. I resist using my wings, but the wind whips and twists and slams me into the walls until I don't know which way is up. My wings spring out on instinct, flapping and using the wind to steady me.

It takes a moment to get my bearings; then I continue the slow progress. I pray no one looks out a window. I glance down again, and instantly regret it. A dark, hulking shadow moves beneath the water. Waves slide over it, revealing its massive, mottled green shell. My hands tremble. I remember how I felt the first time I faced Batu—utter terror. I thought he wanted to eat me.

This creature definitely does.

I'm glad I'm not flying. The dizziness would make that far more difficult here than over land. Concentrating on climbing is hard enough. I force myself to keep moving.

Do not look down, I tell myself, but it's a hard promise to keep. I creep along, buoyed by my wings, and finally reach the lower level. Voices echo from inside the nearby window.

I move toward the next, hoping this room will be vacant. No such luck. The sound of dishwater splattering and hushed whispers comes from it. A third window is farther off, and I move as quickly as possible. The wind picks up, and again I inadvertently look down.

At the very bottom of the cliff, the dark shadow rises, the top of the scaled shell peeking over the rippling waves. A black tentacle stretches out on the rocks. It writhes in the sunlight, revealing the round suckers beneath that attach to the rocks when it slams back down.

That's what it uses to drag the girls to the depths. I shudder, pull my eyes up, and crawl slowly to the next window, arms burning.

I wait above the windowsill for an entire minute, but hear no voices. I peek over the top, and find the room—a servant's chamber—blessedly empty. I slip inside, untie the rope, and rub the tension from my arms. With regret, I toss the rope out the window. My plan is to return by putting to sleep the guards in front of the girls' room, hiding them in an alcove or unlocked chamber, and sneaking in the main door. I can't leave such a telltale sign dangling in plain sight. Greta is ready and waiting to pull the rope back up.

In the shadowed corner of the room, I unfold my crude map. I'm not far from the kitchens, which puts me halfway to the dungeon entrance.

Before I venture into the hall, I check the position of the sun—it took longer than I planned to traverse the outer walls. This rescue will have to be a swift one.

With my cloak settled over my shoulders and my tail wrapped around my leg, I venture into the hall. Voices come from the kitchens, and I hurry in the opposite direction. This section of the palace is as drab as I expect, all stone walls and dirty floors. Candles and rusted steel sconces dot the walls, providing meager light. The shadows are plentiful, which is just how I prefer it. I am a creature of the night and dark corners.

When I hear the tromp of boots on stone, I vanish into an alcove, holding my breath and flattening my body into the small space. The pair of guards passes by, muttering something about food and courtiers. When their steps die down, I wriggle out and head for the dungeons once more.

The trick will be getting in and out without anyone raising the alarm. But I have my ways—and a few tricks left from my time with Barnabas.

As far as Greta knows, the only entrance into the dungeons is through the far tower. I have to duck into two more alcoves along the way, but soon I'm close enough to hear the sound of the guards' laughter trickling into the hall. My pace slows. A wide doorway gives entry to the room, and I catch a glimpse of several men at a table in the center.

I wait in the shadows, eavesdropping. Two more voices join the others. They made the rounds in the dungeons, but now rejoin their friends. A smile slides over my face. Perfect.

I pull the last vial of sleeping powder that Barnabas made from my belt. I know now it is magic, not science, that gives it power. But today, that power will serve my purpose, not his.

I slip out of the shadows and toss the vial inside.

It shatters, and sounds of confusion follow. A guard tries to run out the door, but the white smoke follows, curling around him until he's engulfed. It seeps into his skin like water into a sponge. He drops to the floor and I drag him back inside the guardhouse. I steal a set of keys from the largest man, who is hunched over the table snoring. The guards were gambling, and their gold and silver sit in a pouch on the table. I pocket it and dash down the stairs into the dungeon.

The walls are dank and grimy, which I discover when I reach out to steady myself on the narrow descent. I wipe my hand on my cloak in disgust.

The stairs take me to a warren of cells and halls. Men and women with hollow eyes, distended bellies, and parched lips stare at me as I pass. No Ren. What crime did they commit against Ensel? I wish I could come back and free them all, but I can't risk attracting that much attention.

Not until the girls are safe.

Perhaps someday I will be able to free them from Ensel's cruelty.

After passing four halls with no sign of Ren, I begin to despair. The last conversation I overheard about him was yesterday. Is he dead? Did he find his own way out? A faint hope blooms, but is quickly extinguished. The prisoners are chained to walls at the backs of the cells. They can't even reach the doors.

No, Ren is either here or dead.

I scour the next two halls, and my diligence is rewarded. At the end of the last one, a boy with brown hair, now dirty from the dungeon grime, is balled up on the floor with his back to me. My heart soars.

With no time to lose, I fly down the hall. "Ren!" I hiss, and his head snaps up.

I try the keys until I find one that fits the lock, and the cell door swings open. Ren stumbles to his feet, chains clinking.

"You came for me?" He stares in amazement. His clothes are ill fitting, hanging off him strangely. The king must not feed his prisoners well, if at all. "But I betrayed you."

I smile sadly. "I know."

He shakes his head, holding out his shackled hands. "Do you have anything to help with these?"

I fumble with the keys, then give up and use my claws instead. To my surprise, Ren doesn't flinch at the sight of my animal parts.

"Come on, we have no time to lose. You need to be free of the palace before I get the girls out."

Ren stands up straighter. "I'm coming with you. Delia is my responsibility."

"She's my responsibility too."

"You don't understand, I—" He runs his hands over his face and sighs. "Rosabel. When she found out the wizard was coming for her, she left a letter, asking me to look after Delia if the worst happened. I'm doing a fine job of it, aren't I?" He scowls at the floor.

"I will get her out. I promise. But I need your help."

I take Ren's hand and lead him from the dungeons up the narrow stairs to the guardhouse. It's so strange to feel the warmth of his fingers, after everything that's happened. Yet it still thrills me to be near him.

The burning hatred he felt last week seems to have cooled. Perhaps someday he will forgive me completely.

Ren marvels at the slumbering guards, poking one with his foot and grabbing a sword from another. I motion for him to follow me to the side door and creak it open and glance outside.

"The coast is clear. You'll have to run for the trees, and make your way down the path to the village. Are you well enough to do it?"

"Yes."

"Good. When you get to the village, see what you can buy with this." I hand him the gold I swiped from the guards, "A cart and a donkey would at least aid our getaway."

He pockets the gold. "Where should we meet?"

"In the forest, by the twin trees." I peek out the guard-house door once more. "Go, and be careful."

He smiles fleetingly, and steps through the door. Before he goes, he turns back and whispers, "I'm sorry."

Then he is gone.

It doesn't take long to pile the sleeping guards' bodies in the corner of the room. Returning to the girls' chamber is another matter. It is getting late, and I nearly make up my mind to attempt a flight back, but the wind howls louder than before. The waves crash higher, and thick black tentacles creep up the side of the cliff.

I can't bring myself to risk it. Not now.

I can't risk a shortcut that might end my life when we're so close to freedom. I must live so I can free these girls.

Instead, I tiptoe through the halls, ducking out of sight at the slightest hint of footsteps or voices. It is painfully slow going. I spent longer than I'd hoped in the dungeons and the sun creeps closer and closer to the horizon.

When I reach the stairs, footsteps ring over my head,

and I scurry to the crawlspace beneath it. My hammering heart threatens to break my rib cage. My tail and claws ache to be of use.

But here they are useless. The guards left unconscious in the guardhouse are bad enough, but I cannot leave a trail of sleeping bodies in my wake. Not if I want to get everyone out alive.

I hear a snippet of the conversation, and the name Barnabas brings me to full attention.

"Should be here within the week, they say," a woman's voice drawls.

A man sighs. "I do not like him. He makes the king even more insufferable."

Barnabas is on his way here. Even more reason to hurry.

When their footsteps fade, and no one else appears on the stairs, I bound up two at time.

Our hallway is in the unkempt area of the castle, far from the finery of the throne room and dining hall. Two guards stand on duty in front of the door to the girls' room. Few compared to the guardhouse, but effective nonetheless. The room has a single door, and the only other way out is the window that hangs over the cliff.

I slip into a nearby room to check the trail of the sun.

It is almost dusk. As soon as the sun disappears from view, Ensel and his guard will come to retrieve us.

According to Greta, they don't just take one girl—they take everyone up to the tower and make them watch. It's a sickening display of power, designed to torment the girls into submission. *Be good, and you might not be next* is the message they drill into them.

I don't have much time, and I need those guards out of the way. Our door is halfway down the hall—perhaps I can distract them. I search the room for something I might be able to throw down the stairs, causing enough noise that they'll investigate, but not enough to rouse the whole palace.

But before I find anything that would work, heavy boots tromp down a hall at the front of the palace. Guards, several of them. The sun slips away outside.

I'm out of time.

My stomach knots. I have no choice but to fly to the other window.

As though reading my mind, the wind slams the shutters open, startling me and sending me airborne.

Instinct. I may never fully get the hang of it.

I settle on the windowsill. The sound of boots grows louder. I leap off, catching the vicious wind in my wings. It buoys me up too high, too fast, and I spin out of control. It takes all my strength to avoid crashing into the castle walls.

I fly hard against the ocean wind, never looking down this time, eyes constantly focused on the window several yards away at the midpoint of the castle. I ride the air currents up, until I'm above the window. Then I plummet down, praying Ensel and the guards haven't reached the girls' room yet. The wind picks up as I get closer, making my stomach do flips.

I reach the window and grab onto the sill, digging my claws into the frame with all my might. The wind tries to rip me away, but Greta and Millie yank me inside.

"We've been worrying about you for the last hour. Haven't left the window since the sun began to set," Greta says.

"Thank you," I say, untangling my cloak from my body and trying to make myself presentable. "That wind is deadly." I shiver. "And so is that beast."

Greta's face turns grim. "You saw it?"

I nod.

Millie shudders. "Those tentacles."

Bree, skittish little red-haired Fay, and several others surround me, talking all at once. Even Delia, who has largely avoided me, draws near.

"Did you do it? Is Ren out of the castle?" Delia asks quietly. If she were not at my elbow, I'd never have heard her.

"Yes, he is. He's going to meet us in the forest."

Men's voices and the sound of the iron latch outside our door being removed echo from the hall.

"We're ready?" I ask Greta.

She smiles. "As ready as we'll ever be."

The girls hold out the dull spoons we've spent the last few days sharpening into knives, then bury them back in their skirts. I'd prefer they not need to use them, but I fear that will not be possible.

Any loss of life is on my head.

When the guards arrive to round us up and bind our hands, we are ready and waiting, and pretending to be the docile girls they think we are. Ensel is not with them. On the trek to the tower, we are silent. I know the plan is to offer Delia and me to the Sonzeeki, and I try to say something encouraging to her. But she simply nods and gives me a thin smile in return.

It's best she doesn't yet know I'm her sister reborn. She's too jittery as it is. Ren's rescue has calmed her somewhat, but finding out her older sister was transformed into a monster would only unbalance her further.

The trip feels shorter this time, probably because I know what lies at the end. I count a half dozen guards, including Ensel's captain, Albin, in the room when we arrive, making an even dozen with our escort.

Most I can subdue, and the older girls will overwhelm the rest. The little ones like Emmy will take cover where they can.

King Ensel stands by the window as we're ushered in, examining his "pet" with undisguised glee. My stomach turns. He enjoys this too much. I wonder if the rumors are wrong, if he angered the Sonzeeki purposely.

No wonder he and Barnabas are allies.

He greets us. "Welcome. Not a minute too soon. Our friend in the cove is getting impatient. Good thing we're giving him two meals tonight."

Greta and I exchange a look. The ropes tying the hands of the oldest girls are already loose and ready to rip free— the ends of those spoons are filed to an edge thin enough to surreptitiously cut through them while we journeyed to the tower. We've left just enough rope unsevered to keep the bonds around our wrists for the benefit of the guards.

Delia and I are dragged to the row of windows overlooking the cliff. The night wind tugs at our hair. Delia sends me a wild glance, and I put on my bravest face.

I will get her home.

Outside the window, the top of the Sonzeeki's shell glimmers in the moonlight far below. The glistening black tentacles work their way up the cliff face, and the heaviness of an evil presence weighs on us all.

As Ensel gestures to the guards holding us, my tail sneaks out from under my cloak and stings my unsuspecting guard in the leg. His face shifts from shock to slack and in seconds he sinks to the floor. The moment his hands release me, I leap onto the guard holding Delia and sting him, too.

The girls swarm, using anything they can grab as weapons. Millie trips a guard with a kick from her long skinny legs, while Greta tussles with another in an effort to steal his sword. Bree ushers Delia to the corner of the room where the youngest girls are, swiping a dropped shield on the way. Even Fay brandishes her makeshift weapon with only the slightest hesitation.

I've stung seven guards, when out of the corner of my eye, I see Ensel and Captain Albin open the trapdoor in the tower and slip away. I lunge forward, sliding one claw under the stone to keep it open. I switch to my cat's eyes and peek into the tunnel. Ensel and his man do not lurk below. Their footsteps ring, softer every second, from one direction in the passage. It's only him and Albin—if we go in the opposite direction, we may be able to get out before he can circle back with reinforcements. His entire guardhouse slumbers, which should delay them further.

What a cowardly king. He didn't even stay and fight.

The girls have either knocked out or tied up the remaining guards. Almost everyone bears the cuts and bruises of battle. We may not have size, strength, or weaponry on our side, but together we have disarmed and overwhelmed them with sheer numbers. I'm quite proud of my girls.

A quiet cheer ripples through the room. I can't help grinning, too.

Greta kneels next to me, squinting to see inside the tunnel. "Which way did they go?"

"To the right. We'll go in the opposite direction. Ensel is not a fighter. He'll have to go deeper into the castle to get help, which is exactly where we don't want to go. It looks like the other direction should take us to the cliffside near the forest. I incapacitated the other guards when I was in the guardhouse. Ensel will not have an easy time finding reinforcements to stop us and block the exits. It will be tight, but we can escape that way if we are quiet and swift."

"That is what we shall be." She squeezes my shoulder, and motions to the girls to gather around the trap door.

I leap down first, and signal it is safe and help the girls down one by one, until the tower above holds only sleeping and tied-up guards.

The girls rush past me into the long stretch of hall that slowly slopes downward, but Greta hangs back as she closes the panel. "Thank you," she says.

Hope spurs all of us through the passage.

It doesn't take long for Greta and me to come to the same conclusion: the passage circles the entire castle and has several offshoots that split the fortress like wheel spokes. What we need is one that goes all the way down, but we haven't found it yet. At regular intervals, peepholes appear by various rooms. I pause at each to determine where we are in the castle. The ballroom, a courtier's private chambers, another bedroom, and another.

As we walk, a memory of another castle struggles to surface. Bryre. A corridor like this, but better kept up. The once-me would come in handy here. She knew all about castles, and Bryre does have secret passages. I stop and close my eyes, focusing on breathing in and out, in and out. The images grow clearer. A boy running in one direction, a little girl in another, and I in yet another. Someone counts up to one hundred; then the sound fades. A grand room catches my eye and I duck in, breathlessly throwing back the ornate carpet. I pull up on a wooden handle embedded in the floor, revealing a passage below.

A passage down.

In the vision, I run as fast as I can, until I can smell the rose garden. I wait at the end of the hidden passage, giggling as the other children call my name . . .

"Kymera, what's wrong?" Greta's hand on my arm startles me back to the present. I lean against the wall. My face is slick with sweat as though I truly was running.

"You look like you're going to pass out," Millie says, her ghostly pale face hovering over Greta's shoulder.

"We need to find the king's private chamber. That's

344

where the exit will be."

Greta's face brightens. "Of course. They put it there so the king can escape if the city is attacked."

"This time it will be us," I say.

Greta grins. "We passed it on our last circuit. It is too full of finery to belong to anyone else. And it is the last place he would think to hunt for us."

"Well, let's get moving," Millie says.

I pause to listen, but hear no signs of pursuit. My tense muscles relax slightly. Ensel must have raised the alarm by now; if we don't find our way out soon, we never will.

Greta leads us to the room she saw through the peephole. As in each of the rooms we've passed, a door is carved into the wood of the wall or stone of a fireplace. For Ensel's quarters, it is a grand fireplace that revolves to let us inside a sitting room. It swings open easily. Ensel uses this often.

Greta directs a handful of the older girls to spread out. She hushes the younger ones, reminding them to tiptoe and stay near her. If I were a king, where would I want my escape route to be? Close at hand. Even in the middle of the night.

The bedroom. That must be it. The images from the once-me repeat in my mind—it was hidden under a rug directly next to the bed. A long, finely woven one runs the length of the bedroom. I roll it back.

The once-me was right.

"Greta!" I hiss. "I found it."

She gathers the girls while I pull the handle and open the passage. The youngest girls squirm with glee. Little

Emmy stops sucking her thumb long enough to grin in my direction. Even Bree looks pleased. I watch them with a twinge of sadness. How wrongheaded must I have been to think taking them from their home city and sending them off to a foreign country was a good idea?

I lower them each onto the stepladder and watch as they land on the dirt passage floor. When everyone is accounted for, I close the trapdoor behind me with the faintest of clicks.

This corridor doesn't see as much use as the main passage. It's dirty and damp; rats and spiders skitter in the shadows. Soon I smell the tang of salt air. A door lies ahead of us and we break into a run. I can't help thinking I hear footsteps behind us, but it's only the echo of many girls' feet.

We burst through the door into moonlight, a few feet from the edge of the cliff. The ocean spreads out ahead of us.

Millie utters a small gasp, and her skin takes on a greenish hue. I remember her telling me how much she fears the ocean.

"Take them down the path," I tell her, pointing to the steep path leading away from the castle.

She swallows hard, but does exactly as I ask. I hope having a task will help her stay focused.

Footsteps clomp from the passage. I spin into a crouch, dropping all pretense of keeping my cloak closed. Anyone coming down that passage will be terrified of me. That will work to my advantage now.

The girls file down the steep path, but Greta stands with me. "Go!" I hiss.

She glances from me to the girls and back to me. I shake my head. "Go!" She does, but checks back every few seconds. The footsteps draw closer and I curse under my breath. The girls' progress is slow and impeded by overgrown plants on the path. I focus my attention on the tunnel as our pursuers step out.

Albin leads, his white tunic a beacon in the shadows, with Ensel a few feet behind. Several more guards file after them, but not as many as I feared. I must have incapacitated at least half the palace's reinforcements when I rescued Ren.

"You took the girls," King Ensel howls. He stalks toward me, his captain matching him step for step.

"You have no right to make them pay for whatever mistake you made to anger that creature." The Sonzeeki swirls below us, no doubt getting hungrier by the second.

"Oh, but I do. I bought and paid for them, you see." Ensel and his captain edge closer. A handful of guards fan out at the tunnel entrance behind them as best they can. Only a few feet lie between them and the cliff's edge. I resist the urge to glance over my shoulder. Greta knows the plan—flee the city, then find the twin trees in the woods where Ren waits. I just need to buy them the time to get away.

"If the beast doesn't get a girl tonight to feed on, it will flood Belladoma," Ensel says, with a touch of real fear. "Homes will be destroyed. People may even die. That will be on your head."

I cannot tell whether Ensel has simply been making up

the tale that the monster will only eat girls, but right now he surely seems to believe it.

The guards begin to move toward the path and I cut them off, keeping ten feet between us and spreading my wings to their full span. Tail at the ready, cat's eyes and claws out, I draw myself up to my full height and hiss. Half of them turn tail and run back into the tunnel.

All the while my eyes are glued to Ensel and his captain.

"You cannot have them," I growl.

The king considers me, glowering. "That was a nice trick, putting most of my guards to sleep like that. You're one of Barnabas's, aren't you?" The glint in his eye disturbs me. "He told me about you, but I didn't really believe he succeeded. You even fooled me when you snuck into my castle to steal my girls." He and his captain move forward. "Albin, however, will retrieve them."

Albin circles, trying to draw me off the path, but I cut him off at every attempt. When I move to sting him, he feints away, grinning wickedly.

Ensel laughs. "Do not bother with that. Your father gave me the vaccine against your sting. I had enough to vaccinate my captain, too. Just in case something went wrong and you decided to run amok in my city." He *tsks* and shakes his head. "We could not have that, now could we?"

I crack my knuckles, wishing my claws had sharper points. Especially since Barnabas dulled the bite of my sting. He did the same for Darrell. All his minions protected against me. I wonder if he was afraid I'd find out too soon, or simply that I'd be furious when he finally delivered me into the clutches of Belladoma's villain king and his sea monster.

I position myself at the head of the path. "Barnabas is not my father," I say through gritted teeth. Ensel snorts.

"There is more of him in you than you realize. You are both so dedicated when on a mission."

At a nod from Ensel, Albin pulls a sword from the scabbard at his waist. Moonlight glints off the blade and my stomach flips. My tail has little effect on him. If I try to strangle him with it, he'll just hack it off.

I bristle and my body tenses, muscles coiling in my legs.

Albin feints at me, but I dodge him. Ensel's horrid, fleshy smile only grows wider as he watches, lighting a fire in my chest.

Albin lunges again. The blade sings past my arm and cuts a few feathers off my left wing. Pain ricochets through my body, but I refuse to cry out.

He catches a feather and tucks it into his belt. "A memento," he says, looking me straight in the eyes, "of the strangest kill I've ever made."

Prickling fear runs through my veins, but still I hold the entrance to the path. I must buy time for Greta and the others to escape, no matter the cost.

The vast weight of the ocean next to us bears down on me. If I can just get him off balance . . .

I lash out with my tail several times in quick succession in an attempt to knock Albin off his feet, but he lurches backward out of the way. Then he barrels toward me, determined to knock me off the cliff and end this fight. As I duck, I kick up—hard—and launch him into the air.

A thick black tentacle shoots up from the cliffside and yanks Albin, screaming, from midair and plunges back into the depths.

Ensel edges back to the tunnels. "If we cannot use the girls I bought, I will have to send one of the maids off the cliff."

Rage, long simmering below the surface, explodes. I scream and hurl myself at the king. The few remaining guards bravely try to intercept me, but I sting as I plow through them. One by one they fall to the side, some over the cliff, others on the path.

I do not care. They helped Ensel and Barnabas.

The king cannot move his large form back to the tunnel fast enough. I catch his leg with my tail and he slams to the ground. He yowls and unsuccessfully tries to skitter backward. I yank him toward me, then coil my tail around his waist and neck and squeeze.

"You do not want to do this," he sputters. "I can give you gold, jewels. I have magic charms and potions to offer. Anything!"

I stare into his pleading eyes. Not a shred of kindness lives in them.

"Power! Is that what you want?" he yelps. "I'll give you the seat of mine. I took it from the Sonzeeki—"

I squeeze harder in response, cutting off his fruitless offers.

I may not be able to kill Barnabas without being burned up by his magic, but at least I can stop *this* man.

"All I want is for you never to hurt another girl ever again," I say.

Ensel struggles against my grasp. "No, no—"

Before he can get out another word, I hurl the king off the cliff.

He sails into the air, eyes wild with terror, arms flailing uselessly. Then he drops like a stone. The sea catches him in its maw and swallows.

DAY SEVENTY-ONE

AFTER MEETING REN BY THE TWIN TREES, WE RUN ALL NIGHT, SKIRTING
Belladoma for as long as we can, then cutting back through
the main thoroughfare to the mountains. Ren managed to
buy a donkey, now laden with food and blankets, for the
smaller girls to take turns riding when they get too tired to
walk. In a few days, the girls will be home.

Not me. I don't have a home. I haven't decided where
I'll go once we return to Bryre. Perhaps Batu will take
me in.

The girls' excitement grows with every step we take
away from Belladoma. Emmy, who was the saddest of them
all when I first took them from Bryre, trots along beside me
for a time, chattering about her mother. Millie, taller than
everyone, keeps running ahead, though whether it's from

joy at being free or a desire to put as much distance between herself and the ocean as possible I could not say. Bree has ceased her scowling and even managed to shock me with a thank you.

I saved them. For real this time.

Ren spends most of his time with Delia, helping her down steeper paths and keeping her from tripping over roots. I miss his easy laugh and sparkling eyes. The smell of baking bread dusted with cinnamon. The boy he was before I took Delia away. Before he knew what I am.

Ren glances in my direction on occasion, but quickly looks away if he meets my eyes. I cannot tell whether he is still disgusted with me or embarrassed by his behavior in Belladoma. Perhaps it's a bit of both.

Delia still avoids me, but sometimes she offers me a strange sad smile. I can't fathom what it means, but I hope perhaps she's warming up to me.

A hand slaps me on the shoulder and startles me out of my reverie. I bite my tongue to prevent myself from stinging Greta.

"How much longer until we reach Bryre?" she asks, tugging Emmy along behind her. The little girl smiles around her thumb. I understand better what Ren meant, why he had to go after Delia. He was responsible for her, like I am responsible for them.

"A few days? Not long." I stretch my arms. "We'll have to march steadily over the mountains, but it can be done." I have not told them about the conversation I overheard in the halls. That Barnabas is on his way to Belladoma. The hair on the back of my neck prickles just thinking about it—I don't need to scare the girls, too. They're already on alert in case Belladoma's guards come after us. But without King Ensel to lead them, I doubt they will.

Emmy squeals and Greta picks her up and spins her around, kissing her cheeks. "See? We'll be home in no time!"

"I can see Mama and Papa soon?"

Greta laughs as she plants the girl back on the road. "Yes, and they'll be overjoyed to see you."

"As am I." The gravelly voice forces me to whirl and land in a crouch, claws splayed.

Darrell.

He got free. The merchant friends he mentioned must have finally rescued him. From the glint in his eyes, I imagine he's out for revenge.

The girls scream and run in all directions, but he grabs the nearest—Emmy—and clutches her to his chest. She whimpers. Ren appears by my side, barely contained rage on his face.

"This one should get me a fine price in Belladoma. Again," Darrell says.

"Let her go," I say. Blood rushes to my head as he pulls a knife from his pocket and presses the point to Emmy's neck.

"No," he says. "I don't think I will."

"Ensel is dead," I say. "There is no one to buy her. Let her go!"

He laughs and it rattles my bones. "I ran slave routes long before I met Barnabas. Ensel isn't the only one who'll

354

buy a good young slave."

Ren draws his sword, while the girls cry in the bushes down the road. Red fury clouds my vision. I won't let him hurt her. I growl.

"You can't touch me. Or else she dies."

I freeze with indecision. If I strike, Emmy will be dead before I reach him. My eyes burn, but I can't move. Darrell backs away into the trees that cover the mountains.

"We have to get Emmy back, Kym," Greta screeches as the other girls swarm us, pleading and crying. "We have to! I promised her!" Her face contorts, causing her tears to run in a zigzag pattern down her cheeks.

"I'm going after him," Ren says, but I grab his arm.

"No," I say.

He stares, shocked. "What do you mean, no? We can't just let him take her!"

"I won't," I say. "I need you and Greta to get the girls home safely. Guards may be coming after us. The girls need protection. And Barnabas might be in these woods, too, on his way to Belladoma."

Both Ren and Greta turn several shades paler at the mention of the wizard's name.

"What can we do against him?" Greta whispers.

"Evade him. Do not let him see or hear you. Keep the girls quiet and move as swiftly as you can. Do not light a fire; just eat the bread, cheese, and jerky in the supply bags."

Ren and Greta exchange a brave look, then nod.

"Good. I'll hunt Darrell down and get her back." Greta's lip trembles and I place my hand on her shoulder. "I promise

I'll do everything I can."

"Thank you," she murmurs.

I run to the forest, but glance back at the girls. Their faces are filled with desperate hope. I can't fail them again. We're too close to Bryre and freedom.

"Don't stop until you're inside the city gates," I say. "I'll follow with Emmy as soon as I am able."

I track Darrell until dusk settles in the mountains, the waning light covering everything with odd colors. Strange shadows loom at every corner and I switch to my cat's irises. The forest becomes clear—as does Darrell's trail. The broken brush, hoof prints, and ruts carved in the forest floor show he's dragging poor little Emmy in his cart. He must have bartered for a new horse. It's the only way he could have gotten ahead of me.

Emmy must be terrified. Was I terrified when Barnabas first took me? Did I know I was going to die? Or was I already dead before he brought me anywhere? I search my memories, but this one remains locked away.

I wish I could force it to the surface, even though it will be painful to bear. I need to know the girl I was.

I stiffen. Darrell's scent is stronger here. So is Emmy's. They're close. A scan of the forest reveals no other sign of them. I flutter between the huge trees, not wanting to be taken unawares again.

Fire crackles nearby. I must go higher. I leap into the nearest tree and scramble as high as I can and still have an unobstructed view of the forest floor.

About forty paces to my left is a depression in the forest, masked by an outcropping of craggy rock. Part of Darrell's cart peeks out from beneath the outcropping.

I alight on the ground, then fly to the top of the rocks. I flatten myself on the cold, hard surface. I can see over, but my cloak should conceal me from Darrell in the gathering darkness. Even with the fire.

He rests just beneath my hiding place. Emmy sits next to him, tied to a wooden chair that was once inside the cart. She's frighteningly still and pale.

I hate this man. He must be stopped. By any means possible.

With my claws at the ready and tail tense, I swoop down.

Emmy screeches. Darrell gasps as I pin him down. He laughs, and the flame of rage in me explodes into a bonfire. Furious instinct takes control. My body acts of its own accord, until that horrid smile is gone from his face.

The frenzy slips out of me like a ghost into thin air.

I whirl. "Emmy!" Her chair tipped over in the struggle. She doesn't move. I shake her, but stop when I realize how limp she is. Blood seeps through the front of her dress.

How can she be dead? She was fine a moment ago when I attacked Darrell—

A blade is embedded in her back.

Leaden numbness spreads through my legs. I gently move Emmy and examine the chair. A rope extends from the back, leading to Darrell's mangled body. It's sliced off now, but it was tied to him once. The smallest crossbow I've ever seen is secured to the frame of the chair.

It must have been set with the blade now sticking out of Emmy's back. The trigger was tied to Darrell. One flick of his wrist and she was dead.

My attack caused more than a mere flicking.

Grief hollows out my insides.

Flashes come fast and furious, wrenching me down to my knees.

Father—my real one, Oliver—calling my name, *Rosabel, Rosabel,* over and over.

A woman screaming, crying, cloth ripping.

Silence.

Barnabas looms above, and the once-me chokes. His hands squeeze my throat. I gasp, kick, scratch. His wretched smile freezes the breath in my lungs. Then darkness and ice.

Barnabas—the man I loved as a father—killed me with his bare hands. His awful, taunting eyes were the last thing the once-me, Rosabel, saw.

He lied to me. I was not collateral damage.

This is all my fault. Emmy is dead because I wanted Darrell to pay for his role in Barnabas's scheme. I gave in to revenge. Just like Barnabas. Had I stopped to consider a better way to rescue her, she might still be alive.

All she wanted was to see her mother. I failed her.

Her unseeing eyes stare up at me, more in confusion than accusation. I close them gently, my own tears springing forth as I cradle her small, limp body in my lap.

She'll never look on her mother again.

DAY SEVENTY-TWO

I WANDERED THROUGH THE FOREST ALL NIGHT, TRAILING THE PATH OF the moon and now the sun. I carry Emmy, bundled in an old cloak I found in Darrell's cart. The heaviness in my chest and the dull needling in my head plague me as I flutter between the trees. For a time I flew over the forest, but I am unaccustomed to flying long distances and now walk to rest my wings.

Spears of sunlight dash through the trees, striking my eyes every few steps. It must be midmorning by now. I've been creeping through the mountains for hours. My feet and wings ache. I must rest for a few minutes. I'm deep in the mountain range, no road in sight. Only trees, moss, and rock surround me.

An outcropping lies ahead, and I hike toward it. I set

Emmy's wrapped-up form in the shade of trees, then clamber onto the top of the rock and lie down. The sun peeks through the foliage, but all I feel is cold. Every time I close my eyes all I see is Emmy's pale, unmoving face.

But when I realize the rock beneath me is warm and it wriggles under my weight, I roll off.

"Batu?" I ask the mass of glittering granite scales, unfurling into a giant beast. I had not expected him to find me so far from our appointed spot by the river.

Sister. I was worried about you. His large yellow eyes look down on me with concerned affection.

Relief floods through me like a cooling balm, an emotion shared between us. "I was worried about you, too. When the city folk burned the forest, I wasn't sure you got out. And with the wizard on the loose . . ."

Batu huffs. *I wondered the same about you.*

Happiness trills over me as the dragon's emotions whisper in my head. I place a hand on his scaly snout. My heart is so full at seeing my dragon brother. "I missed you."

Batu leans into my palm. *I missed you, too, sister. Do not worry about me. When the wizard wanders the countryside, I hide. He has been out more than usual.*

"He may be out now," I say, remembering the courtier's words. "He was on the road to Belladoma just a few days ago. You must be careful."

As should you.

I can't help agreeing.

"I must apologize. I pleaded with you so many times to release me from the blood oath, so I could tell my false father about you." It grows harder to breathe with every word. "You were right; keeping you a secret was the only way to keep you safe. If you had released me, I would have led the wizard right to you."

The unpleasant taste of shame sours in my mouth.

Batu bobs his head at me, as if he's nodding. *You understand.*

Then an odd thing happens. A weight lifts from my chest, my skin tingles for a moment, and suddenly it's gone.

"Did you just . . . ?"

I have released you from your oath. It is unnecessary now.

I squeeze Batu's snout. "Thank you, but I don't think that is necessary either. My only interest is in keeping us— you, me, and Bryre—safe."

We would be safer if we hid together, sister.

My heart pinches. Hiding away with Batu, forgetting all these troubles with Bryre, is tempting. The girls are on their way home, after all.

Except for one problem: Barnabas. Who will protect Bryre if I abandon them?

"I wish so much that I could. But I have to stop Barnabas. Permanently."

Batu snorts. *That will not be an easy task.*

I hold my breath. "Will you help me? Together we could defeat him. I cannot do it alone."

A shot of dank, warm air blows over me.

My survival depends on outliving the wizard. And that is what I intend to do. I will live as I am now. In my homes, by the rivers and the mountains. Join me. My nest is empty without my clan.

Despair pools in my chest. "We have little chance against him without your help. I've heard what they say, that the one who kills a wizard will be burned up by his magic. Only another wizard or one made from magic can absorb it and survive."

Batu's yellow eyes consider me. *Are you not a magic creature?* he muses. *Killing wizards is dangerous business, but you may have more of a chance than you think. Still, I wish you would not risk it at all.*

I stare at my multicolored flesh. I had not thought of myself that way before. "I may be stronger than a human, but not like you. There cannot be much magic holding me together. I may thwart him for a time, but without you, Bryre will always be at risk of another attack. We could free so many people who live in fear of him. And then we could live wherever and however we want."

The giant granite body settles back against a tree. Batu sighs another shot of dank air in my direction.

You are so devoted to these humans. Are they truly worth risking everything?

Tears burn the backs of my eyes. I remember the glimmer of mischief in Ren's face when I first knew him, the kindness in Oliver's, and the shy hope in those of Delia and the other girls I saved from Belladoma. I think of all the shattered memories of my former life as Rosabel and how I treasure each one.

"Yes," I whisper, my throat suddenly reduced to a pinhole. "I was human once. I loved the city then, and I love it even more now. I set so many things wrong, and it is my responsibility to make them right. Leaving them to the mercy of the wizard is something I cannot do."

You know they would not do the same for you?

I nod, choking back a sob at the truth of it. I'm a monster. Perhaps a few in Bryre, like Ren and the girls, may forgive me, but most would not see past my wings or tail.

Batu swings his huge head down to eye level. His metallic scent fills my nostrils. *They do not deserve you, sister. If you change your mind, come to the river, and I will keep you safe in my lair.*

A rustling in the trees behind me draws my attention away from Batu. A sweet scent, like honey, lingers on the air.

It is not safe here anymore. I must go, and so should you. Farewell.

"Good-bye." I place my hand on his snout as Batu shimmers and fades, magic tickling my fingers. He is gone too quickly.

The hollowness inside of my chest expands. What if I fail to protect Bryre? What if I never see Batu again? Have I made the wrong choice?

Instinct flares, drowning out my doubts. Something is wrong in this forest. Something that scared away a dragon.

I need to get as far from this place as possible.

I gather up Emmy, and I run until the trees grow thinner and I can spread my wings. I must be close to the road by now.

I halt in my tracks. Voices and footfalls come from the direction I believe the road to be. Many people are traveling through the mountains today.

That is not normal.

As I sneak through the trees, I notice the men walk in a highly regular fashion.

It's an army. Headed directly to Bryre.

My blood curdles. Who would bring an army to Bryre? And why? King Ensel is dead—I should know, I killed him.

Barnabas. It must be him.

The uniforms the men wear are just like the ones the guards wear in Belladoma. Barnabas must've reached the city and rallied them as soon as Ensel's murder was discovered. But so quickly? It doesn't seem possible, yet here they are crawling through the mountains.

Magic. There is no other explanation. The speed at which the troops have overtaken me is unnatural.

I'll follow them, find out what they're about, then fly to Bryre to warn King Oliver. My real father. I will not let Bryre be massacred.

I need speed and stealth to warn Bryre before the army reaches them, so I find a place to bury Emmy's body—a grove filled with wild rosebushes. I think she'd like it, if she could see it. She looks so peaceful as I cover her with the earth, golden curls falling over her face. If not for the dark stain on her dress, she could be sleeping.

I regret that I can't bring her home. I hope Greta and her family will forgive me.

It is dark when the troops stop to set up camp. I circle the perimeter, staying just out of sight of the guards as I flutter between the trees. I must find the largest tent. The leader will be there. It's strange how memories return at the oddest moments. I know I've seen tents like this before—

The last time Belladoma came to Bryre. Of course. They attacked before I was born and came back again when I was Rosabel.

Perhaps Barnabas couldn't destroy the memories of the once-me; he only suppressed them. It's a powerful spell, whatever it is. But I am strong enough to overcome it.

The camp is set in a U shape at the base of a cliff. As I round another clump of trees, I catch a glimpse of a tent in the very center of the U, set near the rock wall of the cliff. It's bigger than the others and several guards stand at attention outside.

Whoever leads these men is in there. I fly out of the forest straight up the path leading to the cliff. If I can circle around them, I could sneak down the cliff unseen. My cloak is dark enough and they've placed no guards atop the cliff. Only a crazy person would try to sneak down from above.

That's exactly what I plan to do.

I lay my cloak on the ground, spreading it wide. With one claw I cut two foot-long slits in the back panel. My wings need to be free for this to work, but I'll want the cover, too. I secure the cloak around me, slipping my wings through the holes one at a time, and pull up the hood. My yellow cat's eyes slide into place. Black wings flap with anticipation. Claws clench. Tail winds.

I'm one with the darkness.

I'm ready.

I leap off the cliff and soar in a silent spiral to the lowest ledge. Shadowed figures move in the tent, but I'm too far away to hear any voices. I don't dare fly closer. The light of the fires would reveal my presence.

I'll have to scale the remaining distance of the cliff face.

Swinging my body over the ledge, I use my claws and tail to crawl down the last fifty feet.

Halfway there, voices resonate in the tent and I pause, clinging to sheer rock. They're almost familiar. My heart pounds as I risk a glance down. I hold my breath for a full minute to ensure no one is leaving and continue my descent. I hit the grass with relief.

I crouch behind the tent, on the small strip of earth between cliff and canvas. I hear them perfectly now and I peek under a flap. I jerk backward, clinging to the rock again, this time out of a desperate need to touch something solid and real.

Because what I just saw can't be real.

I killed him. I threw King Ensel off a cliff. Yet there he is, plotting inside his tent with Barnabas as though nothing happened. As though he were alive.

How can a dead man come back to life?

Barnabas. That evil wizard!

I was dead and he brought me back to life. Did he do the same with Ensel? Make him into some kind of monster? Or is this another spell that I know nothing about?

"We can take them here, through the back of the castle

walls." Barnabas's words float through the canvas, chilling me to the core.

"What about your spell? It no longer holds?" Ensel asks.

I can hear the smile in Barnabas's voice. "Oh yes. I found a loophole. A person meaning Bryre harm cannot enter through any gate or go over or under any wall of the city. So I destroyed the wall."

I have no doubt what he means. The rabid briar patch. It's been tearing apart the wall behind the palace for months. That's why Barnabas forbade me to investigate the monster plant.

"Brilliant. You're certain they'll be defenseless?" Ensel asks.

"Of course. They do not even patrol that area anymore. The forest is so thick no regular traveler would dare try to approach."

"Then how will we?" A hint of irritation enters Ensel's tone.

Barnabas chuckles. "No normal traveler can level an entire forest with one spell either. My elemental magic can force things to grow fast, or slow so much they reverse."

Ensel cackles. "You intend to ungrow a path through the forest for us?"

"Precisely. I hope to have a new influx of magic soon that will make it easy."

The sound of a hand clapping a shoulder rings in my buzzing eardrums.

"You're an excellent ally, Barnabas. Remind me never to cross you. To your health."

The shadows of two men toasting are cast onto the canvas. Bile threatens to choke me. I take off, straight up the cliff face. I no longer care who sees me. I'll fly due east to Bryre. No one can follow me that fast, not even on horseback.

This news cannot wait for stealth.

DAY SEVENTY-THREE

AS DAWN APPROACHES, I SOAR CLOSE TO BRYRE, LINGERING OVER THE forest. The place I once wandered through with impunity is more intact than I expected. Whole tracts of land have been burned like scars on the earth, but the people of Bryre managed to save most of it. Perhaps the flames just looked larger and more frightening to me because I was so close to them.

I locate my old crossing point and verify the guards are not near. With satisfaction, I notice Oliver has doubled the guard. I leap to the ramparts and back down into the city in seconds. I run through the streets and alleys, the sun now risen over the walls. I know where to find Oliver.

It's the last place I wish to go. And filled with the last people who want to see me, I have no doubt.

It doesn't take me long to find the small cottage that

smells like bread and cinnamon. I bound up the steps, throw open the door, and march to Oliver's chair by the fire. Delia sits next to him, one hand resting on his arm, the other holding a small bowl of porridge. Ren and his family sit around the table. I kneel, ignoring their stalled conversation and shocked expressions. The lines on the king's face have doubled since I saw him last.

"I come with much grave news," I say, never taking my eyes off Oliver. "But first I must know: did Greta and all the other girls arrived safely with Ren?" I've feared for them ever since I first saw the strange men wandering through the mountains. To my relief, Oliver nods.

"Yes, they arrived late last night. They said you'd be coming."

"They didn't mention you might bust our door down in the process," Laura says, earning a pointed glance from Oliver. Andrew places a hand on her arm that she shrugs off. Ren squirms, while Delia shyly swirls her spoon in her porridge.

"The king must hear all I have to say." I tear my eyes away from Ren and Delia, and return my attention to Oliver. "King Ensel's army is camped in the mountains, heading straight for Bryre. They'll be here by tomorrow afternoon."

Oliver sits straight up in his chair, brow creasing. "The girls said he died. They said"—he clears his throat—"you threw him into the ocean. That there was no way he could have survived."

"That is true. I did. But somehow he still lives. I don't pretend to understand it. Barnabas is with him and he plans

370

to bypass his own spells by entering the castle through the wall the briar patch has torn down. It's a loophole in the spell."

Oliver signals to Ren. "My boy, I'm afraid I must ask you to start delivering messages right now. Alert the council elders and have them rally our troops. Every able man must arm himself by dawn tomorrow." The king stands. "We must prepare to meet the invaders. They won't have a chance to get close enough for the wizard's plan to work."

Ren scribbles on a piece of paper.

"Wait," I say, "there is more. Darrell the trader killed one of the girls on the road back. Her name was Emmy. I—I couldn't save her. Her family needs to know."

A gasp slips out from Delia's lips, and Ren's father sets down his spoon. Oliver's hands clench into fists. "I am grieved to hear that. Darrell is a horrid man. We've had a price on his head for years."

"You will not need to worry about him any longer," I say. The king's eyes widen in surprise, but I detect a hint of approval, too.

"I know Emmy's brother and where her family lives. I'll deliver the news on my way back from alerting the council." Ren finishes writing down his messages, then dashes out of the cottage.

I rise to my feet before Oliver. An odd, searching expression creeps over his face, and I wonder if Ren told him who I used to be. I fear if he knows, he won't like what I have to say next.

"I will help you defeat Ensel. And Barnabas."

"My dear, I don't know that—"

"This is just as much my fight—more so, even—than anyone else's."

Oliver considers me for a moment. He nods to Andrew, his steward. They head for the private chambers in the back of the cottage. Oliver gives Delia's shoulder a squeeze as he passes.

But before he turns away, I catch a glimpse of something new in his eyes.

Pride.

DAY SEVENTY-FOUR

BY DAWN BELLADOMA'S TROOPS BEGIN TO APPEAR IN THE FOREST HILLS above the main road. King Ensel and his army do not attempt to mask their approach. They don't need to. The hills and woods provide a natural defense, leaving no good place for King Oliver to make his stand. It will also make it harder for us to find our attackers.

But we have a plan.

Guards surround the city, most heavily at the spot where the briars and thorns consume the wall. Barnabas and Ensel will head straight for it. The king, myself, Ren, and a platoon of soldiers wait between the trees in front of the wall for them to arrive. Ren's parents guard Delia somewhere in the city. Now that she's home, Oliver will not risk her being taken a second time.

Our troops are heaviest at this spot, but we've also bolstered the men at the main gate and the eastern and western gates, just in case Barnabas tries something unexpected.

Since I returned to sound the alarm, Bryre's people have been preparing. Stockpiles of weapons were dragged out into the square for any able-bodied citizen to take up. Farmers, blacksmiths, and bakers alike joined the regular members of the guard. A pallor of grim resignation hovers on every face.

No one can kill Barnabas without sacrificing themselves. No one really believes we can stand up to him and Ensel and win.

But no one wants to be a coward, either. Barnabas is only a man, after all. His skin can be pierced by a sword or arrow, but the magic inside him is what we all fear—what it will do to the person who takes his life.

And so we wait for Ensel and Barnabas to make their next move.

I stand apart from the battalion, avoiding the looks of fear and resentment that continually plague me in this city. Ren and I assisted the council with arming the city. I had to swallow my fears of these men who, not long ago, wanted to kill me. They only tolerate me now because they have been ordered to do so by the king.

But I hear them whispering. Many are convinced I am here as a trick. A spy for the wizard. The constant press of the crowd's gaze on my back makes me want to curl up somewhere cold, dark, and empty. But this is my mess, my fault—my fight. They may not welcome me, but I will defend them.

Restless not-quite-soldiers creak and mutter in their ill-fitting armor while the sun beats down on us all. Not long before midday, a commotion begins within our ranks. Someone shoves through the guards and meets with resistance. With a quick nod to Oliver, I flutter off to investigate. Several guards struggle to hold back a girl with a sword from entering the front lines.

"Greta?" I say, amazed. The guards loosen their hold and she shakes them off.

"Did you really think you could get rid of me that easily?" she huffs. "After what that trader did to Emmy and the horror Ensel put us through, I've got just as much of a stake in this fight as any of you."

My cheeks flame with anger and sorrow. "I'm sorry, I tried to save Emmy, but I . . . I could not." I can hardly look Greta in the eye. I made her a promise, but I could not keep it.

She squeezes my arm. "You tried. That is all anyone can ask." Despite her bravado, grief shines in her eyes. "Now take me with you to the battle. I refuse to sit idly by while Ensel kills us all and takes the city for himself."

I have to admit, Greta is a fierce ally. I lead her back to our group by the hole in the wall. Greta gasps when she sees the monster briar and the gaping hole in our defenses.

"What happened?"

"The wizard's enchanted plant—part briar, part creeping

vine—has been pulling this wall down little by little every day for months. Barnabas has been planning this attack with Ensel for some time."

"What a devil," is all she can say.

Soon sounds of skirmishes and striking swords ring through trees. Ensel's men have met our scouts. I itch to join the fight, but I'm determined to defend the king. My once-father.

I'll do anything to keep Barnabas from succeeding in his plans.

The sun is high in the sky when the first soldiers appear in the trees, but the thick forest makes it nearly impossible for our archers to shoot. Dark clouds gather overhead as more and more soldiers weave through the woods.

Barnabas must be near. My heart stutters an uneasy pattern, and my claws unsheathe of their own accord.

I've debated all day and night what I should do. Batu declined to help us fight the wizard, but someone has to stop him. I've never wanted to kill someone so much in my life, far more so than when Barnabas told me half-truths of how the wizard destroyed my family. He did much worse.

But killing him has a price. And it's terrifying.

Our archers hold their bows high, ready to fire at the king's signal. But when the trees begin to thin and vanish into the ground, they lower their bows. It's as though the trees' lives unwind until they are nothing more than seedlings. Several men flee into the city. No one wants to die the horrific death that comes with killing a wizard. The rest shift uncomfortably, but stand their ground.

I smell him and his corrupted magic before I see him. The familiar, sickly sweet, honeyed scent.

Barnabas enters the tiny clearing he's made in front of the wall, wearing a heavy black cloak I've never seen before. It moves strangely, as though it is made of shadows. His silver hair is wilder than ever and his eyes have a faraway look in them. The air around him shimmers, like he is not quite in focus. His hands move in circles, and the storm clouds above us expand and darken. A flash of lightning crackles over our heads, and thunder rumbles loud enough to shake the ground. Fear swims through the ranks. Everyone's nerves are strung as tightly as bowstrings.

Ensel, flanked by several guards, guides his horse a few feet behind Barnabas, relying on him to elicit enough fear to get them close and clear the path in the thick woods. All of our battalion save a few brave souls shrink back, forming a line of people in the hole eaten through the wall. The foundation, though covered with briars, remains intact. I only hope it is enough to keep them out.

Ren lunges forward at the sight of them before I can stop him. A line of guards blocks the path to the wizard and their king with swords raised, and Ren halts, growling.

"Ren!" I cry. "They'll kill you!"

Oliver puts a restraining hand on my shoulder. "You will only distract him. That will indeed get him killed." His voice is tight with anger as he glares at Barnabas.

A balloon swells inside me, threatening to pop. Oliver is right, of course, but that has no bearing on my desire to protect Ren.

Greta stands beside me, sword at the ready, silent and strained. I have no doubt she wishes to do the same thing. But it is my duty to protect them all. I seethe quietly, waiting for an opening.

Ensel laughs from behind his host of guards and shouts to Oliver. "What's this? Sending your best?"

Ren charges again, but Barnabas waves his fingers and Ren soars through the air, smashing into the city wall. He slumps to the ground, blood trickling down his cheek, as the force of the wind shoves our guards back and whips my hair around my face.

I don't move an inch. Barnabas hurt Ren.

A flash of lightning strikes the ground just in front of the wall's foundation, scaring the guards back a couple more feet.

A howl escapes my throat. Red is the only color I see. I'm swallowed up in it.

Red. Blood. Fury. Instinct.

I take off into the air, claws drawn, tail poised to strike. I hate this man more than anything. He hurt Ren. He wants to hurt my real father. My sister, my friends. He wants to hurt my city.

He lied to me to make me hurt them too. That is unforgivable. I may not be able to kill him without dying, but surely I can incapacitate him in some way.

As I swoop down at Barnabas, I dig my claws into his back, ripping his black cloak in the process. I land on my feet behind him. He turns to stare at me for a moment, stunned. Then he laughs. It ricochets through my brain, fueling my anger.

Shadows curling out from his hands yank my feet, sending me crashing down to the forest floor. Ensel's soldiers swarm me. Out of the corner of my eye, I see Barnabas attempt to pass through the wall, and hesitate at the foundation. I lash out with my tail and kick and scream, desperate to get to him, but there are too many hands, too many men charging me.

I am animal. Instinct takes over.

My body moves according to its own will, thrashing and clawing and stinging. Screams surround me. I crouch, quivering, on the forest floor, scanning the area for any other trace of attack. Blood coats my face, my hands, my tail, even my feathers. More than a dozen mangled bodies lie at odd angles between the trees.

Near the wall, Barnabas's scowling form shimmers and fades from view. "No!" I cry. But it is too late.

Oliver and the Bryre guards gape, as do Ensel and the rest of his troops. Frustration explodes inside my chest. I settle my gaze on Ensel. He tries to guide his horse back farther into the ranks of his guards. I lock on my new target and pounce. I knock him off his horse, and we tumble to the ground. Ensel scrambles to his feet, wild eyed and red faced once again.

The coward runs.

I am the fox, and Ensel is the rabbit. We careen over the rocks and trees and leaves, ever faster and desperate.

Behind me, more fighting breaks out near the hole in the wall, but I can't help Greta and Oliver now. Ensel can't be allowed to escape.

A landmark I recognize lies ahead—a blind drop into the ravine. It comes up suddenly, so it's easy to miss unless you know what to look for. Ensel will have to veer in one direction to avoid it.

I can take the path ahead and cut him off. He'll come right to me.

I aim for the grove about twenty paces from the ravine, flying straight up into the trees. My tail is taut and prepared to sting. Just because Barnabas gave him the antivenom doesn't mean the sting won't hurt.

I want to hurt him. I want him to feel all the terror of every girl he paid Barnabas to steal.

I don't wait long. The second he enters the grove at a breakneck pace, I drop like a stone. He stumbles and splays on the ground, but I remain standing. Barnabas used to say I land like a cat—upright and cocky. He was right.

Ensel scrambles back, reaching for the sword that slipped from his grasp when he fell. I step on the hilt. His hands scrabble at it, but it doesn't budge. I place my other foot on his chest.

I sting. And sting. Until his shirt is shredded and bloody, and his eyes are dull.

By the time I reach the city walls, dusk hovers over the monster briar. Scattered boot prints near the wall are the only remaining trace of Ensel's army, and Oliver, Greta, and Ren are nowhere to be found. I clutch the arm of the nearest guard. "Is the king alive?" I hold my breath until he nods with wide, frightened eyes. "Where is he? Where is

Ren?" I choke out the last word.

"The—the king went back to the palace. Ren was taken to his home. I think that girl went with him." I release the guard, then run straight to Ren's house and burst into the kitchen. Laura doesn't stir from his cot by the fire. Only when I fall to my knees by Ren's side do I realize Oliver is back in his usual armchair. Greta and Delia huddle on a settee near the fire and glance up at my entrance.

I clutch Ren's hand. His face is ashen, and a strip of bandage winds around his head. He doesn't move. Despite the pallor, his face is peaceful. Hope blossoms in my heart.

"How is he?" I whisper.

"The doctor says he'll recover. He's been unconscious since he got here. His father is delivering messages across the city in his place." Laura's tone is clipped. She doesn't want me here. One glance at my bloody clothes, and I can't blame her.

"Kymera, my dear," Oliver says. "The attack is over. You terrified Belladoma's mercenary army. Most of them deserted after you took out that entire regiment in seconds. Once word arrived that Barnabas had vanished and King Ensel was dead, they ran."

Greta smirks. "No mercenary will keep fighting if the man paying them is no longer around to do so."

Oliver takes my free hand—despite the caked blood and flesh. "I know you suffered because of what Barnabas tricked you into doing. But thank you. You have my deepest gratitude."

My jaw drops as my skin turns a deep shade of red.

"Thank you, sire. What about Barnabas? Do we know where he went?"

Laura spits at the mention of Barnabas's name. I ignore it and focus on Oliver.

His expression hardens. "Barnabas was up to his usual tricks. He distracted me and the guards by wrapping tendrils of weed grass around our ankles while he tried to cross the boundary. Thank heavens the foundation was enough to prevent him from entering the city. By the time I got free, he'd vanished." Oliver examines me with an odd expression. "Are you hurt, child?" It takes me a moment to realize he's asking how much of the blood on me is actually mine. My ribs hurt a little and scrapes zigzag all over my body from running through the forest without regard to branches.

"No—at least I don't think so."

He waves to Laura. "Would you draw a bath for Kymera, please?" She leaves the room at once after a curt nod. "I'm sure she will wash your clothes, too, and help if you have any wounds that need tending."

The thought of bathing here makes me oddly uncomfortable. "I don't know that I could. I should not impose. I just wanted to talk to you. There's much I need to tell you, sire."

He places a soft, warm hand on my cheek. It almost reminds me of Barnabas when he was pretending to be my father, but with Oliver it is different. The difference between genuine care and a mask of lies. "I insist. We can talk more tomorrow. Tonight we must rest. Who knows what the morning will bring?"

Delia smiles shyly at me, and Greta places a firm hand on my arm. "I'm glad Ensel is gone. And I'm glad you're on our side."

I smile. "And I'm glad you're on mine."

Laura reappears and ushers me down the hallway into a steaming room. My body aches for the water and to relax, even for an instant.

"You can take your things off behind that screen. Scrub until all that guck"—she wrinkles her nose—"is off you. I'll put a fresh towel and a nightdress out."

I do as I'm told, but before I can slip into the water, a scratching at the window startles me. Curling my wings around me, I tiptoe over as the scratching gets more frantic.

Hovering outside the window is Pippa. I thrust it open and she zooms inside, nearly knocking me over with her frenzied flapping and tongue licking at my cheeks. I bat her away, laughing. I can't believe she lives. I was so sure she had perished in the cottage fire along with the chickens.

I scratch her between the ears, just like Barnabas used to do. She whines happily, leaning into my hand. "I missed you, too," I say.

The tub is just big enough to accommodate my tail, wings, and girl's body. Pippa curls up by the side of it and proceeds to snore up a fearsome storm. I pop the bubbles with my barbed tail as I let the warmth work its way into my sore muscles and feathers and scales.

We're safe. For now.

DAY SEVENTY-FIVE

I PACE THE GUEST ROOM IN REN'S HOUSE, WAITING TO BE CALLED FOR breakfast and meet with the king. Pippa paces with me, hovering a foot off the ground. I woke with the sun, and the later the hour gets, the more impatient I become. The king has been so kind to me. I've decided to tell him everything.

That I'm his daughter.

That Barnabas made me from her parts and the parts of the other girls, too.

That I'm monstrous. A killer, a beast.

Then I'll beg his forgiveness.

I don't know where I'll go after that. I could share Batu's cave, but Barnabas is loose and that makes me uneasy. The only home I remember is with that evil man. The cottage in the woods with goat-chickens that was burned to ash by the city folk. I don't belong in Bryre, however much I may want to stay here.

When I smell porridge cooking over the fire, I fly through the door and down the hallway. Laura is there, but no one else.

"Where is everyone?"

"They went to the palace," Laura says, stirring. "The king decided the council is wrong. He won't hide anymore."

"Already? Wait, Ren is awake?"

Laura smiles. "Yes, and well enough to walk, too."

I fly out the door before I hear another word. I don't bother with the palace gates but land on the marble steps. I try to compose myself, but I'm too excited. Ren is fine. He's awake and walking and talking and—

And probably still disgusted by me, too.

More people than I've ever seen here mill around the palace and grounds. They crowd the hallway, buzzing with chatter, waiting for something. I push through in spite of their gasps and protests, while loud whispers spread through the crowd like wildfire. The guards at the entrance to the throne room part when they see me.

It's just as I saw in my visions. Sunlight on silver, everything glowing with glorious light.

Oliver sits on his throne with Delia on a low bench beside him, while Ren and his father stand a little ways behind them. I kneel before the king. A hush falls over the crowd at my back. The weight of hundreds of gazes presses into my wings.

"Kymera, I hoped you'd come this morning."

"What is all this, sire? I thought the palace was closed." I whisper. I had not anticipated the audience, and its presence threatens my resolve to confess everything. But I must.

Oliver waves a hand. "I felt it would be best to address my people's grievances today. It's been a hard year for us all and I've been away far too long. Now what can I do for you?"

"I must ask your forgiveness." The tips of my ears burn as a low murmur rolls through the gathered people.

"Whatever for?"

"For everything I've done, everything I am." I twist a wayward thread on my skirt around my finger, uncertain where to start. "I helped Barnabas steal the girls and send them to Belladoma. He tricked me. He told me we stole them from the wizard and sent them somewhere safe, but I should've known better. I just—I couldn't tell what was true." My hands clench in frustration; I'm already making a mess of this. And publicly, too.

"I know, Kymera. Ren told me. He was quite angry with you for a time, though I believe he's coming around."

Ren stares at the marble floor, while a hint of red creeps up his neck. Could that be true? Could he have forgiven me? That's more than I dared to hope. But I must confess everything.

"You know I killed Darrell the trader, but what you don't know is that Emmy died because of that. He had her tied to a chair rigged to stab her in the back. When I attacked him, it set it off." Sweet little Emmy, who only wanted to see her mother and father again, and I couldn't save her.

A murmur runs through the crowd, and it turns my stomach.

"There's more. I also accidentally killed one of the girls. She wasn't strong enough to withstand the venom of my barb. It's only supposed to put people to sleep." Tears slip from my eyes, as I remember her still form in the cold box in the lab and my horror at seeing her body in the city. "I'm a monster."

"I know."

My pulse quickens. My mouth is waxy and dry. The crowd is dead silent, like they are all holding their breath. This next part I'm certain Oliver doesn't know.

"I . . . I was your daughter."

The room goes perfectly still. Oliver's advisers, huddled in one corner at a long table, gape in my direction.

He reaches for my hand. "I know that, too."

I gasp. "But . . . but . . . how?"

A spark flares in his eyes. "Because I know Barnabas. What better way to punish me than by transforming my firstborn into a monster and using her against me? He's deranged and it's just the sort of thing he would do. I suspected the first time I met you. You had such a vague past and your eyes were—are—so familiar." His face softens and he squeezes my hand. "What he did to you, it is not your fault. You were Bryre's princess and my daughter, and owe no one an apology for that madman's crimes."

The murmurs return and swell into an outright rumble. My entire body is aflame with embarrassment. I should have waited until tonight and spoken to Oliver privately. Here

I'm only providing fodder for the gossip mongers, though it's much too late to turn back.

"I'm sorry for everything I did. If I could take it all back, I would."

Oliver straightens up. "One thing in all this struck a chord with me. In everything you did, you were motivated by a desire to help others. To protect Bryre and its people."

My mouth drops open.

"Granted, you were gravely misguided, but your intentions were pure. That's why I want to make you an offer."

My gaze snaps up to meet Oliver's. "What do you mean?" The rumbling audience grows louder.

He leans forward and whispers in my ear. "I know you don't have a home here in the city. I imagine you're feeling rather alone now, are you not?"

I bow my head, not sure what to say.

"You were my Rosabel once. I'd like to fix that." He leans back and speaks louder, his eyes shining more than they did before. "Kymera, will you accept the title of City Guardian and swear to protect Bryre and its occupants as long as you live?"

I don't have to hide. I can help, and I won't have to conceal what I am. I stand, wings flapping and tail twitching.

"Yes."

To my shock, this is met with cheers and applause. I whirl around, staring at the people gathered in the room. They are . . . smiling. Clapping. Gone are the fearful stolen glances. Replaced by something else—could it be pride? Could these people possibly want me to remain in the city?

Happiness blooms under my ribs, the pressure bringing tears to my eyes.

"Then it is so." Oliver turns me back around to kiss my hand. He whispers, "Go. Enjoy the beauty of a late-summer day while it lasts. We will make plans to defend Bryre again soon enough."

"Kym," Ren places his hand on my shoulder, this time without flinching. It's the first time he's been able to do that since he discovered what I did. It warms me and I cling to that euphoric feeling. "You belong with us. My family, and your family," he says. Delia grins at me from over his shoulder, actually meeting my eyes this time. "We all agree. Even my mother. Our home is yours."

DAY SEVENTY-SIX

ONLY ONE FULL DAY PASSES AFTER ENSEL'S DEFEAT BEFORE KING OLIVER summons me to the palace. That is all the time it took for rumors of the wizard to reach the boiling point. A scout was found wandering in the forest only this morning, disoriented and devoid of all his memories. His wife and daughter are beside themselves because he no longer remembers who they are.

Now that I'm Bryre's defender, I must find my false father—and a way to destroy him.

My feet tap of their own accord as I wait for the guard to let me into the throne room. I have always loved the city, but for the first time in this life, I finally feel at home here. I can run freely through Bryre. No one hunts me now. No one is allowed to.

I'm astonished at the welcome I've received. Even Laura has become less prickly toward me. I could not ask for more.

Yesterday, after I settled into the guest room in Ren's family's home, we explored the city in daylight—at last!—but it was marred by the dark cloud of the wizard hanging over us.

Barnabas will come back to finish what he started sooner or later. If the reports are true, it seems he already has.

The city's guards remain on high alert and have begun repairing the outer wall where the briar plant ate through. The work they do today will be torn down by tomorrow, but at least it should slow the process. My hope is bolstered by the fact that the foundation kept Barnabas out.

King Oliver and Delia have been practically inseparable since she returned. It both pleases and saddens me. Oliver shows me great kindness, but it cannot be easy to feel real affection for a monster.

I've peppered Ren with questions about Rosabel. It's strange to hear about one's former self and not recall most of it. Some things he says trigger memories, and they are as precious to me as the new ones I make now. Sneaking out to the market through a tunnel in an old broken-down fountain. A thick maze of hedges with a small, secret garden at its heart. Ren and Delia and I stealing sweet rolls fresh out of the oven from the kitchen, then gobbling them down in the alcove beneath the stairs before the cook could catch us.

Barnabas destroyed that. All his frustrations, taken out on poor King Oliver and his family. And on me.

Me, the monster girl made up of the pieces of Bryre's

children. Does a small part of them remain in me like Rosabel and her foggy memories? Who am I really? While I may have begun as Oliver's daughter, I have since become something else entirely.

I was created to destroy—but I learned how to love instead. Barnabas twisted that love for the city into something wretched and evil, but I overcame that. I rescued the girls, I earned back Ren's trust, and the respect of the king.

Now the only thing I want to destroy is Barnabas. For Bryre. For all the people who died at the wizard's hands. I am them, and they are me. And most importantly, for all the people I love who still live.

When the doors open, I rush by the guard before the words "The king will see you now" are even out of his mouth.

I slide to a stop in front of Oliver and kneel at his feet. "My king," I say. The words cause a thrill to course through me. I have a king, a country, and a real purpose now. I'll do anything to honor that and keep them safe.

"My dear, there's no need to stand on formality." Oliver motions for me to rise and I sit on the stairs by his feet.

"You summoned me because of the guard who lost his memory, yes?" I ask.

Oliver nods. "I did, in part. First there is something I want to show you." He offers me his arm.

Puzzled, I take it. Oliver leads me into a sector of the palace where I haven't ventured before, then down into the depths of the building. While some areas of the castle are pristine, many more than I remember are now slowly being eaten away by the briar. It grows steadily colder as we descend. The lack of light doesn't trouble me with my cat's eyes, but I marvel that Oliver seems to know it by heart. The walls are a somber gray stone, as is the walkway beneath our feet.

We turn down a long hall that leads to a vast chamber. The walls are honeycombed with alcoves, many of which are half destroyed by long, clinging roots poking out at odd angles and wrapping around the stone columns that hold up the ceiling. These roots are pitch black, reminding me of the Sonzeeki's tentacles. The monster briar plant is deeply embedded in the city. It will not be easy to get rid of.

Oliver walks directly to a raised dais in the center of the room and suddenly I understand why he knows this path so well.

It is the royal crypt.

His wife—my mother—is in the largest stone box on the dais. I run my hands over the form carved in the lid of the marble grave. Her face with its wide eyes and high cheekbones feels familiar. My skin tingles as a new memory rushes forth, taking over my vision.

A woman with bright gold hair and sparkling blue eyes gazes at me. Her soft hand whispers across my cheek. "I know it is hard for you to stay in the palace. But sometimes queens must make the hard decisions. Someday, when you are queen, you will understand."

Oliver clears his throat, and the vision slips away. I realize I hover close to her face with my hand resting on her cheek. "Her name was Aria, and she was just as beautiful as the song she was named after," he says.

I blush. "I'm sorry," I say. The warmth from the memory trills over me. Warmth, mixed with Rosabel's frustration and deep love for her mother. No, not just Rosabel's mother—my mother. In the memory, she wore that blue dress I've remembered before.

"Do not be sorry. This is why I brought you here. What Barnabas did to you is abhorrent, but you should know where you came from. Who you really were. I know you do not have many memories left of your mother. Ren told me you cannot see her face in any of them." His eyes shine. "I am so sorry Barnabas stole that from you too."

I take his hands. "He didn't take everything. I remember pieces. Some of you, and Ren, and Delia when she was very young. Someday they might all come back. Even the ones of my mother. In fact, I think this just shook one of her loose. She seems as kind and lovely as I'd hoped."

Oliver squeezes my hand and smiles. "I am very glad to hear that. If . . . If I can help in any way, say the word. Sometimes it is hard to speak of Aria and Rosabel, but having you here, whatever form you may have been put into, is like a second chance."

"Thank you." I swallow the lump in my throat, and turn my attention to the smaller box.

Rosabel. I hover over the carved image of my former self. If it is true to life, it means I was beautiful too.

"Do you remember that you—she—tried to save us?" Oliver asks. "She decided to give herself up to the wizard because we could not. But he got here first, and in the end it did not matter anyway. He is evil to the core."

As I stand face to face with my own empty crypt the world sharpens into a single point of purpose.

Rosabel was prepared to do what I've been unable to. Give up her friends, her family, her life to keep them safe. She was ready to make the ultimate sacrifice.

Instead, she became me.

I've hemmed and hawed long enough. If Rosabel had the courage to be so brave, I do, too. She loved these people. This city.

I love them, too.

I can ensure Barnabas never does this to another girl, another family, another city again.

If what Batu said is true—that I have a substantial amount of magic in me—I might have a chance of survival. Of living out my days with my human friends and family, and my dragon brother.

But even if I don't survive, it is the only way to keep those I love truly safe.

Rosabel understood it was the right thing, the only thing, to do.

And now so do I.

"Come, child," Oliver says, placing a hand on my shoulder. "I did not mean to upset you."

My face is wet, and I brush the tears away, filled with renewed determination. "No, I needed to see this. Thank you."

He leads me away, back to the throne room. My thoughts return to the matter of finding the wizard.

"Do we know where Barnabas hides?" He must be somewhere in the forest, but I have yet to smell a trace of his scent on the wind.

Oliver shakes his head. "No, but we have patrols in the forest."

"He does not have many places left to hide. He'll attack soon. I just wish we knew when."

He sighs, but his grip on my arm tightens. "Barnabas never was one to make things easy."

"He's still in the area for you and me, and probably Delia for good measure. Aria's refusal to marry him, and your refusal to hand over Rosabel when she was a baby, ruined his careful plans to steal all the realm's magic. He's fixated on revenge. He'll finish what he started."

We reach the main hall, and Oliver settles onto his throne. "I have no doubt you are correct, and with the foundation almost gone where the briar tore through the city wall, he will attack soon. Even with the work our people do, the more they build it up, the faster the briar tears it down. If he tries to get into Bryre again, that's his only possible entrance. I have guards stationed there around the clock, though he is more likely to strike at night. Dark magic is more powerful then, and he will do anything to have an advantage."

"Then I'll join the guard tonight. He may be able to trick them with magic, but he won't slip past me."

I turn to leave, but Oliver catches my hand. "Be careful, Kymera." A mix of pride and fear resides in his eyes.

"I will. So should you."

He lets me go and I stride out so fast I may as well be flying even though my wings are furled. The moment I hit the palace's rose garden, I take off. Barnabas will be at our gates all too soon.

It does not take me long to prepare. Ren is off delivering messages for the king and council, leaving me here by the fire with his mother, Greta, and Delia. The latter two hardly knew each other before Belladoma, but have since become great friends. I help myself to a bit of bread and cheese from the table, while Pippa whines by my side for scraps. I scratch her head absentmindedly, then wander off to my room. My mind is abuzz, and I do not feel much like talking.

Barnabas is somewhere nearby, just waiting for the right opportunity.

And I will be there to stop him.

The city guards prepare their weapons, but I have no need for such things. I *am* a weapon, and besides, I have precious little to call my own. I spread out my meager possessions on the bed. In addition to my satchel, belt, and cloak, I have the clothes on my back and the pressed form of the last rose from my garden at the cottage. It has dried now, but the bright red hue clings to it still. Ren's mother found it after I left it on his pillow and kept it along with the book of fairy tales. When she discovered it was mine, she insisted I have it. I both love and hate the memories it carries in its fragile form.

"Kymera?" a soft voice behind me says. I drop the flower on the bed as I spin around, pulling my hands behind my back so whoever this is won't see that my claws have shot out at being taken unawares.

Delia hovers in the doorway, the fingers of one hand clutching the frame while the other fiddles with her long blond curls. My sister. Who I no longer resemble in the least. Who has every reason to despise me.

"Yes?" I finally say. We have avoided each other ever since my return. She ducks into her room when I am in the hall and vice versa. Her smile in the palace court when Oliver pronounced me Bryre's protector is nearly the only contact we've had since Belladoma.

I simply don't know what to say to her.

"Good luck," she says. "I think if anyone can defeat the wizard, it would be you."

"Oh, well, thank you." Awkwardness hangs between us while I struggle to find something else to say.

"I'm sorry," she says.

All the breath leaves my lungs. "You're sorry?" I cannot fathom why she thinks she should be sorry. She has done no wrong.

She stares at the floor, the window, the doorframe— everywhere but at me. "Yes. You saved me and those other girls, and I—I have not been very welcoming to you."

I retrieve my things from the bed and stuff them in my pack. "You do not have to apologize for that. I could hardly expect you to be. You would not have been in Belladoma in the first place, if not for me."

"But I should. You're—" She stops short and balls her hands into fists at her sides. "You were my sister. It's just that

I thought I was getting past her—you—being gone, and now you're back." Her brow furrows as she considers my monstrous shape. "Sort of."

My long-lost affection for this girl stirs deep in the pit of my stomach. It is a warmth, like a tiny ball of sunlight. Only a hint, but that is enough. For now.

"I wish I remembered you better." I do, terribly. Flits and flashes are all I have. Lately most of them are of Ren, since he's been telling me about Rosabel, but every so often I catch a glimpse of a small, blond girl, too.

She steps fully into the room. "Your eyes are hers. Exactly. Right down to the tiny brown fleck in the left one. The shape of your face resembles hers a little, too. Everything else is . . . different."

"It was the magic the wizard used. He tried to make me this way so many times, it burned up all but the parts you recognize." Fear trembles down my neck. Please don't let this girl ask where the rest of me came from.

To my relief, she just nods.

"I'm sorry, too," I say, because I must, however ridiculous it may sound. "I'm sorry for stealing you from the hospital and sending you to Belladoma. The wizard tricked me. I thought I was doing the right thing."

Delia shivers and takes an unconscious step back. "Yes, I remember when you explained how you thought you were saving us. And when you found out that was wrong, you came with Ren to save us for real."

She remains in the doorway, still shivering. I can do nothing but gaze at her miserably. Would Rosabel have embraced and comforted her younger sister? I cannot imagine Delia would welcome that sort of comfort from me.

Yapping and flapping distract us both from our circling thoughts. Pippa soars into the room. Delia ducks, startled by the flying sperrier. She laughs as Pippa skids to a landing at her feet and yelps for attention.

"What an odd little thing!" she says, scratching Pippa right between the ears just as she likes best. The sperrier leans into Delia's hand, practically purring. Then Pippa flies up and lands in Delia's arms. Her nonstop tail wags her entire body. Delia laughs and grins over Pippa's wings.

I grin back. I may not know what will happen to me or whether we'll save Bryre, but it warms me to see that Pippa—and Delia—will be in good hands.

When I move to pet Pippa, too, something draws my attention to the window instead.

Screams. My heart burns in my throat.

Barnabas must be back already. So early! I was sure he'd wait for nightfall.

"What is it?" Delia asks.

"I don't know, but I fear the worst." I fly by her and out the cottage door. Greta and Delia's feet pound after me. I make it only a few yards before I realize what is happening.

City folk have come out of their homes, and are staring, pointing at the sky.

Batu circles overhead, his great granite-hued wings spread wide as he soars. He is truly a majestic creature. Slowly, he circles down to the street level and settles onto the cobblestones, careful to fold his wings and curl his tail around the street corner. He is taller than the buildings.

Delia and Greta finally catch up, panting. "D-dragon!" Greta exclaims. "Kym, get back! He'll eat you alive!"

I grin back at them. "Not this dragon."

Sister. Hot air brushes over my face in a comforting, familiar breeze.

"Batu!" I say, amazed. "What are you doing here?"

My dragon lowers his head to my eye level. *I heard rumors of the forest by the city being unmade, and knew the wizard had to be near. I realized you were quite serious about fighting him, and I came to a decision.*

"What decision is that?" I place my hand on his scaly cheek.

I am alone. I have been alone, and scared, for too many years to count. But since I found you, my life has felt full. I decided I would rather risk dying with you than go back to living alone.

My heart swells and I throw my arms around Batu's snout.

"I am so glad you're here." I pull back and take in the sight of all the quivering city folk. "Batu, I think I should bring you somewhere less exposed. Did you see the palace when you were circling?"

Batu nods.

"Good. Go to the garden there. You'll have more room to stretch out, and a smaller audience."

He launches off the ground, and I follow suit, fueled by renewed hope.

Batu reaches the palace garden first and lands with his tail amid the hedge creatures and his head on the grand front steps. The ground trembles when he lands, and the guards come running, swords drawn, only to halt and gape.

"It is all right," I say, landing in front of Batu. "The dragon is with me. Which means he is with us. Please, get the king."

"The king is already here," Oliver says from the wide marble entrance. The guards immediately step in front of him. Ren appears behind the king, his face ashen when he sees Batu.

"It's real," Ren chokes out.

"Of course it is," I say.

"Kymera," Oliver says, looking like he just realized he swallowed something poisonous, "what is the meaning of this? Dragons are dangerous. They are notorious for destroying cities like ours and—"

Actually, Batu says in his think-speak, *that would be fire dragons. They always were temperamental. No rock dragon has ever destroyed a city.*

Oliver gapes. Ren leans against a marble column for support. They both must have heard Batu.

Delia and Greta race down the garden path, panting. "Kym, have you gone mad?" Greta says.

I sigh. I never did stop to consider what the Bryrians' reaction might be to a dragon in their midst when I begged Batu for help. "He is here, at no small risk to himself, I might add, to help us defeat the wizard."

Oliver's eyes go wide. "You cannot be serious?"

"You can't trust a dragon. He would eat you as soon as look at you!" Ren says.

I shake my head. "I am serious and no, he will not." I smile at Batu, placing a hand on his snout. "We are like brother and sister. We protect each other."

"I must say I share Ren's concern," Oliver says. "Dragons are not tame creatures by any stretch of the imagination. They may be wise, but they can be vicious. They are feared for good reason."

I glance at Batu—his rocky shimmering scales, the dank breeze of his dragon's breath, his pure hatred of wizards. And his kindness. Batu saved my life; he is my friend. "I don't fear this one. And neither should you. The wizard murdered his whole clan. Every member of his family, his entire race. Barnabas has been chasing him for years. He has just as much stake in this as any of us."

I swear on the mountains I mean you no harm, King Oliver. Unlike my fiery brethren, I have little desire for wreaking havoc. All I want is to live freely and without fear.

Delia and Greta stiffen, exchanging a stunned look as Batu speaks.

Oliver takes a step toward Batu. He quietly considers the beast on his steps for a few moments.

"I trust you, Kym. That's why I named you Bryre's guardian. If you swear this dragon is here to help, I don't think I have much choice but to believe you. Who can say no to a dragon?" He reaches out to take my hand. "With the wizard bound to arrive at our gates any hour, we are in no position to turn down assistance, especially from something that has a real chance of defeating the wizard for good."

"You won't regret it, I promise," I say, squeezing his hand. Batu inclines his head as if in a bow, and huffs his acknowledgment of the king's approval.

"Be careful. Even with this unexpected help, Barnabas is bound to be angry now, and that makes him more dangerous than ever before," Oliver says.

"Don't worry, I will never let my guard down again."

Soon we'll be free from all this madness. With my dragon by my side, no wizard can stop us.

DAY SEVENTY-SEVEN

BATU AND I HAVE BEEN GUARDING THE WALL WHERE THE MONSTER BRIAR
burst through since the sun set earlier in the evening. Now
it is well past midnight. The wall keeping our enemies out
is down in one spot, just wide enough for two men to walk
through. The foundation is in more of a shambles than the
last time I saw it, and between the rubble and clog of briars,
it's now nearly impossible for the repair workers to reach.
I suspect Barnabas prepared for that sort of thing. And I'm
sure he already has a plan to get around it.

Batu barricades the way into the city proper with his
massive body where the briar gives way to the street. The
night is bright and clear, and I try to pick out constellations
in the stars. It reminds me of another time I gazed up at the
night sky, with Ren. It feels like forever ago.

What do you see in the sky, sister? Batu asks.

"The stars." I lean against the scales along his tail. "Once a friend told me that when people die, they become stars. My mother and the girls the wizard took are all up there watching over us. I'd like to think the dragons and other creatures he killed are up there too, but I don't know if you have to be human to become a star." I worry my bottom lip. I don't know if I'm human enough anymore to qualify.

Humans, dragons, hybrids—we are all animals in some form. And we all return to the universe when we pass from this life. Batu points with his tail to a group of lights in the sky. The outline of a form suddenly comes to mind.

"They do make a dragon!" I say. Tears of relief cloud my eyes and the stars blur together in a sweeping brilliancy. Someday, I can rejoin the family I lost to the wizard, even if it is only to look down upon Bryre from above.

Branches rustle in the dense woods nearby. Up until the small clearing Barnabas created by ungrowing the trees, it's impossible to pass by in silence. I crouch lower in my hiding spot near Batu, concealed by a nasty patch of thorns.

A shadow-cloaked body steps through the gaping hole in the wall, past the boundary that thwarted the wizard's plans for years. The air buzzes with the hum of magic thrumming beneath the surface of his skin, and the briars shrink back to let him pass. My pulse quickens. I despise him. He can't be allowed in any further.

A revolting grin crosses Barnabas's face when he spies Batu.

"Ah, my old friend. I thought I caught your scent in the

woods. This is better than I had hoped."

I step out into the open where he can't miss me. Barnabas's eyes widen.

"Both of you? Of course, you would have befriended a dragon. Get out while you can, Kymera." A sly grin creeps over his face. "Or you could join me. You were so helpful before."

I struggle to maintain my composure, letting the anger boil inside, but keeping it focused on one thing: finding an opening to sideline him for good.

We block his path into the city streets. The briar clogs any other route in. Hidden from view in the streets behind us, ten men with lassos, maces, and crossbows lie in wait. I can smell their fear, but they're not here to kill him; their purpose is to distract and slow him down if he gets past Batu and me.

Barnabas raises an eyebrow.

"We won't let you hurt any more girls," I say. Batu growls, a sound like rocks grinding together.

He laughs. "I never cared about the girls. They were a means to an end. Oliver must pay for services rendered one way or the other. More importantly, he must pay for taking everything that should have been mine. Aria. You. The magic I could have wielded if I had spilled your blood when you were an infant. He ruined all my plans. He will suffer for it, and he will watch me destroy his entire city."

"Oliver did nothing wrong."

"Nothing? He promised me you, did he not?"

I bristle, but try not to let it show. "Only because you

tricked him. We won't let you hurt him. You won't kill anyone ever again."

"I will kill whoever I please." He leans in. "You have made it easy for me. Everything I need to take my revenge on Bryre is right here waiting for me. I could not have planned it better myself."

At the flick of my tail, Batu attacks, leaping past the briar with huge, sharp teeth and talons bared.

Dark light spews from Barnabas's outstretched hands like glowing shadows. The ground and city walls shake when it touches them. Batu shimmers and fades in and out, feinting and ducking at Barnabas.

My dragon is glorious, wings stretched wide to their full span, scales glittering in the half-light, yellow eyes ablaze.

He is also afraid. Though he looks terrifying, the way he carries himself makes me certain of it.

One of the dark coiling lights strikes Batu on his wing, and I can't help but shriek. I clap my hands over my mouth, terror rooting me to the spot. Barnabas is determined to hurt everything I hold dear. Rage comes on like an ocean wave slamming against the rocks. My claws are out, my tail taut, and I burn for his blood.

Our plan is for Batu to fight Barnabas first, with me keeping him trapped between the wall and the briar if he tries to run into the city. I don't know how much longer I can stand back, yet I don't want to get in Batu's way, either.

Batu's left wing smokes where he was hit, and it folds against his side. He cannot maneuver as easily without it. Barnabas hits his paw and side in quick succession with his magic, but Batu claws Barnabas's arm and knocks his feet out from under him as he flickers out of sight.

Barnabas laughs from where he fell and meets my eyes.

I fly straight for him.

No, Kym! Batu reappears behind Barnabas, his yellow eyes focused on me. Barnabas mutters something I cannot make out.

Suddenly, my body jerks and I hit the ground, the breath knocked from my lungs. I twist to see a briar vine curling around my leg. Barnabas's evil magic has brought the beastly plant more to life than ever. It grows at an alarming rate, new vines appearing every second, slithering toward us.

I scream and thrash, but the briars pull harder. I slash at the one wrapped around my ankle and the stung plant recoils. I scramble to my feet, but the vines still approach—reaching, prickling, stabbing—and they curl even more tightly around me again.

More shadow ropes approach Batu along with briar, but he does not vanish like he did before.

"Batu, flee! Go!"

I cannot. Something stops me.

"It was foolish to bring the dragon into the open, Kymera. Did you not think I would know all their tricks? I have more than enough tricks of my own."

"No!" I lunge forward again, but the vines hold me in place. I swing my tail, trying to gain enough momentum to rip free of the hateful plant.

Though I can sense Batu's fear, he does not give up. He leaps into the air, then crashes to the earth, making the ground tremble and crack. He yanks huge chunks out of the wall with his tail and begins hurling them at Barnabas.

Barnabas rises to his feet, neatly dodging the cracks in the earth, unfazed. As a boulder hurtles toward him, he casts his dark light, and the rock ricochets back to the dragon. It strikes Batu square in the side, but then something odd happens. It doesn't hurt him as I expect—he absorbs it. Wide-eyed, I watch while his curled wing unfurls again, now whole.

The rocks may make my rock dragon stronger, but Barnabas is barely slowed. If anything, he redoubles his efforts. Before Batu can take flight, Barnabas lashes out with a glowing shadow coil, and it wraps around the dragon's neck. One yank, and Batu's giant craggy face is slammed to the ground. More shadow coils and twisting vines snake around his body and legs and wings. He attempts to stand, but the vines pull tighter and tighter and force him back down. Batu struggles to breathe. I clench my fists against my sides and a low keen rises in my throat. The briars that hold me are alive with writhing black shadows and they move as one deadly entity. It burns cold where they touch my skin. I struggle violently, desperate to break free and help Batu.

Barnabas draws closer to the dragon caught in his web. The briar vines speed their growth until they cover Batu entirely. Drops of blue, glittering liquid—dragon's blood— dot the ground. He stops moving.

I am sorry, sister, he says.

Tears sting paths down my cheeks. "No, no!"

I tried. Sometimes that is all you can do. I shall miss you. Farewell.

"I will miss you, too," I whisper.

And then he is gone.

Bang!

Brilliant light fills the street. Barnabas stands stock still, arms lifted above his head, welcoming the onslaught. It pours into him until he's lit up like the sun. His body contorts, leaving him crooked and bent, but with a horrid gleam in his eyes.

Beside him, Batu's body crumbles into shimmering dust.

"Good-bye, my dear," Barnabas says with a tilt of his head. He vanishes into the street.

A howl tears from my chest, mournful and furious. My heart twists with grief. Batu's kind, wise yellow eyes and craggy face. The sun glittering off his granite scales. The way he called me sister.

He was my dragon, my brother. I was so certain Batu could defeat Barnabas. The dragon was right to be so wary for so long.

Batu ventured out into the open for me, for my cause.

I refuse to let his death be in vain.

The shadow ropes have vanished with the wizard. With a burst of renewed strength, I rip my arms from the briars' hold and claw my way free. I collapse for a moment on the pavement, gasping to catch my breath.

Barnabas may be gone, but I know where he is headed.

The palace. For Oliver. For revenge.

At the end of the abandoned, briar-infested alley, I find the ten palace guards trapped by the vines. I cut them free and together we run into the nearest clear street. The briar vines slither slowly after us, like a living creature.

"Go, alert the council," I tell the guards.

Ren and Greta barrel around the corner, nearly colliding with them.

"Don't go down there! The briar will eat you alive." I grab Ren's arm and they both stop.

"He's here already? Is that what we heard?" Greta asks, eyes wide. "The ground was shaking horribly!"

"He set the vines on us and got away. He—he killed Batu." I choke out the words. "He's going to the palace, I'm sure of it."

"We're coming with you," Ren says, hand tightening around the hilt of his sword.

"Ren, Greta, you—"

"We know. We're still coming with you."

The determination on their faces makes it clear I won't be able to get rid of them except by force. I hate the thought of either of them in harm's way, but at the same time I'm relieved not to have to do this alone.

When we reach the gates of the palace, it's clear Barnabas has already been here. The gates are blown off the hinges, pieces scattered in the street. We slink in, keeping to the walls and hiding behind the massive hedge monsters.

Barnabas stands in front of the palace, all his attention on the person before him.

The king is suspended above the marble stairway between the reaching arms of two hedges. A centaur and a mermaid fight over him as the rest of the plants try to tear him in two. They've come alive, spelled by Barnabas's magic. A silent cry rises in the back of my throat.

Barnabas is making good on his threat and giving Oliver the most perfect, painful vantage point to watch his city's destruction.

Vines and thorns from the briar snake through the garden and carved iron door, winding around hedges and roses alike. If we don't stop him, the briar will consume the entire city in one night.

The harpy we hide behind turns a leafy scowl on us. As it reaches its limbs out, I shove Ren and Greta to the side. The branches curl around my chest, lifting me up in a crushing embrace. Flecks of light dance before my eyes. I thrash, struggling to breathe through the pain, but it squeezes harder. Nearby, Ren and Greta are caught by a giant minotaur and faun.

My tail wraps around the limb and I pull as hard as I can. It cracks and creaks and the harpy's scowl deepens. But its grip loosens and that is all the advantage I need. With one hand free, I slash at the branches until they finally break and I drop to the ground.

A glint of silver catches my eye—Ren's sword, lying where he dropped it in the attack. I scoop it up and toss it to Ren, then wrap my tail around the minotaur's legs. It takes only a minute of squeezing before they break in half and the creature topples over. Ren extricates himself from the foliage and attacks the faun without pausing to catch his breath. Moments later, Greta is on her feet again.

With our backs to the wall surrounding the palace, we pause to regroup. So do the hedge creatures. A menacing line forms in front of us, blocking our path to the king and Barnabas.

I glance at Ren and Greta, and my heart swells. Barnabas will not stop until every person I love is dead or enslaved. Until Bryre is reduced to rubble. Rosabel understood this. Despite his efforts to squash my memories, he made a fatal mistake by leaving one part intact: love of my home. His awful plan required my utmost devotion to Bryre and its citizens. Even if I don't remember everyone I knew before, I'll do anything to protect them.

I swallow the lump growing in my throat. I could not protect Batu. I must protect those who remain.

Horrid laughter echoes through the garden.

"Have you come here to save him?" The laughter vanishes and Barnabas's tone is quietly mocking. He glances over his shoulder and that hateful smirk consumes my vision. He may have turned me into an abomination, but he's the real monster.

"You think they care about you, is that it? Oh, they might play at it, my dear, but they do not know you. They could never care for a monster."

Fury burns in my chest like a candle tipped into a haystack—small at first, until it bursts all over. Ren squeezes one hand, and Greta squeezes the other. The hedges, roses, and vines smoke from the excess magic in the air. Thunder rumbles and dark, vicious clouds gather over our heads. Barnabas uses everything he has to keep the king suspended by shadow ropes while he taunts him, letting the hedge monsters tug as viciously as they please. Each grunt and cry from Oliver only makes Barnabas more absorbed in his task.

Barnabas has no fear. He knows no one will challenge him.

I step toward the line of hedge creatures.

"Kym." Ren wraps his fingers around my wrist, sending streams of warmth up my arm. "What are you doing?"

"The only thing I can." Heady with an odd mix of fear and bravery, I force myself to step away, and take off into the air, swooping over and around the hedges. Seconds later, I land a few feet behind Barnabas. He sends the shadow ropes spiraling into the air, and a hedge centaur catches them, pulling them taut to keep Oliver suspended. Barnabas turns his gaze skyward, and a bolt of lightning strikes the marble steps behind Oliver. I crouch low, claws out, tail poised.

"What did they promise you? A role protecting them? That you would have the honor of keeping them safe?" Barnabas advances slowly, and I match him with a step back every time, waiting for my opening. Shadows trail from his fingertips like strange, glowing smoke.

"They offered me kindness," I say, though his words prickle. Faint sparks flash in his palms.

"Kindness? Of course they are kind. You terrify them. They have no idea what you are capable of, and they never wish to find out." He stops and places his hand over his heart. "I, on the other hand, know you as no one else can. I made you."

"You know nothing of how they feel." I cling to the memories of Oliver taking my arm without flinching, of Ren and me running through the streets hand in hand, of the city folk cheering as I was proclaimed Bryre's protector, of my mother's face carved into marble—and of my own former self. He's wrong, I'm certain of it. Perhaps I scared them once, but no longer.

"You are useful tamed, but you will always be a monster." Wind kicks up behind me. I edge near the line of hedge creatures, but they're too close together and I can't see beyond them.

"I wasn't a monster to Batu." A new jolt of rage trills through my blood, and I focus on that with razor-sharp clarity. "You killed him."

Confusion colors Barnabas's face for a fleeting moment. Then he laughs. "You named the dragon?" A roar comes from the west, growing louder by the second. "I have been hunting that one for years. Thank you, dear daughter, for luring it into the open."

"I am not your daughter," I say through gritted teeth. A briar vine twines around my ankle, but I yank my foot away.

"Yes, you are. You and I, we are dark creatures. Do not fight it. Together we could wield more power than any kingdom."

He splays his hands wide, and shadow ropes slink from his palms toward me. At the same time, a huge funnel cloud

416

rips the western wall to mere rubble, sending bricks in all directions.

Not one hits Barnabas.

The funnel cloud shreds the western side of the garden, destroying several hedge creatures in the process. And Rosabel's roses. Leaves, twigs, and petals swirl in the cloud and fall to the ground like rain.

"I've never wanted that sort of power." I struggle to keep my voice even. He either toys with me or he's truly delusional, and believes his pleas to join him might have an effect.

The funnel cloud peels the roof off the fancy portico entrance, knocking over two of the marble columns and breaking the other two in half. The raging wind pulls at my cloak and hair, and flings leaves in my face. The ground trembles beneath my feet.

"That is very disappointing." For one moment, he looks genuinely sad. A lightning bolt zings the ground by my feet, forcing me to jump back. The shadow ropes advance, coiled and ready to spring.

So am I.

I duck under the coils, rolling in the grass and debris, then leap to my feet and take off into the air.

I circle twice over the scene to get my bearings, avoiding the funnel cloud and dodging lightning. I swoop back down to the earth and curl my tail and arms around Barnabas's gnarled form, pinning his arms to his sides so he can't use his power on me. The magic has warped him in body and mind. It took me so long to see that. But now everything is clear.

Ignoring Barnabas's howls, I shoot into the air and soar until I graze the rumbling, darkened cloud bank. He's heavy and awkward, and his cold shadow ropes curl around my neck and arms, threatening to choke me. I let the fierce winds spin me in the sky, keeping him and his magic tricks off balance. But the shadow ropes are odd things. Where they touch my skin, freezing pain sears, more so than before, and I bite my tongue to keep from screaming. It is a bizarre pain, and with every second that ticks by, I feel a little weaker.

"You will not hurt me," he sneers. "I made you. If you kill me, you will die too. You are too fond of that fool boy and the other humans. I know you do not want to die."

Before he can free his hands to place them on my forehead and make me forget, I release my grip on his body and drop him into his own funnel cloud. Lightning crackles and sparks out of it, illuminating the debris caught in its pull.

Then it spits him out.

He plummets with a wild look in his eyes, before landing on the top of a broken pillar. In seconds his body crumbles to dust.

Now, as I soar over the garden, a brilliant light envelops me and a warmth rises from the tips of my toes and presses down from the crown of my head. Rather like the warmth I feel when I look at Ren. The tingling heat swells and spreads like a great beam of sunlight, until it swallows me up and nothing remains to see or feel.

EPILOGUE

THE BLINDING LIGHT WEAVES AND TWISTS AROUND THE MONSTER GIRL
while the pair of children below run to free the man trapped
in twining branches over the broken stairs. They gape at the
sight above them as they help him to a bench.

The light fades to a shimmering, and the air crackles
around the form as it drifts back to the earth. Arms, legs,
wings, and tail curl inward, taking on a greenish hue. Claws
and barbs become thorns. She transforms before their eyes,
growing more compact every second, until finally alighting
on the top of a broken pillar.

The princess who became a monster is now a rose about
to bloom, with all the magic of the wizard stored in the tiny
beating heart at the base of her stem. The evil presence that

hung over the land for so long is vanquished, canceled out by an act of love.

The roots of the rose burrow through the marble column, digging deep into the earth of her city. Unknown to the three humans watching, the creeping briar at the back of the palace withers and recedes until it crumbles into dust. The protective wards, damaged by the machinations of the wizard, heal over, and the rubble by the hole in the city wall begins to knit back together brick by brick. Ribbons of magic flow through the ground, mending all the things that were torn apart. The palace, its walls and halls and crypt. The garden maze behind it that was the first to be consumed by the pitiless briars. The streets and alleys and houses, now renewed by magic in the hands of a kind user. The guardian rose's roots run deep, healing and protecting the land with her magic. And there she will remain, watching over her beloved city forever.

While the three on the bench watch in wonder, the green stem and leaves unfurl, rising higher into a tight-fisted bud. The flower blooms, and its petals open, exhaling toward the stars.

ACKNOWLEDGMENTS

I FEAR IT'S AN IMPOSSIBLE TASK TO THANK EVERYONE WHO HAS encouraged, supported, and believed in *Monstrous* within the span of only a couple pages. The writing community, especially the kid-lit community, is made up of a multitude of kind and supportive writers and readers, many of whom have cheered this manuscript on from the very beginning. Such unflagging support is a true gift, and I'm very grateful for every second of it.

There are, of course, a few who stand out, and without whom *Monstrous* would never have landed in readers' hands. To those listed below, you have my deepest gratitude for all that you do.

My editors, Rosemary Brosnan and Andrea Martin,

for being patient, brilliant, and especially for insisting that this book needed more dragon (they were correct!). *Monstrous* blossomed under their kind, yet tough, guiding pens, and it's been a pleasure and an honor to work with them. Also, infinite thanks to everyone at HarperCollins who has touched this book in any way, shape, or form—the people behind the scenes play a much larger role in bringing a book to life than most people realize, and the team at Harper is exceptional.

My literary fairy godmother (a.k.a. agent) Suzie Townsend, for loving this book as much as I do, and for making dreams come true. Also, everyone at New Leaf Literary & Media for being the most supportive, fabulous champions of a book a writer could possibly ask for.

My most stalwart critique partners: Mindy McGinnis, whose hilarious (and—sadly—utterly inappropriate to print in the back of a middle grade novel) frustration at the ending of an early draft of *Monstrous* convinced me it needed an epilogue; and R.C. Lewis, who speedily read my first editorial revision of *Monstrous* (among other drafts) and reassured me that I had, in fact, not ruined the book. Many thanks to these ladies for allowing me to flail in their direction whenever the need arose!

My critique group and beta readers: Cat, Derrick, Ríoghnach, Stephanie D., Sakura, Jordan, Eric, Chris, Melodie, Stacy, and Tracy. Without their excellent feedback on this book (and many other manuscripts over the years), *Monstrous* simply wouldn't be the same.

The wonderful folks at AgentQuery Connect, my second home on the internet. This is where I learned what a query was and how to write one (though not without extensive trial and error), and found like-minded writers, friends, and critique partners. AQC is a beacon of reason and a bounty of resources in the rough sea of publishing advice that resides on the web. I would have drowned without it.

The children's book community (both online and off) whose awesomeness never fails to astound me. In particular, thank you to Krista, Brenda, Monica, and the pseudonymous Cupid who ran the first Writer's Voice online contest. The outpouring of love for my entry from the judges and contestants gave me the nerve to query the weird little book that was *Monstrous*. It was just the push I needed, and I honestly don't know that I would have without it.

My best friends, Trish and Chandra, who were there through all the highs and the lows on the crazy journey to publication and cheered me up when I needed it. Espinaca and Indian food are the cure for all woes.

The loving support of my entire family, but especially my parents, for encouraging me in every dream I ever had, no matter how ridiculous (even that time I decided I'd grow up to be a traveling farmer who lived in a motor home). They let me believe anything was possible. And of course, many thanks to my sister and nephew for being my first nonwriter readers.

And finally, Jason, for happily letting me have the time and space to write whenever I needed it, for listening to me babble on about plot twists with no context whatsoever, and for keeping me in writing fuel (otherwise known as coffee). You are always my favorite.

READ ON FOR A SNEAK PEEK AT
MARCYKATE CONNOLLY'S NEXT NOVEL

CHAPTER 1

THOUGH I SIT BY THE WARM, WELCOMING HEARTH IN THE HOME OF THE king's page boy, Ren, one small sentence is all it takes to drag me back to that awful place. To my nightmare.

"We are sending aid to Belladoma," King Oliver said moments ago, propelling us all into confusion.

Belladoma.

I stand in the tower again, the nauseating smell of sea brine stinging my nose, and a guard's hands pinning my shoulder to the rough windowsill. Below us, black water swirls against the cliff's edge and one long tentacled arm gropes up the rocks.

All those other girls King Ensel holds captive as meals for the sea monster, the Sonzeeki, are too soft, too coddled.

I have to help them. I have to try, no matter how futile it seems.

1

But every month we're taken up to the tower like clockwork,
and terrible, helpless rage curls around me like a strangling cloak.

"We are sending aid to Belladoma."

"You must be joking," I say. The mere thought of that place makes my stomach lurch. I grip the edge of my chair, nails digging into the wooden frame.

Laura, Ren's mother, bristles in the chair next to me. I've known her almost as long as I've been friends with her son; she hates Belladoma too. "Greta's right. Why should we help them? They murdered our children. They aided the wizard."

How can I forget those empty-eyed courtiers in Belladoma, or the poor who hid, safe in their houses, while King Ensel sent yet another of my friends off the cliff to sate the ravenous beast in the bay? They did nothing to help us. Why would they? Without us, the beast would destroy their city with floods unless they sent their own children to the Sonzeeki. The sea monster that haunts every Belladoman child's dreams has spread like a disease to disturb the slumber of Bryre's children too.

I don't need to look at Ren to know what he is feeling. He tried to save us only to fall victim to Belladoma's evil king too. Out of the corner of my eyes, his hands clench and unclench, much like my own. But he doesn't say a word to the king he adores and serves. In spite of everything.

And there is Delia, who should be as disgusted by this idea as any of us. We were both among Bryre's stolen girls. But she simply stands beside her father the king, staring at her feet. Her golden hair drapes in such a way that I can't see her expression.

King Oliver sighs. "I do not expect any of you to be happy about this. But it is not the people's fault their king was a horrible man. He was a usurper, and he was mad; he was never going to be a good ruler. The people of Belladoma have long suffered, and we can help. Now that Ensel is dead and no one feeds the Sonzeeki, it floods their city every month, poisoning the soil with salt so nothing can grow."

He stands, and for a moment he resembles the king I recall from when I was a child. Tall, strong, decisive but kind.

If only the transformation wasn't on behalf of Belladoma. Bryre—our own city—needs its king's full attention now more than ever.

"They starve," King Oliver says. "The few children they have left who weren't victims of King Ensel's sacrifices are dying. I will not stand by and watch."

I cannot bite my tongue like Ren and Delia. "*They* joined forces with the wizard and his evil magic. *Their* king woke the angry sea monster with a taste for young girls. The wizard stole Bryre's girls, my friends. Haven't *we* suffered enough?"

"She's right," Laura says, putting a hand on my shoulder. "We should show them the same measure of kindness they showed us."

The disappointment in the king's face sears my heart.

"It grieves me to hear that," King Oliver says. I can't

meet his eyes. The emotions twisting inside will explode from my chest if I do. I wrap my arms around my middle, and Ren's mother rubs my back. At least someone here understands.

The king sighs again, then bows and leaves the cottage silently. Delia follows like his shadow, but her betrayal lingers, needling over my skin like tiny knives.

"Greta, Mama," Ren says to Laura and me. "I don't like it any more than you do, but if the king says we must, we have no choice."

"If the king said we must give over our girls to help them, would you go along so easily? Our focus should be on our own city, on Bryre. We need our king here, not running off to some other place."

Ren frowns, and it pinches my heart. "Belladoma is repulsive to me, too, but we can't let people die needlessly."

"But how can we help another city, when we can't even help ourselves?" I stand, pulling my cloak around my shoulders.

Laura pats my arm. "Just wait, perhaps the king will see reason tomorrow. Belladoma might refuse our help. They've always been a proud people."

The fire flickers, throwing shadows all over the small room. "I can't bear to watch it happen." A buzzing in my ears, like frenzied waves crashing, grows louder with every second.

"Greta." Ren tries to follow, but I flee. This is worse than the nightmares that still plague me after all these months.

But the worst part is that our own king would offer

4

help to the city that attempted to destroy us before healing Bryre's own deep wounds.

Our city may have come back to life, but its occupants have a long way to go.

I wander through the city streets, meandering toward the palace, trying to escape the sound of waves crashing that won't let me rest. I know what draws me in, but it's foolish. This won't help a whit. And yet . . .

The guards know me well now. Ever since I fought against King Ensel and the wizard with Kymera the monster girl, they have treated me with more tolerance than they ever would have before as a commoner. They let me into the gardens without batting an eye.

While I have visited the palace many times since the battle with the wizard, there is one place I have avoided.

A strange flower lies at the edge of the garden not far from the palace steps. A beautiful red rose that's always in bloom, never closing up for the night to sleep. It never wilts, and probably doesn't need watering, though the gardeners water it anyway. After the battle, it rooted in a broken pillar, and King Oliver built the Altar of the Rose around it in an enclosure of fine silver-veined white marble, with a skylight to let in the moon and sun and rain.

Strange occurrences are often followed by rumors, and Bryre's rose is no exception. A steadily growing faction in the city claims the rose has the power to grant wishes, to fulfill unspoken needs, and to right wrongs. They visit the flower regularly to leave offerings and pay respects, their red cloaks marking them as followers of the rose.

But I don't believe in rumors. I believe in myself, and what I can do with my own two hands. Yet the righting of wrongs, the tempting idea it might be possible, now draws me in at last.

I enter the alcove, the moon high above, its light piercing through the skylight and illuminating the rose in all its perfect beauty. Just seeing it quiets the ocean in my brain.

There's just enough room inside for a handful of people to circle the rose on a marble walkway. The walls have shelves from floor to ceiling, and many of the city folk, not only the cult, leave tokens and offerings here. There are a few statuettes of dragons, and many carved in the monstrous likeness of a girl with claws, a serpentine tail, and black wings. Other oddities line the shelves too—dried flowers and roses mostly, but also bits of bone, thorns, and pottery of dubious shape and origin. And there on the bottom row lies a book of fairy tales.

I kneel on the marble path, a foot away from the flower. The petals are like soft velvet; its leaves are green and strong, and its thorns are fierce.

"I don't know if you can hear me," I say. An odd desperation has settled in my chest: if the rose does look after Bryre, it would not approve of the king's plan, I'm sure. "But I don't know where else to turn. Our king wants to help Belladoma, to give them supplies and food. They can't feed the Sonzeeki any longer, and it has been terrorizing and flooding the city." I ball my fists in my skirts as the image of that awful black shell rising from the depths dances in front of my eyes. "I pity them, but I can't stomach the thought of helping them. They sat idly by and did nothing while King Ensel held us captive, while he threw my friends off the cliff. They don't deserve our help." Unwanted tears burn the backs of my eyes.

The night breeze brushes over the petals of the rose.

"Would you aid the people who tried to destroy your city? If you have any power to stop the king, I beg you to do it. He hid from the wizard for so long, and now Bryre needs him here. We need him *more*."

The rose doesn't answer, but a cloud passes over the moon, removing all the light from the altar chamber. I leap to my feet.

My hands quiver. It's only a rose. Nothing more.

A single beam of moonlight pierces the cloud, striking the book of fairy tales on the alcove shelf.

A memory stirs within me. The book reminds me of something an old friend once held dear. I kneel by the wall and put my hands on the book. The clouds shift again and moonlight fully illuminates the room. The change is so sudden it startles me and I drop the book. A pressed rose slips from between the pages, and as I pick it back up I realize the book is filled with the pressed flowers.

Someone treasured this book once. I'll take the fairy tales—my brother, Hans, will love them—but I don't feel right taking these.

I carefully remove each pressed rose, making a strange sort of bouquet. When it's complete, I tie them together with a piece of string I find and rest the flowers back where the book once stood.

It must be the wind whispering through the palace garden, but I think I hear a sigh as I put the book in my satchel and leave the Altar of the Rose.

CHAPTER 2

I SPEND HALF THE NIGHT WANDERING THE DARK CITY STREETS AND reliving my nightmares.

Once I had a family, a loving mother and father, and a younger brother. Mama and Papa were long gone before I was sent to Belladoma. Hans was all I had left.

Then the wizard's disease curse infected me and I was tossed into quarantine with the rest of Bryre's sick girls. That's when Kymera, the monster girl created by the wizard, stole me and unwittingly sent me on my journey there. If only she'd known what really waited for us in that city.

Belladoma.

The memories creep in around the edges of my vision and I shudder. Like water, they flow through every barrier I put in their way. My parents raised me to believe in the kindness of strangers. But the people of Belladoma merely watched while their wicked king sent us over the cliff, slowly killing every ounce of that belief.

Finally, I reach our cottage on the outskirts of Bryre. It isn't a large house, but it's too big for just my brother and me, and it's fallen into more disrepair than I can fix easily. The roof needs thatching, and the front window frame is cracked from a recent storm. But the house is painted a pretty blue and the walkway is neat and free from the weeds that would threaten it. I tiptoe into the cottage as the dawn crests the trees with hues of pink and gold. I checked that Hans was asleep before I left to see Ren and the king. The last thing I want to do now is wake him.

Hans suffered enough while I was captive. Reduced to begging for scraps, even stealing on occasion, his only other source of food was the small garden I planted behind our house. When I finally returned, he was so thin, I feared he'd never recover. I wasted no time volunteering to help out the local baker and butcher, if only to justify the scraps I took home. I promised never to leave him again—unlike our parents.

Up until the day they left, we were happy together.

Happiness is not something I'll ever trust easily again.

I hang my cloak on the rack by the door and rub my sleepy eyes. The anger I felt at Ren's house has dulled to embers, leaving me exhausted and hollow. I should sleep for a few hours before another day of trying to coax the old Hans out of his new shell. Perhaps today I'll have better luck.

About a year ago, our parents vanished. No note, not a whisper of where they might have gone. Did they abandon us? Or did something terrible befall them? Are they out there somewhere, alive and waiting for us to join them, or are they already in their graves? If not for my brother, I would have chased after them, hunted down some small trace. But Hans needed me here.

I miss the Hans who was full of life and wonder, constantly curious. It's been my personal mission to bring that boy back. He grew sullen and more frightened after they left. His laughing eyes dulled to a somber gray. Lately, he's become more stubborn than ever—and taller, too. Sometimes when he gives me a rare smile, hope trills over me, but his smiles are few and far between and always fleeting.

I shuffle across the worn boards of our kitchen floor toward the back of the little house where our bedroom lies. We still share a room as we did when we were young, even though our parents' room lies empty. Neither of us has opened the door since that day. It would be like reopening a raw wound.

But after my night of wandering, I've made up my mind. Hans and I will leave Bryre. There's no reason to stay. Mama and Papa are not coming back. And I cannot stand by and watch while my friends help the people who held me captive and forced me to watch other girls die.

We're better off in the woods.

When I wake, we'll take our belongings and the little money we have to buy a few hens and a goat. Build a little cottage deep in the woods. No one will trouble us there. We won't have to pretend our parents are still around. It's been over three months since the battle with the wizard; the days tick by and it makes me restless.

Careful not to wake my brother, I pry our door open. Dawn trickles in through the windows, casting light on the sight that stops me in my tracks.

Hans's bed is empty.

Panic rises in a thick, suffocating stream up my chest. The doorknob rattles under my hands.

"Hans?" I whisper, hoping and praying for an answer. None comes. "Hans!" I yell and fling myself into our room. His bed is tousled and messy. Could something have woken him? Why would he have wandered off in the middle of the night?

I can't help thinking of our parents' disappearance. Hans wouldn't leave me too. We need each other. I toss off the bedclothes to ensure he isn't asleep somewhere deep under the covers. No luck.

Under the bed—the same. I rush to the closet and throw it wide. Again nothing. His clothes are all there, but no Hans hiding inside.

He can't be gone. He *can't*.

Fear crawls under my skin, worming its way over my body. I run through the house, wishing to find something that will let me escape this nightmare. But our cottage is small. There are not many places to hide. I check every single spot we used to play hide and seek as small children. The pantry in the kitchen is empty of all but some potatoes and carrots. The cupboards have a few handfuls of rice and dried beans that I would have cooked for our supper. The nook under the front stair. The hollow in the oak tree out front.

Nothing, nothing, nothing.

At last, only one place is left to check: our parents' room.

I stand outside the door, focusing on breathing. This is too eerily like that terrible day a year ago, when Hans and I returned home from school to the same: nothing.

Maybe Hans got the ridiculous notion into his head that he needs his own room. Maybe I'll find him sleeping soundly on their bed, cranky because I woke him.

Or worse, he won't be there at all.

I close my eyes, heart trembling, and reach for the doorknob. It turns slowly and the hinges creak and groan as the door swings inward. I don't want to look for fear of what I might see. When did I become so afraid?

Everyone I grow close to vanishes. I refuse to lose Hans. He's all I have left.

I force my eyes open.

Hans is not here. Everything is just as my parents left it. Clothes neatly stacked in the closet. Bed perfectly made. The only addition is a thin sheen of dust coating everything. No, Hans has definitely not been in here. Not since they vanished.

I flee the room, slamming the door behind me and sinking down to the floor. Water rushes in my ears, threatening to pull me under again.

Gone. Just like Mama and Papa. Visions of my family waltz before my eyes. Mama cooking in the kitchen, Hans

12

playing with blocks on the floor or sneaking into their room and jumping on the bed. Papa scolding Hans for rumpling the bed stuffing.

And me, wide-eyed and hopeful that life would bring adventure and a happily ever after. Papa taught me how to use a hammer and a sword, and Mama taught me how to grow my own food and shoot an arrow. Everything I'd need to be resourceful. I took to all of it, but Hans was never quite as good. Mama and Papa always told me that when they were gone, I'd have to look out for him.

Above all I am a sister, and a fierce one at that.

I will find my brother.

I push myself up off the floor and return to the room I share with Hans. There must be some hint, some clue as to what happened. Hans wouldn't just leave. I sit on the edge of his bed, smoothing over the blankets. No note lies hidden between the sheets or on his pillow. Not even on the floor.

Wait.

A yellow and brown feather lies on the floor, half hidden by the bed. It looks like it came from a chicken, except it is much larger than any chicken feather I've ever seen.

Puzzled, I walk over to the window. Caught on the outside of the sill is another feather, as though the window closed on a bird's tail. Several more dot the small yard beyond. A block of ice hardens in my gut. It can't be a coincidence that the feathers have appeared just as Hans has vanished.

They make a trail right up to the wall separating Bryre from the forest. Unlike Ren's cozy home, our cottage is on the outskirts. That was useful. It kept us from being noticed when our parents disappeared.

But now I'm certain. Something bad is in the forest. It has my brother, and I won't rest until I have him back.